PRAISE FOR

WE RULE THE NIGHT

★ "The **richly textured world, painted in snow and fire**, filled with disparate, diverse people who all want to win the war, is background to **a powerful, slow burning story.…A fierce and compelling breakout debut that should not be missed.**"
—*Kirkus Reviews*, starred review

★ "Bartlett's **electrifying feminist fantasy** debut uses keenly wrought characters, harrowing action sequences, and creative yet economical worldbuilding to explore misogynistic military culture and the human cost of war."
—*Publishers Weekly*, starred review

★ "**Rich characterizations** and an enemy that, while it looms in the background, never feels quite as threatening as the country the girls are fighting for complete a story set against the bright, brutal backdrop of war. A **breathless** [debut]."
—*Booklist*, starred review

★ "Full of sharply realized characterizations, **intriguing** magical elements, and twisty plots."
—*SLJ*, starred review

"**A riveting tale** of feminism, friendship, and a fight for survival.… **Bold**."
—*The Globe and Mail*

WE RULE THE NIGHT

CLAIRE ELIZA BARTLETT

LITTLE, BROWN AND COMPANY
New York Boston

Little, Brown and Company
Hachette Book Group
1290 Avenue of the Americas, New York, NY 10104
Visit us at LBYR.com

Originally published in hardcover and ebook by Little, Brown and Company in April 2019
First Trade Paperback Edition: March 2020

Little, Brown and Company is a division of Hachette Book Group, Inc.
The Little, Brown name and logo are trademarks of Hachette Book Group, Inc.

The publisher is not responsible for websites (or their content) that are not owned by the publisher.

The Library of Congress has cataloged the hardcover edition as follows:
Names: Bartlett, Claire Eliza, author.
Title: We rule the night / Claire Eliza Bartlett.
Description: First edition. | New York ; Boston : Little, Brown and Company, 2019. |
Summary: Seventeen-year-olds Revna, the daughter of a traitor, and Linné, the daughter of a general, must use forbidden magic to fly planes in wartime despite their deep dislike of each other.
Identifiers: LCCN 2018022805| ISBN 9780316417273 (hardcover) | ISBN 9780316417266 (ebook) | ISBN 9780316417280 (library edition ebook)
Subjects: | CYAC: War—Fiction. | Women air pilots—Fiction. | Air pilots—Fiction. | Magic—Fiction. | Fantasy.
Classification: LCC PZ7.1.B37287 Our 2019 | DDC [Fic]—dc23
LC record available at https://lccn.loc.gov/2018022805

ISBNs: 978-0-316-41729-7 (pbk.), 978-0-316-41726-6 (ebook)

Printed in the United States of America

LSC-C

10 9 8 7 6 5 4 3 2 1

To my grandmother Lorene Bowling, who worked for the US Air Force and never let her male-dominated society—or anyone, for that matter—dictate how she would manage her life.

1

NIGHT WON'T PREVENT US

Revna didn't realize the war had come to them. Not until the factory stopped.

She sat at her conveyor belt like a good citizen, oblivious to the oncoming storm from the west. The organized cacophony of industry filled her to the brim. Shining war beetle parts drifted past, twitching and trembling with fear and faint traces of magic. As the belt slowed, the voice of her supervisor emerged from the din. "Girls!"

The hissing, ratcheting, and clanging died away. Revna's fingers were half-buried in the oily bones of a leg that shivered and twisted of its own accord. She soothed the living metal, trying to keep the sudden spike in her heartbeat from infecting it with her own unease. In her three years working at the factory, she'd never heard the machines go still.

She turned her wheelchair away from her workstation and pushed toward her supervisor's voice. Machines towered around her like trees, frozen in the act of spitting out legs, carapaces, and antennae. Revna rounded the base of an enormous sheet press to find Mrs. Rodoya standing at the door to her office, hands clasped over her belly. Other factory girls crept out from behind conveyors and riveters, ducking under cranes. They clustered together in front of the sheet press, gripping one another with slick fingers.

Mrs. Rodoya took a deep breath. "We need to evacuate. Get your things."

God, Revna thought reflexively, even though Good Union Girls weren't supposed to think about God anymore. They would evacuate for only one reason—the Elda. She imagined regiments of blue-and-gray men marching through the smoke, bringing the hard mercies of conquest. But the Elda wouldn't march into Tammin. They'd obliterate it from the sky with Dragons of steel and fire.

And when they came, they'd aim for the factories.

Mrs. Rodoya sent them back to their workstations for their War Ministry–approved survival kits. Revna strapped her kit to the back of her chair, then wheeled over to the factory door. She could walk, but Mrs. Rodoya had doubted her ability to stand on prosthetics day after day, and Good Union Girls deferred to their supervisor's judgment.

The girls lined up in pairs at the door, clasping their survival kits in one hand and their partners' hands in the other. Revna went to the end of the line. She had no hand to grab, no one to whisper that it would be all right. She wasn't going to the shelter for good citizens, for Protectors of the Union, but to the alternate shelter for secondary citizens and nonworkers. She'd sit in the dank cellar and play with her little sister, Lyfa, and try not to see the worry in every line of Mama's face.

Revna heard a low hum, like an enraged cloud of insects. Elda Weavecraft. Her heart jumped. The primary citizens' shelter was a five-minute trip, but hers was ten, and Mama worked even farther away. Revna wanted nothing more than for Mama's hand to be the hand that clasped hers now.

Mama would find her in the shelter, she reminded herself. They'd be together there, and surely safer than out on the street with the Elda and their aircraft.

Mrs. Rodoya opened the factory door and counted each pair with a bob of her head as they went through. Then she grabbed the wooden handles of Revna's chair and began to push without asking. Anger boiled up like an allergic reaction, mixing with Revna's nerves and making her feel sick. She could get herself to work every morning—she could walk it, for that matter. Her living metal prosthetic legs had been called a work of art by Tammin's factory doctors. But Mrs. Rodoya didn't care what Revna or the doctors thought. "Now, now. We want speed over pride, don't we?" she'd said in early practice raids. A different Revna would have punched her. But this Revna wanted to keep her job. As long as Revna had a job, there was money to set aside and extra rations for Lyfa.

"I'll take you the first part of the way. But once the routes split I'll have to look after the other girls. You'll be on your own," Mrs. Rodoya said. She'd said this every drill. But now her voice had an edge to it and climbed a little too high as she called out to the rest. "Quickly, now." The factory girls began to move. Mrs. Rodoya and Revna followed, lurching as the back wheel of Revna's chair caught on a loose stone at the edge of the road.

The factories of Tammin Reaching spat out legs, carapaces, rifles, helmets, all that was needed for the churning Union war machine. Oil and dirt coated everything—the brick walls, the windows, the streetlamps that never turned on anymore.

Even the propaganda posters developed a coat of soot a few days after the papergirls plastered them to the sides of the factories. Revna rolled past image after image of Grusha the Good Union Girl, her patriotic red uniform already spattered with grease and mud. DON'T CHAT. GOSSIP WON'T HELP BUILD WAR MACHINES, said one, showing her scowling with a finger to her lips. NIGHT WON'T PREVENT US FROM WORKING, said another. PRACTICE MAKES PREPARED, declared a third.

Revna found that laughable now. She'd practiced her trip to the shelter so much that she could go there in her sleep. But real life had surprises. Real life had Dragons.

The eternal lights of the factories flickered out around them and twilight deepened the cloudless sky above. The moon hung like a farmland apple, fat and ripening and surrounded by stars. A few palanquins scuttled from place to place, grim-faced officials perched at their fronts. There was no army waiting to protect Tammin, no squadron of war beetles assembled and ready. They'd have to wait out the attack in shelters and hope something was left when they emerged.

The line of girls undulated as their unease grew. "Calm," Mrs. Rodoya said.

Calm was easy during a practice raid. With the hum of aircraft resonating against the buildings, calm became a whole lot harder. Revna clenched her hands until she couldn't feel them shake. *Don't be such a coward,* she told herself. But she hadn't been brave in a long time. Sometimes she thought when the doctors cut off her legs, they'd amputated her courage as well.

Maybe the Elda would pass overhead, on the way to do reconnaissance or bomb another target. She knew how selfish it was, hoping that someone else would die so that she might live. But she wasn't thinking only about herself. Every quiet moment meant that Mama was closer to the shelter, too.

They made it to the end of the street before the first explosion hit the edge of town. The ground trembled and a sound like thunder washed over them. Two girls screamed. Revna's pulse throbbed in her ears, drowning out the whine of aircraft. The girls ahead quickened as the balance between order and panic began to destabilize.

"Calm, girls." Did Mrs. Rodoya have to keep saying that? "Left," she called, and they turned, joining the current of workers who emerged from the factories and hurried, heads down, toward their designated shelters. Maybe PRACTICE MAKES PREPARED after all. A few men and women sped ahead, carrying rifles. Every Protector of the Union took required rifle practice, and some were designated first responders, on guard for any opportunities to fire back during a bombardment. Mama had excelled with her rifle until Papa was arrested and their Protector of the Union status got revoked. Now their guns were in someone else's hands.

A crack split the sky and the ground shook again. The Elda were getting closer now. Smoke blotted out the twilight and Revna heard a faint buzzing, like a swarm. Her nose twitched as she smelled the sharp heat of burning metal. Open flame was the enemy of a factory town.

The line stopped. Someone at the front gasped. "Girls—" Mrs. Rodoya said.

A man stood in the road. A man in a silver coat.

Revna's living metal prosthetics shook. His coat made him unmistakable, as did the blue star pinned below the collar. He was part of the Skarov unit, the Extraordinary Wartime Information Unit. The last time Revna had seen a Skarov up close was the last time she'd seen her father. In the years since, she'd wondered if they would come back for her, too. The Information Unit was always in and out of Tammin, carrying messages and supplies. Occasionally carrying off people.

The man's eyes flicked over the group. "Get on with it," he snapped. "You haven't got all night." Above them, the hum grew louder.

Compared with a Skarov officer, the threat of the Dragon was less immediately terrifying, but direr in consequence. The girls in front took the risk and edged past him. When he did nothing but roll his eyes, the line began to speed up. For once it didn't bother Revna so much when Mrs. Rodoya pushed her chair.

No two people agreed on what the Skarov could do. And since GOSSIP WON'T HELP BUILD WAR MACHINES, they discussed it only

6

when their supervisors weren't around. Even though the memory of her father's arrest was a fresh scar in her mind, Revna couldn't recall any proof of their alleged magic. She'd heard they could read minds, change shape, know a girl's name by meeting her gaze. Revna didn't believe all that. But when the Skarov's eyes locked on her, she couldn't look away. His eyes were a strange brown, almost tawny in the dying light. A thousand fears and confessions raced through her brain.

The Skarov looked down to where her prosthetic feet poked out of the cuffs of her work trousers. For a moment his lofty arrogance was replaced with a more familiar but no less unwelcome expression: pity. The chair rolled past.

The humming around them grew higher, more urgent. The girls ahead broke into a run. "Don't—" Mrs. Rodoya began.

Revna didn't see the Dragon. But for a terrible moment she heard its deep, haunting cry as its port opened and the bombs fell. It sounded like the mating call of some haughty creature. A creature that brought dust and fire.

The street next to them exploded.

Revna threw her arms up as heat rolled over them. Mrs. Rodoya released the back of her chair and the world rocked, trying to shake them from its surface. A spray of gravel tore through her factory uniform and bit at the arm beneath.

Someone gripped her shoulder and Revna opened her eyes. Mrs. Rodoya bent over her, lips moving soundlessly. "Revna," she mouthed. A flurry of words poured out of her, lost in the haze and the high whine in Revna's ears. Then she turned and ran down the road after the others, disappearing into the smoke.

Dust and panic lodged in Revna's throat. Buildings leaned out over the road. Garbed in their peeling propaganda posters, they looked half-demolished already. She tried to take deep, slow breaths, but how could she with the wreckage of Tammin threatening from all sides? She pressed her hand over her mouth. She had to identify the problems, as Papa used to tell her. Clear thought led the way to real understanding. *And you can't overcome a problem if you don't know what the problem is,* he'd said.

Problem: Mrs. Rodoya was gone. If Revna wanted to get to the shelter, she'd have to move herself. Which had never been an issue before, when the skies were clear and the Dragons were a distant threat. She tried to push herself into the street, but her wheels caught on the rubble.

Problem: If she didn't get to the secondary citizens' shelter soon, she'd be locked out.

The city was silent for a breath. Maybe the Elda and their Dragon had already gone. Maybe they'd left a little greeting as they made their way to some other target. Or maybe she couldn't hear them dipping through the smoke to come find her. In the gray half-light of the world, she could hear nothing, see no one.

Which meant that no one would see her if she used the Weave.

The Weave sat like an extra sense in the back of her head. Invisible strings aligned the world, crisscrossing like crowded threads on a loom. Loose threads hung ragged where the bomb had torn them apart, though they already reached for one another, trying to smooth over the gap. Revna could feel the threads, even grasp them. They shivered with magical energy. She could make it to Mama if she used its power.

But the Weave was illegal magic. While spark magic gave energy to the world, Weave magic distorted it. The Union declared it immoral and unlawful. Tonight, it might be the difference between life and death. And what did it matter if using the Weave warped the fabric of the world? The world was a mess as it was.

A better daughter of the Union, the good girl who took her cues from propaganda posters, wouldn't even think about it. She would place her own life far below the well-being of the land, and not for dread of the Information Unit or of a long sentence on a prison island. She would do it for the love of the Union. But Revna didn't love the Union. It had taken her father and worked her mother twelve hours a day. It had put her in a dirt-lined cellar for secondary citizens instead of one of the strong, concrete shelters built for the other factory girls. To the Union, she was a burden.

Revna pushed herself out of her chair and started up the street. She picked her way around the debris scattered over the road with her hands extended, ready to grab the Weave if she lost her balance.

An explosion rumbled somewhere behind her, and she caught a high scream through the cotton feeling in her ears. Her heart pumped liquid terror. Mama might still be out here, fighting to reach the shelter through closed-off roads and Skarov checkpoints. The shelter would close soon. But if she made it there, and Mama didn't—

The world thrummed. The Dragon was making another pass. Ash fell on her upturned face like snow, the little flakes clinging to her sweat-soaked forehead.

The old half-timber house next to her sagged, as if hundreds of years of standing upright had taken their toll at last. Fire bloomed behind its windows. Shingles tumbled from the roof. Revna stopped, transfixed.

A silver blur grabbed her by the arm and the Skarov officer began to haul. His fingers dug into her shoulders hard enough to leave a bruise. "Come," he shouted.

His voice seemed so far away. Revna stumbled after him, wheezing as ash filled her mouth, bitter and hot.

She didn't know whether to pull the Skarov closer or push him away. Her hands clawed at his coat. *My mother*, she tried to say, but when she opened her mouth nothing came out. Her ears filled with the sound of her heart.

The world began to darken. A massive shape dispelled the dust and ash—death streaming in for a final kiss. Certainty seized her like a vise, certainty that she was going to die. And it might be her fate—it might even be what the Union expected of her. But it wasn't what she wanted.

The cloud parted. The sky fell.

She didn't think about finesse or delicacy. She didn't think about whether she'd be shot later. She wanted to live.

Revna reached for that sense at the back of her mind. She grabbed two threads with one hand and looped her arm around the Skarov's waist. Then she pulled with everything she had.

They shot forward. Revna clenched her fists until her knuckles pushed against her skin. The threads slid against her fingers, trying to break free and rejoin the Weave. She didn't dare let go. She floated in her own thin universe of dust, of smoke, of destruction, and for that moment it was hard to tell whether she was living or dead.

The Skarov yelled, digging his fingers into her arm. Living. She was definitely living. The threads of the Weave slipped through her hand, and the world rushed up to meet them.

She hit first, landing hard on a pile of rubble and rolling onto her back. Dust puffed up as the Skarov came down beside her.

Loose pieces of brick and mortar bit into her spine. Pain shot through her calves and the bottom of her residual limbs. Her torso was agony. Her phantom feet burned. She blinked through her tears. Pain was good; pain meant her back hadn't broken in the fall. She tried to push herself off the rubble, but her hands only scraped on gravel and brick dust.

Her prosthetics. Had they broken? She fumbled for the straps.

A shape disturbed the smoke around her. The Skarov officer had gotten to his feet and was dusting off his coat. But his strange eyes never left her face.

She should have known she couldn't hide forever. Weave magicians were evil. How could she think that she was special, that she was different? What right did she have to ruin the world?

It's already ruined, she thought. Then she thought, *I never meant for it to go this far. I don't want to die. God, I don't want to die.* But there was no God to beg. So said the laws of the Union.

The Skarov stepped forward, bracing his back foot on the ground and leaning in to grab her by her prosthetics. She groaned as they twisted and scraped on her residual limbs. He'd break them if he wasn't careful. "Stop," she pleaded, coughing ash.

His hands moved up, gripping her waist just under her rib

cage. And then she stopped worrying that he might break her legs, and started worrying that he might break *her*.

I saved you, she tried to say. *Please*. But the words wouldn't come.

He pulled her to her feet. "Walk," he said with iron in his voice. He gripped her shoulders, steering her.

She could do nothing but obey.

2

I GIVE MY SON GLADLY

Linné stood at attention outside her colonel's office, cursing herself. Colonel Koslen's voice cut through the thin walls, and she caught words such as *honor*, *disgrace*, and *stupidity* as he blasted the unlucky Lieutenant Tannov with the full force of his wrath. Linné's blood sang. She'd be trembling if she let herself relax. But that was her secret to being in the army: Never let your guard down.

That *had* been her secret to being in the army. Then she'd been stupid and allowed her guard to slip. Now she was here.

The few men who walked by shot her curious glances. She ignored them all, as she'd ignored the catcalls from those who thought the humiliating discovery of her sex was somehow hilarious. When she realized the game was up, she'd swiped some brandy from under Tannov's bed, hoping to fortify herself. She'd taken only a swig or two, but now she couldn't decide whether it was the brandy or the fear that turned her thoughts upside down.

The slate sky gave way to a bleed of color with twilight, and the temperature was fast dropping toward night. Clouds piled on the horizon, as they always did in early autumn, becoming darker and colder until they finally rushed in to unleash the first howling storms.

The shouting ceased. Linné wished she'd had time for a rascidine cigarette. Maybe she should've taken the rest of Tannov's bottle.

The door creaked. Tannov's voice came from over her shoulder. "The colonel wants to see you, Private—" He stopped. "Um, miss."

Miss. He said it like he didn't even know her. They'd served together for three years. Tannov had screamed at her, sworn at her, threatened her, punished her. She'd gotten him drunk the night before his promotion, and she'd shot the Elda by steadying her rifle on his shoulder. When she roared at a charging Elda soldier, he'd laughed and called her "little lion," and everyone in the regiment followed suit. Once, they'd sworn they'd get their Hero of the Union medals together. Now he averted his eyes and stepped smartly to the side, leaving the door open for her.

March, soldier, she told her feet. She could do that, at least, even with the cocktail of rage, nerves, and brandy inside her.

Colonel Koslen's office smelled of sweat, earth, and oil. Papers lay scattered across his desk, the aftermath of a bureaucratic war. Koslen stood behind the desk, clenching and unclenching his ham hands as Linné came in. The colonel cut an impressive figure, tall and broad and with biceps the size of Linné's head. Tannov and their friend Dostorov had joked that before the war, Koslen was a goatherd who liked the smell of goats better than the smell of women. Linné preferred to mock his glorious mustache, waxed to a curl. It twitched whenever he spoke, whenever he sighed, whenever he lost his temper, or whenever it seemed a particularly difficult thought was pushing itself through the sludge of his brain. After any ordinary disciplinary action, Linné would return to the barracks with her finger over her upper lip, wiggling it back and forth as she described Koslen's temper.

No one would laugh at the joke now. They'd laugh at her.

Koslen studied her round face, her dark hair, her thin body, searching out the little touches that branded her as female. Linné pushed her shoulders back, daring him to say something.

They stood that way for several long moments. Then he sighed. "Please, take a seat." He gestured toward his chair, the nice chair. "Would you like some tea?"

Linné's palms began to burn. For three years he'd treated her like a soldier. And suddenly she was a girl. A *miss*. She fought to keep her face neutral. If she took his offer, she'd be relegated to the status of a woman, an outsider, unfit to serve. If she refused, he could claim that she was incapable of following orders.

Koslen went over to a silver samovar, squeezed onto a side table next to the company's hulking radio. Wasting precious metal had become a serious offense around two years ago, when the heads of the Union had realized just how bad the war was about to get. But officers always managed to squirrel something nice away.

Linné slid into the hard chair reserved for the colonel's subordinates, sitting rigid with her wrists propped on the desk. "Thank you, sir."

Koslen stopped midstep toward the chair she'd taken for herself. Then he turned and went to his own as though he'd meant to all along. He placed one cup of pale golden tea in front of her and took a sip from the other.

"You've turned our little regiment quite upside down, miss." His tone was all exaggerated courtesy. A gentleman could never shout at a lady.

"Have I, sir?"

Koslen frowned. The mustache twitched as he inhaled, slowly and deliberately. He could smell the brandy on her. She should've left it alone.

He was silent for a moment, and behind his eyes she saw some sort of argument raging. Then he seemed to make up his mind. "I'm not going to waste time. If you have no shame for your actions, perhaps you should consider how you have endangered the men of your company."

Linné pressed her lips together. Arguing got a soldier latrine duty, or graveside duty, or watches for the witching hours.

Perhaps he mistook her silence for contrition. "War is simply not women's work, miss," he said.

Though apparently it is goatherds' work, Linné thought. She couldn't help herself. She imagined her next words running along an iron beam, strong and steady. If her voice shook, Koslen might think she was close to tears instead of holding back her rage. "I have served faithfully, sir. I have been loyal to the Union and the regiment."

"You have distracted the men," Koslen replied. "They cannot

spend their time at the front worrying for your safety. Don't you understand? You don't just endanger their lives by coming out here. You endanger their minds, their ability to think."

Cowards. She recognized the lie, even if Koslen didn't. The men were afraid that she could no longer do her job. They were afraid that she'd never been able to do her job. That every mistake she'd ever made was because she was a girl, and not because she was human.

"I admire your heart. And your courage. And the Union appreciates the...enthusiasm with which you have risen to serve."

"Then why not keep me?" she burst out. Damn it, she had to stay calm. She wouldn't let Koslen's last memory of her be some hysterical thing who confirmed his suspicions. "We've just lowered the draft age. Again. I can fight better than the new recruits."

Koslen's jaw clenched. "Everyone has a place in this war, miss. And I'm certain we can find a role for you. A role that suits you, that helps the men focus and provides stability and strength to the armed forces. Won't that be best for the Union?"

A *role.* He was bullshitting to get her to agree to be some administrator in the city while her friends went to the front. No one won a Hero of the Union medal by sitting behind a desk. Heat pricked at her eyes, and for the first time Linné worried she might cry in front of the colonel.

She had to say something before her fate was sealed. But she didn't know what.

Koslen pulled out her file. He examined the photograph, then her. Then the photo. Her bronze skin was washed out by the flash, which only made the freckles across her nose more prominent. The photo made her look defiant. It dared anyone who saw her to underestimate her. "It *is* me," she said.

"I beg your pardon?"

"The photograph. I didn't fake it or anything."

"I see. But I presume Alexei Nabiev is not your real name." Koslen dipped a smooth, glass-tipped pen into an inkwell and drew a line over Linné's alternate identity. Three years of her life, three years of faith and loyalty, erased from record. "Whom do I have the pleasure of addressing?"

"Linné Alexei Zolonov," she said. She deliberately left the feminine *a* off the end of her name.

His pen jumped across the page, trailing a streak of thick black ink. Koslen cursed and blotted at the paper. Linné turned her snort into a cough, though her amusement stalled as he scrawled her real name in a free, unblemished space. He focused on her photo again, but this time he was looking for someone else. He was trying to see her tall, pale father in the lines of her face and figure. He wouldn't find the resemblance. She took after her mother in far too many ways, including her looks. "Your father's name?"

"Alexei Ilya Zolonov," she confirmed. General. Hero of the Union. Second commander of all land units in the armed forces. He'd been called the fourth-most-powerful man in the nation. At home he'd once joked that it was lucky he had such influence over the first three.

His voice rose to a squeak. "Does...your father know that you are here?"

Linné took a moment to savor the sheer panic on his face. "Of course not." Her father was powerful, but even he had rules.

Koslen's eyes rested on the scrawl he'd made. She could see the battle raging behind them—or perhaps, more important, behind his mustache. "Would you wait outside for a few minutes, miss?"

"Yes. Sir," she added. Koslen ignored the jab. As she left she heard the whir of the radio starting up.

The air outside was crisp and thin compared with the stuffy interior of the colonel's office. Linné took a deep breath. Maybe if she thought of a convincing enough argument, Koslen would reconsider. She could tally her confirmed kills, her sharpshooter skills, her last score on a spark exam. She could remind him of the time she'd saved his life by caving in the skull of an Elda soldier. Not that she particularly wanted to remember that herself.

Her thoughts evaporated. Tannov still stood outside the office, with the patient expression of a soldier who might, at any moment, be called back in for another verbal beating. Dostorov stood next to him, his stoic look marred by the dead end of a cigarette clamped between his lips. He'd once said he joined the army to save money on rascidine, and Linné was only three-quarters certain that was a lie. The sour smoke drifted in a perpetual cloud around his head. The fiery hues of sunset had turned to deeper colors behind them, and no doubt they had better places to be. What were they doing here? *Don't let your guard down.*

"So," Tannov said at last.

So what? she wanted to ask. But that would invariably lead to

So, you're a girl, which would be a stupid way to start a conversation after he'd been the one to walk in on her with her shirt off. And enough bureaucratic garbage had spewed from Koslen's maw to fill her with rage for months.

Dostorov spat his cigarette butt into the dirt. The barracks were quiet around them as the men went in for dinner on the other side of the base. The few living metal constructions that passed were little messengers, scuttling like brainless spiders as they ferried notes and small supplies. Linné forced herself to ignore the boys next to her rather than to wonder at their strange, silent vigil.

They stayed that way for some minutes. Then Tannov said, "How'd you do it?"

"What?"

Light crackled over Tannov's fingers, tiny pops of spark magic that flashed as they disappeared into the Weave. He'd always been the worst of them with his spark. But he wasn't paying any mind to the way it flickered. He gazed at her with earnest, too-bright eyes. Maybe he'd been at the brandy himself. "*Three years*. I never thought—I never suspected—" He turned to Dostorov. "Did you know?"

"Course not," said Dostorov, looking up at a break in the cloud cover, where the first bright stars of night peered through.

What little hope Linné had shriveled away. Maybe they didn't catcall, but she wasn't good old Alexei anymore.

"I've never even seen you piss. I mean, um, urinate," Tannov said. Dostorov punched his shoulder. "I mean—"

"Just stop," she snapped.

Tannov stiffened. He looked hurt in a way he'd never looked

when she'd lost her temper, or hit him, or stolen his cigarettes or beaten him at cards. And she knew why. And all the things she needed to say bottled up in her throat, refusing to come out as anything but righteous fury.

Linné's palms itched. She was as good a soldier as Tannov. Better, even, in some ways. She could hit a bull's-eye every time she tried. She could shoot that ridiculous mustache off Colonel Koslen's face without drawing blood. And she could let out a blast of spark that would knock an Elda soldier back ten feet. Yet Tannov and Dostorov and their fumbling magic would be at the front again in a few days' time, and she would be headed north to an office and the displeasure of her father.

The itch in her hands became a burn. She knew she shouldn't, but she brought them forward, letting her spark form into a hot glowing orb in front of her. Women weren't forbidden from doing spark magic. Perhaps she could set Tannov's shoelaces on fire. He'd be sloshing around in unlaced boots for weeks until he could requisition new ones. Or she could blow up the new cigarette that Dostorov was failing to light with a flicker of his own spark.

Why are you here? she wanted to scream. Would they swagger back to the mess when she was gone, reenacting the downfall of Alexei Nabiev?

The door of Koslen's office opened. They dissipated their spark like three guilty schoolboys. It flashed along the lines of the Weave, and Linné let hers go.

Colonel Koslen watched her, with his eyebrows—and, somehow, his mustache—raised. "You two," he said to the boys. "If you have so much time to waste, you can waste it on pot duty in the kitchen. Get out of my sight." His voice turned slightly soft, slightly sweet. "Would you care to join me inside, miss?"

"Yes, sir," Linné replied. He stepped aside, and she had no choice but to let him hold the door for her. When she looked back from the threshold, Tannov and Dostorov had already disappeared in the fading light.

Maybe she should have said goodbye to them. But the old Alexei wouldn't have, either.

She and Koslen sat again. "I've spoken to your father's staff," Koslen said.

"That was quick," Linné murmured.

She hadn't meant for him to hear, but Koslen said, "He's quite concerned with your welfare. He was under the assumption that you were at a school."

Which demonstrates exactly *how much he cares.* She had never worried that her father might come to look for her when she'd run away. His life and love was the war, and it left him no time for children.

"It turns out that you are very much in luck, Miss Zolonova." In luck. That probably meant her father was coming to pick her up personally. "It is still an unofficial decision at the moment, but..."

"But what?" Linné leaned forward. Too late she remembered she should call him *sir*, but he didn't seem to notice.

"There has been a decision to found a regiment devoted to women's service at the front," he said.

Don't get too excited. It was probably nursing, or preparing the dead for burial, or something else that involved staying behind the lines.

"What do you know of flying machines?" he said. His mouth twisted, like the very speaking of it left a bitter aftertaste.

Her heart crashed. "Airplanes? The Weavecraft of the Elda, sir. Illegal witchcraft."

"Hmm. Well, the commander may still have a use for you. She's searching for girls with experience in engineering, weaponized spark, or—" Koslen hesitated, frowning. "Other kinds of magic."

Other kinds of magic. He could only mean Weave magic. The thought of it sent a shiver along her skin. The Weave blanketed and protected the world. But those who used it pulled its threads out of order, warping them so that swaths of land lay dead and abandoned, while the tangles fostered a dangerous crush of magic. The Elda worked the Weave and didn't seem to care about the consequences. But Weave magic had been illegal in the Union since before it had become the Union. Were they so desperate that they'd turn their backs on their principles?

Or perhaps they were only desperate enough to let the women turn their backs on their principles. Linné fought, once more, to keep her voice steady. "With all respect, sir, I would serve the Union better stationed with the regular army." She knew how to fight, knew how to take care of her friends. Knew how to advance and how to try her luck for a Hero of the Union medal. And she knew that what she was doing was right. She was saving the Union, not destroying it.

"If you serve on the ground, then you shall serve in the offices of Mistelgard," Koslen said. "It's the best I can do."

So that was it. If she joined the women's regiment, she'd be forever tainted by her connection to the illegal Weave. If she said no, she'd be sent back to her father a failure. A disobedient failure, at that. Two things her father despised, all rolled up into her.

"How can I be a pilot if I've never used...other magic?"

"If you'd rather go home, I can arrange for you to be on the next transport." The colonel turned toward the radio.

"No." The spark flashed through her, so hot she thought it would burst from her clenched fists and make a smoking hole in the office floor. She couldn't go home. She couldn't be a secretary. She couldn't leave her friends at the front to face the Elda while she sat locked in her house, serving penance to a father who didn't care what she could do. Who cared only how good she made him look.

Koslen half turned to study her. His finger brushed the knob of the radio.

Bitterness filled her throat and she clung to her rage. If she let go, even for a moment, it would come crashing out, and Koslen would declare her unfit, even for an experimental regiment, even for an illegal one. "I would be honored to join the regiment, sir." She squeezed her fists until her nails cut her palms, until the sting drove her spark back in. She'd made a promise to herself, years ago, to fight like her father, to fight despite her father.

And I will, she thought, glaring at the top of Koslen's bent head. *No matter how many men like you get in my way.*

3

SEIZE YOUR CHANCES

The latch scraped on Revna's front door around midnight. Mama came in, a gray shape with a sleeping Lyfa in her arms. She let out a sigh as she leaned on the door to close it.

"I'm home," Revna whispered from the bed.

Mama half screamed. "Oh my—" She clapped her hand over her mouth, banging Lyfa's head against the door. Lyfa began to cry.

"Here." Revna reached out, and Mama came forward, depositing Lyfa in her lap. Mama's face was as gray as her uniform. Dust and ash coated her hair, ringed the inside of her nose, powdered her lips. When the tears spilled over, they left tracks on her cheeks that smeared when she palmed at them. She bent down and pulled Revna into a hug so tight that Revna could feel the trembling in her arms, her legs, her shoulders. Lyfa sobbed between them, confused and tired and rubbing her sore head.

Mama wrestled out of her coat while Revna held Lyfa, rocking her gently. "Lyfa," she murmured, and her sister's wails diminished. Her hearing was coming back, though she could think of better ways to find that out. "What's your favorite constellation?"

Lyfa sniffed. "Oryxus Brenna," she said in her small voice, still sticky with tears. She was four years, three months, and she could say star names that Revna had never known.

"Good job." Revna squeezed her tight. Lyfa would be a brilliant astronomer when she grew up. If they made it to the other side of the war. If they could afford to buy her books on physics and astronomy and mathematics. If they could persuade the men-only science academy to take her. And how was Mama going to do all that once Revna was arrested for using the Weave?

As Mama washed Lyfa with a cloth and changed her into a nightshirt, Revna wriggled out of her uniform. Then she took Lyfa and lay down. Stripes of pain still wound their way up her leg. Her prosthetics rattled against the wall, weary and terrified. She focused on the sound of Lyfa's breathing, trying to match it as it slowed.

Mama ran the wet cloth over herself, then slid into the bed on the other side of Lyfa. Normally she slept in the loft, in the bed she'd shared with Papa before he'd been taken away. Now she pulled Lyfa close and cupped one hand around the back of Revna's head, stroking her hair.

"What happened?" she said.

"Our route got bombarded...." Revna told the story in halting whispers, choking out the words when shame threatened to close up her throat. She'd been such a coward. Why had she thought about the Weave before her family? What would happen to them once she was branded a traitor? But she had to tell the truth. If she was going to be arrested, Mama deserved to know why.

The Skarov officer had taken her home after their near miss, depositing her at her front door with a muttered "Stay inside" before he fled. Revna still didn't understand. Was he waiting for her family to join her so he could arrest them, too?

"Oh, my darling," Mama said when she was finished. She and Papa had admonished Revna whenever they'd caught her using the Weave. They gave her spark tests instead, encouraged her to practice the one form of magic that was legal in the Union. But she hadn't been able to keep away from the Weave. She'd used it when no one was watching. She'd learned how the threads could move her over the ground, and once, she'd even pulled herself up to the loft where Mama and Papa slept. But the Weave was dangerous, and she'd stopped herself for love of the Union.

"I'm sorry," she said. She shouldn't have been so resentful after Papa was arrested. She shouldn't have kept working the Weave, even a little, in secret. She'd probably be dead now, but at least Mama would get a few days off work for mourning.

"When they locked the bunker, I was so afraid you'd—" Her hand tightened around the back of Revna's head.

"It's okay," she said, wiggling closer. It wasn't okay—they both knew that—but what else could she say?

"And Mrs. Achkeva, whining about her dog, how unfair it was that she couldn't bring him down. As though we had air in the bunker for all the creatures on God's earth—"

"Mama," Revna warned her gently.

"I know," Mama said, flapping her hand. Mama had been the spiritual one, going to temple every seven days. She didn't pray anymore, but she called on this god or that one a little too often for a good Union citizen. "But you were missing, and you weren't the only one, and all this woman cares about is her poor dog...." She sighed.

Revna echoed her sigh. It was cozy in the bed with the three of them. She wished she could be relieved that they'd all made it through the raid, but she still couldn't quite believe it.

"I'll write to your father in the morning," Mama said. "If you want to add to the letter."

Revna didn't answer. The lump in her throat had grown too large. Of course she wanted to add to the letter. Papa wasn't allowed to write to them, but they could send him mail, no doubt heavily edited by some bored Information Officer on the prison island.

"He'd be proud of you, you know."

Revna let out a soft sound, somewhere between a laugh and a snort and a sob. "For breaking the law?" A tear slid over the bridge of her nose.

"For saving a man's life," Mama said.

"Even a Skarov's?"

28

Mama brushed her tears away with a thumb. "Especially then. It takes a lot to save a man you hate." Her breathing evened, and before Revna could think of a suitable reply, Mama was asleep.

✳

The Union frowned on superstition and pointless tradition, but Revna had grown up with superstitions, and she even had one about herself. She was a curse. And her family was cursed with her. Every time something good happened to her, something bad seemed to happen to them. When Papa had used factory scrap to replace her old prosthetics, she'd walked better than she had since before the accident. Then he'd gotten arrested. Every time she had a good day at the factory, Mama or Lyfa came home crying. And now she'd survived outside in the air raid, caught using the forbidden Weave, and Mama was going to be branded as the woman with two family traitors.

Revna didn't think she'd be able to sleep, but somehow the swirl of dread turned into dreams of dust and silver coats, and when someone finally banged on the door, light peeked around the blackout curtains. Mama woke up and gave her a worried look, but slid out of the bed and combed her fingers through her hair before opening the door. She murmured to whoever stood outside, then shut the door and pulled the blackout curtains back. Lyfa grunted and wriggled farther under the blankets as light flowed into the room, but Revna sat up.

"What's happening?" she croaked. Her voice had thickened in the night.

Mama picked up her uniform and scrubbed at a palm-sized

orange stain. "The factories are running," she said. "Extra pay if we come to work today." She was a cook for one of Tammin's explosives factories, and she came home stinking of garlic and cabbage every night.

Revna leaned back against the headboard, gathering a blanketed Lyfa in her arms. "The Elda didn't hit them?"

"Not one." Mama put wood into the stove and grabbed the blackened teakettle. "So much for their Dragons."

Revna thought of the buildings crashing around her, the smoke parting like a ghostly curtain, revealing the end of her life. She set Lyfa down and scooted to the edge of the bed to retrieve her legs. Mama looked up from where she leaned over the spitting fire. "What are you doing?"

"If the factories are open, then I'll get extra pay, too," Revna said.

"Oh, no." Mama brandished the kettle at her. "You don't need to be attracting attention to yourself. Whatever miracle saved you last night, I don't want to chance it."

Miracle, curse. She knew Mama wouldn't want to hear her talk like that, so she grabbed her uniform off the floor and said, "The Skarov know where I live, not where I work," and she got on with it.

"You're making it cold," Lyfa complained in a muffled voice.

Revna patted the lump of blanket next to her. "It's light, Lyfa. Time to get up. You can help me with my legs, if you want."

As Lyfa poked her nose out from under the blanket, Revna finished buttoning her uniform and reached for her prosthetics. She pulled on her socks first, modified tubes made from old flour sacks. They protected her from the slim sheet of living metal that slotted over her legs next, tightening on her calves. There was a pin at the bottom of each sheet, which snapped into the outer legs. She let Lyfa draw the straps at the top of the outer legs tight, threading them through three buckles at her calf and knee. The living metal did the rest, pressing against her like a firm hug. She winced. Her legs were still sore from the night's action, and her prosthetics still shivered with fear. She rubbed at the area around the buckles, trying to send calming thoughts. But her mind was filled with the Skarov, and the Skarov never brought calm.

Mama pursed her lips as she watched. "You were caught out of the bunker. There's no shame in taking a day off."

"If I don't go, someone else will pull a double shift." *For the glory of the Union.* Worse, the Skarov would have one more reason to arrest her. And perhaps worst of all, no one in the factory would blame her for staying home. *Poor girl tires easily,* they'd say behind her back.

Mama sighed through her nose. She ushered Lyfa into an oversized coat and took her to the neighbors. By the time she came back, Revna had gotten up and poured herself a cup of tea. Her uniform was stiff with dust and crackled whenever she moved. It stank of smoke and heat. Then again, the whole city smelled of fire. She'd fit right in.

"I'll take you before I go to the kitchen," Mama said. "Where's your chair?"

"Under someone's house. I can take myself."

"And then Mrs. Prim Rules can fire you because you didn't come in your chair?" Mama rolled her eyes and got the extra chair out of the cupboard. It rattled Revna back and forth on anything but the smoothest roads. But Papa had made it, and she loved it.

Before she'd gotten hit by the cart, Revna had hated to sit down. She'd run everywhere and not even Papa could keep up with her. And that was how the accident had happened. She'd been nine, running free, flying over the ground. Then she'd woken in the Tammin factory hospital, on fire from the calves down.

Her right leg had been amputated just above the ankle, her left leg just below the knee. The phantom pains visited her every day at first, pricking where her feet and ankles used to be, as though they'd gone to sleep and needed a good shake. The sight of the crude wooden legs Papa made for her, little better than stilts, had nauseated her. She'd learned to walk on them, though, and when she outgrew them, Papa made her new ones. Each time he replaced them they got a little better, a little better, and then he'd brought home enough scrap metal from the factory to fashion the living metal legs for her. He'd adjusted them after her last growth spurt, and the metal tried to take care of her in its own way. She could walk, nearly as well as anyone else, but they'd kept the chairs for when she got tired, and now her job depended on them.

She buttoned her coat and got her clean scarf from the peg by the door. Mama tucked it under her coat, then leaned in and kissed her on the forehead. "I'm glad you're here," she said.

"Me too," Revna replied.

A second knock sounded. "Yes?" Mama said, wrenching open the door.

A man in a silver coat pushed her aside. No, *the* man in the silver coat. The Skarov Revna had saved. And he had two others with him.

Problem: She was about to be arrested.

She'd expected it. She'd spent half the night thinking about it. But that didn't stop the shaking in her hands, or the involuntary squeeze of her prosthetics against her calves.

"Revna Roshena?" said the first. He looked as if he hadn't slept all night. One of his companions sported a black eye, while the other fiddled with the torn hem of his coat.

"What do you need, sirs?" Mama asked. She held her hands clasped in front of her and her head cocked, all politeness and curiosity. But Revna could see the whites of her knuckles, the way her throat bobbed when she swallowed.

The Skarov's eyes never left Revna. "We have business with your daughter."

Mama lifted her chin. "Then you have business with me, as well."

"It's all right," Revna cut in. Mama couldn't go around antagonizing the Skarov. She had Lyfa to think of. "You'll be late for your shift."

The Skarov glanced at his companions. Then he said, "You may come, if you wish."

"Mama," Revna began.

"Get in your chair," Mama said.

Revna knew what Mama was doing. She was trying to make Revna look helpless and innocent. If Mrs. Rodoya could be fooled into underestimating her, why not the Skarov? Revna didn't think it would help them this time, but she got into the chair and let

Mama push her out the door. Her gaze lingered on the things she wanted to remember. The stove. The lopsided ramp that Papa had stuck over the sagging front steps. The birch tree that defiantly broke through the stony ground in their yard. She'd climbed that tree, before the accident. She'd always intended to try again. This was probably the last time she'd see it.

Tammin was a bizarre mix of ruin and order. Buildings stood proud next to heaps of brick, all that remained of some people's homes and livelihoods. First responders and living metal flatbeds had cleared enough rubble that people could make their way to and from the factory quarter. They stopped to observe the strange little entourage as it passed, and Revna knew the news would be around Tammin before sunset. The traitor's daughter had been carried off, too.

Revna folded her hands in her lap and tried to ignore the whispers that followed them. This was how they would remember her. Not as the girl who was always on time, not the girl who worked hard and stayed late. She'd never given Mrs. Rodoya any reason to discipline her, nor given any of the girls on the assembly line some excuse to dislike her. She handled living metal better than anyone else on the factory floor, and most times she could calm it with a touch. No one would remember that. She was the disabled girl who was as traitorous as her father. GOSSIP WON'T HELP BUILD WAR MACHINES, but apparently it fueled Tammin.

The Skarov wove through the city, backtracking and second-guessing as they took streets that dead-ended in ruin. Mama and Revna fell behind, but they finally passed the munitions quarter and made their way to the nicer parts of town. Here the damage was worse, and the houses drooped, moments from collapse. First responders and young citizens picked through the wreckage, calling to one another when they thought they found life. Mama's hand rubbed her shoulder as they passed a team pulling a limp body from a collapsed house, and for the first time since last night, Revna was glad she'd used the Weave.

Tammin wasn't the first civilian-heavy city targeted by the Elda. Four years ago the Elda had flown their first prototype planes over Goreva Reaching, a mining town at the edge of Union territory. By breakfast, war had been declared. Everyone in Tammin had thought that the twenty-year truce between Elda and the Union meant peace, but the first bombing put an end to that.

The Elda had swooped in hard and fast to save the God Spaces, the holy sites where this god or that was said to have blessed the earth. Supreme Commander Isaak Vannin said there was no God, they wrote, so why should he be entrusted to take care of the God Spaces? According to the old traditions, Goreva was blessed by the goddess of the morning. The Elda decried the way the Union stripped the earth to pull gold and silver and living iron out of its depths.

Revna had always found it strange, though, that when the Elda took Goreva, the mining didn't stop. The resources had gone to Elda instead. And they'd used those resources to make Skyhorses and Dragons that could fly farther and farther north, all the way up to Tammin and its farmland, and the Teltasha Forest around it. And in some way that led to Revna being paraded through town, and what next? The family earnings cut again for Mama, the shadow of secondary citizenship dogging Lyfa's steps as she grew. Even if the war ended in the next few years, Lyfa would be punished—in which schools she attended, which jobs she could take. *Don't cry*, Revna told herself. The Skarov would think she was afraid. And she was. But more than that, she was angry.

Their journey ended at an impromptu military compound that had sprung up in the night. The wide double-story houses of the governor, the factory owners, and the wealthiest merchants hadn't escaped the Dragon fire, but a few stood with little damage. Dust coated their pane windows, and debris had been swept between ridged decorative columns. More men in silver coats directed the rebuilding effort, checking papers and generally doing whatever it was they did when they weren't arresting people and shipping them off to the far north.

The Skarov led them to a grand structure with a green tile roof. The front garden held a few battered flowers, clinging grimly to life. Nothing had escaped the fine sheen of dust from the bombardment. In peacetime Revna would have wept for such a house. Now she was glad for a less ostentatious one in a neighborhood the Dragons had ignored.

Mama wheeled her up the little flagstone path to the front door and eased the chair over the threshold, jostling Revna into the entryway. The front hall alone dwarfed any private residence she'd seen before, but the finery couldn't outshine the chaos. Muddy footprints crusted a wooden floor inlaid with a stark geometric pattern. A dark stain crept up the blue wallpaper, though the exact nature of the stain was something Revna didn't dare contemplate. A tree heavy with tiny green fruits had been overturned in the corner, and no one had bothered to sweep up the dirt or even turn the pot right side up. Bottles lined the grand stair—empty bottles, if she had to guess—and the entire foyer had a sour smell to it. Upstairs, someone screamed. Revna's hands clenched around the arms of her chair.

The Skarov with the torn coat trotted up the stairs. "Your chair, miss," said the tired one. A slim hall next to the staircase stretched to a series of rooms beyond. Her bulky old chair wouldn't fit.

"We'll have to carry you, miss."

"No," she replied, before she thought better of it. The word came out strong and angry. She flushed. But if this was her end, she didn't want to meet it in the arms of an enforcer. "I'll walk."

She gripped the banister at the bottom of the stairs and pulled herself up, taking care as she disentangled her feet from the little shelf her father had carved for them. When she had her balance, she looked back at the Skarov. The tired one stared outright at her legs, frowning at the pointed metal toes. The bruised one looked everywhere but her feet. Neither of them met her eye.

"This way," said the tired one, shoving past her.

✳

She'd expected to be taken into an interrogation room. She hadn't expected it to be so ... pink. The walls were a paler shade than the couch, which had a rose pattern woven into the silk and likely hadn't been in style since before their last war with the Elda. A walnut desk had been pulled into the center of the room to act as the interrogation table. The Skarov she'd saved took an upholstered chair. The bruised one shut the door in Mama's face.

The tired one gestured to the couch. "Take a seat."

Revna sank into an overstuffed cushion. Papers had been dropped on the floor in an unceremonious stack, and more had been shoved over the books on a small bookshelf in the corner of the room. Through the window she could see a square of hazy blue sky. The city jail must have been bombed. Why else would she have been brought here?

"Revna Roshena," Tired said, picking up a file on the desk and flipping it open.

He paused as if she was supposed to say something. "Yes?" He must've known who she was, and the file in his hand must've told him exactly *what* she was—child, traitor, amputee, factory worker.

"Age?"

Doesn't your fancy paper tell you? "Seventeen," she said. Her hands knotted together in front of her. It was getting hard to breathe.

He checked her face as he ticked off her physical description, and for a few moments the room was silent aside from the scratch of his pencil. His companion leaned against the door. Revna bit the inside of her cheek to hold back a hysterical laugh. After expecting the Skarov threat in every back alley, in every official building, she was about to meet her fate in an ugly pink room, sitting on a squishy rose-patterned couch.

"How long have you been experimenting with the Weave?"

"I—" *Never. Six months. A year.* She'd practiced each of these replies, and all of them were so obviously wrong.

"There's no point in lying." He looked at her for the first time since he'd come to the house. "I was there."

"I don't know anything," she blurted out. Which was a ridiculous thing to say, because everyone knew that she did.

"I flew twenty feet through the air because of you." He tapped her file on the table. "You saved my life."

"I didn't mean to."

He raised his eyebrows. "Didn't mean to save my life?"

No. "Everything was dark, and the buildings were falling, and we didn't have shelter—and I never knew I could do it. I've never done it before, and I'll never do it again." The words tumbled out of her, and as she watched him lick the end of his pencil and press it to paper, it all became worse somehow. She wanted to be proud, to own the truth and accept her fate with grace. But she kept talking, hoping to talk until she said something that saved her. "I'm useful here. I've never done anything wrong and I've never been late for my shift. You can ask my supervisor. Mrs. Rodoya. I do factory work, for the army—"

He leaned forward. "*I don't care,*" he said, setting his hand on the table. Revna stopped, mouth half-formed around a word. They sat like that for a moment. Then he drew back. "Your father taught you to use the Weave?"

"No." They couldn't pin another crime on Papa.

"Your mother, then."

"*No.*" Panic flushed her. "I taught myself."

"Impossible. You used a complex tactic—"

"My mother never knew—"

"*Don't* interrupt me," he snarled. His features twisted into something enraged and animal.

39

Revna's spine turned to ice. This was when they broke her limbs and scored her skin until she told them all about her life. She wondered how thin the walls were. Would Mama hear her scream in this makeshift cell? Revna wanted to think she'd stay strong under torture, for her family. But she couldn't be sure.

The latch clicked as the door opened. Revna jumped. Then she drew a shaky breath to tell Mama to get out.

But it wasn't Mama who stepped through the door. The woman who came in was short and dressed in a sharply tailored uniform that said *army*. She wasn't what Revna had expected some Skarov bruiser to look like. In fact, something about her was familiar. Revna wanted to recognize her but didn't quite know from where.

The woman looked from Revna to the bruised one to the tired one. "I told you to let me know when she arrived."

The bruised Skarov shifted, as if he was trying to edge out of the room without attracting attention. The tired one leaned back, clasping his hands in his lap. "We have a very particular procedure."

The woman smiled. It wasn't a kind smile, like Mama's, or even a patronizing smile, like Mrs. Rodoya's. It was a smile that begged the Skarov officer to take one more step in the wrong direction. "My procedure has precedence. Or would you like to check that with Isaak?"

His lip curled up, but he said nothing. He wasn't the same kind of predator that he'd been with Revna. He shoved his chair back. "I was sick of listening to her, anyway."

That was it? Some big interrogation and retrieval, all to be abandoned on an ugly rose couch?

The bruised Skarov slid out, and the woman stepped aside to

40

let the tired one pass. "Shut the door when you leave." She waited until it had slammed before she took a seat in the vacant chair. "Sorry about that. The Extraordinary Wartime Information Unit can be pushy. But I was the one who wanted to see you today. Not them."

Revna's head swung between the door and the woman. The woman stuck her hand out. "I'm Tamara Zima."

Revna felt her jaw go slack. The woman seemed familiar because her image had been on every newspaper and magazine cover; her words had been branded into the minds of thousands of young girls. Tamara Zima was the foremost aviator in the Union, practically the *only* aviator in the Union. She'd flown the very first Union plane to the war's front lines, she'd crossed the Union in a twenty-hour flight, and she was on record as being the only person to have told every general on Isaak Vannin's staff to go stuff himself.

Her hand was still outstretched. Revna wiped hers on her uniform and shook.

"You've pleased our Skarov troops," Tamara said. Revna couldn't help checking the door. "Believe it. They put on a stern face, but they were impressed. Otherwise they wouldn't have called me. I heard about you, and I had to come down to see for myself."

She was in league with them. As Tamara flipped through her file, Revna tucked her hands under her thighs and waited for the first question.

Tamara seemed to notice her unease. She leaned forward, crinkling her eyes in a smile much warmer than the one she'd given the Skarov. It was the kind of smile that made Revna want to smile back. But she didn't. This was only another technique in the

Union's interrogation arsenal. "You can relax, Miss Roshena. No one's here to arrest you. In fact, we're quite interested in you."

Revna didn't answer. Of course they were here to arrest her. They were interested in her because they wanted to get as much out of her as they could, before breaking her irrevocably.

"You have something the Union desperately needs," Tamara said.

That did give her pause. "Sorry?"

"What do you know of Elda aircraft?"

"They fly?" Revna guessed. Tamara raised an eyebrow, and Revna flushed. "I mean, they distort the Weave, and they use it to fly."

Tamara tilted her head. "Mostly true. In fact, what they do is an elaborate version of what you did last night. Which is why we find you so interesting."

So that was the game. "I'm not a spy." The words came out sharper than they should have. The Union could accuse her of treason all it liked. They weren't going to call her a turncoat, too.

Tamara took a deep breath. She scratched at the pages of Revna's open file with a pen. "I think we're coming at this from the wrong angle," she said at last. "I want to help you."

"Why?" Mama would have hissed at the impertinence of the question, but Revna was curious. When had the Union ever tried to help her?

"Because the Elda are winning this war from the air. If we want to fight them, we need air regiments of our own, and Weave pilots to help us. We need people who can do what you do. What *we* do," Tamara corrected herself, meeting Revna's eye.

"You use the Weave?" Revna said.

"How do you think I fly my own plane?"

She hadn't thought about it. "But—you're famous. Everyone knows you. And you're Isaak Vannin's—" She stopped just shy of saying *lover*. That was only rumor, anyway. "Good friend," she finished.

"I learned to fly in Elda, before the war. And what I learned there convinced me that the Weave's not as fragile as we think. Isaak Vannin believes that the risk is worth the reward, and he's given me permission to recruit as I see fit." She leaned forward. "I want you to help me save the North. Will you do it?"

Her eyes sparkled with promise. She seemed so certain, so sincere. All the same, resentment bit at Revna's belly. Tamara Zima had broken a law that was hundreds of years old, and she had a Hero of the Union medal. Revna's father had taken some unwanted scrap, and he'd pay for it the rest of his life.

Perhaps Tamara noticed her reluctance. She pressed on. "As a junior pilot, you'll be paid twenty-three marks per month, with room and board and a bonus for every successful mission. And..." She drew out the *and*, tapping the file in front of her. "Only Protectors of the Union are allowed to serve, so your family will be regranted status. As long as you're not discharged dishonorably... or convicted of treason."

She'd added that last part a little too casually, like an afterthought. Revna didn't care. The sound of her heart—the sound of her hope—could have drowned out the roar of a Dragon. "You can do that?"

"I've already put in the request. I'm *really* hoping you'll say yes." Tamara winked conspiratorially.

Revna had never imagined a life at the front. She'd never wanted one. She'd never wanted to work in the factories, or anywhere the Union could press down on her with its suffocating fingers. After all, it hadn't wanted her, with her metal legs and traitor father. But... *Protector of the Union*. All this time she'd been a curse, and now Mama and Lyfa could get something back. They'd regain their status, be provided with firearms and an extra ration card and entry into the safe shelters for good Union citizens. As long as she fell in line, it was a status they could keep.

Of course, Tamara might have talked to the Skarov first. She could have arranged to terrify Revna so that her timely offer would be even more miraculous. Knowing one way or the other wouldn't change Revna's answer, though.

"What do you say?" Tamara pressed.

You know what I say. But she said it anyway.

4

FOR EVERY GIRL A PLACE

Intelgard was *not* the front. The nearest front was over the mountains to the south, close enough for planes to fly there, but far enough that the regiment could tear down the base and retreat if the Elda marched over the mountain range.

The front had been muddy, cold, terrifying. But her friends had been there, and she'd always known what to do. Here Linné felt helpless, and her new comrades dismayed her. The girl recruits disdained their breakfast, complained when they had to march to the field, complained when they had to march *around* the field, and one was stupid enough to ask Colonel Hesovec what time they'd be served lunch. The only thing they could all wrap their heads around was the firing range. Given that citizens were registered for mandatory firearms practice from the age of ten, they impressed no one. When Colonel Hesovec was forced to supervise them, his criticism rained like bullets. But he never gave them instruction. He was waiting around, Linné thought, for the first opportunity to remove them from his base.

The girls took it personally, of course, and they clamored for Zima. The name Tamara Zima rang in Linné's ears from breakfast to dinner. Every girl wanted to see her, and Linné was no exception. She'd never met the woman her father called "Isaak's harpy," and she wanted to see the legend who controlled the Supreme Commander's heart and wore an army uniform as a woman without consequence.

Linné had been the first girl to arrive at Intelgard. The base had consisted of one long building for the men to sleep in and another to eat in. She'd been refused when she reported to the construction crews, so while the rest of Intelgard rose up around her, she and two staring raw recruits had inventoried supply palanquin after supply palanquin. She'd slept under a blanket in Hesovec's office until a separate barracks had been built—then she had that hall to herself, while the men crammed two to a bed. For three weeks all she'd heard was mumbled *miss*es from the soldiers and inventory notes from the colonel. When the rest of her regiment arrived, she welcomed them with enthusiasm...for about five minutes.

She hadn't expected the girls to be so *girly*. While she sewed up tears in her jacket, they embroidered their cuffs and buttonholes. They used their spark to make ice roses that melted at a touch. They'd brought dresses and fancy shoes. Olya even had a crystal radio to listen to her favorite radio play. When Linné warned her it would get confiscated, Olya smiled in challenge. Didn't they know *anything* about being soldiers?

46

Of course not. They hadn't jumped through hoops and cut their hair and bound their breasts and learned the foul language of the marching army. They hadn't walked an extra half kilometer to pee to make sure they weren't spotted. They'd sauntered in and expected to be treated like ladies.

Linné tried to help them at first. By evening she gave up. She sat alone, ate alone, and went out for inspection alone.

✳

The day's assignment saw them on the far side of an unused laboratory, crammed together with a map of the western Mariszkoy Mountains and orders to memorize peak heights and notable landmarks. Linné got to work. The others burst into complaint as soon as Hesovec left.

"I don't see the point," Olya said, shoving her topographical map away. She had fine fingers and the sort of soft face that adorned the pinup pictures Linné had seen in her old regiment. She pushed her curly brown hair out of her eyes. And she kept smiling at Linné as if she wished Linné would drop down a well shaft and never come out. "I was chosen to make bombs, not draw routes."

Linné couldn't let it be. "The Elda are on the other side of those mountains. What if you lose your way on a flight back? What if you crash?"

Olya smiled wider. "I can survive the mountains. I was at the top of my outdoor class in preparatory school."

"Surviving a park in Mistelgard isn't the same as getting lost in the mountains in wartime."

Olya kept smiling. The other girls weren't even pretending to work; their eyes darted between Linné and Olya as if they were watching a competition. "You always take the boar's side," Olya said.

"Don't call him that," Linné warned. Hesovec might make an ass of himself and waste resources, but it didn't mean the girls could make a habit out of bad-mouthing their superiors.

"Ha," Olya said. She probably thought Linné was only proving her point. "Why bother kissing up to him? He's never going to like you." She pulled the map back toward her and ran her hand through her short hair again. "No matter whose daughter you are." Olya had been the first to ask if Linné was *that* Zolonov. Linné's status seemed to make them hate her a little, and she struggled not to return the favor.

✳

Inspection took place on the airfield, which lay fresh and green and, most important, empty. Intelgard was the second air base on the southern front, and what few aircraft the Union had scrambled to put together had been sent to the first. No one screamed orders, and the day's construction hadn't yet begun. Little mechanical messengers scuttled from place to place, and the flat-backed palanquins that normally acted as people movers carried cheap board panels to build the base's administrative offices.

Linné watched the Union flag flap from a pole at the edge of the field, letting the cold kiss the back of her neck. The golden firebird flew on a field of red, wings outstretched, beak open to let out a war cry. Stars shimmered above its wingtips. She could see it small, pinned to her chest as a Hero of the Union medal, with a gold ribbon dangling like a burning tail. She could see the crowded hall, full of everyone who'd ever doubted her. *This*, she reminded herself. She was here for the Union and for glory. Not for anyone or anything else.

The men joined her right on time, trotting up and clustering a few meters away. A couple of the girls came, too, but most arrived after Colonel Hesovec started to pace along the line. The latecomers pelted up and tried to stand at attention. It would have been funny if Linné were allowed to laugh. But Hesovec didn't find it amusing, so neither did anyone else. He swelled so much that she thought he'd pop the bottom button of his uniform. Then he spoke to the girls.

"Late. Again. Always. And to make matters worse, not one of you is in uniform." Linné stared down at her issued boots and clenched her fists.

A girl at the end of the line piped up. "Excuse me. Sir." Linné leaned forward to eye her. The girl who spoke had half a head of height on most of the boys, long frizzy hair, and a friendly face. "We still don't have any uniforms."

Hesovec stopped and glared at her. "Why didn't you make a request?"

The girl looked around, bewildered. "For what?"

"Uniforms," he snapped. "What else?"

She considered. "May we have some uniforms, sir?"

Linné watched Hesovec's mustache twitch as he worked his lower lip. Apparently he'd attended the Colonel Koslen school of mustache expression. "What's your name?" he said at last.

"Magdalena Chuikova."

"And why are you here?" he said.

"I'll be an engineer," she replied.

Hesovec let out a short huff. "Good. You can spend the morning assembling the laboratory." He stepped back and raised his voice. "As for the rest of you—this sort of behavior will not be tolerated. You have asked to participate in the war, like men. If you truly want to, you'll have to act like them as well. Be timely, respect the discipline of the base, wear your uniforms, which I will assign forthwith, and attend to all duties given by your commander. Once Commander Zima is here, she will direct your pursuits. But until her arrival, I am in charge of the base and everyone on it. And I *will* send you away if you give me a reason. Clear?"

"Yes, sir," chanted Linné and the men. "Yes, sir," the girls chorused an instant after.

"Good. First things first: Everyone who was late this morning can practice their march around the yard. Zolonova, come with me. The rest of you, report to your platoon commanders for your morning assignments. Get this base built by the end of the day."

The girls set out across the yard with woeful faces. Some of them tried to emulate the march of the men, strutting across the field with their arms swinging like pendulums. Linné resisted the urge to put her face in her hands. Nearby, one of the male soldiers smirked. "I never thought the front would be a place for comedy."

"Shut it," she replied, and stalked off. The girls needed to be put in their place. They didn't need to be mocked.

"Zolonova," Hesovec mused as she approached. His eyes flicked over her form, dismissing her from head to toe. "You don't resemble your father much, do you?"

50

I hadn't noticed. "No, sir." Comments like that had followed her from childhood. When she was four, the Minister of Agriculture had joked, "Are you sure she's yours?" at an informal dinner. Her father had laughed, but three days later the minister was gone.

Hesovec led her past the barracks and office buildings, dodging metal constructs as they hauled cheap materials to the skeleton of a warehouse. He went into a finished warehouse and sparked the lamp inside. The interior smelled like damp pine and cold metal. Yellow light flickered over crates, piled haphazardly and stamped with the Union's firebird and stars. She'd stacked the uniform crates against the wall herself.

"Each girl gets one, and if any of you come back for a replacement, you'd better give a good reason for why. You'll have to take care of your . . . female needs yourself. Don't take too long sorting."

Oh, no. "Sir, I don't have much experience—"

"You can report back when you're done." There was a knock, and Hesovec wrenched open the door. "What?" he said to the cluster of silhouettes in the doorway.

"She says she's here for the girls' regiment, sir."

Hesovec's voice practically bled scorn. "Another one? Zolonova will show you where to go." He jerked his head and stomped away. Two shadows detached and fled after him.

The remaining figure peered through the doorway. Linné turned back toward the crates. "Come and help. We have to haul these to the barracks, anyway."

"What are they?" The new recruit had a soft, uncertain voice. A heavy tread, though. Linné expected a tall girl to correspond, but when she turned, she saw that the girl was shorter than her.

51

The new recruit had a pale, heart-shaped face framed by a tangle of black hair knotted at the nape of her neck.

Linné wrestled a crate off the top of the stack and dumped it with a thud that sent up a cloud of dust. "Clothes," she said. The girl leaned away, coughing. She didn't smile at Linné, and Linné didn't bother to smile at her. She didn't need to be anyone's mother hen. "Who are you?"

"Revna," the girl said. "Revna Roshena." She swallowed her last name like a curse. Linné could sympathize with that.

"Well, Revna, grab a crate. I'll show you where you sleep."

Linné led the way out of the warehouse, glancing back every so often to make sure Revna was keeping up. Was she limping? Linné caught the flash of strange, steel-toed shoes under her factory uniform, but when the girl caught her looking, she turned bright red and said, "Go ahead," a challenging glint in her eye.

"The army's no place for dawdling," Linné said. "You're going to have to work on that."

Revna opened her mouth to reply. Then she seemed to change her mind. But Linné felt resentful eyes on her back all the same. It seemed she'd failed, yet again, to make friends. Why had it been *easier* when she'd been a boy? She missed her old regiment. She missed Tannov and Dostorov. She even missed that buffoon Koslen.

By the time they got to the barracks, most of the girls had returned from the field. Linné shouldered through the door.

"What's that?" Pavi said. She was the smallest of them, short and slim, with dark brown skin and quick eyes and a black braid that fell between her shoulders. Her southeastern accent marked her as a girl from the edge of the Union.

"Uniforms. Organize yourselves from tallest to shortest," Linné said.

"And who's this?" Katya looked past Linné to the threshold, where Revna wobbled under her crate. Katya looked as if she belonged in a glossy magazine, not on the front lines. Hesovec had already told his men off for whistling after her. "Come in, come in. What's your name?"

Revna came in. And tripped over the threshold.

The *thunk* of metal on wood filled the room, quickly followed by the crash as Revna dropped her crate. All eyes moved to her leg.

Linné'd thought Revna had metal-toed boots, but that wasn't right at all. She had metal feet. Linné could see two steel toes, pointed and caked with dirt. The toes were longer and broader than flesh toes, forming a Y and attaching to a wide base that acted as the ball of the foot. It was wider than most shoes and capped with rubber. As Revna righted herself, Linné spotted a fat cylindrical heel, also capped in rubber. The steel toes dug into the ground, midjoints twitching with an odd precision. They were living metal feet, Linné realized. She had to stop herself from leaning forward for a better look.

The other girls gaped. But they weren't here to peer and frown and poke. Linné cleared her throat. "Revna's our newest recruit. And like the rest of you, she's going to be fitted with a proper uniform. So line up—"

Revna's dark eyes swam with tears. With every thunk of her

feet on the floor, she seemed to go more rigid. Katya took Revna by the elbow and led her over to an empty bed. She smiled like a film star, brushing her platinum curls over one shoulder. "Welcome, Revna," she said, and threw Linné an angry look over her shoulder. "Don't worry about Linné. Her father's a general, so she thinks she's in charge. But she's not, so you don't have to do what she says. Where are you from?"

Revna sat down and put a hand to her calf. Then she saw the girls all staring at her and jerked it back. "Tammin Reaching," she said.

"I'm from Tammin," Magdalena said. She'd finished her assignment suspiciously fast, Linné thought, and she suppressed a sigh of irritation as Magdalena lifted the dropped crate. Magdalena hauled it to the middle of the room, then went over to shake Revna's hand. The Linnés of the world got to carry their crates themselves, evidently. "Why didn't we come down on the same palanquin?"

"Had to process some paperwork," Revna said.

"What happened to your legs?" said another girl.

Revna stiffened. "An accident." Her tone was light, but she drew her lips together, and her legs curled under the bed.

"We're running late," Linné reminded them.

Katya turned on her. "Let her settle in."

"Welcome to the regiment," Linné told Revna. "Consider yourself settled and take your old uniform off. The rest of you have more crates to haul."

Katya rolled her eyes but beckoned the others. Linné heard them laughing behind her as she led them back to the warehouse. She told herself she didn't care what they were laughing about.

The uniforms consisted of a cotton tunic and trousers with a high-collared jacket for everyday use. Another crate contained wool coats, scarves, and gloves, and yet another held socks and belts. Everything was in the same shade of olive brown, except for the tin buttons on the jacket and the patch on one sleeve, decorated with a simplified Union star to mark them as enlisted. "We'll assign uniforms by size," Linné said.

Katya scoffed. "I don't need you to tell me what size I am. I can dress myself, thank you." She pursed her lips as she pulled out a canvas belt that could wind around her waist twice.

Linné had intended to match the large to the large and the small to the small. But soon it became apparent that small was a matter of opinion. Everyone but the towering Magdalena looked ridiculous.

"I can't use these," laughed Galina, a stocky brown-haired navigator. She'd worn a dress on her first day, to no end of amusement from the boys. Today she'd managed to find trousers, and she even wore boots, one of which she compared with her issued boot. The issued boot was at least six centimeters longer.

"Stuff it with socks," Linné said. They had plenty of those.

"Can't I wear the boots I brought? They fit, and they're nice." Galina wiggled her ankle.

"The army requires orderliness and sameness," Linné snapped.

"Which is why I'm going to bring it all in," Katya added. She held up a measuring tape and handed her writing kit to Elena, a quiet girl with a strong face. "Arms up," Katya said, and a bemused Pavi obeyed. The tape circled her waist. "Sixty-five," Katya said. Elena scribbled it down.

"You can tailor them on your own time. We have work to do," Linné said as Katya moved up to Pavi's bust.

"Like what?" Olya said.

Like reporting to Colonel Hesovec. Like doing whatever he told them. Like proving that they could act like soldiers, even though they couldn't.

"No one can be expected to go out in this." Katya held a pair of trousers up next to Olya. "Are we going to trip over the enemy?"

"You can take care of it tonight. Right now we have to report to Hesovec." Linné turned to go. She would do her job, no matter what. Maybe if the others proved themselves especially incompetent, the project would be abandoned and they'd all be sent home. *Except me.* She still had to get to the front.

"Should we report in or out of the uniforms?" Katya asked.

"Why don't you ask him? He'll be glad to give you another marching lesson, no doubt."

Katya snorted. "I'd rather march my boot up your—" Someone knocked at the door. Katya's eyes narrowed. "What did you do, tell on us before you even got here?"

"I didn't—" Linné started.

The door opened and a boy ducked inside, red-faced and tugging on his cap. "Sorry," he said. "Sorry. But Commander Zima's here. And she brought a plane."

5

OUR SOLDIERS MARCH
ON YOUR FAITH

For once, Linné wasn't the first out to the field. She marched while the rest of them ran—tripping over uniform legs and with one arm of their jackets flapping out behind them. She wanted to slink out of sight. But that wasn't what you did when your commanding officer arrived. She lifted her head and pretended she didn't see the boys sneering as she passed.

She got to the edge of the field and lined up next to Katya, who tucked a lock of pale hair behind her ear. Olya brought her hands in front of her, then behind. Others fidgeted in their own ways. Magdalena looked the most at ease in her uniform, like she belonged.

Tamara Zima's famous plane, *Winter Witch*, sat on the green. *Winter Witch* had been the first plane to fly from the western edge of the Union to the eastern one, the first plane mobilized in the war, the first plane to do practically anything. Not that they had many planes to go around. Zima stood in front of it, grinning.

Linné's father had spoken of Tamara Zima as though she were a giant, too large for the law. But she had a small frame, a round, smiling face, and more energy than the sun.

"It's wonderful to see you all," she said. She practically glowed, radiating the sort of happiness that Linné had rarely seen on the front lines. "You are the great success of a long war waged already, and you will be the success of this one."

All around her the girls straightened, like birds fluffing their feathers. Linné felt a swell of her own hope. But then she remembered being a new recruit under Koslen, trembling with nerves and an arrogant need to prove herself, listening to the veterans cover their disbelieving snorts with coughs as he ranted about the superiority of their soldiers. All commanders said this sort of thing.

"The Elda have a tactical advantage. They've had years to hone their Dragons, while we've had to work with what we can steal from the battlefield. But with special permission from Commander Vannin himself, production has started on our own line, which you will use to combat the Elda in the air."

The girls leaned forward, eager to drink up every word. When Zima drew breath to speak again, Linné recognized the telltale signs—the sagging mouth, the forced cheer, the deep, steeling inhale—that pointed to a commanding officer putting a positive spin on something. "The Elda have designed their Dragons as machines of force and power. They are intimidating, but they are slow to gain speed and slow to maneuver. Skyhorses are faster, but often less precise. These are the ways in which we seek to bring them down. I have been asked to form a corps of night bombers, and you are my choice. We will work counterpart to the men here: They will fly during the day, and we during the night. Our targets will be the camps, the front lines, anything that will hold the Elda back for one more day, anything that will break even one cog in their war machine. Soldiers, I have the highest faith in you. We will work hard, we will train hard, and we'll be at the front before the Elda even hear we can fly."

The girls cheered. Linné clapped but she didn't join in. Zima made it sound so easy, a matter of waltzing up to the Elda's aircraft and blasting them to oblivion. But Linné had seen Dragon fire turn the land black, burn palanquins and the men inside them until no one could tell what was metal and what was flesh. She'd seen the Dragons spew choking smoke and gas along the front line; she knew the terror of fumbling for her gas mask as she heard the final sounds of the men who hadn't found theirs. Sometimes she'd listened to them scream through the night. Sometimes she thought she could still hear them.

Something in her warmed horribly at the thought of repaying the Elda for her memories.

"There will be three of you for each plane. Pilots to steer the plane. Navigators to power and fire and plot the course. Engineers will be responsible for keeping her going, even when the night is cold or we've suffered enemy fire. If you're a pilot, report to Colonel Hesovec. Navigators to the map room. Engineers to the laboratory. A permanent schedule will be in the mess tomorrow morning. If you have any questions, please come speak with me at any time. I'll be assembling my office this evening." She beamed at them. "Welcome to the One Hundred Forty-Sixth Night Raiders Regiment."

The girls cheered again. The way Tamara Zima spoke filled Linné's mind with fire and victory, explosives dropped on a nameless foe, a triumphant return to a grateful Union. She could almost feel the fingers of Commander Vannin as he plucked the edge of her coat, the pressure as he pinned a shining Hero of the Union badge to her chest.

She wanted it to be real. Could it be real?

The noise abated. Linné watched as the others turned toward one another, toward the warehouses, toward their assignments— and away from her. Everything seemed suddenly wrong. Everyone else knew what to do, and she was in the dark.

Commander Zima stood with a paper in one hand, worrying the end of a pencil between her teeth with the other. She looked up as Linné approached. "What do you need?"

"I beg your pardon, sir, but I don't know where I should go now." Linné frowned even as she said it. She would never have begged a senior officer's pardon when she was a boy.

"Are you a pilot, a navigator, or an engineer?" Zima asked around the pencil.

"I don't know," Linné said.

"Ah. What's your name?"

"Zolonov, sir." The name still had to be pulled out of her. She missed being Alexei Nabiev, with no notable family, with nothing to her but boldness and rawness.

Zima must have recognized the name, but she didn't react. Maybe she thought there were plenty of Zolonovs in the Union. "Yes, I remember. You were the only one I didn't have a chance to meet." She stuck out her hand.

Linné stared at it. After a moment she understood and shook it uncertainly.

"It's a pleasure to see you at last, Miss Zolonov. Colonel Koslen wrote that you excelled with a rifle and had uncanny precision with your spark."

"Yes, sir," Linné said.

"I've marked you down as a navigator. I understand you have a little more army experience than the rest of the recruits?"

"I've been in the army since I was fourteen." It felt like admitting to a crime.

"Maybe we should make you a commander," Zima joked.

"No, sir," Linné said. Not with recruits like Katya and Magdalena.

The commander's mouth twitched. "You don't have to keep calling me that."

"Should I call you ma'am, sir?"

Koslen would have glowered. Hesovec would have told her off. Tamara Zima laughed. "Can I tell you something?" She looped one arm through Linné's as if they were two friends going for a walk around town. "I've never been in the army. I've never been called 'sir.' Hardly anyone calls me ma'am, for that matter. I'm here because I flew the *Winter Witch* from coast to coast, and I flew relief for Goreva Reaching. Isaak needs someone with my abilities to train you, not an army commander."

61

This was getting worse and worse. No wonder Hesovec wanted them all off his base.

"I'm not interested in the traditional army way," Zima said. "But sometimes I have to put on a good show. If you're willing, you can help me with that. And perhaps with guiding some of our new recruits."

No. Definitely not. Her first glimmering of command was not going to be sabotaged by unruly subordinates who didn't know how to obey.

Then again, Zima could send her back to Mistelgard if she said no. She hadn't recruited Linné. She'd been stuck with her. "Your methods sound interesting," Linné managed.

"They are." Commander Zima smiled.

Was Linné supposed to smile back? Was this the untraditional army way? She nodded as though she understood the situation completely and waited for an order.

Zima stood there, looking at her. After a few moments she raised her eyebrows. "Would you be willing to help?"

"Of course, sir," Linné lied. Because no matter what she said, Zima was still the commanding officer. And a superior commanded, even if she did it in nice language. Even if there was nothing Linné wanted less. And there *was* something she wanted less. She'd rather be here at Intelgard than up north. *Faith and loyalty. If the Supreme Commander believes in her, so can I.*

"Good. Go change into the nicest uniform you've got. We'll have to see if we can find smaller ones to fit some of the girls, but for now make yourself as presentable as possible. Then report to me."

"Yes, sir," said Linné before she could stop herself.

Zima nodded in satisfaction, patted her shoulder, then strode off. She wasn't even marching.

✳

Linné found her clean long-coat and walked down to where she thought the commander's office ought to be. She found it when she spotted men and machines hauling stacks of paper, tangles of wire, and an enormous silver samovar. Even the nonofficers seemed to be able to squirrel something away.

The door was open. She knocked anyway.

Zima looked up from where she supervised two men putting a table together. "Good timing. Nikolai's palanquin has been spotted approaching the base, and we don't have much time. Move the supplies behind my desk. Nikolai won't want to see the clutter."

"Nikolai Tcerlin?" Linné guessed.

"You're not intimidated, are you?" her commander said with a sharp look.

Something in her bristled. So Zima *had* connected her to her father. "I'm not intimidated, sir."

"Good. You'll be my aide tonight. Our itinerary is an inspection of the planes, followed by dinner and a tour of the base. I'm afraid it won't do to have you sit with us for dinner, but I can promise you a plate when the evening's over."

"That's very kind of you, sir."

Zima shook her head. "I think you'll do wonderfully, Linné." Linné couldn't tell whether the commander thought this was a good or a bad thing.

A nervous recruit poked his head around the door. "He's here, ma'am."

Zima straightened and left the room at such a pace that Linné broke into a jog to catch up with her. Suddenly Zima was not the friendly head of the regiment, smiling and asking permission to give orders. She walked with a purpose—not quite marching, but with the same energy, the same concept of a place to go and a time to be there.

What if Nikolai told her father about the sloppiness of her new regiment? What if he said it didn't reflect well on the Zolonov family? If she played her part well enough, Tcerlin might think the regiment operated perfectly. Or adequately, so that he wouldn't go back to Mistelgard and mock her father or give a nasty report to Vannin. Tcerlin didn't need to know that the regiment couldn't stand on its own two feet. Or that Tamara Zima wanted to be Linné's friend more than her commander. Or that Colonel Hesovec would be looking over their shoulders and wiring all their errors to Mistelgard.

A stone seemed to settle in her stomach. Tonight, her mission was to make regiment 146 look good enough. Tomorrow, she'd have to make them *be* good enough. Good enough to get her transferred to a ground unit.

Nikolai Tcerlin's palanquin sat on the airfield, steaming in the cold afternoon. It was sleeker than the usual Tammin-made army models, with a long green neck that extended elegantly into curved metal jaws. Its body undulated, serpentine. A dozen men could fit inside. The design imitated the Elda Dragon, though it was made for the ground, not the air. Five men stood next to the palanquin, loose, wary. Hungry. Even though they didn't wear the infamous coats, Linné recognized the amber eyes of the Skarov who acted as Nikolai Tcerlin's bodyguards. They turned those eyes on Zima and Linné, assessing the threat. Linné's father had warned her about the Skarov when Vannin approved their development for the war. *They look like men, but they'll prove their true nature soon enough.*

A man emerged from around the side of the palanquin. Nikolai Tcerlin, barrel-chested, grayer than Linné remembered, with a coat covered in service decorations. The last time she'd seen him, he'd been in the parlor of her father's mansion, arguing. He always argued, especially with her father. Now he gripped Zima's hand and leaned down to give her a hug and a kiss on the cheek. She looked like a doll next to him.

Linné stood behind, waiting for him to notice her. He didn't.

He released Zima and thumped her on the back, nearly knocking her over. "My last stop on my way back from the front," he said. "All to deliver some very special items to you."

"Oh?" the commander replied. She peered around him at the empty field.

"They'll be along, they'll be along." He laughed. "They're being brought in from the Eponar air base, full of new parts. But they'll be a couple of hours or so."

"We can adjust the itinerary," Zima said. "Are you hungry?"

"Famished. Unless it's you who's cooking." He chuckled at his own joke and turned to Linné. Here it came. She steeled herself for the wide eyes, the recognition. "You ever tried anything your commander made?"

He still didn't know her. She supposed it wasn't so strange—she'd last seen him years ago, and she didn't exactly look the same in her soldier's uniform. "No, sir." She kept her eyes trained on the empty field.

"It's probably why you're still here," Tcerlin said, and elbowed Zima. "She cooked for Isaak once. We nearly put her on trial for attempted poisoning. Then we gave her a medal instead." Still laughing, he made his way off the field, hooking his arm through Zima's so that she was dragged in tow.

Linné followed not far behind. She couldn't help thinking that the last time she'd seen Tcerlin, he hadn't seemed like such an ass.

"I doubt you'll find Intelgard to your liking," Tcerlin said as they toured the base. "I requisitioned as much of the field for you as I dared before the other squadron commanders started muttering about murder." He guffawed again. Linné knew full well if anyone had breathed so much as a syllable of discontent, they'd be off to the mines before their subordinates could finish saying thank you for the promotion. But to Tcerlin it was all a joke. Linné remembered his laugh from when she'd attended party functions as a child. Back then his laughter had a way of making everyone feel more comfortable, of putting her father and Isaak Vannin and the other volatile heads of state at ease. Here, it was the opposite. When he laughed, others had better laugh with him.

"Intelgard is a lovely place," said Zima. "And the gentlemen aviators have been nothing but kind."

Tcerlin surely recognized the bald-faced lie. Linné expected his face to darken, his laughter to fade. *Lies are the greatest enemy of the*

Union, he'd once said in an address at Eternal Square in the center of Mistelgard. But Tcerlin said nothing. He merely nodded.

Zima must have sweet-talked the regimental cook, because when they went back to her office, a cart waited with thick reindeer steaks so rare they still leaked red. Bowls crowded her desk—cabbage, string beans, and a thick gravy. A pale-haired girl named Asya laid the plates between them, then retreated to the corner. She shot Linné a sharp, almost resentful look as Linné found a bottle of wine with two silver cups. Linné poured for Zima and Tcerlin, who toasted the health of the Union.

"How's the front?" Zima said.

"Which one?" Tcerlin paused to take a long drink. "They're about how you'd expect. Everyone's miserable; the fight goes on. The southern front is mostly stationary, the western front is covered in Dragons, and the sea front lacks for men. We have them surrounded in the Berechovy, but it looks like they might blow it up before they give it back."

"So much for their love of God Spaces," Zima said. The Berechovy Forest had been one of the most sacred places in the Union, back when they'd had sacred places.

Tcerlin nodded. "They've used blackout gas over the entire area. My guards wouldn't even let me enter the base. They couldn't see more than five meters in front of themselves."

Linné hadn't encountered blackout gas, but seasoned soldiers said it stuck to you for days, like a lingering shadow, and even hot spark couldn't get rid of it. Men in a blackout zone often panicked, shooting indiscriminately.

"They're training the spark there for more precision," Tcerlin said. He held a hand up until a thin, bright sliver of spark stabbed out a few centimeters from his fingertips. It sputtered, fighting to turn into a full blaze. "The fighting's all close quarters, since no one can tell who to shoot. This works almost as well as a bayonet."

Linné had practiced with the spark in her old regiment, hurling projectiles and imbuing bullets until they glowed. She'd seen some men wind the spark around a weapon. But she'd never seen this, the making of a blade. How long could a weapon like that get? Her fingers itched to try.

"Interesting technique," Zima said. "I'm sure my girls would be keen to learn."

"Oh, I don't think they'd be able to learn that," Tcerlin said with a wave of his hand. "It requires enormous concentration."

On the other side of the room, Asya frowned. Linné thought of the ice roses the others conjured and destroyed with a few quick touches, and waited for Zima to tell him where to stick his fancy tactics. But she only said, "And Mistelgard? Is all well there?" Linné hoped to the Union that Zima was choosing her battles instead of rolling over.

"Much the same," Tcerlin replied. "Once a week, someone tries to kill me, or Isaak or Alexei. Once a month, someone tries to surrender to the Elda. The war makes us all desperate in different ways, and the southern reachings have been hit hard."

"That's what we're here for," Zima said. "To get them back."

Tcerlin smacked at his cabbage and cleared his palate with a gulp of wine. "Not every minister is convinced your squadron is necessary in the operation."

"And why is that? Is the war going so well?" Zima smiled over her wineglass, but her voice held a tone that Linné hadn't heard from her before. She hid a core of iron beneath her smiles.

Tcerlin didn't answer. He didn't smile, either. He set down his knife and fork and regarded Zima silently. Linné recognized his look. Her father called it the last-chance look. The speaker had one last chance to smooth the waters.

Zima continued. "We are a strong country. We are a proud country. But we do not have an unlimited supply of young men, and our allies are tied up in conflicting interests or wars of their own. Women have an equal love for the land and deserve the chance to defend it. You can't deny that you need us, not when you've lowered the draft age to thirteen."

Tcerlin's eyes hardened. He breathed deep, a demon readying to spew fire, and Linné saw how angry a man who laughed so much could be. He could pack Zima off to the mines or even shoot her here in the office. But something held him back. Maybe it was the truth of her words; maybe it was the rumors of her involvement with Supreme Commander Vannin.

He picked up his wineglass, and by the time he swallowed, his composure had returned. "A number of ministers are concerned by the influence that a women's squadron might have on the men. Some say it will distract them. Others feel it is unthinkable to watch their sisters or wives die at the front. War has never been women's work. Why is it now?"

Zima smiled again. "Is this your way of telling me you haven't brought my planes?"

Again, Tcerlin paused before he spoke. "The planes are on their way," he said at last. "But I would forbid any daughter of mine from flying them."

"What about your sons?" Zima said. "None of these girls came to the front thinking it would be easy. They are determined to make a difference, and they have skills. I'm told that Linné here was the best shot in her previous regiment."

Tcerlin looked over at Linné. "Previous regiment?"

Asya's eyes widened. No doubt she'd run back to the rest of the Night Raiders with this news. Linné waited for her commander to come to her rescue, but Zima raised an eyebrow, as though surprised by her impertinent silence. *Why* was she bringing her into this? "Yes, sir," she said, hoping she sounded confident and not arrogant or nervous.

"I wouldn't mind seeing your skills," Tcerlin said.

"It would be an honor, sir," she said, though she suspected he'd rather like her to prove her incompetence.

"What do you say, miss?" said Tcerlin. "Is war women's work?"

She fought to keep her face free of the disgust that her father had so often shown when speaking of Tcerlin in private. "War is everyone's work, sir, as long as the Elda are still here."

His mouth split open and a laugh rumbled out. "Spirited," he said. "Very spirited. Are all your recruits like this one?"

"All the girls are enthusiastic, but Linné was so keen to go to war that she dressed as a boy and enlisted in the Thirty-First Night Guards before she joined us."

Anger twisted in her gut. So this was Zima rolling out her grand battle plan. Linné had thought she wanted help, but she had Asya for that. Linné was no more than a prop for her political statements. Tossed to Tcerlin like a scrap, no matter what Linné thought about it. No matter what situation her father would be in because of this.

Tcerlin pushed back from the desk and approached her. She forced herself not to retreat. She'd only run into the wall, anyway. But he loomed a lot taller than she remembered, for all that she was the one who'd grown. As he came closer, she caught derangement in his eyes, a look that came from fear and power and the constant pressure of no right decision to be made. And in that moment, she had a flash of sympathy for her father, as much as she didn't want it.

"What is your name?" Tcerlin said.

"Linné Alexei Zolonov."

His eyes unfocused as he sought to remember her. "Alexei's girl?"

"Yes, sir."

In a split second, the derangement was gone. Tcerlin threw back his head and laughed as though it were a joke better than any he'd heard before. He clapped her on the shoulder with a force that nearly sent her to her knees. "Did you know your father says you're at a fancy school? He told me last week what an accomplished young lady you've become."

Linné spoke before she considered the wisdom of her words. "The greatest accomplishment of any lady is to give her life for her homeland."

Tcerlin laughed even harder. Linné couldn't find it in herself to laugh with him. She'd defied her father, but that didn't mean she wanted to give Tcerlin any power over him.

When Tcerlin's laughter subsided enough for him to speak, he grabbed her hand and pumped it up and down. "Your spirit is noble," he said. "I shall tell your father that you are doing well, and that he must be proud of you."

She doubted he'd say it in those exact words. "Thank you, sir." Was her father proud of her? Angry? Too shocked to be either? *What does it matter? I'd need a medal before he acknowledged it.* Definitive proof that she belonged.

"So, are you convinced?" Zima said, standing as Tcerlin returned to the desk.

"My dear, charming lady, you've already convinced Isaak. I was merely here to oversee the arrival of the planes."

✳

Linné had expected the planes to roar in, a declaration to the world that a new weapon of war was here to stay. She was surprised to find them on the field when she accompanied Tcerlin and Commander Zima out after dinner. Enormous flat-backed palanquins made their pendulous way off the base, assisted by drivers who powered the machines with their spark.

The arrival of the planes had drawn a crowd. Both girls and boys clustered, for once heedless of one another, craning to get a good look at them. They were covered in canvas sheets.

Colonel Hesovec came out to see the affair, and his chest puffed as he recognized Tcerlin. He brushed past Zima and strode forward, hand outstretched. "General, it is an honor—"

Tcerlin grabbed Hesovec's wrist and pumped his arm up and down a single time. "Pleasure," he said, and moved along.

Linné bit her lip so hard that it bled as she passed Hesovec. He couldn't see her smirk.

They stopped on the edge of the field, and at Tcerlin's instruction, two men jogged out to the nearest plane and tugged at the canvas covering until it fell away.

The plane sat low to the ground, propped up by two claws. It was perhaps two or three times as long as Linné was tall, with a fat body of wood and canvas and wide double wings lined with living metal. The open cockpit revealed two seats and a tangle of steel mesh barely protected by the windscreen. This was their response to the monstrous power of the Dragons?

Zima walked up to the plane and crossed her arms. Tcerlin followed her, motioning for Linné to stay put.

"Is this our temporary consignment?" Zima said.

"They're your permanent consignment," Tcerlin said.

"Impossible." Her smile mirrored Tcerlin's but pulled at the edges of her face. "Strekozy were designed to carry seeds, not firepower."

"They are the aircraft we have available," Tcerlin replied.

"You said yourself you'd never let your daughter fly in one."

"I wouldn't," said Tcerlin.

"Then get us others."

"There are no others."

Zima stepped close to him and her smile disappeared. Linné strained to hear her. "Paper planes," she said. "That's what the Elda call them. The Dragons and Skyhorses can send them to the ground with one hit. You can't expect a crop duster to take down a Dragon. The Elda designed them, and they don't even want them in service. I can't imagine that Isaak—"

"They're the only planes available. If you want something else, you'll have to sign up for it. And you won't be pushed to the top of the list because you're Isaak's..." He paused, lip curling. "Good friend."

For a moment Linné thought Zima might hit Tcerlin. She squared off against him, shoulders wide and arms away from her body, making her seem a little bigger against his massive frame. Her anger was a heat that threatened to burn anyone who stepped too close. It was the same anger Linné had felt when Colonel Koslen had sent her here. No right choice, no way to win.

Colonel Hesovec chose that moment to approach again, chest puffed like a pigeon's.

"Yes, my good man?" Tcerlin snapped.

Hesovec was brave in his persistence. Linné gave him that. "I couldn't help but overhear. Is there some issue?"

Zima continued as though she hadn't heard him. "You can't condemn my girls to die this way. There must be something better."

"Did you truly think that each of your pilots should have a plane like yours?" Tcerlin said. "They're soldiers. Isn't that what you wanted to show me? They get what we can spare. And it's lucky that we have enough Strekozy on hand."

"My men are happy to take the consignment, if it harms the ladies' delicate sensibilities," Hesovec said.

Zima's eyes widened as she saw the planes slipping through her fingers. "That's not your choice to make."

Hesovec spread his hands. "We've been stationed at Intelgard longer."

"Waiting for superior aircraft, which we have no chance of getting," Zima snapped. Her face was flushed, and in the heat of the moment, her voice carried past Linné to the soldiers loitering at the end of the field. They edged together, closing ranks.

Tcerlin looked Hesovec up and down. Dislike for the interfering sycophant crossed his features. "Your aircraft will be here soon enough—unless you'd like to trade your place in line for the Strekozy."

There was a moment of silence. Hesovec paled. "With respect, sir, the men have been training for much more complicated machines. I believe it would be wise not to let that training go to waste."

"And you." Tcerlin turned back to Zima. "Isaak isn't here to grant your every whim, and he isn't here to keep you in line. You have me to deal with. Do you want to fly the Strekozy, or do you want to send your girls home?"

The look Zima gave him could have stripped paint. She turned and walked to the edge of the field, beckoning to the girls. They flocked around her.

"This decision is yours, not mine," she said in a trembling voice. "I won't lie to you. The Strekozy were designed as farming planes. They're slow, slower than some palanquins, and they don't hold much in the way of bombs or firepower. They must fly low to the ground, which makes them more susceptible still. But they're the only planes we can have." She sucked in a breath and closed her eyes, as if she couldn't bear to see their faces. "If you wish, you may get on the supply palanquin headed north at nine bells, and no one will blame you."

The girls glanced at one another. Then Elena said, "There must be some advantages to it."

The commander's smile was brittle and brief. "Some," she said. "But not enough."

They were silent for a few moments more. Linné watched resignation fill Zima's face and felt a pang of sympathy. She might have been a great leader had she ever gotten the chance.

And I might have stayed at the front, kept my friends, won my distinction, and shown my father. Army girls, it seemed, didn't get real chances.

"I'm staying," said Revna. She flushed as thirty-odd heads swiveled her way, but she crossed her arms and kept her gaze locked on Zima. Linné wouldn't have figured Revna to be the first to speak up, but she saw a need in her eyes, the need to stay. The need to distinguish who she was now from who she'd been. Linné could understand that.

"I'm staying, too," she said, ignoring the incredulous looks the other girls threw at her. Nothing waited for her in Mistelgard except for paperwork and the punishment of a lifetime when she finally went home.

Magdalena smiled. "Surely we can find some way to equip them."

"Things are starting to get interesting," Katya said.

"I want to fly. I don't care what."

One by one, the girls of the 146th Night Raiders Regiment spoke up. They spoke from their hearts. They spoke with their want shining plainly in their voices.

Maybe serving with them wouldn't be so bad after all.

6

KEEP FAITH IN YOUR UNION

Thirteen countries formed the Union of the North, and girls had come from all of them to join the Night Raiders regiment. Revna came from Rydda, the Union's solid core. Rydda had been hit first and hardest, and from the things Mama and Papa had whispered about politics, Revna wouldn't have expected their sister countries to come to their defense so quickly. But when Revna entered the warehouse for her first flight lesson, she saw pilots who'd traveled from Kikuran in the east, Ibursk in the far north, the Parsean Peninsula at the edge of the Tsemora Sea.

She hadn't worried much about training. She'd worried that she'd be judged on her legs, or that everyone would find out her father had been sent to prison. She'd worried about spies, about being sent home, about more bad news from Tammin. She'd worried about using the Weave in public. Yet as they waited for

Tamara, everyone's raw nerves clamored against one another and she felt the air humming.

"Hey," whispered Katya, the dazzling pilot who had defended Revna the day before. She'd somehow managed to curl her hair, and it hung in perfect ringlets around her round face. Revna had already pegged her as one of *those* girls—the girls who took special care to sit down next to her, to make sure she had someone to talk to who didn't care about her legs. Usually they were trying to make her feel normal, and usually they were nice enough. "Look." She brushed her hands over her jacket collar. She'd lined it with soft gray rabbit fur, making a fashionable trim.

Revna ran her finger along the lining. "It's lovely." And not something she'd think of making or wearing as a factory girl. Katya must have money. "Where did it come from?"

Katya stuck one foot out and waggled her boot. "I took the lining out. I have warm feet anyway. I could make one for you," she offered.

"I don't have boots to borrow from," Revna said. The toes at the ends of her prosthetics twitched.

Katya turned slightly pink. "I'm sure we could find something."

This always seemed to happen with people who tried to ignore her disability. Revna was spared having to refuse her again when Tamara came in. They all stood up to greet her and she smiled at each of them, though she raised an eyebrow at Katya's new collar.

"Welcome," she said at last. "The eleven of you have been singled out and brought to Intelgard for a very special reason. Either I or my allies have noticed a powerful affinity in you for Weave magic."

Revna winced. Tamara said it so openly. Like a preference for sugar beet rum over vodka. If Revna had wandered around Tammin speaking of the Weave in such easy terms, she'd have been shipped off to the far north like Papa.

"We have one of the war's most challenging tasks: We need to beat the Elda at their own game. They've been flying longer than we have, and Weave magic's been legal there for years. Since we've been given permission to develop our own Weave corps, we can work on catching up. Most of our planes, including the Strekozy, are modified Elda models. Known Weave practices will be effective when flying them. Once we have improved our strength and precision, we'll study the machines themselves and pair off with navigators."

Tamara began to pace. "Accomplished Weave users are adept at maneuvering themselves with the Weave. Elda pilots extend that concept of self to the planes they fly, and that is our goal. The most capable Weave magicians can even manipulate the movement of others, though it must be at a short distance and through great concentration." She caught Revna's eye. Revna felt her stomach flip. Even now, something in her wanted to retreat to the corner, to beg *It wasn't me* until someone finally believed her. "We'll work on finesse, but sometimes the only way to get yourself out of a situation is through strength and force of will."

The pilots started with pulling crates or knocking coats off the shelf. Easy enough, but when they had to move one another, that was a different story.

Revna could feel the Weave if she concentrated. It ran through the whole world, thick threads and thin ones, passing through mountains and cities and people all the same. She could see a glimmering of threads, but they felt greasy and slick between her fingers, like warm butter. Revna and Katya joined hands. She could lift herself a few inches straight up, but Katya's weight was too much, and the threads slipped away from her before she could get a good grip. The Weave disliked human meddling.

The others didn't have much luck, either. Pavi was the quickest to pull her partner off the ground, but she couldn't manage more than a couple of seconds before she flopped back down again, wincing as her tailbone smacked the dirt.

Come on, Revna thought to herself after the fourth failed attempt. *You've done this before.* As a child, she'd played with the Weave all the time. Had she forgotten how? Maybe pulling herself and a Skarov away from a falling building had been a fluke.

Maybe the secret was not thinking. She watched the others' techniques and the way they stumbled over thin air. Then she tightened her hand around Katya's sweaty fingers and yanked.

They whipped forward, lifting halfway off the ground. Then her prosthetics dug in. She hissed as she came back down hard.

"Are you all right?" Katya said, face pinched in concern. "Maybe I should try."

"Give me a minute," Revna said. Through her residual limbs she could feel her prosthetics tremble. The last time she'd used the Weave this way, she'd thought she was going to die. Did her prosthetics remember, or were they afraid of something else now? Of getting thrown out and letting her family down again? Of getting arrested and sent north? The Weave was illegal, after all, and as the propaganda posters said, THE LAW COMES FOR EVERYONE.

There's nothing you can do about it now. Her powers were no secret. The best she could do was make use of them for Mama and Lyfa, and hope the Union didn't arrest her anyway.

She yanked herself forward once more. Her hands slipped on the thread and she tumbled into Katya. Her shoulder knocked hard into Katya's nose, sending Katya's head flying back. For one glorious moment Revna was in the air. Then she came down, chin-first onto the hard dirt.

Pain exploded in her abdomen and phantom feet. Across the warehouse someone shouted, and the girls scrambled over to them. "Ooh," Katya groaned next to her. "I think I'm seeing colors I've never seen before."

Someone ran for a drink of water. "Sorry," Revna said to Katya, wincing as she pushed herself up. She wanted to check on her prosthetics, comfort them and try to massage the ache out of her calves. But all the girls were watching, and then Tamara came over.

"We're fine," Revna said before Tamara could ask. She didn't need to be pitied the way she had been in Tammin. And she couldn't afford to be the weak one of the Night Raiders.

Tamara looked at Katya. "Don't worry," Katya said, touching her nose. "It's not even bleeding."

Tamara didn't seem convinced, but she nodded. "The brute force is good, but as you can see, you need to be versatile with how you use it. Don't rely on the same tricks every time." She folded her arms and said pointedly to the other pilots clustered around them, "Keep practicing. It will come."

It didn't, not for any of them. Revna didn't try any more

violent pulls, but working slowly and carefully yielded no results. Her arms burned and gave up. She almost groaned in relief when Tamara called them in. "It's no easy task, what I ask of you. But if you do not possess the strength to do this, you do not possess the strength to handle the Strekozy in battle." Her voice held the steel core Revna had heard when Tamara had rescued her from her Skarov interrogation. "If we cannot fly, we cannot even the odds. If we cannot fly, we've lost the war. And that's why we'll come back tomorrow and we'll get it right."

"How could Tamara possibly have learned?" Revna asked Katya as they left the warehouse for dinner.

"She's got her own special magic," Katya replied. She leaned in and lowered her voice. "With Commander Vannin." Revna snorted. Katya was a little frivolous, but at least she wasn't party line.

✳

The crisp air and the bitter scent of oil hanging over the field couldn't dispel their fatigue. All the same, as they opened the mess door, every back straightened and they lifted their chins as one. No matter how tired the Night Raiders might be, there were some places they had to go looking as fresh as ever.

They shared the mess with the 146th Day Raiders—also known as the boys. Tamara said they would have the chance to promote friendliness in the regiment and get the men used to having some "sisters." But everyone had witnessed Hesovec and Tamara arguing over who got the Strekozy, and as far as the boys were concerned, superior planes meant nothing if they had to wait to fly. They'd been training for weeks and had yet to see their promised aircraft. The friendly burble of conversation dropped as the girls entered.

Revna shuffled in between the chattering Katya and Elena. Elena always looked solemn and mournful. She had the sort of long face required for it, with a hooked nose and eyes that seemed faraway, as if she were weighing each word that went through her mind. "Do you need assistance?" she asked.

"I'm fine," Revna said. "Thanks." She was too tired to even think about rolling her eyes, even when she had a small tug-of-war with Katya over who got to carry her tray.

"What did you do today?" she asked Linné, who was in line in front of her.

Linné gave her a blank look. "I worked."

"Never mind." Revna wasn't quite sure what to make of Linné. She hadn't made any comments about Revna's legs, but anything she did say was terse and unhelpful.

Revna followed her fellow pilots over to the end of a long table, and together they dug their spoons into a less than delectable dinner of pale yellow carrots, barley, and greasy fowl. It was the first meat she'd gotten since Papa was taken away. She'd expected to savor it more. The Union really could ruin anything.

"How was your day?" Magdalena dropped her tray next to Revna, spraying them both with gravy. She'd come in laughing with the other engineers.

There wasn't much point in spoiling Magdalena's good mood. "It was fine."

"We took apart explosives," said another engineer. "Magda almost got us killed."

"I wanted to see how the mechanism worked," Magdalena explained. "Someone mentioned to us that the Strekozy had sticky release triggers."

"Like it matters," said Elena, raising her ponderous eyes heavenward. "We'll never even get them in the air."

"Don't say that," Katya told her, leaning around Pavi. She waved her spoon at the other side of the mess. "If the meatheads over there can do it, why can't we?"

"Because we'll be thrown in prison?" Revna suggested. Tamara had promised her that the Weave was acceptable now. But in the Union, truth seemed to wriggle and squirm like an angry snake, hard to pin down and keep hold of.

Katya shrugged off her worry. "They won't arrest us after the war. They'll still need pilots. And I'll be happy to volunteer."

"You don't want to go back to what you were doing?" Magdalena said.

"I only helped my father. He's a hunter," said Katya. She waggled her fingers. "I used to disrupt the birds for him. I could knock eggs out of a nest fifty meters up." Revna couldn't really imagine Katya tramping through the woods with her meticulous white-blond curls and eyebrows darkened with kohl. She'd assumed Katya came from one of the big reachings, where she could go out and listen to state-approved jazz every weekend. "I was recruited to sew parachutes when the war started, but someone reported me for Weave magic. I thought I'd be sent to Kolshek Prison.

The Information Unit brought me here instead." She turned to Pavi. "What about you?"

Pavi swallowed her mouthful of stew. "I applied."

"Applied?" They gaped at her. You didn't write to the army and say you could use illegal magic.

"Yes." Pavi made a face at her plate. "In Kikuran no one cares whether you use the Weave or not. There weren't that many of us, and I was the only girl who'd practiced much. Tamara and General Tcerlin visited to recruit. They took away fifteen boys, and me."

"How can no one care? It's illegal to use the Weave in the Union," said Nadya, a navigator who came from Tyrniakh, toward the Union's southern center. Everything about Nadya seemed severe, from the tight bun at the back of her head to her sharp nose. She'd even managed to make her rumpled and oversized uniform look austere.

Pavi looked Nadya up and down, dark eyes flashing. "We're not part of your Union. Kikuran is an allied state."

"You still have to follow Union laws," Nadya said. "The Weave has to run its natural course. Using it makes it tangle."

"Most tangles resolve themselves in twenty-four hours," Pavi said.

"According to who?"

Pavi flared her nostrils. "Why are you even here if you think using the Weave is so bad?"

Nadya blushed but stuck her chin out. "Tamara asked for me specially."

"Why you?" Katya asked.

"I can spark-power a factory washing machine with my right hand for six hours."

With Nadya's credentials established, they turned to Magdalena. Tamara had seen her test scores at the technical school in Mistelgard and tracked her down in Tammin, where she'd been sent to improve palanquin design. "That's what the university gets for rejecting women," Magdalena said.

Next up was Elena. "I, um, asked."

"What, you walked up to Tamara on the street?" Katya laughed.

"No." Elena shifted uncomfortably, stirring her spoon around and around in her bowl. "I went to her office."

"You're ruining your own story," said Asya, a tiny girl from up north in Ibursk. She had short pale hair and eyes like ice, and scars crisscrossed her fingers, winding up under her cuffs. "Tamara wasn't home, so Elena waited for three days and most of a fourth. I thought she was ridiculous. But Tamara said yes, so her ridiculousness paid off. I was Tamara's secretary."

"Secretary?" Olya challenged. Asya's scars were as easy to miss as Revna's prosthetics, and her coldness didn't really scream secretary material.

Asya ran her hands over her scars. "Yes." Her glare dared the rest of them to disagree.

So Revna told her story, how she'd been caught up in the bombardment of Tammin. The others *ooh*ed appropriately before moving down the line. Revna felt a weight lift from her heart with every story. More and more, it felt as if they were in this together.

Revna liked her new friends—well, she wasn't sure about Linné, who seemed to spend most of her time getting into arguments about who should do what. The rest were all right, though. And she liked Magdalena the best. Everything in Magdalena's heart came straight out of her mouth, and most of the stuff in her brain did, too. Over the course of dinner she deliberated the year's crops (good, considering), predicted the outcome of the war (over by the end of winter), criticized the Union's leanings in nationalist poetry (soppy), and discussed Isaak Vannin's latest gift for his wife (a bear). Revna had an opinion on none of it, though she'd heard different news about the crops. This didn't seem to bother Magdalena, though. It meant she could talk and talk, and never had to argue. She had such an easygoing manner that Revna couldn't imagine her in the heat of battle. And though other girls pushed on with different conversations, Revna couldn't help thinking that Magdalena had her own sort of charm, bouncing from one subject to the next with consistent enthusiasm. Revna spent so much time trying to keep up she could almost forget how she missed home.

✳

Routine became law. Revna ate breakfast with Magdalena, then trained with Tamara and the other pilots. Every time Revna pushed herself, she imagined the Skarov hiding right around the corner. She couldn't decide whether they were waiting to arrest her for using the Weave or waiting to discharge her for not using it well enough.

"Chin up," Magdalena said at dinner one evening. "No one should be expected to fly a plane in only a couple of days."

Whatever the expectations should have been, the pressure was strong. By the end of the first week, the engineers had worked out a new hinge for the Strekozy to carry bombs under their wings. By the end of the second, the navigators had begun target practice, blasting their spark to set empty crates alight from ten meters. In between their specialized work sessions, the girls trained together with firearms and gas masks, and on survival skills, semaphore communication, and more. Revna tried to use Papa's approach to problem solving, but all she could think was *Problem: I am a failure.* And she had no solutions for that.

At the end of the third week, Elena rushed into the mess and pulled them away from breakfast. "Come out to the field," she said, pale and thin-lipped. They left in a clatter of spoons and metal trays.

The air outside was brisk, and an overnight rain had muddied the ground and slicked the boards. Angry shouts drifted from the officers' quarters.

"Is that Tamara?" Magdalena turned back, distracted.

"Just come," Elena said.

As they approached the Strekozy, a wave of revulsion washed over Revna, forcing her to stop. She felt ugly and hot and closed-in all at once, and even deep gulps of cold air couldn't draw it out of her. Her prosthetics constricted around her calves.

"What *is* that?" Katya said. Her hands went to her temples. She looked green.

Revna knew what it was. She'd felt it a few times in the factory when someone farther up the line was having a bad day. And if her secret practice with the Weave had done nothing else, it had helped her learn living metal. Large strands of the Weave ran through the ore and permeated it with semisentience over tens of thousands of years. Living metal could feel angry, anxious, excited, even offended—tied to the people who worked with it. Sometimes you pushed your emotions onto it, and sometimes it pushed its emotions onto you.

Someone had been out here, pouring hate into the Strekozy. And now they radiated that hate, so simple and so powerful that her stomach turned and her mouth flooded.

Revna's legs trembled in sympathy. She forced herself to move forward, one hand over her mouth to keep from throwing up. The air seemed to grow thick and fight against her.

Graffiti was scrawled on the canvas plane covers. It ran from wing to wing, from nose to tail. There was a slogan for every girl in the regiment.

CARRY BABIES, NOT BOMBS.

YOU COOK BETTER THAN YOU FLY.

CAMP FOLLOWER WHORES.

GO HOME.

The words ran together. In some places they weren't even legible. But that didn't matter. The Strekozy had absorbed them, and long after the graffiti was gone, the hate would remain.

No one had to guess who'd done it.

"We're not going to stand for this," Elena said. "Right?"

"We'll go to Tamara," Nadya offered.

"Tamara already knows." Linné stood at a distance, eyeing the planes. She was still as stone, but a golden glow peeked through her clenched fists. "What good is it going to do to tell her again?"

"We should go to Hesovec, then," Nadya said. "Demand that he—"

Linné cut her off. "You don't demand things in the army. And Hesovec already knows about it, too. Who do you think she was shouting at? If he doesn't listen to her, he won't listen to you. He'll punish you for wasting his time."

"Forget being official," Pavi snapped. "Rules are only rules when somebody's watching. We have to show that we can't be run off. Harm them like they harmed us."

But the men's planes hadn't arrived yet. Katya wanted to sabotage their rifles; Asya wanted to destroy the ramshackle bar they'd constructed behind their barracks. Linné only said no.

"What do you think we should do, then?" Magdalena said.

Linné chewed on the inside of her cheek. Then she took a deep breath. "Nothing." The spark retreated up her arms.

Asya flared her nostrils. "We're not going to do nothing."

"Do you think you can out-prank a soldier? Everything you want to do—complain, destroy army equipment, make demands— proves that we're immature, overreacting, and that we'll never fit in." Linné kicked a rock. It bounced over the ground and *plink*ed off the body of a plane.

"It's not our fault we can't even get close to these planes now," Asya said.

"But we'll still be called weak for it. And then we'll be sent home, and then it won't really matter whose fault it is."

"But that's not fair," Revna said.

Linné snorted. "You joined the army because you think life is fair?" She crossed her arms. "Don't start a war. You won't win it."

They stood in furious silence, leaning away from the hateful Strekozy.

"You depress me," Magdalena finally said to Linné. "I thought you should know, considering how hard it is to get me depressed about something."

Maybe this was it. Maybe they would be sent home. The pilots hadn't made much progress, and the war seemed to creep on somewhere far away from them. But Mama and Lyfa were protected as long as Revna was here. Something hardened inside her. Her father had been pushed out of the Union, and she wasn't going to go the same way. She'd come here to ensure that her sister could grow up and her mother could grow old. She wouldn't lose to a bunch of boys who thought their hate was funny and clever. She'd think of the problems.

Problem: We can't get revenge.

But they could get even.

"We have to reverse it," she said. The others turned to her. Revna swallowed. Usually when this many people were looking at her, it was because of her legs. "And then we have to practice, and pass our flying test, and go to war. That's how we'll get revenge."

It would be impossible to dismiss them then. Impossible to insist they couldn't handle the pressure.

"But how are we supposed to reverse it?" Katya said.

"I used to do it all the time in the factory." If a riveter was having a bad day up the line, an angry antenna or stray leg ended up in her lap. She'd ensured they were fit for service, which included making them calm.

"We're not talking about a couple of spare parts," Asya pointed out.

Revna was trying not to think about that. She moved forward, and the others followed her. The rage pressed against them. *You know how to handle this.* She pushed on, fighting nausea. Even when she began to feel ugly, tiny, worthless, she wouldn't stop. It wasn't real.

The planes quivered and Revna's prosthetics trembled in sympathy. The more complex a living metal machine was, the more it needed human direction and the more attuned it was to human emotion. It would take a lot of work to return the planes to a functioning state, more than she'd ever tried at the factory.

Magdalena ripped the tarred canvas off one wing. "Let's start with the covers," she said.

"Start what?" Linné called from the side.

"They can't stay," Revna agreed. The hateful words would cement the emotions the regiment was trying to uproot.

"So you'll do what, burn them?" Linné scoffed.

They glanced at one another. Nadya flicked her fingers and spark blazed at the end of her hand.

"You can't," Linné sputtered. "That's army property."

"It's been defaced," Magdalena said. "If we burn the evidence, we're doing the boys a favor, really. What can Hesovec say to that?"

"A lot," Linné said. But she didn't run off to report them as they bundled the canvas and hauled it to a dry patch of earth at the corner of the field. She even joined the other navigators as they burned their spark hot and threaded it toward the stack, pushing until the blaze had caught and was higher than Magdalena.

Together they watched it all burn. Linné stood next to Revna, her hands still bright. "Too much vengeance for you?" Revna asked.

Linné's eyes darted away. "Not enough," she replied. "But it's all I'll get."

I, not *we*. Even when they were on the same side, Linné seemed insistent on being by herself. And if she'd wanted revenge so badly, why had she been dead against it? She never backed down from arguments with the other girls. The general's daughter was a complicated knot, one that wanted to stay tangled.

✳

Visiting the planes became part of their routine. The Night Raiders went to the field after dinner and rubbed them down, washed them with bristle brushes, and spoke softly to them as though they were wary animals.

Pilots took specific planes without being assigned. Pavi sang to hers, and Katya painted the nose of hers in bright swaths of red and orange. At first Revna's plane grew hot and prickly whenever she touched it, especially when she ran her finger along the steel-edged wing or approached the mesh inside the open cockpit. But living metal didn't retain emotion forever, and after their first few visits, Revna could walk onto the field without the ugly anger pressing in on her from all sides. The male aviators hadn't been back, as far as they knew, and the new covers Tamara requisitioned remained pristine.

Revna liked to sit on the wing of her plane with Magdalena, letting the engineer talk while she warmed the space next to her with her spark. She couldn't use it like the navigators could, but she could make her hands glow warm. Living metal seemed to like that. The Strekozy were barely less flammable than a match, though, and if she set hers on fire before she even took it for one flight, she'd probably be shot for treason.

"The bombs are going to be heavy, no matter what we do. Tamara says that's a problem," Magdalena was saying, "but I think if we could cast a thinner bottom, that might help with some of the weight. And the gas bombs are the easiest, obviously. But Tamara says they can't break against the plane by accident."

Revna was half listening. The twilight had turned to full night and soon they'd have to go in. Her fingers were already stiff in her gloves, but her residual limbs sweated. The long days of marching, running, and smacking herself into things with the Weave were starting to take a toll on them, and on most nights phantom pains prickled where her feet used to be. A blister had formed at the bottom of her right calf where she'd been smashing it on the ground all day. They were practicing precision. She'd never had to be precise as a child, only unseen. As other pilots showed their strengths, she started to wonder what would happen if they were all ready before she was. How long could she keep her family safe if the army lost faith in her as an asset?

"I wanted to make some kind of spark extender, so the navigators could fire from a greater distance, but—what was that?"

Magdalena was staring beyond the military chain fence. Beyond the base lay Intelgard's remaining farmland, and beyond that the plains stretched flat and dark, all the way from the Karavel Mountains, jutting up on the southeast, to the northern edge of the world. A star burned bright, far to the west.

Not a star, Revna realized. It drifted too close, too bright. Too... yellow. Then it was gone.

The regiment scrambled off their planes. Magdalena hopped to the ground and held out her hands for Revna, who ignored the offer and climbed down more cautiously. They moved toward the fence.

More pinpricks of light burst where the mountains became hills. A thin tongue of flame blazed down. "What is it?" Elena whispered next to her.

"It's a battle," said Linné from the other side. She pressed her face into the fence, as if trying to push herself through.

"Will it overtake us?" Revna said, thinking of Tammin. She hoped no one else could hear her voice tremble. They weren't ready yet. She hadn't even gotten the chance to sit in her cockpit.

"I doubt it. They have targeted the town of Troiya," Tamara said from behind them. She joined them at the fence, pulling her folded arms against her belly. A bright flame burst again. "That's an Elda fighter."

Silence fell, thick and heavy. Revna strained to see the fighter's shape, a darkness in the darkness. But from here, the aircraft were as invisible as their flames were bright. Finally Katya asked in a tremulous voice, "Are they all Elda?"

Tamara didn't answer right away. When she did, her voice was weighted with grief. "No. Each explosion was one of our night fighters from Tereshkogard base."

Was. As they watched, more night fighters combusted, more streams of fire jetted from the air to the ground. For a long while, that was all they could do. When Tamara spoke again, her voice seemed to echo into a vast silence. "One Dragon can turn a battle against us," she said. "Just one. Our night fighters are precious and too few. Every time a Dragon appears, the night fighters must choose between fleeing to save themselves and their equipment, or dying to give the troops one more moment to turn the tide. It was the Dragons that leveled Goreva Reaching, the Dragons that set fire to the Berechovy Forest. The Dragons will win the Elda their war if we don't find a way to stop them. Isaak thinks the Strekozy will be key."

How? Revna thought. But no one dared to speak when Tamara fell silent.

The Elda went on and on about the gods, but they were here to take the fields and the mines, and to burn the rest. They didn't care about the sacred places of Rydda and the other Union states. They'd come not for the God Spaces, but for the farmland and the fatherland. They didn't want to protect; they wanted to demolish.

So the Union had resorted to people like Revna—secondary citizens and women they never thought they'd need. Pavi from Kikuran, Asya from the ice-steppes. All of them called the Union home. This war wasn't about the Skarov or the men who'd tried to turn her plane against her. It was about more than buying Mama and Lyfa a spot in a real bomb shelter. Revna's fight belonged in the skies, where she had the chance to make sure that no one else's family got rejected or torn apart. Even though the Union had torn apart her family and rejected her.

Tamara thought Revna could turn the tide. The Supreme Commander of the entire Union thought Revna could do it. And she had to do it, for that faraway dance of fire that claimed its dancers one by one.

They watched the battle for half an hour. When it was over,

Revna was stiff and had all but fallen against Magdalena's shoulder. But she couldn't tear her eyes away. It was her second look at war, and this time she wasn't consumed with how to survive.

Now she wanted to know how to bring down a Dragon.

All the lights on the horizon had gone out. Tamara stood with her hands at her sides, and when she spoke, her voice was clear and strong. "Our Strekozy are more agile than the Dragons," she said. "And the difference in speed might make it difficult for a Dragon to catch us. That is what is said among the generals and tacticians in Mistelgard. I don't know if it's true. But every day we don't fly, their power grows."

Her face glistened with tears in the spare light of the moon. "The boys on this base will tell you again that they don't need you, that they don't like you. The things they say don't matter. As long as *that* is happening"—she pointed beyond the fence—"they need us. They need every fighter they can get."

The wind tore at her words. It carried the scent of ashes.

She turned away, and her shoulders seemed to slump. "Go to sleep, girls," she said. "I'll see you again in the morning. Don't lose heart."

They got up the next day without complaining. They did their work not with optimism, but with grim determination. They practiced, and they practiced, and they slept, and they practiced again.

And they got better.

7

COOPERATION IS
INFORMATION; INFORMATION
IS VICTORY

Linné woke every morning in a state of despair. She got up in despair; she ate breakfast in despair; she trained in despair. Before she got caught, she'd been too tired, too stressed, too intent on passing as a man or surviving a battle to let her emotions rule her. But now the endless loop of training, battle, and recovery had been traded for training, training, and training. And basic training at that. Zima had officially named her a supervisor and, if anything, it made her life worse.

Midautumn arrived with a vengeance, all wind and sleeting rain. The most recent crop of male recruits was being sent out today and replaced with another. The men shipped in from the front for Weave and spark training before shipping out again.

Until Hesovec's planes arrived, his regiment was rotated. And every time new recruits arrived, a new kind of trouble arrived with them.

Zima had reserved the range for target practice. Linné would have preferred to try General Tcerlin's spark blade than waste ammunition on scarecrow targets, but she had to set an example. She could work on her cold spark anyway; her spark had always run hot and angry. Hot spark could keep an engine running, hot enough could ignite a fire, but sometimes soldiers wanted to put out fires or cause frostbite.

But her bullet didn't seem to take to the cold spark, and the other girls hardly helped her concentration. For all that the Night Raiders could shoot, their discipline was abominable. Galina and Nadya were burning spark, threading energy out to steam the rain as it fell around them. Katya and Pavi tried to coax a hissing cat out from a hole in the sandbag wall that separated them from the range. Revna sat on a crate, swinging those metal legs of hers back and forth.

Magdalena was the worst. She leaned next to Revna and squinted down the barrel of a rifle. "What do you think of making some sort of gas bullet?"

Revna started to reply but seemed to lose her nerve when Linné sloshed over to them.

"Don't tell me that's loaded," Linné said. The last thing she needed on her watch was Magdalena blowing off her face. Zima wouldn't take excuses, and the girls would be far too happy to blame Linné.

Magdalena looked up coolly. "It's not cocked."

Which meant that it *was* loaded. Couldn't Zima have screened for common sense? Linné ripped the rifle away, making sure that the barrel pointed toward the target straw men on the range. "Didn't either of you take shooting lessons?" She checked the rifle and presented it to Magdalena, butt first. "Go up to the wall and try it properly."

Magdalena squeezed Revna's hand. "No."

Honestly, they acted as if this were some sort of holiday. Without thinking, Linné leaned forward until her nose was an inch from Magdalena's. "I'm your supervisor. Do it before I report you."

Wrong thing to say. Magdalena took up the challenge with flashing eyes. "So report me. I'll tell Tamara we'd rather be supervised by someone else."

Linné nearly choked. "That's not how the army works." She'd said it so many times recently it came out without thinking.

"I'll do it," Revna said, sliding off the crate. Her prosthetics squelched in the mud. Whoever made them had been a real craftsman. The toes even splayed fractionally to support her. Though how Revna could afford them as a factory girl was another mystery.

Revna took the rifle and made a clumsy shot that missed the man she was aiming for and struck another in the shoulder. She sagged in disappointment and sent Linné a furtive glance, as if she expected a rebuke.

Linné gave her the chance to try again, approaching Katya instead. "You keep tipping the barrel too far up. Your bullets are going everywhere."

"Straw man wins," Katya said, rolling her eyes as she aimed. "It's not like we're going to have space for rifles in the plane."

Linné gritted her teeth and tried to remember why she should keep her temper. "One day you might need to shoot, and how are you going to hit something if you don't keep up your practice? I'm only trying—"

"To make us look foolish," Katya said. "I know."

"You don't need help for that," Linné replied.

Katya's soft, pretty hands clenched around the gun. The embroidery she'd stitched into her military sleeves glinted like fire in the weak light of the cloudy day. Linné could taste the fight on the air. But Katya never got her chance.

Someone at the edge of the range cleared his throat loudly. They all turned to see a small knot of boys standing next to the sandbags. Linné wasn't sure how long they'd been there. The one at the front—a dark-haired, tan-skinned man with a trim beard—gave them an indulgent smile. No one returned it.

The paler man next to him seemed more disdainful. "Argue somewhere else, if you don't mind. We have practice."

"If *you* don't mind, we've got practice of our own," Katya said, letting some of her ire flow out onto this new foe. After the stunt with the Strekozy covers, there was no question of who their worst enemies were. "Clear out—we're working."

"Doesn't look like it to me," someone said. Snickers erupted from the back of the group.

Linné's hands burned, but she forced her face into a smooth mask. "Haven't you been assigned your own shooting range?"

"Overcrowded," the dark-haired soldier said. His easy smile widened as he took her in. "Long way from the steppe, sweetheart."

Linné's jaw clenched. Her mother might be Ungurin, but

that didn't mean *she* had anything in common with this bastard. She picked up her rifle and made a show of loading it, as if she didn't care. But spark danced at her fingertips, betraying her. "I'm from Mistelgard. I've never seen the steppe. And don't call me sweetheart."

He lifted one shoulder. "Dolosh, dolosh."

Linné had never mustered the courage to ask for Ungurin lessons from her father, so she had no idea what that meant. She sneered at him to cover her bases. "Our superior gave us orders to be here."

"Tell that to Colonel Hesovec," said the light-haired one. "I'm sure he'll set everything straight." He wore the classic good looks of Rydda well: a sharp profile, blue eyes, thick honey-colored hair. His was the kind of face that got sketched on the bulletins that were tossed from palanquins, paired with words like FOR OUR HEROES or MAKE ME PROUD. But Linné was forming a different opinion of him, mostly determined by what came out of his mouth.

Katya leaned her gun on the sandbags and folded her arms. "We've earned our right to be here."

The good-looking ass smiled like his four-year-old sister had done something amusing. "Men are needed at the front; men get priority. We don't have time to sit around and show you how to use your guns."

"We can use them," Revna said, though her voice faltered as their heads swiveled around. Their collective gaze slid to her legs, looking for some crease in her trousers that might show where her flesh ended and the metal began. She flushed but didn't back down. "We've been training here for two months."

Good-Looking Ass snorted. "Sounds like a waste of resources, then."

Linné felt the familiar burn, the anger that was never far away. It dared her to do something stupid. She flipped the safety off her rifle and fired. Most of the men jumped. Two of them swore. On the edge of the range, the farthest straw man rocked as her bullet pierced his shoulder.

For a moment no one did anything. Then Olya began to applaud. The rest joined in, eager to emphasize the achievement. *Hypocrites*, she thought, but all the same she had to clamp down on a smile.

"All this practice and the best you can do is moderately wound one stuffed doll? Looks like dumb luck. You couldn't do it again," said Good-Looking Ass.

The dark-haired soldier elbowed him. "How would you know, Krupin? You couldn't hit a Dragon if it were parked right in front of you."

Laughter rumbled around the group. Someone near the back shouted, "It's true!"

Linné didn't laugh with them. She looked between the Day and the Night Raiders, twirling another bullet between her fingers to imbue it with heat. Rain started to collect under her collar. If the boys hadn't shown up, the Night Raiders would be talking about how much they wished they were inside. She also knew the boys wouldn't walk away and leave her to her victory. They wanted to win, and they'd use humiliation, trickery, or excuses if they had to.

The dark-haired soldier stepped forward, primed his rifle, and took a shot. His cold-sparked bullet punched the torso of a straw man midfield, frosting blue over the hole. His friends clapped for him. It was a good killing blow. But she could do better.

He held out his rifle. "No tricks. Same gun." Linné nodded. His fingers brushed over hers as they traded. "Match that, sweetheart."

"Don't call me that," she said again. As she loaded the rifle, she checked to make sure he hadn't blocked the barrel while she wasn't looking, or disengaged the hammer, or let some of the rain in. When she was satisfied, she took aim and blew the straw man's nose off his straw face. His head smoked as a puff of flame fought against the rain.

Applause circled around. Her opponent waggled his eyebrows. "Perhaps this competition is too simple for you."

"It's not a competition," Linné replied. If it were, she'd wipe the floor with him. Heat flushed her. "Go away."

"You're giving up?" His eyes widened in mock disappointment. "You can't let me win so easily, sweetheart."

"Don't call me that."

"There." He pointed beyond the shooting range to a postage stamp–sized cabbage field, all that remained of Intelgard's original purpose for the Union. A cart was parked in the middle of the field, piled with cabbages. "I bet that I can shoot a cabbage off that cart and you can't."

"How much?" Linné said.

He pulled a cigarette case from his pocket and opened it. "Half the week's rations."

Temptation tugged at her. The girls got a smaller ration than the boys, and she'd never been good at saving hers. She could almost taste the sour rascidine on her tongue.

She primed and aimed. Rain lashed her cheeks. The world stood still for a moment, and in that moment she was certain. This was a setup. He would trip her, or jerk the gun, or call her sweetheart, or even slap her ass. Anything to put her off her game and make her miss.

She waited for it. And waited. And then she took her shot.

The cabbage at the front left of the cart exploded and toppled from its perch. A few other cabbages wobbled from the force, rolling off the cart into the mud. The girls cheered and the boys clapped. Linné's opponent smiled. "Nicely done," he admitted.

"Hand them over." She tucked his rifle under her arm and pulled out her cigarette case, a bright silver monogrammed beauty she'd swiped from her father's desk the day she'd run off.

His hand lingered on his case. "One more time."

"That wasn't our agreement."

"Krupin could be right—it could be a fluke," he reasoned.

"Tell me which one to shoot," Linné said. "Tell me, and I'll do it." She loaded his rifle a second time.

He came around to stand right behind her, leaning in. "That one," he murmured, pointing to a cabbage near the top.

"Front right corner," she confirmed. "Two from the top, three from the side. Step back—you're impeding my movement."

"Sorry." His breath tickled her ear before he moved away.

She rubbed at the side of her head and focused.

She didn't hit the second from the top, third from the side. The bullet tore into the cabbage next to it. Someone at the edge of the field, presumably the farmer, screeched a curse as precariously placed cabbages began to tumble, knocking their neighbors down with them. Damn it.

"One more time," she said.

"What are you doing?"

Everyone turned. Three figures strode toward them through the rain. The one in the front had a red face and a colonel's stripe.

She needed to come up with an excuse, and fast. She snapped to attention and saluted. Rainwater washed down her back. "Ah," she said.

"Answer me," Hesovec snarled, spit flying from his mouth.

Linné couldn't answer him. She couldn't think of anything except the two men behind him. Two men in silver coats that buttoned up to their chins, their blue stars proudly pinned where everyone could see. Skarov.

Hesovec noticed her paralysis and turned to look. "Ah, yes. *Ladies*, allow me to introduce the representatives of the Extraordinary Wartime Information Unit. They'll be keeping the capital apprised of our progress. They weigh in on our deliberations regarding who is ready for combat, and they ensure the base is secure. With that in mind, I'm sure you can tell me: *What were you doing?*"

They couldn't be. They couldn't be Skarov. Not those two. Her legs began to tremble. She couldn't let it show.

She recognized them. She recognized them more than she'd ever have wished.

Dostorov stood on the left, as gloomy as always, dripping in the rain. Dostorov, who'd signed her up for Koslen's regiment.

Dostorov, who smoked too many cigarettes and never spoke if he could get away with shrugging instead. His dark hair flopped into his eyes. She could tell that it irritated him, but he wasn't going to fidget with it. He seemed so out of place in his long gray coat.

Next to him stood Tannov, light-haired and light-eyed, cheerful as always. Tannov, who'd always made the worst jokes. Tannov, who'd caught her and reported her. Now she'd never be able to give him the kicking he deserved. Her father had once said that becoming a Skarov stripped all the smiles out of a man, but Tannov's smile was as free as it always had been. His eyes flicked around the cluster of girls. They rested on her briefly—a little longer than on everyone else, maybe? She clenched her hands around the rifle behind her back, cold spark skittering down her fingers. *Don't blush.* Maybe he wouldn't recognize her.

"Answer me," Hesovec hissed.

Revna, of all people, tried to save her. "They pushed her to do it, sir—"

"To do what?" He rounded on her like a feral bull.

She stared at her feet. "They said we were wasting time and we couldn't shoot, and Linné wanted to show them."

Don't say my name, Linné thought furiously, swallowing a lump of panic. Had her old regiment learned what she was called?

"So you were showing off." Hesovec pointed to the cabbage cart and the distraught farmer rushing toward it. "That is army property. Showing off is no excuse for damaging *army property*!"

"They—they interrupted us," Revna sputtered.

"Do you think I care about petty arguments?" he roared.

Flecks of saliva speckled her coat. Revna flinched, and even the

Skarov behind him raised their eyebrows. She took a deep breath. "But they challenged her—"

"Do you?"

The range was silent for a moment. "No," Revna said at last, barely above a whisper.

"No what?"

"No, sir."

Hesovec glared at them all, chest heaving. The men did their best to look as if they'd ended up at the range by mistake.

Tannov made a small, polite noise.

Hesovec jumped. With some effort, he schooled his expression. "Perhaps Officer Tannov would like to do the honors," he said.

Linné's stomach twisted. She couldn't possibly get arrested for shooting a cabbage.

Tannov seemed to feel the same. "Continue," he said with a smile and a wave of his gloved hand. "We're merely here to observe."

The Skarov didn't observe. They hunted. They hunted information and they hunted people, and used the same ruthlessness with both.

Hesovec licked his lips. When he spoke, Linné could see the sweat that beaded at the edges of his mustache. "Zolonova. Roshena. You will go out to that field and you will pick every last cabbage leaf off the ground. You'll pay the farmer any damages from your own wages, and I'll report this behavior to your commanding officer." His mouth twisted as he said *commanding officer.*

"Yes, sir," Linné said quickly, staring at her boots.

Revna picked up on her lead. "Yes, sir."

The colonel turned to the other regiment. "When recruits have reserved the firing range, it's theirs to use. If you make them wait, they make the next batch wait, and nothing gets finished on time. You can think about that as you take three laps around the field."

"Yes, sir," they chorused, like a proper unit.

"A moment," Tannov said. Everyone froze. Linné heard Revna's breath hitch.

Tannov's boots squished into her line of sight. Had he recognized her? And *what* was he doing here? Why had he left the Thirty-First, and why to become a Skarov, of all things?

"We're sure it will be a pleasure to work with you all," he said. His voice was deeper than she remembered. "We're here for the same reason as you—to win the war. Remember that lies and secrecy are the enemy of the Union, and if you have questions or concerns, our door is always open."

After a second half-hearted "Yes, sir," the boys marched smartly off the field.

Tannov's boots disappeared at last, and Linné dared to raise her head. Tannov and Dostorov stood with their backs to her, facing Hesovec. "Shall we continue the grand tour?" Hesovec said to the Skarov, in a voice that clearly indicated he'd rather be anywhere else.

"Let's go," said Tannov. Dostorov shrugged, and they set off without looking back.

The sight of their retreat was eclipsed by the approach of the dark-haired soldier, who'd broken off from his unit and circled back around. "Need my rifle back," he said, his voice full of apology. She handed it over without a word. She didn't blame him for abandoning her to the attention of the Information Unit. But when he said, "Thanks, sweetheart," she gave him her best withering look. He winked in return. Then he trotted off to catch up with his comrades.

The others let out their breath as one. Revna was pale as a corpse. Katya had made little crescent marks in the skin of her wrist with her fingernails. Olya sighed. Her hand went to her hair, smoothing her short dark curls. "Wow," she said. "They're not bad looking."

"The Skarov?" said Asya. "They'll send you up to the mining colony for sneezing wrong."

"They can't do that. Rules are rules, even for them," Nadya said, letting her cold spark fountain up. It returned to the Weave in little flashes of silver-blue, redistributing along its grid and flickering from sight.

"If all their agents look like that, it's no wonder they get so many people to snitch." Olya smirked and raised her eyebrows. "Now Miss Zolonova will have someone who listens to her when she complains."

Linné ground her teeth, but for once she didn't have to stand up for herself.

"Leave her be. Linné's the hero of the hour." Katya turned to Linné and folded her arms. "Never mind what that boar said. We'll tell Tamara—"

"Don't," grated Linné. It came out harsher than she intended, but what difference did it make? The girls would go back to hating her tomorrow. And they'd only hate her more if they found out she knew the two new faces of the Information Unit.

"The boys were the ones breaking the rules," Nadya said. "You didn't do anything wrong."

"We *did* do something wrong. I destroyed army property. And Revna talked back to a superior officer, in front of the Information Unit." Linné motioned to the still-pale Revna as she addressed the rest of them. "Don't start shooting till we're back. The only way this could get worse is if someone gets hit by a stray bullet. Practice cleaning your rifles, check your powder, that sort of thing."

"Nah, we'll come cabbage picking. It'll go faster if we all do it," Katya said.

Linné nearly groaned. "If you come, you'll get into trouble. The point is to punish *us* for what *we* did wrong."

"We want to help," Olya said.

"Well, don't." She didn't have the patience to try to make them understand. "Let's go," she told Revna.

Magdalena squeezed Revna's arm. "Are you sure you'll be okay? In the mud and everything?"

"I've gotten these legs muddy before," Revna said.

"All right," Magdalena replied, though she didn't sound convinced.

The others turned away grudgingly and sat against the sandbags to clean their rifles. Linné and Revna started off over the field.

Tannov and Dostorov. Why had they left the regiment, and why to become Skarov? Trading in a life of camaraderie for a life of bullying, monitoring, ruining lives for the slim chance of protection. Destroying a country to ensure it never fell. This was the Skarov initiative.

She needed a cigarette. By all that was good in this world.

She realized she was walking alone. Revna lagged behind,

picking her way through the field with care. Linné stopped to wait. Over the sound of the rain, she called, "Can't you go any faster?"

"Have you ever tried walking through mud on stilts?" Revna replied.

The rain had intensified, and fat drops pounded the earth. Something unpleasant squelched in her sock. "No."

"It's nothing like that anyway." Revna took another careful step on the uneven ground. "But I'm not really interested in embarrassing myself and getting my uniform covered in mud. So I'll go at my own pace, thank you."

"Well, maybe you should think about that before you butt in on someone else's argument," Linné said, adjusting her jacket. Rain slid down her back.

Revna snorted. "Sounds like you could learn a thing or two about flirting with soldiers when on duty."

"I wasn't flirting." Linné felt herself turning hot. "He challenged me." And he'd walked away with her cigarettes. The Skarov could penalize them for gambling with army resources, so she found it hard to blame him.

"You may be good with a gun, but you're not good with people. Trust me—he was flirting."

Had he been? Linné tried to remember. But when she thought about the dark-haired soldier, she pictured the silver coats and the men underneath them instead. "I didn't ask him to." It didn't matter. He'd probably flirted to distract her.

Revna shrugged.

"Why *did* you stick up for me?" Linné said.

Revna looked back at the rest of the girls, who fiddled with their rifles and laughed as Katya waved her arms about. No doubt Katya was talking about Linné. "No one else is looking out for us here. So we have to look after each other. We're a team, aren't we?"

"Even in front of the Skarov?"

Revna looked at Linné for a moment, judging her in some way. "Especially in front of the Skarov."

They finished their walk to the cart in a silence Linné couldn't bring herself to break.

When they neared the farmer, Linné went forward to apologize. His face became rigid as she explained. "Not a very funny joke."

"No, sir. We—" She glanced back. Revna had disappeared behind the cart. Linné's goodwill evaporated. Revna wouldn't get out of paying that easily. "I apologize."

His face softened at her *sir*. Though laws of the Union stated that all men were equal, a lot of gentlemen forgot this inconvenient fact where the people of the land were concerned. But Linné's father had always advised her to treat the common people with respect. *They will form the bulk of the revolution*, he'd said. *And the best way to survive a revolution is to be on the winning side.* "I hope you won't make a habit of it?" he grumbled.

"Definitely not," she said. Her salary wasn't near enough to buy Intelgard's entire supply of cabbages.

"So long as it doesn't happen again. You can pick up the cabbages and we'll settle for the two you shot. I can't sell them now."

Linné paid him and gathered the pieces of the demolished cabbages off the field, then went around the back. "You owe me twenty coruna," she began, then stopped. Revna sat on the lip of the cart, sagging against the grayed wood. She was even paler than when she had been facing off against Hesovec. As Linné watched, Revna reached out and pulled on thin air. A cabbage rolled rather nonchalantly under her feet. "What are you doing?"

Revna eyed the delinquent crop. "Picking up cabbages."

Linné bent down and began to scoop them up. "I can think of easier ways."

"I wanted to practice." Revna flicked her wrist again, and this time a cabbage sailed over her head, landing with a thump that dislodged two more. She caught them before they hit the ground and shoved them on top of the pile. "If we don't improve, we don't fly. If we don't fly, what are we doing here?" She wouldn't look at Linné. "I'm not going home."

Finally, something Linné could relate to. She didn't want to be here all day, though, so she picked up more cabbages by hand, and Revna gave up on her Weave-working and bent down to join her.

Linné wanted to think of something nice to say. Couldn't she manage one compliment? "Um." Her mind came up blank. All words fled. But Revna was looking at her, raising a questioning eyebrow. "I'm intrigued to see you fly."

Revna's mouth twitched. "I'm intrigued to see you fire."

✳

Linné left the range soon after. She was finished with Olya's snide comments about the Information Unit and Katya's huffed indignation that she hadn't been allowed to help pick up cabbages. Magdalena confirmed that Revna was all right, then ignored Linné and proceeded to sketch out plans for her gas bullet. The way

115

the others spoke—laughing, teasing, supporting one another—ignited a resentment in Linné that threatened to blaze out into the cold air. When she walked off, no one even bothered to ask her where she was going.

She focused on her hands, trying to form her spark energy into a blade the way she'd seen Tcerlin do it. The spark whipped out in slim threads, grounding itself on the Weave and disappearing before she could solidify it. *Come on.* Maybe she should have taken Koslen's suggestion and gone to be a secretary at Mistelgard.

She couldn't harbor that thought for long. She was born to fight. She had to believe that they would succeed and that Tamara Zima would get them to the front. Or she had to believe that Zima would fail and that she could make it back to the front on her own. She pushed on her spark, willing it to obey.

"Excuse me, miss!" A figure in a silver coat strode toward her. Another stood a few meters behind him, attempting to light a rascidine cigarette.

She cast about desperately for an excuse to bolt. She could say that she had to use the toilet—feminine problems, she was learning, could get you out of a lot. She could say she'd been called to Hesovec's office, and she couldn't dawdle. But her training pushed against her. They were Skarov. You kept your mouth shut.

Tannov's hawkish nose was a little larger than she'd remembered it, though his face was still smooth, almost babyish. His straw-colored hair had grown out from its regulation cut. Maybe the Skarov didn't care if you forgot to trim it.

Too late to run now. She tucked her chin. Was it stupid to hope he hadn't caught a good look at her?

"You're one of Zima's girls. Kindly direct me to her office." His voice wasn't only deeper. It held the clipped, clear tones of someone used to giving commands and having those commands obeyed without question. Not three months ago he'd paraded around the field with her, stuffed Koslen's pipe with dried cow dung, and snuck out after curfew to practice night shooting.

Now he wore the blue star of the Extraordinary Wartime Information Unit dangling from his coat. And that meant that he didn't obey regimental orders anymore. His orders came from a separate source, and no one with intelligence questioned that source. It was Tannov's job to notice who was likely to defect, who needed to be transferred, and who needed to be quietly taken care of. And now he'd noticed her.

Without raising her head, she pointed to the cluster of offices and tried to pitch her voice low. "That way, sir," she said. "Light blue shutters."

"Don't mumble, miss," he said. "In the army we put our heads on top of our shoulders, like we're proud to be here. No one's going to—" He stopped, leaning in. She tucked her chin farther, but it was too late. "Alexei?"

She might as well try to salvage some dignity. She straightened. "It's Linné now."

Tannov clapped her on the shoulder so hard she staggered. He pulled her arm out from behind her and pumped it up and down. "Screw me sideways," he said. "I never thought I'd see you again. And certainly not on military ground." He laughed the good-natured laugh she'd heard the first time she met him. It was an open sort of laugh, the type that invited everyone to join in. It didn't fit at all with the uniform. As he turned around, she found herself peering at his ears and neck, looking for any evidence of the fabled shape-shifting everyone whispered about. But there was nothing to indicate his change except for his golden eyes. He called back to Dostorov. "Look who I found!" he shouted. "Alexei!"

Dostorov shrugged.

"Alexei Nabiev," Tannov clarified. "*Girl* Alexei."

That got Dostorov moving. He stomped forward, splashing through the mud. Wind tossed his hair into his eyes, but he was too busy holding on to his battered cigarette to push it away. "Miss," he muttered, and turned back to the task of trying to light his cigarette.

Linné tamped down on the hot spark that rose at the word *miss*. *Skarov*, she reminded herself.

"How did you end up here?" Tannov said. He hadn't let go of her hand. "Does that pompous windbag in charge know who you are? Are we getting you in trouble? Again?" He elbowed Dostorov. Dostorov kicked him back.

"Everyone here knows who I am," she said.

"And you're calling yourself Linné," he said, working the name around in his mouth. Finally he shrugged and smiled that broad, open smile. "It'll take getting used to. But I guess it's smart for you to have joined Tamara's force." He waggled his eyebrows. Dostorov shook his head at Tannov's expression.

"Well, Koslen wouldn't keep me," Linné said. She didn't know whether to grin or try to extricate herself. Tannov was as blunt as ever, it seemed. How had he ended up a Skarov?

"And Tamara trusts you to fly experimental planes?" he said, one corner of his mouth pulling up.

"She trusts me to spark things and drop bombs," Linné replied. And rain fire down on the Elda. "Someone else gets to fly."

Tannov finally let go of her hand. He elbowed Dostorov again, causing him to fumble his cigarette. "You know, Dostorov almost got demoted for recruiting you. Koslen screamed at him for an hour. Said he damaged the reputation of the army."

And that's how you got to be a Skarov? she thought, but she didn't say it. Everyone at her old regiment had stories of friends who joined the Information Unit. Who changed. Now she could gather some stories of her own—not that anyone cared to hear her tell them.

But she still couldn't believe it of these two. Tannov's straight-forward manner was the exact opposite of the typical shadowy Skarov figure. And bumbling Dostorov was even worse. How was *he* supposed to crack codes and break spies?

Tannov reached out a hand and tugged on a lock by her ear. "You're growing out your hair." He frowned at it, head cocked to one side. "It suits you."

She knocked his hand away. "Screw you."

Tannov and Dostorov gawked. Clearly becoming Skarov had changed the way people talked to them. It was supposed to change the way *she* talked to them.

Then Dostorov snorted. The snort turned into a laugh as he fished his cigarette case out of his pocket. "Same old Alexei," he said as he put his much-abused cigarette away.

"Same old Alexei," Tannov agreed. He was smiling, too.

She opened her mouth to correct them. But maybe it was better for her to be Alexei. She'd rather be Alexei than this stranger, Linné.

They stood for a few moments without speaking. Then Dostorov nudged Tannov. "It's colder than a witch's tit," he said. "Let's go."

She led them to Zima's office. The yellow light inside promised warmth and comfort, making her ache.

Tannov clapped her on the shoulder. "Got to get to work," he said. "But why don't you get a drink with us sometime?"

No one ever "got a drink" with a member of the Information Unit. No one ever said no to them, either. "How long will you be here?" she said, trying to evade the question.

Tannov spread his hands. "Who knows? I'm sure we'll see you. It's a small base."

It was a base so small that everyone would know she'd been talking to the Skarov. Apparently it wasn't enough that everyone thought she was an arrogant sycophant. Now she'd be branded the regimental snitch.

Their talk was the first nice conversation she'd had since she'd arrived.

8

STRIVE FOR YOUR UNION

The next day was their first in the air. Revna pulled her sore limbs out of bed to the sound of the sirens, put on her kit, and trotted outside, rubbing her eyes. She lined up at the edge of the field with the rest of the girls.

Wind wound in cold ribbons about their wrists and jerked at the Strekozy covers. Gray clouds soared in from the mountains. But Tamara didn't seem to notice any of this. Her cheeks blazed with something more than the cold, and her brown eyes were bright.

"Pilots!" she shouted. "Remain with me. The rest of you, to your usual stations."

The navigators and engineers left in a flurry of whispers. Magdalena grinned at Revna as she passed. *Good luck*, she mouthed.

"We'll have to fly them one at a time, I'm afraid." The girls fell silent at once. "Colonel Hesovec has...other arrangements," Tamara continued, in a voice that clearly indicated her disdain, "and you can't go up on your own. We'll be using today to apply what you've learned to a larger world. Why don't we start with you?" She beckoned Katya, who barely controlled a squeal.

Three pilots wrestled the cover off Katya's flame-painted Strekoza, and Katya and Tamara clambered up on the wing and into the cockpit. A few moments later its landing claws pushed it into the air. It wobbled and stabilized as spark blasted through the engine at the back of the plane, flashing yellow and orange before redistributing along Weave lines. Revna was surprised by its silence; the Dragons that flew over Tammin had thrummed and roared like beasts. The Strekozy were no louder than the palanquins that shuttled men to and from the front.

The Strekoza wound like a lazy bird around the field. It was even slower than Revna would have guessed from Tamara's descriptions.

Katya didn't care. "It's incredible," she gushed after she'd landed and disembarked. "You'll be terrified at first. But don't worry."

One by one they went out, and at last it was Revna's turn.

Tamara scratched her leg as she frowned at Revna. "We'll have to boost you into the cockpit," she said.

"Sorry?"

"You can't climb up the wings like the others. You'll need a boost."

Something hot stabbed at her belly. It took her a moment to realize it was anger. When she'd left Mrs. Rodoya and Tammin, Revna thought she was done with all the superiors who assumed they knew more about her legs than she did. "I think I'll manage."

"Are you sure?" Tamara said.

Revna planted one hand on the wing of the plane and grabbed for the Weave. She pulled herself up and tumbled gracelessly into the cockpit, banging her prosthetics against the dashboard and making her residual limbs sing in pain. It was worth it, though, for the way Tamara hopped up behind her without another word.

"Shall we?" Tamara's voice sounded right next to her ear. A speaking tube allowed pilot and navigator to communicate, and Revna didn't even have to turn her head to say, "Ready," with more confidence than she felt.

Maybe I wasn't meant for this. But she thought of the battle they'd seen from the ground, and when her heart faltered, she set Mama and Lyfa firmly in her mind.

"Tell me what you know about living metal," Tamara said.

Revna had hated being called on in school. She'd always second-guessed herself, as if she were being asked a trick question. "It knows I'm here. It can sense me." She felt a bit foolish, as though she were talking to thin air.

"And?" the thin air replied.

"It's alive because of the Weave."

"And?"

"It's heavier than normal steel, and more durable. It's susceptible to the mood around it. It knows when it's being worked, and it can help or hinder the smith. It likes physical contact." As long as it liked the person it was in contact with, anyway.

"Good. All good. Each of these planes was modeled off an Elda prototype, and we don't have a lot to spare. If you crash it, you'd better have a good reason for doing so."

Revna could hear the grin in her voice, and she opened her mouth to respond but stopped, unsure of what to say. The air prickled all around her.

"Sorry," Tamara said, and the prickling faded to a grumbling undercurrent. "A bit of war humor. We won't be doing anything fancy on this flight. You need to acquaint yourself with your plane, get it used to your style. The engineers of Mistelgard have made a couple of adjustments that mean you'll also be able to see a few things from the plane's perspective, too."

The cockpit was cramped and cold. Revna barely had space to shove her feet underneath her chair. The short dashboard held a compass, and the windscreen came up to the top of her head. Revna tugged her leather helmet over her hair and set her goggles. They slipped down her nose. Wind edged around the gap between her helmet and her ear.

"I have a throttle back here," Tamara said. "That controls the power. You'll need to trust your navigator to operate on her own, but don't hesitate to give instruction. We can prepare to use more spark to accommodate a faster engine, or diminish our output to slow down. I'm going to clip into my harness now."

Revna couldn't find a harness for herself. Her seat was surrounded by long, slim metal rods that resembled nothing so much as the fingers of a giant. They were even jointed, dozens of little metal plates welded together. Two enormous leather gloves, lined with more metal, sat before her. She slid her hands into the gloves, stopping only when she touched the metal tips of their fingers and their cuffs brushed her elbows.

"Elda planes take advantage of the fact that living metal can interact with the Weave far more effectively than we can," Tamara said. "The Strekoza is designed to tap into you, and you into it. It should help you manipulate the Weave and should feel like an extension of your body. Your navigator will feed energy into it to keep it going, and the plane, in turn, will feed energy into you, to keep you going." She took a deep breath. "I'm going to fire up now. Are you ready?"

"What about them?" Revna looked at the silver-coated men standing on the edge of the field. She didn't really need to ask. Everyone knew the Information Unit was here to report on them, to learn who could use the Weave and put them on some special list so they could all be rounded up after the war. *Except Linné.* Katya had seen their so-called supervisor talking to the Skarov in a friendly manner, and while Revna knew better than most not to believe everything she heard, she also knew that a last name like Zolonova had a power of its own. A power that would protect Linné even if everyone else in her regiment had to face the firing squad.

"Don't worry about them," Tamara said. "Focus. Are you ready?" Without waiting for Revna's reply, she activated the plane.

A burst of energy brought the Strekoza to life. Then the giant hand closed around her, pinning her to her chair.

She gasped as something slid between her shoulders, piercing the skin of her neck. Tiny jabs, like the needles of a bitter seamstress, bloomed at her chest and midriff. Revna twisted and tried to pull her hands from the gloves. But the metal fingers only bit deeper. They squeezed her until she thought all breath would be pushed out of her. She opened her mouth to scream.

And then—

—and then, her heart slowed. The sounds of the world became something new. The biting wind was a tickle; the chill, damp air became soft. When she inhaled, she could smell the sweetness of coming rain, the fresh dirt, the biting smoke from the engineers' laboratory, gunpowder from the firing range. She felt light, as though the wind could pick her up and take her far over the mountains. Something massive rose in her, breathed with her. She was a great beast awakening from slumber.

"Open your eyes." Tamara's voice came not from behind her, but from someplace *inside*, someplace she both wasn't and was.

She obeyed. Silver strands spread out around her, slim and strong, crisscrossing the air. Some strands were as thick as her arm, pulsing where they intersected and fading as they disappeared into the ground. Some were thinner than a line of spider silk. Under the modified gloves, they were the softest, finest thread she'd ever touched. She plucked one and it undulated, rustling against the threads around it before sliding back into place.

"I'm going to increase power," Tamara said. "You'll need to hook us on a diagonal cross-thread. Can you do that?"

"Yes," Revna said. *Hopefully.*

"Easy," Tamara said. "She's sensitive."

Revna felt the gathering excitement of the Strekoza as the engine grumbled. She didn't pull on the Weave so much as coax the plane to hop away from the earth, light as a bird, and fold its landing claws up into its body. Tamara guided her onto a stronger strand, and they were off.

They drifted up, resting on the wind and the Weave like the

crows and magpies that flitted along Tammin's roofs. The Strekoza had looked fat and ungainly on the ground, but it was meant to be in the air, meant to be felt from the inside. When Revna flexed her hands, the wings of the Strekoza responded, its simple steel frame adjusting in tiny increments as the flying gloves hooked into the tiniest strands.

She'd been worried that the plane would still hate her. Now she knew it would never turn on her again.

"Good," Tamara said. Revna could feel her smile.

They made a low circle around the base, almost low enough to scrape the top of the fence or drop a coruna on the hospital roof. From above, the world was a patchwork of brown—chicory roofs, dark mud, beige boards stained with soldiers' footprints. The Weave flashed silver as Tamara's spark fed into it.

What would Tammin look like from the air? The city she'd lived in all her life, the city she'd learned to use the Weave in. Would the palanquins and war beetles feel the pull of her as she passed? She imagined flying over the factory that once stifled her, over the cluster of houses that held Mama and Lyfa and their neighbors. And the next time the Dragons came to Tammin, she wouldn't be a curse, panicking in the dust-choked street. She would meet them head-on, and she would use the Weave with pride.

Tamara talked her through the landing as they set down lightly and cut the power. Revna felt the last pieces of their shared emotion slip away, until all she had left was fatigue, satisfaction, pride. The Strekoza's pilot cage loosened around her chest.

"Is it true?" she said, twisting around to look at Tamara.

Tamara's eyes shone, reflecting Revna's elation. "Is what true?"

Could it be legal after the war? Revna licked her lips. "Won't we make tangles when we fly?"

"Tiny ones," Tamara said. "Most tangles resolve themselves in twenty-four hours." Like Pavi had said at dinner after their first practice. "The major tangles, the magic-distorting, monster-making tangles, take more Weave activity than a hundred Strekozy. The excess spark that comes through the engine will return to the Weave as well, making it stronger." She smiled as though she knew what Revna was trying to say. "If we can prove it now, we can keep flying after the war. I promise."

If we can prove it now. They still had work to do. And now Revna was more determined than ever to do it.

She used the Weave to help pull herself out of the cockpit, fumbling as she came down. She slammed on the ground. Her feet prickled and her residual limbs throbbed.

"Well done," Tamara said, shaking her hand. Then she was off to collect Pavi.

Katya and Elena rushed to her side. "Are you all right?" said Elena, gripping her by the arm as though she might fall over if she tried to take another step.

"Fine," Revna said. And though she limped off the field, she *was* fine. She was better than fine. Her body felt different, as if she were so much bigger and she'd never known it.

Tamara took them back to her office after practice was over. The pilots crowded into the little room, rubbing their hands together for warmth as she poured tiny cups of tea from her samovar. She topped off each cup with a dollop of fermented mare's milk.

"My dears," she said, and saluted them with her cup. They saluted back and drank up. Revna tried to keep her mouth from twisting at the sour-bitter taste of the milk. Mama had never been much for drink, and Papa had preferred sugar beet rum freshened with mint. Mare's milk was a farmland liquor, and Tammin was a factory town. But the rite of passage was more important than the drink itself.

They sat quiet for a few minutes, savoring the warmth of the room and the spiked tea. The others might be suspiciously Good Union Girls, Revna thought as she sipped, but they were all pilots now.

"I never really thought we'd do it," Pavi said at last.

"I always knew," Katya said. "We can do anything."

That was the secret they shared as they held out their cups and got another splash of strong tea and tangy liquor. That was the secret they smiled over when they went to dinner. Not that they could fly, not that they could use the Weave. *We can do anything.*

✳

Dinner was full of a giggling flock of pilots. No one told Linné what was going on, and she didn't ask. Her day had been wretched enough. The navigators had been given whatever spark-powered machines the base had on hand and had practiced running them. Linné could still feel the prick of the mess generator's long needle as it slid through her skin, the way her life seemed to suck out of her in a thread. She'd never felt sicker in her life. When her old regiment trained with the spark, she'd had power and control, and now she had neither.

Worse, no one else had complained. The others had chattered away, theorizing about the pilots and their first flight today, without an apparent care for the spark they lost. She'd been too afraid to ask Nadya how she did it, even though the somber girl read a technical manual while she powered machine after machine.

Linné kept one eye on the door of the mess in case Tannov or Dostorov made an entrance. They never did. Maybe the Skarov ate something better somewhere else. She got through dinner without a word, which she considered a personal victory. Then she went back to her bed and flopped down on the hard board.

The so-called Night Raiders would never make it into battle. And if they did, the war would break them.

The door slammed open and Elena trotted in. She stopped when she saw Linné, her face reddening.

Well, Linné didn't know what to say, either. If she had, she might have been a more sociable dinner companion. After a moment she heard the creak of Elena's bed as she sat and kicked off her boots with a sigh of relief.

Linné tried to ignore her. All she wanted was to lie there in peace. She'd gotten used to sharing her life with the boys of Koslen's regiment—a little too used to it—but at Intelgard she felt shut up tight.

Elena rummaged around in her pack. She looked over and caught Linné watching her. "Not going to the mess?"

"Why should I?" said Linné.

"Why indeed," Elena muttered. She found what she'd been looking for, a pair of black heeled shoes and a wool dress. She unbuttoned her uniform and stripped down until she wore nothing but her bra and underwear. Linné rolled over to face the wall. That was another thing. The girls had no shame. She'd spent years slinking around, changing where no one could see, looking over her shoulder whenever she took off her shirt. She'd gotten up an hour early to bathe and slip shaving foam on her razor. She'd washed her menstruation rags in the middle of the night. She couldn't bring herself to stop binding her breasts, as though quitting would be an admission that she really did belong here. And though it was wrong to blame Zima's regiment, Elena's cavalier attitude seemed off. Un-soldier-like.

Something clunked on the floor, and Linné turned back over. Elena had dropped her shoes. Her sky-blue dress was more suitable for summer than autumn. Her bare legs would freeze outside, but that didn't seem to concern her. She slipped her feet into the shoes, grabbed her army jacket, and left without another look at Linné.

Where was she going dressed like that? The first image that sprang to mind was of a boy waiting somewhere with a flower and a smirk. A blaze crept up Linné's neck. The Thirty-First would have ranked the Night Raiders according to various lewd themes. She wouldn't put it past any boy here to try to use sex to prove that women didn't belong in the army.

Linné slid off her bed and put on her boots. She willed spark to pool in her hands. If she got into a fight, the case would go up to Zima and Hesovec, and rumors would wash through the regiment like a flood. But if she let loose with her magic a little, she might only have to frighten the offending boy. She could always blame it on an incompetent mistake.

She didn't bother lacing her boots. She grabbed her coat and hurried out.

Elena was halfway across the yard, moving as fast as she could in her nice shoes. Wind whipped Linné's hair into her eyes. The sun had dropped behind the mountains, turning the night a deep cobalt. Her sparked hands steamed.

Elena went to the mess. But instead of sneaking around the side, like Linné expected, she pulled open the door. Linné heard the soft croon of a trumpet before Elena disappeared within.

Curious now, Linné went up to the mess and opened the door herself. The warm blast of air was a welcome feeling after the numbing wind. Elena, still at the threshold, registered Linné with a raised eyebrow before turning to Katya.

Tables and chairs had been stacked along the side of one wall to open up a wide swath of floor. The stove burned merrily, casting light and warmth over the room with the help of a few lamps. A crystal radio played music, faint under the chatter and clack of shoes on the floor, but those who danced seemed to pick out its beat. The girls danced alone or with each other. Linné didn't spot a boy among them.

Magdalena came up to her with a broad smile. "What do you think?" she said. Her wild hair was pulled back in a ponytail, and grease streaked her face and uniform from the day's work. "In celebration of our pilots."

Linné searched for a suitable answer. *It's nice* would sound too fake. *No one invited me* sounded too whiny. "Does Commander Zima know about this?"

She wasn't sure what she'd meant to say, but she definitely

hadn't meant to sound like a pompous ass. Which was exactly how Magdalena took her comment. She rolled her eyes. "Lighten up." Which meant, Linné reflected as she watched Magdalena stalk away, that Zima probably didn't know.

The other girls shifted, enough for Linné to notice they were getting out of her way. They moved when they could and turned their backs to her when they couldn't.

Well, that was fine. She didn't want to be friends. And she *should* go to the commander. She'd keep a clean record and maybe the rest of them would learn something for once.

They'd be expecting that, of course. It was why Elena ignored her, why Katya tossed her pale curls, why Olya smiled extra wide, and why Nadya shrugged one shoulder. Linné had never told on anyone in Koslen's regiment, and she wouldn't become known for tattling in this one. Even if she did want to go back to her old life, she wasn't going to do it by becoming a snitch. When she'd served under Koslen, she'd snuck out after hours with Tannov and Dostorov to poach rascidine cigarettes from the officers' quarters and drink confiscated brandy.

She hated to admit it, but dancing wasn't the same.

Revna watched the dance floor with a wistful expression. Not quite knowing what to do, Linné sat down beside her. Revna's eyes widened in alarm; it was too late for her to pretend that something interesting had happened on the other side of the room. It almost made Linné laugh—the only person who would talk to her was literally her captive audience.

If only she could think of something to say.

Everyone else made it look so easy. But Linné's lessons in

discourse had taught her more about politics than small talk. She kept her mouth shut and waited for Revna to say something instead.

Revna tapped her finger on her thigh in time to the music. The idea that she might be trying to ignore Linné was more irritating than her silence. "Enjoying yourself?" Linné finally said, even though she thought the question was stupid.

Revna paused, giving Linné a sidelong look that indicated she agreed. "I loved dancing, before," she said. "I was never much good at it, but it's more fun to be out there than to be sitting on the side."

Linné thought of asking what sort of an accident Revna had been in. But she remembered Revna's expression when she'd arrived in the barracks. The way she winced every time the sound of her feet made someone look down. Instead, Linné kept her eyes on Olya as she paraded a bemused Nadya across the squeaking boards. Olya's laugh was different tonight, free, more genuine than Linné had ever heard it. "That would never be me," she said. "If I had to dance formally one more time, I'd probably saw off my—shit." She caught herself far too late. "Sorry." The apology came out insincere. She really should have listened to her tutors more during the conversational lessons.

"I guess you're not fond," Revna said stiffly.

Linné searched for something else to say. "I was such a failure that my tutors hired someone to teach me martial arts instead."

Revna looked at her. "Really?" The judgment had slipped from her voice, revealing curiosity underneath.

"Mostly kicks and stances," she replied. "Our housekeeper

never let me do anything that would bulk up my arms like a peasant." Shit again. Though the laws of the Union officially proclaimed that all were equal, she'd sounded like a would-be aristocrat of the worst type.

Revna cocked her head and scrutinized Linné's arms. "It didn't work."

Magdalena appeared in front of them. Her cheeks were flushed from dancing. "Is everything all right?" she said to Revna, tilting her head toward Linné.

Linné rolled her eyes. If Magdalena wanted to talk about her from two feet away, she could have picked a better code.

"Everything's fine," Revna said. She turned back to Linné. "Did your father really let you learn to fight? He didn't mind?"

"He wasn't around much." Linné fought the urge to squirm. It was one thing to talk about home, another to talk about her father. And she didn't want to think about him, about what he might say if he saw her now. "Why did you join up?" she asked, more to divert attention than because she cared.

"Tamara asked, and the money's better than the factory wage." Revna took a breath to add something, then seemed to change her mind.

"Tamara Zima saw you in person?" Linné said. "And she didn't care that you can't walk?"

Wrong thing to say. "I can walk," Revna said, and her tone had a definite frosty edge. She lifted one steel leg, turning it so that Linné could see the ball of the ankle. "And you don't need flesh legs to use the Weave."

She had a point. "But have you ever used them in battle?"

Linné knew that it was a cruel and unfair question. But war was unfair. It was messy and filthy and bloody, and it belonged to the people who could fight it. Revna might be a genius with the Weave. Being in a war was not the same as fighting one. And for all they claimed victory tonight, these pilots hadn't seen anything yet. "How long will it take you to get to your plane every night?"

"Leave her alone." Magdalena moved closer, folding her arms. Using her size to intimidate. "She has as much right to be here as you do. Maybe she has more. Dozens of girls could take *your* place."

"And no one would suffice for yours?" Linné said. "What your rights are has nothing to do with it. What matters is whether you *can* do it."

And then she was there, with the thick summer rains lashing, cowering inside the carapace of a war beetle that wouldn't press forward no matter how much spark the driver poured in.

She was shooting the man who'd walked into the minefield because he needed a midnight piss and he went the wrong way.

She was defying Colonel Koslen as he told her to leave a casualty behind. She was pulling the man through the mud. She was feeling him die anyway, against her shoulder.

She was on the retreat in her first-ever battle, running for her life as snipers took out their regiment from the rear forward.

"What happens if we have to abandon the base? What do you do when we have two minutes to get to our planes? What happens if we have to jump out as fast as we can, when something's wrong and we have to bail? How fast can you run on those feet?"

Her heart pumped as though she'd run laps for Colonel Hesovec. A cluster formed around them, muttering. Their eyes bored into her. She needed to fix this. To calm herself and the others down.

As with dancing, she'd never really gotten the hang of it.

"She's a great pilot," Katya said. "Revna deserves her spot."

"It's not about what she can do in the plane," Linné snapped. "The war doesn't just happen when we're in the plane." And people who thought they were ready for it, that they were special somehow—they got the worst shock of all.

Revna had begun to tremble. Magdalena put a hand on her shoulder. "If you're only going to criticize, you should go. You can run to Tamara if you want—we don't care. Leave Revna alone."

Linné squared her shoulders and met Magdalena's eye. "Would you fly with her?"

"What?" Magdalena said, stunned.

"Would you be the navigator? Would you risk getting killed because she can't run fast enough? Would you risk watching her die for the same reason?"

There was a moment's pause—a moment too long. It gave enough time for Linné to see the emotions play their way across Magdalena's face, shock and shame and anger. Finally she said, "I'm not a navigator. But if I were, I'd fly with her."

"That's easy to say when you never have to prove it." A cold, bitter triumph bloomed in Linné's belly. She hated that she was right. She hated that it satisfied her.

"Leave," growled Magdalena.

The trumpet on the radio turned to a melancholy piano. No one danced to it. Some stood around Revna, hands on their hips, shielding her. Others watched the conflict from a safe distance. Outraged expressions abounded. But the silence spoke, too.

Linné left them there. Let them be self-righteous and hypocritical. She was mean, cruel, heartless, and all the other names they flung at her. But she was honest. They worshipped a commander with no experience commanding, but they didn't even want to look at Linné. This war would destroy them and they hated her for saying it.

The wind outside had turned even more bitter. *Tomorrow will be worse than today*, she thought as she fought against it. She went back to her bed, and she lay down, but sleep didn't come.

Near ten bells the door opened and Revna's telltale footsteps thunked across the room. Linné probably imagined that they paused as they passed her bed. But she couldn't mistake the sniffling sounds that the other girl tried to suppress in her pillow.

She'd done that. Maybe the rest of them hadn't helped, but she'd done it. She felt sick.

A couple of hours later they filed in, speaking in hushed tones. Linné was still awake. Revna was still crying.

Nobody said anything to either of them.

9

UNITY IS STRENGTH

Revna refused to act like a victim after Linné's display in the mess. It had been years since someone had attacked her and her disability so blatantly. Usually people acted like the rest of the girls—silent when they needed to be noisy, faithless when they needed to show loyalty. She imagined Linné with her jaw on the ground, watching Revna soar. Linné could spark, but so what? Everyone had the spark and thousands of people could use it. Only a few could do what Revna did.

Win one war, and you'll win all of them, she reminded herself. She was at Intelgard for a reason, and it wasn't to get pushed around, belittled, or arrested.

And when she ended the war, she wouldn't do it for the Union or people like Linné. She'd do it for her family, for her friends, for herself.

Flying invigorated her, though doubt still needled in when she put her hands in her pilot's gloves. Every time the Strekoza's giant fingers closed on her, she trembled and her prosthetics twitched. But her Strekoza loved her, and when Tamara powered up, Revna lost herself to this glorious new creature that could go anywhere, do anything. The Weave limned her sight in silver and showed her the Ryddan countryside as she'd never seen it before. The farmland was churned by never-ending autumn rain, and the plains beyond the base wove gold and green together as the grass and the scrub took over. It was easy to believe that some god of the land had painted it in bright swaths, heedless of the snow that would blanket it two-thirds of the year.

Revna learned to steer the plane with the slightest movements, adjusting to the wind and the weather. She learned to make the plane roll and flip, to pull it by brute force. She learned to see Intelgard's ramshackle mess for what it was, to recognize the plains beyond it and the southeastern Karavels ridging the horizon. Twice they flew beyond the Karavels, though they always turned back before they could catch even a glimpse of the front.

Tamara flew with every pilot, and the pilots spent long hours practicing techniques on the ground while they waited. She flew up to twenty-two times a day, pouring her spark into the throttle. Her hair turned dry and brittle, her skin ashen. The Strekozy sucked the spark from her greedily, teasing out her life one needle prick at a time. Whenever she rolled up her sleeves, the girls could see bruise after bruise and dozens of tiny dots where the blood had risen to the surface, like a tattoo. But she never stopped. Once, she fell asleep behind Revna, and their plane grew so heavy Revna thought they'd drop straight out of the sky. She had to yank on the Weave with all she had as the aircraft drifted down.

Tamara came to with a start. "Good use of force," she said in such a crisp voice Revna almost believed she hadn't nodded off. "I know it's not something we like to talk about, but if something happens to your navigator, you'll feel it. You won't be able to fly the plane for long, so your safest bet is to set down in home territory and send up an emergency flare."

Revna knew she was trying to cover for her exhaustion. Mama did the same thing. And what else could Tamara do? Hesovec wouldn't help them.

It took Tamara another week to approve them to fly with navigators. When she told the pilots, they sent up a cheer that rattled the weak walls of her office. They trooped to the mess as if they'd already won their first battle. "Here's to us not crashing and dying tomorrow," Katya said, raising her tin cup as they sat down.

"Hear, hear," they chorused. Nadya released a shower of cold spark that bloomed like fireworks, and they shrieked as it fell on their heads and necks. She could do anything with her power. Revna supposed it was too much to hope that Nadya might partner with her.

Some of the men laughed derisively on the other side of the mess. Linné, sitting alone against the wall, snorted and went back to reading her survival manual.

"Miserable hag," Magdalena said in a low voice. "Her life must be unbearable." She choked on a bite of gristly pork. "Like this food. Pass the salt."

Katya handed it over. "She looks like she can't decide whether to kill herself or the rest of us."

"It doesn't look like things are so bad for her," Revna said, nudging Magdalena. The dark-haired soldier who had challenged Linné to a shooting contest sidled up to her.

"I can't believe it," said Katya. Her spoon clattered to the table. "That's the third time this week." The table fell silent as every head craned to get a good look.

The dark-haired soldier caught them staring. He smiled, a little self-conscious, and saluted them. Then he walked back to the unofficial male side of the room, leaving a red-faced Linné glaring at all of them.

Revna pretended to examine her allotment of dry bread. "Anyway," she said, even though she didn't know how to continue. Linné went back to her book. But she didn't turn the page, Revna noticed.

"Flying," Katya prompted them, letting a thin stream of greasy stew fall from her spoon into her bowl.

"Come on," said Pavi, rolling her eyes. "It's nothing she doesn't deserve."

Katya leaned forward. "How is it that she's the first of us to land a boy?" she said, not quite softly enough. Revna saw Linné's hand crumple the book's corner.

"Maybe pretending to be one gave her some insider knowledge," Pavi said.

"She's not landing a boy. I'm not defending her," Nadya said when Katya shot her an incredulous look. "But rules are rules. And if anyone knows the rules..." She nodded in Linné's direction.

"And we don't really know what he was doing there," Revna added. She didn't have to defend Linné; Linné wouldn't do the same for her. But she still remembered what it was like to be whispered about.

"Don't be ridiculous. We all saw him at the firing range," Olya butted in. A bitter smile turned the corners of her mouth. "'Be a nice, sweet girl, Olusha. That's what men like.' I should never have listened to my mother."

"Maybe I should have listened to mine more," sighed Katya, playing with the cuff of her uniform. She'd embroidered a firebird entwined in a ring of ivy, and it danced in the light of the lanterns.

Revna shrugged. She'd never ached for someone, not in a way she thought a girl ought to when she was in love. And when boys looked at her, they looked at her legs first. They always saw the rest of her after. "It's one man," she said. "It's not like they're all falling over themselves to get at her."

The blond man in the Skarov coat walked past. All sound cut off, like a radio switched to silent. Revna bit back her next sentence, and she wasn't even thinking anything incriminating. That was the Skarov effect on people. When they walked by, you shut up.

He nodded to them. He was the friendly-looking one who smiled at everyone he saw. It didn't put Revna at ease in the least. Her fingers clenched around her spoon. For a terrifying moment she thought he would sit down among them. She wouldn't break bread with him. She couldn't do much for Papa, but she could do that.

He passed their table and went right up to Linné. He leaned in, and though conversation had come to a standstill, he spoke too softly for Revna to hear. But whatever he said, Linné shut her book and grabbed her tray. They walked back across the mess together.

"I knew it," Olya said.

The Skarov stopped.

Olya froze, eyes wide. Revna felt a flash of pity for her. Didn't she know that the Skarov heard everything?

"I beg your pardon?" he said, taking half a step in her direction. His words were like a knife stabbing into a thick blanket of silence. No one moved. Revna could barely breathe. They were flouting Union law as it was; couldn't Olya resist making snide remarks?

The man waited, all politeness. As if he had posed a perfectly innocent query.

"Nothing," Olya finally squeaked.

"My mistake." He inclined his head in a little bow.

Linné stomped out of the hall. The entire table exhaled as the Skarov followed. Someone across the room made a joke, and the mess filled up with noise.

Olya let her head drop to the table. Questionable stew slopped over the side of her bowl. "I'm a dead woman," she moaned, digging her fingers into her hair. Giggles erupted all around her.

"Cheer up." Magdalena patted her shoulder. "You'll probably only be mildly tortured. Keep your cool and all you'll lose is a couple of fingers."

✳

"It looks like you've made a few friends," Tannov said as they left the mess.

"Shut up," Linné said, tilting her head to the sky. Sleet spattered the wooden boards, the first advance of Commander Winter toward the front.

"Is that any way to address your dedicated Information Officer?"

She didn't care. Maybe she'd regret it later, but right now Tannov could think what he wanted of her. Everyone else did—the dark-haired soldier who'd badgered her three times this week, the girls who huddled in defensive groups whenever she passed. "If you came to get me for interrogation, then it hardly matters what I say now. If you came to be my friend, then you can be a bit nicer about it."

"Why does everyone think that my job is to torture people?" Tannov said. He lit a rascidine cigarette and offered one to Linné. She never said no to a free cigarette. "I want a drink. A real one. Come on."

The base bar had been a supply closet before an enterprising soldier found a couple of tables and a portable radio. As they squished up to the hut, she caught the sour smell of too many drunk men crammed into a small space, sweat and puke and piss cutting a sharp undertone to the constant stink of sulfur that marked out the engineers and their experiments. The propaganda posters had even made it here. On one, a line of soldiers proudly proclaimed, WHILE THEY REST, WE MARCH. Another showed a man with a blaze of spark between his hands. FIRE AND GLORY TO THE HEROES OF THE WAR.

Linné stopped in front of the proud profile of a strong Union boy, blue eyes shining, blond locks curling under his aviator helmet. A red-and-gold monstrosity flew over his head, scarlet maw snapping out fire. OUR REALM IS THE AIR.

Typical. The men didn't even have planes, but they got propaganda. Linné wondered if the public even knew Tamara Zima's regiment existed.

"Stop gawking. I'm cold." Tannov pushed the door open and nodded inside.

Linné hesitated on the threshold. She was tired of the looks, as if she'd crossed some horrendous line whenever she did anything. But it had been a long time since she'd enjoyed someone's company, and a long time since she'd tried some contraband alcohol.

And she was with Tannov. What would anyone dare to do to him?

Only three men were in the bar, and one stood behind a makeshift counter. Empty crates were stacked to provide shelf space for the bottles that got smuggled onto the base, and a haphazard collection of tin cups littered the bar.

The men eyed her warily but didn't comment. "Find a seat," Tannov said.

Linné took a spot in the corner at a table piled high with bulletins. Each one told another story of the bravery of their boys, their victories at the front. No talk of defeats or setbacks. Lies were the enemy of the Union, but demoralization was the enemy of the army.

She'd drunk from bar glasses enough to know how often they were cleaned on average. She gave Tannov her issued mug and he returned with it, full and steaming. The best drink for autumn was sweet-spicy ginger tea, and the best of that was spiked with sugar beet rum. Linné took a sip that burned all the way down her throat. The men watched Tannov carefully as he poured a dollop of tea onto his saucer and slid it under the table. One of the little base cats darted beneath them and settled in, lapping.

"So," he said, scooting his chair in, "you're not too fond of being one of Zima's firebirds."

Firebirds, for the girls who shot fire and flew through the air. She'd heard worse terms for women. "Is that what you call us in the Extraordinary Wartime office?" She took another drink. The ginger reminded her of nights at home, sitting across from her father as he imparted his wisdom from behind his study desk. She'd never been allowed the strong stuff, not when he was watching. She'd gotten her alcoholic education when she joined up.

"It's what everyone calls you. When we're feeling charitable," he said. "You've certainly earned a reputation among the regulars."

"Impossible. We haven't even seen combat yet."

"That's part of it."

She didn't have to press for details. According to the army, the Night Raiders took up a lot of time, a lot of attention, and a lot of money and had far too little to show for it. Tannov told her jokes he'd heard about new shoes for every woman, aviation dresses, makeup in the Strekozy cockpits. Linné detected a hint of resentment underneath it all.

"Of course they resent you. You use resources. You take planes, even if they're *those* planes. And Tamara Zima's not military. Everyone knows she was given a command post—and this assignment—because of her...political ties. No one thinks you deserve to be here."

"Shouldn't we fight?" she said.

He raised his hands in a conciliatory gesture. "You asked me to tell you."

She sighed, trying to cool the spark burning in her palms, and tipped back her tea. "Go on."

"Officers from the front to the capital want to delay getting you into action. Some are campaigning to scrap the entire effort."

Her temper flared again. "So we should leave the secret of flight to the Elda?"

"You should leave it to the men, they say." He shrugged, as if he didn't believe them.

"What men?" She laughed. "The draft age is lower than ever."

"Maybe our allies will help," Tannov said.

"Batinha's too busy fending the Elda off themselves to help us. Ojchezna won't risk losing trade benefits. Kotimaa always hated us, and Sokoro has a civil war of its own. If anyone's going to come to the army's rescue, why not women? Why not the One Hundred Forty-Sixth Night Raiders Regiment?"

"They don't want you here. You have to face facts, Linné. War is a mess, especially this one. No one wants to be pulling your carcass out of a burning plane." He shrugged again. "The men would rather die themselves."

"So they claim."

"I don't doubt them." He set his cup down and regarded her with frankness. His eyes had been blue before, she remembered, clear reflections of the sky. Now they gleamed unnatural and tawny, proving his ties to the Skarov every time she looked at him. And he was scrutinizing her entirely too much for her liking. "It's been our job to run off and die for years. You're the people we're supposed to be dying for—and now you want to be out here with us."

Linné didn't like his use of *you*. She'd been the lion of Koslen's regiment. Had Tannov truly forgotten her? She ran her finger around the rim of her cup. "Plenty of women have gone to war. Nadya Noreva, the Blood Duchess, the Huldrani dryads—not to mention normal people like me."

"Half the stories are legend. The other half are outliers. Nadya Noreva joined—well, the way you did." Except Nadya had become a heroine and had been given prizes of land and money for uniting the North. And Linné had been pushed off to the nearest sideline. "Let's all hope the Blood Duchess was a fable. Most women who have gained fame in the army have done it through magic or command, not for their individual prowess. And no one has ever tried to make it easier for women to join on a large scale."

"We've never had a war on this scale. And we need the Strekozy. Who else is going to combat the Dragons and Skyhorses?"

"The regiment's reserve aircraft are nearly finished," Tannov said.

"But they're not here."

"Have you seen a Dragon around these parts?"

"Excuse me." The bartender stood at the table, clutching a cloth between his hands. He looked as if he'd rather be standing before an Elda firing squad than before them.

"May I help you with something?" Tannov asked. He spoke the same way as always, friendly and open and genuine. But the man flinched as though he'd drawn a pistol.

"I'm sorry, miss," the barman said.

Here we go.

He gulped. "I'm sorry. But you're not allowed to be in here."

"The lady is my personal guest," Tannov said.

"I'm sorry, sir. And miss. But Colonel Hesovec's particular orders. No women."

He did look sorry, in his own way, though whether he was sorry for her or sorry for bringing himself under the scrutiny of an Information Officer, Linné couldn't say. And it wasn't his fault if Hesovec gave him the order.

"I hope you're not attempting to interrupt a dedicated Information Officer during the course of his duty," Tannov said.

The barman swallowed. "Of—of course not. I didn't realize—"

"What's your name?" Tannov said. His voice was soft, and though he smiled, it held no hint of warmth.

Linné stood quickly. "I'm finished. And this place smells like piss."

"Whatever you say." Tannov followed suit, still staring at the barman. The barman stuttered an apology and fled.

They walked away from the makeshift bar in silence. The rain had let up a little, enough for the little stray cat to make a dash from the bar to the warehouses. Linné didn't know whether she ought to thank Tannov for sticking up for her or tell him off for abusing his power.

He caught her eye. "Your turn for a cigarette."

"Your rations are better than mine," she complained.

"And I'm a more generous soul, accordingly. Don't be stingy."

She'd already seen how petty he could be tonight. She dug her cigarette case out and let him take whatever he wanted.

"What's wrong?" he said as he stuck the cigarette in his mouth.

"Nothing."

"You gave me a funny look. And you flinched when I took a cigarette."

She hadn't realized. But when he activated a flicker of spark at the end of his fingertips to give her a light, she nearly pulled away from him again. *You're different*, she thought. That was the problem. She wouldn't have expected a few months in the Information Unit to change him so utterly. The war claimed lives, one way or another.

Maybe he guessed her thoughts. He smiled a sad smile, a little twist at the corner of his mouth. "It's still me," he said. "I haven't changed any more than you. It's a job." Linné arched an eyebrow, and he let his head flop back. "I'm serious. You think our lives are all about dragging off traitors and spying on the regiment?"

"Also threatening hapless bartenders," Linné couldn't resist adding.

"He was being a prick. Honestly, Linné. The only reason our job's such a mystery is because people like you make it that way."

Linné made a derisive sound. Perhaps Tannov had forgotten who her father was, but she was not some country girl who had learned of the Skarov through the gossip of her friends. The Skarov were built to keep secrets. They were built to *be* secrets.

"I'm serious. Ask me something. Anything about work."

She glanced at him sidelong. What was his game? "Okay. What did you do today?"

"I listened to the radio and I read everybody's mail. So far, your regiment sisters are extremely law-abiding, boring people."

"Have you ever interrogated someone?"

"I've had to practice." He blew a thin stream of blue smoke into

151

the air, letting it mingle with his exhale. "Get the technique right, just in case."

"Tortured someone?" she pressed.

He laughed. "Give me a break."

"Do you really think there are traitors here?" she said.

He shrugged. "Every base needs Information Officers. A lot of them want action near the front. Few of them want anything to do with Weavecraft. What I think doesn't have much to do with it."

There. That was how he'd changed. He didn't answer questions so directly anymore. He spoke openly, like a friend. But he still managed not to say what she needed him to say most.

The glowing end of his cigarette turned her way. Before he could accuse her of flinching again, she said the first thing that popped into her head. "Can you really shift shape?"

His yellow eyes widened. For a moment she swore the pupil changed, elongating into a vertical slit. Then he blinked, and his eyes were back to normal. Well, yellow normal. "Depends on what shape you're asking about." The cigarette-end turned back ahead. "To the mess, or walk?"

Neither of those options included parting ways. In the mess she'd be safer, surrounded by witnesses. Surrounded by girls who whispered and peeked at her from behind their hair. "Walk," she decided, and they set off.

They were the only ones out in the slush, aside from the perimeter guards and a couple of metal messengers, scuttling and slipping in haste to get inside. Even the constructs had more sense than she and Tannov did. She'd have to dry her whole uniform out in front of the little stove in the barracks. But the rain washed away the perennial scent of ash and engine grease.

"Things—aren't the way they were," she said after a while.

"For you, too," said Tannov.

"They want to be soldiers, but they don't think it takes any work. I say things Koslen would never have been kind enough to say, and they hate me for it. The boys think it's funny. I can't—" She didn't know what to say—rather, she didn't know what to say first. The women despised her. The men mocked her. Zima had manipulated her to influence her father's enemy. Hesovec disdained her. Anger pulsed so hot her fingers blazed, nearly incinerating her cigarette.

"We were like brothers, in the old regiment." Tannov smiled his classic open smile. "Well, sort of. It's not the same here, is it, little lion?"

It was only the same with Tannov, and only sort of. And even though her brain told her to *watch out, beware*, she couldn't bring herself to listen tonight. She had only Tannov and Dostorov, and she couldn't pretend she didn't care about them.

She told him everything. It was stupid, but she did it anyway. They walked the perimeter of the base, and her anger flowed out of her with every step. And she felt lighter when she finally realized she had nothing else to say.

"Maybe it will get better," she finished. "In combat. But I can't—" *Be sure. Believe it.* "I don't know if we'll see combat at all." And if they never saw combat, she'd never be able to prove herself.

"You won't if Hesovec has his way. But you're making progress.

153

We'll be watching your first flight tomorrow. And from there it's a short jump to the front. We'll be Heroes of the Union in no time."

She'd been trying not to think about their first flight all evening. It was bad enough using her spark to power Zima's army radio. How was she going to stream it into a plane?

Tannov stopped. They'd reached the long officers' barracks, including the Information office. He fished out a key and held up a finger as he disappeared inside. The rain had stopped, and clouds skated across the sky, taking the storm north. Linné watched them until Tannov returned with a pile of opened mail. "For the aviators." She grabbed it, creating a fat, wet thumbprint on the top letter. Tannov's grip tightened around the pile. "Do you want my advice?"

"The advice of Tannov my boneheaded friend, or Tannov the dedicated Information Officer?" She'd meant for it to sound like a joke, but it came out brittle around the edges.

"The advice of the great Mikhail Tannov, your boneheaded friend who joined the Information Unit." His eyes sparkled. His yellow, foreign, animal eyes. His hand slid from the mail to her cuff. "Colonel Hesovec will do what he can to be rid of you, but if he has to use you, he'll use you. Don't give him any other choice. Convince him that you're ready. Convince someone who can order him around. Make your first flight count, and the one after that. Keep pushing. The bastard's like a wall, but he'll crumble eventually."

10

PRACTICE MAKES PREPARED

Linné was late getting back to the barracks, late enough that she was the last one in and everyone's eyes were on her as she shut the door. She shook the rain out of her hair. "Don't you have anything better to do than wait for me to come home?"

"Always thinking of yourself." Katya tutted as she snipped a stray thread away from a jacket. "All done," she said, tossing it to Olya. "Magdalena, you're next."

"I don't need mine fitted," Magdalena said, a hint of panic in her voice.

Katya had been taking everyone's measurements and adjusting their clothes for weeks. She hadn't talked to Linné, and Linné didn't care. She didn't need her uniform fitted, either, and she didn't need someone else to do it. The others watched in amusement as Katya advanced on Magdalena, snapping her measuring tape menacingly. Even though Magdalena was a good foot taller than Katya, she shrank back against the wall, holding her palms out to ward off Katya.

"You have to put your arms up." Katya laughed. "I need to measure your breasts." Giggles erupted all over the room.

"You'll tickle me," Magdalena said.

"Only if you don't hold still. Nadya, come help me," Katya implored, but Nadya shook her head.

Linné drew the stack of damp letters out of her coat pocket. "I'm dousing the lamp in five minutes," she said, tossing Pavi a letter from her boyfriend. The others leaned forward on their beds, and those who slept at the back of the hall clustered around. Even Katya stopped harassing Magdalena for a moment to see if there was any correspondence for her.

The girls got a lot of mail. It seemed that every sweetheart, sibling, parent, and uncle wanted to know what life was like in the Union's most experimental regiment. Some got more mail than others—Revna seemed to write home every week—but every single girl had received something since training began. Everyone except for Linné.

She didn't need it, she reminded herself as she handed Revna two letters. No one would write to her except her father, and she hadn't needed him since she was five.

As she gave Elena a letter, the high whine of the siren began. Chatter died away.

"What is it?" Revna asked, reaching for the prosthetics she'd stowed beside her bed.

"Either we're under attack or they've rescheduled our first

156

flight." Linné tossed the rest of the letters onto the nearest bed. She grabbed her aviator helmet and headed for the door.

"I wish they *would* send her back to the front," she heard Katya say as the door closed behind her.

She ran, trying to outstrip the others, trying to keep ahead of the growing unease that made her hands shake as she slid to a stop, panting, at the edge of the airfield. She wasn't ready for this. How could this happen? She'd always been ready. She'd been the first out of their supply palanquin when her old regiment went to the front. When she feared something, she ran toward it. She'd never wanted to hide before.

The clouds had broken open to reveal a bright slice of moon. Zima waited until the others pelted up behind Linné. "Good morning, ladies. Now that you're going to start practicing together, you might as well get used to your new night schedule. Navigators and pilots, pair off. Engineers, come with me to assist with takeoff."

The engineers stumbled out of line to follow Zima. The girls to either side of Linné turned away to find their friends, pretending not to notice her. Resentment stabbed her gut. Or was that nerves? She pulled out a cigarette and told herself she didn't care. She didn't look forward to spending hours in a cramped cockpit with a nattering counterpart and a needle sucking her life away.

The girls departed, two by two, for their planes. Until there had to be only one left. That one was still making her way across the field, stepping carefully. Moonlight gleamed on her prosthetic feet.

Linné waited until she was close enough to speak without shouting. "Which one's yours?" she said around a dry tongue.

Revna's shoulders hunched. "You want to fly with me?"

The kind answer would have been yes. But Linné had always preferred honesty to kindness. She shrugged.

Revna stalked past her, chin held high. "This way."

Linné followed, flicking spark out of her fingertips. She didn't know whether to laugh or to scream. *Would you fly with her?* She wondered if Revna was thinking about that now.

Revna stopped at the wing of her plane. It was undecorated, snub-nosed, and ugly. Linné couldn't believe she'd be sparking her life into this clumsy contraption when elegant Skyhorses and powerful Dragons ruled the air.

"You sit in the back," Revna said.

"How are you going to get up there?" Linné looked at the pilot's seat. "No offense," she added. Revna set her jaw. Linné could feel the heat of her rage. "I'll—" *Shut my mouth.* She used the side of the wing to hoist herself up. In front of her, Revna swung herself into the cockpit. She had facility—Linné had to give her that. Maybe she'd been too hasty in her judgment.

Shouts from the field caught her attention. The first Strekoza wobbled into the air, a dark shadow against the lamps on the green. Painted flames caught the light—Katya's plane. The girls cheered.

She watched the Strekoza dip dangerously close to the ground before veering up so sharply that her stomach flipped. This was going to be much worse than powering spare washers and radios. Failure now wasn't a matter of a slap on the wrist or a train back to Mistelgard. Failure meant going home in a box or getting dumped in a hole somewhere.

I've almost died before. Every time Koslen's regiment advanced, she'd been in danger. She should have felt safer here, behind the lines, surrounded by people who were on her side. Maybe if she smoked her cigarette—but as she stuck the end in her mouth, she noticed the wood creaking under her boots and the canvas stretched over the wings. She didn't want to be the one who set her plane on fire before it got off the ground.

The aircraft rocked. She grabbed the sides of the cockpit to steady herself. "Ready?" came Revna's voice next to her ear.

No. "Obviously." Linné took her bearings. Her knees scraped up against Revna's chair. A slot for a map had been nailed to the back, and a compass was mounted next to her right arm. She buckled her harness and turned her head to speak into the tube at her ear. "So. What do I do?"

"You don't know?" The faint tinny ring of the speaking tube couldn't disguise Revna's incredulity.

Linné bristled. She hadn't spent the last three weeks learning the ins and outs of the Strekoza. "I suppose it has something to do with my spark." *Great revelation, genius.*

"There's a throttle. We can't go anywhere if you don't put power into it," Revna said.

The throttle was a long steel tube that slithered up through the bottom of the cockpit, linking her spark to the engine. She'd be firing at the enemy with her right arm, powering the engine with her left. Linné rolled up her sleeve and reached into the tube, gripping the handhold there. She shook worse than the first time she'd been shoved into battle. All the same, she pushed out a thin stream of spark, just as she'd practiced.

She looked up in time to see machinery spasm and close

around the pilot's seat, trapping Revna in a gleaming cage. Her own gasp was cut short by a piercing pain. The living needle had shot from the tube and wrapped around her forearm while she wasn't looking. *"Shit."* She tried to pull back. The Strekoza didn't let go. Her spark choked.

"Language," Revna snapped.

"Are you joking?" Revna looked as if she were being eaten alive and all she cared about was Linné's *mouth*?

The wings of the plane twitched. Something rose up to meet her panic. She needed to relax. If she relaxed, it would be fine; flying was wonderful—

Dread snapped tight in her, scattering the soothing feelings. Her arm trembled so hard that her fingers knocked against the side of the spark tube. This unnatural Weave magic was bad enough on the field. Now it was in her head. "Get it out." She twisted and tried to pull away.

"Stop it. *Stop*," Revna said, and the tranquility surged back, though this time it held a desperate note. "If you don't calm down, we can't fly."

"This can't be happening," Linné whispered. She could feel the dismay of the plane, the nervousness that she pumped into it. And she could feel Revna's influence trying to soothe them both, to send calming thoughts and steady the Strekoza. And, even though Revna didn't say anything, Linné felt her impatience, her resentment and anger, all directed toward Linné, because the others sped into the sky and they were stuck.

Linné had never been the reason for anyone's failure. She

clenched her free hand until her fingers cramped and her palm burned from the imprint of her nails. She felt the plane stabilize.

"Good," Revna said.

The engineers waved semaphore flags, instructing the second-to-last plane to take off. Linné had to control herself. She had to do what the others did. She'd defied her father for this. *I'm the soldier. The one they called lion.* But that had been a regiment, a gender, a life ago. She took a gulp of air and tightened her grip in the spark tube. It thrummed warm and alive. "Tell me what to do."

"Relax."

"Tell me something else."

The engineers ran up to the Strekoza. Magdalena wrinkled her nose at Linné. "What are you doing here?"

"You're the smart one—you tell me," Linné replied.

"If you ruin this for her..." Magdalena began.

Olya nudged her. "Chat later. Work now."

Magdalena cast Linné a final, dark look, then popped up to Revna's seat. A screwdriver flashed briefly as she tightened one of the monstrous claws at the back of the chair. "Ready?"

"Yes," Revna answered.

Linné was going to throw up. The Strekoza shot a mix of impatience and disdain up her arm. *Be ready.*

Two gray shapes appeared on the field. Linné saw the tiny flare, like a star, as Dostorov lit his cigarette. The Strekoza tensed. The air inside the cockpit became suffocating, possessive. But there was no time to think about that. Zima was signaling. It was finally their turn.

"Good luck." Magdalena hopped down and waved. She backed away from the front of the plane, grabbing the semaphore flags she'd tucked into her belt. Even though Linné was responsible for memorizing their instructions, Revna didn't need her help in translating the signal for takeoff.

"Everything all right?" Revna said.

"Of course." Linné filled her voice with scorn, but the Strekoza amplified her anxiety, proving the lie to them both. The tube hummed under her hand, trying to tug her spark out. "What now?"

"Wait." Revna adjusted something in front of her with a click.

Ahead of them the field was lonely without its flock of Strekozy. Linné could see the silhouette of trees at the end of the base, marking the plains that stretched all the way to the blacker-than-black edges of the mountains.

The engineers stepped away. Zima gave the all clear. "Fire up," Revna said.

Linné took a deep breath. She'd practiced this. She'd practiced so many times. She tried her spark again, pushing gradually. But the plane fluttered, lurching as it tried to launch.

"Steady," Revna said.

Linné fought the urge to punch something. She focused on the back of Revna's chair, the only thing that didn't seem to be shaking. *Don't think.* If she kept her eyes on the chair, maybe she could pretend—

They veered into the air. Her spark fired, panicked, and they sped toward the stars at such a pace that a short scream was drawn from her throat.

Laughing. Revna was laughing. Linné aimed a kick at her seat. "Stop it," she whimpered. *Whimpered.* Honestly.

"We're *flying*," Revna said. The plane didn't seem mocking or amused. Linné caught a sense of sheer joy at their free movement through the air. For an instant she soared with it. Then the living metal squeezed around her arm.

The feeling of free movement stalled, and so did they. Linné wasn't part of the team; she was an impostor, an incompetent between pilot and plane. The initial roar of the engine dropped away and they drifted downward. "Increase power," Revna said, and Linné both heard and felt the desperation. Her heart crashed against her ribs. She had to regain control and do what needed to be done. But sweat slicked her whole body, and her spark hid from her.

"Linné."

"I'm trying." She *wouldn't* cry. She pushed on her spark, pushed with her fear and her need to salvage herself. She imagined being sent back to her father. She imagined explaining why.

The plane jerked forward, catching on a stray breeze and turning sharply starboard. Linné pushed again. They bounced.

"Linné," Revna warned her. "Not all at once."

"Would you like to do it?" Linné snarled.

"I'd like to not crash!"

Linné tried to send her spark out the way she'd practiced. The engine sputtered, then blasted, then finally evened. Linné closed her eyes for a moment, sighing. Then she finally peered over the edge of the cockpit.

The Strekoza had scooted its way past the edge of the base,

much farther than they were supposed to go for their first flight. The cold, open air assaulted Linné. Revna turned the plane clumsily, nosing down as they swung, and Linné's whole body lifted off the seat. She gave a short scream and the Strekoza tensed. Her spark sputtered. "Shit," she said, giving it another boost.

The air around her turned hot, prickling at her skin. "Please don't do that," Revna said.

It didn't get better. Linné tried to control herself, but the flight was one long sequence of turns, banks, and dips. She swore, she screamed, she heaved. Her stomach knotted itself five different ways. Thinking of her father seemed to help the most—her stomach convulsed even more, but she could use her spite to center herself. She could push away the shivering feeling that something else was in her head.

And she ignored thoughts of what would come next. As soon as they landed, she'd be the laughingstock of the entire regiment. She was already the laughingstock of her partner.

"We're supposed to be in the air, you know," Revna said. The Strekoza took on a definite smug atmosphere. "Maybe you should have applied for a spot in an infantry regiment."

"You're hilarious," Linné replied through gritted teeth.

They made their way back to the base with a string of curses from Linné and winces from Revna. The Strekoza felt more and more oppressive with each breath. Linné didn't realize how bad it was until they landed safely and Revna gave her the all clear to cut power. The feelings lifted, like breaking through the top of an icy river to discover air on the other side.

Her knees shook. Her hands shook. Even her teeth were

chattering. The thin needle released from her arm as she pulled away from the throttle. A tiny dot marked the space where the needle had tapped into her. She tried not to heave as she rolled her sleeve down.

"Um," Revna said. Linné didn't need the Strekoza's connection to know that she was trying to think of something nice to say. "I'm sure it will get better."

She had to get out of this thing. Linné hauled herself over the side of the cockpit, down to the ground—down to freedom—and put her hands on her knees, head swimming.

"What happened to you?" Magdalena said as she came up beside Linné, making no effort to hide her amusement. And she stood much too close. "Nothing funny to say about your pilot?" Magdalena rolled her shoulders. As if she were getting ready for a fight.

Linné knew she was short, but it had been a long time since she'd felt so small. Her first impulse was to step back. Her second was to throw a punch. "You wouldn't be up there if you had the choice," she said. "No one would."

Katya raced past them. "How was it?" she called to Revna.

Magdalena watched Linné pointedly. "No one?"

The shaking started again. Linné wanted to sink to the ground and let it swallow her whole. "You don't know how it is."

Magdalena leaned in. "You mocked her. You told her she doesn't belong. But from what I saw, you were the one who couldn't handle the assignment."

"The assignment is wrong," Linné hissed. And it *was* wrong— it had to be wrong. She hadn't come this far and defied so many people to wash out from fear.

165

Disgust crossed Magdalena's face. "Unbelievable."

"Girls!" Zima was crossing the field at a brisk pace. "This is practice, not teatime. Switch navigators and get ready to go again."

Linné swayed on the spot. Again. She'd go again and again, laying her life out over the Weave in a series of neatly executed maneuvers. She wanted to throw up. She wanted to cry. Maybe she even wanted to go home. Some navigator she was turning out to be.

War is simply not women's work, miss, said Colonel Koslen's voice in the back of her mind. But she'd die in that cockpit before letting anyone think he might be right.

✳

The Strekozy were far from perfect. They were slow, for a start. Their lightness made them more maneuverable, but the slightest breeze could pull them off course. The first bombs they carried swung like pendulums during takeoff, and the engineers spent two weeks adjusting the weight. The open cockpit let the wind and rain and sleet howl around them, stinging their cheeks and biting at their exposed necks. They had no radio, and they could barely hear each other through the speaking tubes. They had to take their ground instructions via semaphore signal.

The planes were easily weighed down by superfluous equipment, so the girls analyzed the survival kits and tossed anything unnecessary out of the cockpit, much to the rage of Colonel Hesovec. Most of their night missions would be harassing the nearest front, so tinned food was pointless. The planes' canvas wings and wooden noses were vulnerable to spark and Dragon fire, and the Strekozy flew too low to the ground to enable good use of parachutes. The rations and fire starters had to go, too. Soldiers who went missing at the front were assumed to be traitors and deserters, and none of them favored the idea of hiking through the Ryddan wilderness only to see the inside of a prison cell when they made it home. There was no point in taking it with them.

The Strekoza started to feel like Revna's real self. She thought about it as she ate her sunset breakfasts, and it was the last thing on her mind when she slipped off to sleep each dawn. She had wings instead of arms, a tail instead of legs. Outside the Strekoza she saw half the world, but in it she understood everything. She could feel the air currents as they tugged her, the magnetism of the Weave guiding her wings. She could see the way the threads lay flat over the plains and warped to follow the course of the river. She could feel the pulse of life in the cockpit.

Tamara put them on a rotation of flying partners. All the navigators felt different, and their emotions twined with hers until she didn't know who thought what. Galina's moods were light and fleeting, like her gossip. Asya felt so invisible that Revna had to keep checking that she hadn't fallen out. Nadya's presence was forceful, her questions brash and oblivious to Revna's discomfort, and often about Revna's legs.

But worst of all was Linné. Linné shouted and swore from the time they took off to the time they landed. She made the Strekoza nervous, and by the end of each practice, Revna's hands shook— though with Linné's terror or her own anger, she couldn't tell. And when practice was over, Linné stalked off to her Skarov friends. *At least one of us will be safe from the Union after the war*, Revna thought bitterly.

She'd hoped someone would ask to be her permanent partner, but girls paired off all around her and the pool of available navigators dwindled. What would happen to her family if she were grounded without a navigator? When she finally got up the courage to ask Nadya during a practice, Nadya shrugged. "I agreed to fly with Elena," she said. "Sorry." She did sound sorry, but Revna finished practice with Linné's words ringing in her ears. *Would you fly with her?*

Magdalena found a stepladder, but Revna hated using it. She pulled herself in and out of the Strekoza with the Weave, even when her vision blurred after long hours of practice and her chest ached where the living claws dug into her. Sometimes she couldn't hold herself up and she fell out of the cockpit, slamming her prosthetics against her residual limbs and setting her phantom feet ablaze. And sometimes she borrowed a hospital wheelchair when she was too tired to care what pitying looks the others threw her. It didn't matter what they thought of her, anyway. All that mattered was that she could fly.

✳

The evening they received their team assignments was gray and cold. Revna went to the mess for breakfast to find a notice pinned to the wall and girls crowded around it. She stumbled into a table, jarring her legs. The others jostled around her to get a good view, shouting back and forth as they found their names and their partners.

She had to see the list. But she desperately, desperately didn't want to. She needed more time to find a partner she could trust.

But they'd already practiced 150 hours, nearly ten times as long as the aviators Colonel Hesovec trained. She'd had experience with every navigator.

Their permanent teams meant they had only one obstacle left in their training. Everyone was delirious with excitement. Everyone but her.

She waited until the press had cleared a little, then pushed forward to look at the notice.

They were grouped by team, pilot's name first. Revna skimmed the sheet until she found hers.

PILOT: REVNA ROSHENA

NAVIGATOR: LINNÉ ZOLONOV

ENGINEER: MAGDALENA CHUIKOVA

Revna's heart sank. Maybe Tamara thought they were friends. Maybe she'd seen some of their arguments far off and mistook them. Maybe it was bad luck. Or maybe Linné was keeping a close eye on Revna for her Skarov friends.

Or maybe everyone else had put in their requests, and no one had asked for her.

"Hey." Magdalena touched her shoulder. She looked as if she'd been in the lab since the afternoon. Her frizzy hair was knotted at the base of her neck and grease smudged one cheek. "We're together." She walked with Revna to the nearest open seat. "I'm sure we can fend off the worst of her. Sit here. I'll get your breakfast."

Revna's stomach felt heavy. They were one step closer now. She should be rejoicing for her friends and herself. She should be pleased that she was securing Mama and Lyfa their future. She should relish her chance to strike back at the Elda.

She couldn't do that with Linné. She simply couldn't. Linné was everything about the Union that had ruined Revna's life.

Guilt twinged in her at the thought of Linné panicking in the cockpit. Revna could fly with her, even if it was difficult. If Revna forced Linné onto someone else, would she be dooming a different pilot? Then again, she comforted herself, Linné probably wouldn't be so difficult if she were with a friend.

It's Linné, her treacherous mind whispered. *She hasn't got friends.*

✳

Revna went to see Tamara as the engineers prepared for their next flight. Wind had blown every cloud out of the sky, leaving a deep blue dusk behind. Frost was beginning to form, making the hard ground slick beneath her feet. Messenger palanquins slid as they scuttled around the base, and Revna's toes dug into the boards with each step. They were reluctant, like she was. Maybe it would be better to suck in her anger and try to get used to her new partner.

That was the old Revna talking. If she wanted to win a war for her friends and her family, she'd have to fight for herself.

Tamara's office door was ajar, and Revna heard the uneven murmur of voices inside. She wanted to sit—her left leg chafed and she needed to adjust her prosthetic. But good soldiers didn't barge in. *Ha.* Maybe Linné was rubbing off on her.

An impatient "Sir—ma'am—" caught her ear. She knew that voice. That smug, I-know-everything voice. The voice that left her ears ringing like a vicious slap. *Would you fly with her?*

Revna shoved open the door and went inside, grabbing the frame to keep steady as she crossed the threshold. Tamara and

Linné looked up from where they sat. Linné's cheeks flushed pink. Anger gripped Revna, as tight as the Strekoza's metal fingers. Linné was the one dragging them both down. *Linné* was the one who couldn't be trusted. She shook so hard she didn't dare let go of the door frame.

Tamara regarded her calmly. "If you'll wait outside, I'll be with you in a minute."

"I don't want to be her partner any more than she wants to be mine," Revna said. Linné's flush deepened, erasing any doubt. Embarrassment rushed in to hit Revna full force. Mama would give her the telling-off of her life for questioning the order of a superior officer, and for saying that in front of Linné.

Tamara took a deep breath. "I'm sorry that your personal difficulties have interfered with your work. I hope that your objections are purely social, and not because you doubt each other's ability in combat?"

The silence stretched long and heavy. Revna couldn't bring herself to look at Linné.

Tamara rubbed at her forehead. "We've spent so many hours training that I'd have thought you'd be the last people to doubt your own readiness. As things stand now, it will be difficult for me to adjust the roster. The other girls have requested their partners and would need to consent to any change."

Shame squeezed Revna's chest. So she *had* been the only pilot left.

But there had to be another way. What could she do? *Identify the problem*, Papa would have told her.

Problem: Linné. How could she solve the problem when she had to work with the problem?

"Your examination flight is tomorrow," Tamara continued. "General Tcerlin will be the presiding examiner, and he doesn't have time for petty feuds. If you will consent to fly together, I'll see what I can do regarding your permanent assignment. However"—the corner of her mouth twitched—"if the two of you truly cannot work with each other, it would be much better to preserve your safety and the safety of the plane. Shall I remove you from the roster?"

"*No*," they both said. Revna's toes dug stubbornly into the floor, cracking the cheap plywood. She wouldn't be the only one left on the field. She recalled the feeling of the wind under her, the Weave stretched out like a silver blanket before her eyes. She remembered all the reasons she had to fight—for the Weave, for her family, for her friends. Being stuck with Linné was better than being grounded.

She ventured a look at Linné. Linné didn't look back. Her hands clenched so hard that her knuckles stood out. She had a few freckles across the bridge of her nose. Revna had never noticed them before. She'd never seen Linné so pale.

Tamara surveyed them. "Then you can get along for now," she said pointedly.

"Yes, ma'am," said Revna.

"Absolutely, ma'am," said Linné, not to be outdone.

Tamara sighed and pulled her typewriter toward her. For the first time, Revna noticed the bags under her eyes, the hollowness of her cheeks. Shame bit at her again. Her commander was bogged down with other problems. It was selfish to think that this was more important. "In that case, I would urge you to relax. Try to find a common ground. You may take that as an order from your commanding officer."

She dismissed them, which left them with the uncomfortable task of leaving her office together.

"Listen," Revna began as soon as they were out the door. She wasn't sure what she wanted to say, but anything would be an improvement. Anything to get them working together.

"See you on the field," Linné said, and turned away. She headed toward the edge of the base at a pace too quick for Revna to follow.

11

NEVER RETREAT

The final night of practice was torture, drawn out and meticulous and dull enough that Linné could feel every piece of her as it was spun through the engine to dissipate in the Weave behind them. Linné concentrated on Revna's instructions, and thankfully Revna didn't natter like the others. She only said, "Ready." "Increase power." "Decrease power." She let Linné judge for herself when to aim and fire, and while blasting spark over the rim of the cockpit wasn't the same as using her rifle, Linné knew she could pass that part of the test.

The Strekoza felt her discomfort, and it had taken Revna's side. When Linné grasped the throttle, the living needle squeezed her wrist so hard she thought it would break the bones. Sweat dotted her hands and neck, making her shiver in the cold, open cockpit.

The needle released her only reluctantly, and after practice she found herself rubbing at the long welt it left.

Thick clouds rolled in overnight and stayed through dawn, promising snow by noon. The examination was scheduled for the morning, and they would take their first assignment that night if all went well. Linné smoked cigarette after cigarette, grinding the stubs into the ground like a little line of soldiers as she waited for her pilot.

Her pilot. That more than the rascidine left a sour taste in her mouth. Not that any of the other girls had seemed better at flying in practice. And all of them had laughed at her, or worse. She was surprised no one had tried to get her kicked out of the regiment yet.

The 146th Night Raiders met outside the mess and walked to the airfield together without speaking, in a haze of smoke and nerves. The bulk of their test would take place over a borrowed cabbage field, but first they had to greet their general.

A cluster of figures resolved as they approached. Tamara Zima stood between Colonel Hesovec and Nikolai Tcerlin. Tcerlin smiled, as usual. Zima's expression was blank. It made Linné tense to look at her, as if Zima were a bomb that had failed to detonate.

Hesovec didn't smile, though his trademark glower was less pronounced than Linné would have expected, considering how he'd fought to keep them from getting this far. Maybe he was certain they'd fail.

The girls came to order and stood straight and silent, hands behind their backs. Katya, near tears, took rattling breaths next to

Linné. *Don't break down.* She didn't know whether she was directing the thought toward Katya or herself.

"Good morning," Tcerlin said. A few of them mumbled *good morning* back, forgetting they weren't supposed to. Tcerlin's smile broadened, as though the mistake was charming rather than incompetent.

"Pilots and navigators," Zima said, "prepare formation C-one. Engineers, remain for individual assignments." The brusqueness of her voice matched her pale face. This was a test for her, too. To see if she could be an army commander even though she'd never been in the army.

They trooped to their planes. Formation C-1 was among the worst, and they'd practiced it to death. They flew as high as the little Strekozy could go, cut power, and swooped in like birds to drop their incendiaries. Linné could already feel her stomach in free fall.

She hopped into her seat. If she craned around, she could see Revna as she tumbled in, fingers slipping around threads Linné couldn't sense. Sweat glistened on Revna's forehead. "You shouldn't do that so much," Linné said. Using the Weave when she didn't have to would only make her tired.

Revna ignored her. "Are you ready?"

"Are you?" Linné shot back. She'd never be ready. But if this was her only chance to fight, she'd take it.

Magdalena jogged up to the plane with two clay pots. She stopped in front of Revna first. Linné caught the top of her curly head as she peered over the side of the cockpit. "Flash bombs," she said. "Don't look down when you release them. Come back safe."

Revna laughed. "It's only a test run."

Magdalena hooked the flash bombs under each wing. When she straightened, she met Linné's eye. She didn't smile. "Don't ruin this for her," she said, too quietly for Revna to hear.

Anger sent Linné's spark flowing down to her fingertips. The Strekoza shivered as it tapped into her vein. She leaned toward Magdalena. "Would you like to be in here instead?"

"I should be." Resentment blazed across Magdalena's face, sharp and bold and angry.

Linné bit the inside of her cheek as the engine rumbled. She wouldn't show fear to Magdalena. "If you were better with your spark, then you could be flying and we'd both be happier. Whose fault is that?"

Magdalena turned away.

Revna remained oblivious to the exchange. "Think we'll pass?" she said through the speaking tube as she slid her hands into the flying gloves.

"No idea," Linné replied.

"You could have said yes."

"I don't like to lie." And she didn't have the presence of mind for it, either. A foreign trembling resonated up her arms. Was it her, or was the plane skittish?

"Didn't you lie about being a boy to enlist?"

"That was different," Linné said. The discomfort pouring through the plane intensified. But it *had* been different. And if she'd lied more successfully, she wouldn't be in this mess.

They sat in silence until it was their turn. An engineer named Nina waved her semaphore flags—not according to regulations,

Linné noticed—and marked them for the next takeoff. "Increase power," Revna said.

Linné pressed back into her seat. She couldn't fail. The landing claws pushed off lightly and Linné fought the wave of sickness, the feeling that everything was wrong. She thought of her father again, but this time he wasn't in his parlor, waiting for a disgraced daughter. This time, he stood on the steps of the old imperial palace, watching as she got a red firebird medal pinned to her chest. She didn't know whether she wanted him to be proud or cowed, and she didn't care.

The trick worked, and she was able to take a deep breath without hyperventilating. The Strekoza hooked into the Weave and lifted away. Linné risked a look down at Tamara Zima and Tcerlin. They seemed deep in conversation.

An engineer stood at the edge of the base, directing the formation. Linné spoke over the pounding of her heart. "Fall in. Prepare to bear southwest."

They lined up behind Elena's Strekoza and followed it for a couple of laps around the field. The plane pressed in around Linné, taking her nerves and mixing them with Revna's. Beneath them, Zima, Tcerlin, and Hesovec loaded into an open-topped palanquin and sped toward the test site.

The 146th Night Raiders lapped until the engineer signaled again. Then they began to peel off southwest. The noise of the base became a whisper, and soon the only sound Linné could make out was the low hum of the Strekoza on the wind.

She spotted the tattered flag on the pole, barely visible in the gray gloom. Revna began to ascend in line with the others.

Gravity dragged Linné into her seat. But this was still better than what came next. Her dread leached into the cockpit.

The first of the planes reached its peak. Its snub nose tilted in a free dive, hurtling toward the earth. Linné's breath caught. If the navigator was too slow, she'd plow the Strekoza into the ground— but at the last moment the engine roared to life, sending out a wave of spark energy. The plane turned back toward the sky as something dropped from the port wing.

She wasn't supposed to look. But the shot was beautiful. Right up until the flash bomb detonated. "Shit." She clasped her free hand over her goggles. The throttle squeezed her wrist, making her grunt as the Strekoza prickled.

"Do you have to say things like that?" Revna said.

"Yes. I'm blind."

"Magdalena told you not to look. How are you going to aim for the target now?"

"Go stuff yourself. It's already clearing up." The air inside the cockpit became warm, and the Strekoza sped forward as Linné's spark edged out of her. She clamped back on it. If they overflew they might miss their target or hit Elena.

The next plane dove. A shadow flitted across its squat body. There was a hum in the distance, a strange, looping *whoomp whoomp whoomp.*

"Something's wrong."

"Still blind?" Revna asked.

"No. I hear…" Another plane? It sounded like an engine, a much larger engine than the Strekozy had.

Revna cocked her head. "It's probably—"

A shadow fell across the Strekoza's nose. "Something's up here," Linné said. And it wasn't them or the winter birds. The Strekoza twitched, setting her heart skittering. Control the spark, she had to control the spark—

A dark shape dropped from the cloud cover above. Revna wrenched them into a sharp turn. More planes swooped in from the clouds. "What are they?" Revna cried. The Night Raiders' formation shattered.

"What do you think?" They didn't have time for stupid questions now. Linné's mind began to focus, but her hands still shook. "Get me a clear shot at one."

"What about the test flight?" Revna asked.

"Screw the test flight. This is war." Linné leaned over to her side mirror. The sharp point of a fuselage loomed. "There's one right behind us." She'd seen these planes before. They were Falcon class, the smallest of the Elda Weavecraft. They harassed the lines while the Skyhorses and Dragons aimed for strategic targets.

The Strekoza shivered. "What do I do?" Revna said.

Linné couldn't think like the soldier she'd been. Things didn't work the same way in the air as they did on the ground. What had they learned in training? "Shake him. Don't let his navigator get a sight on you."

"Do they have guns?" Revna's voice quavered. The Strekoza began to lose control, jerking from side to side as if it didn't know what it wanted.

Linné imagined a stream of flame gulping them down and spitting them out as twisted heaps of metal and flesh. The panic started to edge back in. Only now if she lost control, she'd kill them for sure. *"Lose him."*

But they didn't have to. The *whoomp whoomp* became a *whoomp, clunk* as the plane behind them lost power. Linné watched it angle down, disappearing from her side mirror. "What are they doing?" she wondered.

The enemy's engine whirred back to life. It sped by beneath, too quick for Linné to aim. "They stalled," Revna realized. "They couldn't match our speed. We're too slow for them."

"Look." Linné gripped the back of Revna's chair. The Falcon was turning around. Another dark shape had stopped harassing a sister plane and was speeding toward them. "We've got to do something."

"Find the problems," Revna said.

"What?"

"We can't go faster, and we can't go higher." She pulled the plane up. "So we're going to dive, like formation C-one. Cut the power."

"No chance. You'll kill us."

"Trust me," Revna said.

Linné's throat closed up. She let her spark wither back into her body. Her skin grew hot. The Strekoza lost all sound as it tilted toward the earth. Spark flashed at her elbow, grounding on the throttle's needle. The plane trembled with their combined fear, but Revna held course. Yellow-red crept up Linné's veins.

"He still coming?" Revna called.

"Still there," Linné said. The world rushed toward them. Pleas

181

jostled at the edge of her teeth, fighting to get out, to beg Revna to save them, to stop this death wish. She could see the grass of the field, the errant threads of the flag, the leaves on each tree, and still they were swooping down. Even the best pilot couldn't get them out of this mess now.

"Still there?"

The whine of the enemy's engine took on a different tone. He peeled out of the dive, up and mercifully away from them. "Gone, he's gone—can we please—"

"*Now*," Revna shouted.

Linné pushed with everything she had. The engine roared back to life. Revna pulled the Strekoza onto a new set of strands and it turned sharply upward.

Laughter bubbled out of them. They sped toward the sky, half choking, half screaming. "I told you I could do it," Revna gasped.

She could do it. She could do anything. Together, they could do anything. The Strekoza danced up, cocky and exulted, toward the enemy plane. Now it was Linné's turn. She had nothing but flash bombs and the fiery spark in her body, but she didn't need anything more. It was time for the Elda to see what they'd brought on themselves. She brought her hand up, waiting for her moment. Heat pooled in her palm.

The underbelly of the plane flashed by in a stream of red and gold. Firebird and stars. *"Shit."* The spark boiled out of her. She twisted so it missed the tail of the plane by centimeters, streaming out into the cold air.

"You missed!" Revna yelled. The cockpit grew warm with indignation. "How could you miss? He was right on top of you."

Linné sagged. "He wasn't Elda."

Around them, the Falcons began to break formation. She saw it again, the star of the Union under one wing, the bird under the other. Her stomach dropped, and this time it had nothing to do with her fear of flying. The new planes sped toward the base, leaving a few confused Strekozy and a cluster of tiny figures on the field staring up at them.

Revna turned in her seat to stare after them, openmouthed. "What happened?"

"We got screwed."

✳

Everyone landed and disembarked before the viewing party got back to the base, and the girls clustered together against a sea of angry faces. Seventeen adapted Falcon-class planes took up most of the space on the airfield, and thirty-four male pilots and navigators stood opposite the Night Raiders.

"Were you trying to kill us?" one of the Falcon pilots said.

"Can you tell the difference between our flag and the Elda's?" said another.

"You're a joke. This whole thing is a joke."

The girls looked as if they wanted to cry. For once, Linné didn't blame them. Anger burned in her belly. But shame crept through her, too. Her old regiment would never have fired on their own. She imagined her father, pale with rage. He'd have said that a soldier took his dressing-down and punishment without complaint, like a man.

But the Night Raiders weren't men, and Linné wasn't her

father. She was their supervisor, and she'd been cheated of her right to a fair judgment. Again.

She stepped forward, pushing her shoulders back, taking charge. "You had no business flying on an active airbase without notifying us you'd be coming."

"Notifying you?" sputtered one aviator. "These maneuvers were arranged yesterday by radio."

"We almost died because you didn't read the paperwork?" said another.

Arranged? Zima would never have surprised them on their examination day. Hesovec must have undermined them. Hesovec, who knew they couldn't afford to look like fools. Hesovec, who wanted them off his base and out of his life.

The palanquin pulled up and settled on its spindly haunches. Men began to pile out. At first Linné couldn't see Zima among them, but her commander soon appeared, running to keep up with a storming Colonel Hesovec.

"Disgraceful," he shouted smugly as he approached. "Engaging your own troops. Unable to distinguish between your allies and your enemies. In the confusion of battle, we would have had a bloodbath. You think you're ready to go to war? You can't even figure out who to shoot."

"Colonel." Zima caught up to him on the edge of the field. "You're being unfair, Colonel. You know this."

"I know no such thing," he snarled. "You want to coddle these girls, but that's not what the war is for. You can't keep lying to them. We all saw what happened."

"Yes, they showed an impressive array of skills and tactics to

184

avoid enemy aircraft." Zima spoke in cold, clipped tones. Her face was white with rage. "They were able to think in the air and discern that the other planes in the sky were not a threat. Many of them completed the planned maneuvers."

"More than one of them fired on my boys," Hesovec said. "Would you call it good skill or bad that they missed, *Miss* Zima?"

"You set them to it. You told them to make the ambush. What does the army say about using resources to damage reputations and prove a point?" she shouted.

"Enough." Tcerlin stood next to the palanquin, having a smoke. The night obscured his face, but his tone was far from friendly. "You men: I presume you're here to drop off your aircraft. Kindly familiarize the pilots who will receive them with their workings. Ladies, there's a field that contains your flag and a few shells. It would be fine exercise to hike out and pick them up. As for the two of you," he said to Zima and Hesovec, "I presume we can finish this inside."

Zima started off briskly. "My office," she said, and Tcerlin followed. Hesovec seethed at the girls one last time before he broke into a trot to catch up.

✳

The Night Raiders' mood was subdued for the rest of the day. They collected their shells and went back to the barracks, but no one could sleep. Revna's anger toward the colonel and his aviators was squashed by an ugly disappointment. She'd thought she was doing well. She'd thought she could finally face the Elda and make her magic something she could be proud of. And in the end,

185

it had all been for nothing. She wondered how long it would be before Mama got the notice revoking their Protector of the Union status again.

She should have known something like this would happen. The Union didn't care about her. It didn't want her to succeed. And it never would.

"How long until they send us home?" said Katya, shrugging out of her jacket and pulling a pile of hairpins from her bag.

Nadya set down her writing kit and began counting on her fingers. "If Tcerlin radios now, we could be grounded by tonight. But it would still take...three days minimum to requisition the Strekozy and take them off the field."

"As long as everyone plays by the rules," added Pavi.

Katya began pinning her hair in too-tight curls. Her normally agile fingers fumbled the pins until she finally put them down with a growl of frustration. "I don't understand," she said. "We practiced so much. How did we get everything so wrong?"

"We didn't." To Revna's surprise, it was Linné who spoke. The room rustled as thirty-two girls turned to look at her. She didn't lift her eyes from her bed. "We were ready. That's why Hesovec cheated. It's why he planned the maneuvers and didn't tell us."

There was a short silence. "Linné," Katya said in a hushed, almost reverent voice. "Are you being *nice*?"

Linné sighed and flopped back onto the mattress. "Screw you." But she didn't sound as if she meant it. Revna felt a warm flash— was it affinity? Perhaps both of them were cursed. Linné to never fight, no matter how hard she tried. Revna to destroy her family, whether that family was Mama and Papa and Lyfa or a flock of ragtag girls from every country in the Union.

The room fell into a gloomy silence. No one wanted to talk about the mess they'd made, so they went through their routines, over and over, as if the repetition itself might finally put them to sleep. Katya took up her pins again. Revna rubbed her residual limbs with a cream she'd requisitioned from the hospital. She loved her prosthetics, but it was nice to give her legs a break at the end of each long day.

As she worked in the cream, she thought about the letter she was trying to write to Mama, but all her news seemed so pointless. *Dear Mama: Today we were tricked, and I've probably ruined your life again. Dear Mama: I know I'm cursed now. Dear Mama: The Union still hates me.* Even though she was trying to risk her life for it. Thirteen-year-old boys were good enough to be drafted, but Revna was apparently so odious that grown men would cheat to keep her grounded.

She'd received two letters in the last mail drop, a detailed one from Mama and scrawled loops that, Mama assured her, meant *I LOVE YOU* from Lyfa. Mama spent three full paragraphs on their new status—the green ration stamps that got them pork once a week, the bunkers with concrete reinforcement and benches, the old rifle she'd bullied out of the commissar. ------ *would have laughed*, she wrote.

Revna could guess what the redacted portion said. Papa would have laughed. He'd often said that the only time Mama yielded to anyone was the day she agreed to marry him. Once he'd been taken away, her will had seemed to wilt. Revna was glad to see some of it returning.

Lyfa was finally gaining weight again, catching up to the height she'd put on in the last few months. Mama thanked Revna for the money she'd sent home, too, but money didn't buy food anymore. Workers were paid in ration stamps at the end of each fourteen-hour shift. No one liked the increase in hours, but there wasn't much they could do. Revna didn't need the redacted portions to see what Mama meant. If you didn't agree to work, you didn't eat. Mama hoped Revna's money would make good savings for after the war.

Longing swept through Revna all the same. She didn't want money. She wanted to press her little sister against her chest and ask her about every star in the sky. But she couldn't go back yet. She couldn't bring the curse of the secondary bunker and the reduced rations.

The barracks door opened a fraction. "Ladies?" Tamara said.

They bolted up, setting their projects aside. Revna tried to push away her thoughts of home and scooted to the edge of her bed.

Tamara entered and sat in the nearest chair with a thud. She rubbed at the deep circles under her eyes. The regiment was around her in an instant, a flurry of well-meaning subordinates offering a little of what they did not really have. Did she need tea? Water? A cigarette? She waved them all away. "I still have to make my report tonight, so I cannot stay. But General Tcerlin has approved your training."

For a moment no one spoke. Then the girls let out a cheer. Someone started to clap, and the applause built momentum until it filled the room.

Tamara held up a hand and the applause died as quickly as it had begun. "Nikolai Tcerlin was not at all impressed by your mistakes. Despite that, he believes you have the necessary heart and skill. But he'll be keeping a close eye on us and he could easily change his mind. Every move from here on out must be impeccable. If I give an order, you follow it. You do not stop to ask questions; you do not argue; you do not think you know better." She rubbed at her temple. "Perhaps if I had treated you like soldiers from the beginning, Tcerlin would not have needed so much convincing to approve you. But I can't change that now, so I must hope that you trust me enough to follow my orders when I give them. And once I have given you an objective, you must complete it. Do you understand? Nothing will be more important than the missions. You must follow through. You must succeed. The fate of your sisters and your Union depends on this." She looked around the room with red-rimmed eyes. "Tomorrow evening at nine bells you will report for your first assignment. Clear?"

"Yes, ma'am," they replied in unison. As if they'd practiced it. As if they were disciplined.

At that Tamara was awake again, smiling, full of the energy she always brought with her. "Soldiers," she said, "we will bring great change with us, wherever we go."

12

WE WILL BRING THEM WAR

They appeared in the briefing room at nine bells and not a minute late. Revna trembled on her nervous prosthetics. The room was hot and primed like a rocket ready to fire. If Nikolai Tcerlin didn't like tonight's report, Tamara Zima's experiment was over, and so were their chances. Magdalena's hand found Revna's and squeezed. Revna squeezed back.

Tamara gave no sign of trepidation as she sifted through communications. Her desk held two neat stacks of papers, a cup of tea, and a typewriter. An enormous map with the Karavel range sweeping across the bottom third covered the wall behind her. The largest peaks had been labeled in a slanting, near-sideways script, and Intelgard base was marked with a hasty *X*. On the other side of the mountains lay the taiga—a snowy forest with only a few settlements—and the plains that stretched down to

Adovic Reaching. An old border fort along the eastern edge of the plains delineated the official divide between Rydda and the Doi Ungurin, though both were part of the Union now.

As the last bell rang, she looked up and counted the girls. Then she nodded.

"The Elda have advanced on the Karavels from Adovic Reaching, with reinforcements from the war on the Ungurin front. Our Seventy-Seventh and Forty-Sixth Night Armies are moving to intercept them on the plains, and they have requested air assistance. If the Elda successfully cross the Karavels, we'll be forced to abandon Intelgard.

"You have your partners, and you have your training. Don't think about your test flight or about what happens tomorrow. Use formation C-one to drop incendiaries on the Elda lines. Focus on the mission. Katya and Asya will take point. Any questions?"

Revna had thousands. Would the Elda be asleep or awake? Would it be hard to find the Elda lines? Did Linné *really* have to be her partner?

But everyone else chorused, "No, ma'am," so she mumbled it, too.

The girls shuffled around one another as the navigators milled forward to collect the localized maps with the latest on troop movements. Linné was first in line; she leaned over the desk and muttered something to Tamara. Tamara's frown grew irritated. "I haven't had time to think about it," she said curtly. "Do your work, and we can discuss it when you get back."

"Yes, sir," said Linné. Her expression was blank and hard. But Revna knew what she'd asked.

So did Magdalena, who began walking with Revna to the

191

Strekoza. The wind had picked up, and her long hair flapped in her face. "Honestly," she said. "What a miserable hag. She should do us all a favor and drop out. Then she can complain to her daddy about the awful Tamara Zima and get us shut down like she wants." She picked out a cigarette from her rations and shoved it into her mouth.

"Not right now," Revna said. She should be the better woman and tell Magdalena to leave Linné alone. The more she resented her flying partner, the harder their mission would be. But Linné made it so difficult to be on her side.

"It's true," Magdalena said. "She's foul. She's been foul since the first day and the harder we've worked, the fouler she's become."

Revna got out a cigarette of her own. Mama would kill her for smoking, but the rascidine helped her body remember that night was day now, and the last thing she wanted was to crash on her first assignment. Working with Linné would be hard enough. "You don't have to convince me, but I don't want to talk about her."

"About who?" Katya appeared on the other side of Magdalena. She held her cigarette as if she were ready to be photographed for the magazines. Even with her aviator helmet on, her curls fanned out perfectly in the wind.

They paused. "No one," said Revna, as Magdalena said, "You know who."

Katya smirked. "I don't blame you. I'd probably try to ground myself if I got stuck with her." She reached for Revna's arm. "Do you need help getting to your plane?"

"I'm fine," Revna said.

"The ground's pretty slick."

"I've got a good grip."

Katya shrugged and blew out a thin blue stream. The wind tore it away from her as if the smoke was a scrap of her soul. "All right, then," she said. "Let's go be heroes."

They started walking again. Magdalena tried three times to light her cigarette with the spark before she gave up and let Katya do it for her. "I'd kill to fly with you, Revna. You're the best pilot we've got. But I'm stuck on the ground, while that entitled little—" She coughed as the smoke hit her wrong. "If she can't work as part of a team, she should go do something else and stop endangering the unit."

"Like what?" Linné's voice cut colder than the wind. Revna jumped. Magdalena turned as if she'd known Linné was there all along.

Katya took a quick step back, then fled to the safety of her own plane. Magdalena tilted her chin, welcoming the challenge. "Anything," she said, folding her arms. Two bright red spots burned in her cheeks. "Anything that puts you far away from us."

A muscle moved in Linné's jaw. For a moment Revna thought she might hit Magdalena. But when she spoke, her voice was level. "Is the plane loaded?"

Magdalena's silence was all the response Linné needed.

"Now who's endangering the unit? Or did you think we'd lean out and ask the Elda to leave?" She stalked off without waiting for a reply.

"I really hate her," Magdalena whispered as they followed.

"Come on," Revna whispered back. "We need to get through this." And as much as they'd like to get through it without Linné, they couldn't. Revna extinguished her cigarette in the snow before lifting herself into the cockpit.

Linné clambered in behind her. "Let's get this over with." The engine started with a grumble.

Get *what* over with, exactly? "It's not only tonight." Revna slid her hands into the flying gloves. She barely winced as the Strekoza hooked into her chest. The lines of the Weave flickered into visibility.

"Sure it is. We'll fly, and tomorrow we'll tell Commander Zima she has to give us new partners."

"Like we did before our test flight?"

"She'll break down eventually."

Linné would go to war against everyone until they gave up out of sheer exhaustion. The Union should send her to the Elda emperor and have her badger him until he agreed to retreat.

Magdalena hooked four glass shells filled with liquid fire under their wings. The glass would break apart on impact and burn through everything in its path until it scorched the very ground black. It was the first time Revna had flown with something so volatile. Unless she counted Linné.

Magdalena appeared on the pilot's side of the cockpit. "It's ready," she said, reaching in for Revna's hand. "Don't let the bombs wobble."

Revna squeezed her. "Thanks."

"Come back safe." Magdalena shot Linné a parting glare, then stepped down.

Revna's whole body warmed as Linné began to feed power into

the Strekoza. She expected fear, and she pushed back. But Linné's anger bit at her, sharp as teeth. Her heart hardened. Linné would never turn the plane on her, not with all the rage in the world. She took a deep breath and jerked them up, just a little. The plane filled with a smug satisfaction as Linné squeaked.

Focus, she thought. She didn't want to end up a blackened smear on the snow because she was careless with her incendiaries.

Ahead of them, Katya and Asya lumbered off the ground. Their Strekoza took flight like a startled duck. "Why are *they* taking point?" Linné muttered.

"Try being more concerned with your job and less concerned with theirs," Revna said.

"Unless you'd like to literally kiss the asses of the girls in front of us, I'm doing everything I'm supposed to right now."

Revna rolled her eyes. She'd have thought that the Zolonovs had a mansion filled with posters of Grusha the Good Union Girl. CLEAN MOUTH, CLEAN MIND had papered Tammin as much as anything else.

They took off facing the mountains, churning up the snow in little flurries that brushed over the windscreen and misted their faces. Magdalena waved in Revna's side-view mirror as Linné increased power. Revna took a deep breath. *Keep the plane steady.* The engine stuttered, quick and shallow, in time to Linné's breath. Revna grabbed at strands to compensate. Her muscles ached without the spark to help the plane glide. "All right. Where are we going?"

"The Karavels," Linné said.

"I was hoping for something more specific."

"Why? You don't need it yet. Besides, all we have to do is fol-low Katya."

The entire Strekoza sagged as Revna huffed. It dipped in the air and she hauled on the Weave a touch enthusiastically, making Linné hiss. They bucked upward and the firebombs swung. Even though she tried not to smile, the Strekoza exuded a bitter satisfac-tion. That might never get old.

"Look, I'm not trying to endanger the unit. This is how I'm supposed to do my job. Can we—do this? Please?"

"Please, even," muttered Revna as she stabilized them. Not because Linné had asked, but because she needed their mission to succeed. Tcerlin would revoke his approval if he knew they used expensive military equipment to fight with each other.

The Weave surrounded them like a net, calming Revna despite the constant nagging of Linné's doubts. She floated on the wind, listening to the sounds of owls and rustling trees. The cold tick-led her.

She brought them around in a smooth line toward the moun-tains. Mama used to say the Karavels were giants, enchanted by the gods to sleep until Rydda needed them. Now that Rydda was part of a godless Union, Revna wasn't sure what that meant. She saw no traces of limbs or features on their sharp faces. The range barely cleared the tree line, a poor obstacle for the Elda.

Katya led them east in a low line along the foothills, gliding with small spark boosts that made the Weave pulse like a heart-beat. Revna spotted a few small tangles, places the Weave had been stretched or warped by the planes ahead of them. Before they flew back this way, the tangles would even themselves out.

The Night Raiders cut through the mountains where the hills turned to peaks. Rock shot up between their wings, closing them in and cutting through her sense of comfort. Below them the valley lay like a wrinkled cloth, cragged and covered in shadow. Ahead of them, the tail of the next plane disappeared around a mountain. Linné's breath came in short pants, and with each one her spark stuttered from her. The Strekoza slipped off course, edgy. Revna's hands cramped around the Weave as she tried to hold them steady. Couldn't Linné do anything about it? *"Increase power,"* she said, and a moment later they evened out a little.

They drifted through the peaks, ghost birds in a land too steep to hold trees or snow. The bare angles of the mountains flashed gold in the light of Linné's spark as it redistributed along Weave lines. Revna could almost imagine that she saw the blurred reflections of the Strekozy in their dark faces. High ridges strung false summits together. The valley floor wound below, crowded with pine trees that bowed and whispered in the wind. Revna tasted the crisp scent of snow. If they crashed now, the chances were high that no one would ever find them. The thought made the plane nose upward, and her muscles tightened as she kept it on course.

They clung to the Weave. Revna plucked lightly, adjusting in increments, feeling the sticky mass where tangles gathered and ripened the air with magic. She separated the strands with sweat-slicked fingers. Her breath hitched every time she slipped.

The Strekoza was hot and prickly from her concentration, from Linné's nerves.

When they emerged from the pass, all three of them let out a sigh. "Tcerlin should have seen *that* in our test flight," Linné said, increasing power to catch up with the rest of the regiment. "He'd never have doubted us then."

"Us?"

Linné's voice was stiff. "Yes. Us."

"We're an 'us' now?"

"We've always been an us."

Revna made a derisive sound. *Despite your best efforts.* "If we're such an us, why do you want another pilot so badly?" Her voice sounded pathetically close to a whine. "I mean, I don't have any great love for you, either, but I'm not trying to distract you in the middle of a mission."

"There's nothing wrong with your piloting skills." Revna felt a stab of embarrassment from her, a flash of something deeper. A memory, maybe? Linné continued before Revna had a chance to work it out. "But in an emergency situation, you're a dangerous liability."

The Strekoza veered left so sharply that they nearly flew back into the pass. Linné yelped at the change of course and the way the throttle constricted around her wrist. The cockpit filled with indignation, but Revna didn't feel Linné's pain, and didn't care. "Don't *ever* call me that," she shouted.

Nausea flared back from Linné's seat. Nausea, self-righteous anger, and shame. Not nearly enough shame.

"I didn't mean—"

"I'm a *person*, not a liability. And in case you forgot, I'm the only reason you're up here. No one else wanted to fly with you." Satisfaction flooded Revna and she didn't try to hide it. Let Linné hear her own words fired back at her.

The cockpit was silent for a moment. Then Linné whispered, "I know."

Her admission didn't make Revna feel as good as she thought it would. Now that the rush of anger was over, her gut twisted and her wings trembled. Maybe if she apologized...

For what? She hadn't done anything wrong. Linné was the one who assumed Revna was incompetent because she was disabled. Linné, the mouthpiece of the Union that had always rejected her. She was as bad as Hesovec. Going on about "emergency situations" when they didn't even have parachutes—

Focus. Mama and Lyfa needed her to succeed. They were much more important than Linné.

They followed the slim Ava River on its southward course, trying to ignore the way the air in the cockpit curdled. Soon they spotted the Elda army nestled in a dip on the plains, overflowing a hamlet of farmhouses. The buildings were crowded with soldiers looking to stay out of the cold, and fires burned out in the open, without much consideration for blackout conditions. Palanquins, war beetles, and little messengers had disrupted the new snowfall by the dozens, churning the ground without any attempt to mask themselves. They must have presumed that the mountains and the Union's famous lack of aircraft would provide them with all the cover they needed. *Good*, Revna thought in a sudden rush of heat. *They don't deserve to see us coming.*

"Palanquin pen," Linné said. A fence of wooden stakes and chicken wire cut off a large square of ground where the living metal constructs sat dormant.

Katya's plane swooped down. As slow as it was, it moved elegantly, like a bird of prey through the flashing Weave. Not like Revna's Strekoza, cringing every time Linné gasped.

The first bomb landed on empty ground, bouncing instead of breaking. But Katya's second bomb shattered against the closed shell of a palanquin and spattered liquid fire onto a group of little messengers huddling for warmth. They flew apart in a blaze of metal limbs.

The living machines around them barely had time to leap up before the next plane dove. Elena and Nadya scored two solid hits, sending a palanquin rolling end over end.

Their turn. "Ready to dive?" Revna said.

"No," muttered Linné.

They dove anyway.

The air was driven from Revna's lungs. She pushed against the terror—*It's not mine, it's not me*—but she felt a genuine panic as the engine coughed. Linné had restarted it too soon. Revna lunged for the nearest strand of the Weave and brought them about. They shot over the heads of the palanquins and narrowly missed a barn. And on top of all that—

"You didn't fire!"

"Of course not." Linné managed to sound derisive.

"That was the whole point!" She jabbed her finger at the palanquin pen. The wing of the Strekoza followed her hand, lunging down. She barely kept them from doing a barrel roll.

Linné made a strangled noise. "You didn't get me a clear shot," she said.

"I would have if you'd waited to reengage the engine."

"You were too close to the ground."

They'd gone through training. They'd gone through testing. They'd logged hundreds of practice hours. But Linné would always think of her as the *liability* before she ever thought of her as a pilot. "I'm the judge of when you spark. You're the judge of when you fire."

Revna brought them around in a loop and came up on Pavi's tail. They were last in line now. The Strekoza constricted around her as they prepared to dive. "Gently," she murmured, trying to push away her anger and send something soothing instead.

The plane faltered. And they were swooping down. Fear pulled, tighter and tighter, until they were so close to the ground that Revna could reach out and touch the antenna of a rearing war beetle. "Okay—"

The engine kicked to life and they shot up again. The whole plane was shaking—but Linné released the bombs with the click of a trigger. They sped away, and as Revna sagged she heard her first sounds of battle.

It was a lot of screaming. The palanquins screamed as they burned. The wind screamed over the front screen, tearing at Revna's helmet and goggles. And Linné screamed incessantly. Her voice streamed out behind them in a bright stripe of sound. And then she ran out of breath, and it was the wind and the cold as they pushed higher and higher.

The Strekoza began to pound in time with Revna's heart.

"Linné." Revna's breath puffed in front of her. The Strekoza shivered. Clouds loomed ahead of them like a thick wall. The world was turning gray. *I can't move.* Was that the Strekoza's feeling, or Linné's, or hers?

Think of the problems, her father's voice whispered in her mind.

Problem: The Strekoza couldn't fly too high without freezing.

Problem: She controlled the direction, but Linné controlled the speed.

"Linné." Revna wrestled for a strand, trying to reach Linné through the Strekoza's connection. "Get a hold of yourself."

"I have a hold of myself," Linné shouted over the hammering fear between them.

"Then slow down," Revna cried.

Panic surged through her. The Strekoza sped up instead.

With a *clunk,* the Strekoza had its final word. Their nose pushed into the clouds, soaking them both, and Linné's spark dissipated in a flash like the center of a lightning storm.

The long metal fingers around Revna jerked loose. Cold slammed into her, searing her lungs as she tried to breathe in. Suddenly she wasn't part of some great entity that could fly among the stars. She was a girl in a small cockpit, going nowhere but down.

"Revna, what's happening?"

Clunk, clunk. Problem: The engine was trying to restart, but something held it back. Revna reached for a Weave strand and missed. Their tail-first fall began to turn into a somersault.

"Revna!" Linné screamed.

The answer snapped into her head. "Hot spark! All of it!"

Linné didn't ask questions. Her spark surged through the

plane, blasting through the ice around the propeller and roaring into the Weave. The cage clamped back over her chest, and Revna pulled with everything she had.

She let the blast push them away from the mountains, farther into Elda-occupied territory. She shook. The whole Strekoza shook. *It's all right now*, she told herself and the plane.

When she thought the aircraft was steady enough, she eased it around. "There, there," she murmured, patting the Strekoza's pulsing fingers. The smell of singed canvas tickled the inside of her nose.

"Are you *talking* to it?" Linné said.

"It's upset." She didn't know whether the defensiveness in her voice was all her own or half the plane's. "It probably panicked, seeing the palanquins explode like that."

"Oh, yes, comfort the monster flying machine. I pushed half my life out of my arm, but don't mind me," Linné grumbled.

"It's also less of a whiner than you are," Revna said before she could stop herself. Her heart still pounded. She wasn't thinking properly. But she'd show empathy for Linné when Linné showed empathy for her.

"Oh, screw you—"

Behind them, something *crack*ed like thunder. Every hair on Revna's body stood on end. A searing pain burned through her, and she felt the plane release a raw scream as it reared up. She grabbed for the Weave, fighting to think past the pulsing agony.

They sped back over the palanquin pen, which burned in a mess of machines that fought the fires, the shrapnel, and one another in indiscriminate panic. A few figures had rushed to the pen to help, but the craft were insensible. One palanquin raised a steel leg and flicked a man ten meters through the air.

By the time Revna could think straight, they were close to the Karavels again. They slipped through the mountain pass, the last of the Strekozy flying back to base.

"What happened?" Her left arm ached as though someone had taken a hammer to it.

"We got shot," Linné said.

"What?"

"We got shot. We flew so low and we flew so slow that someone shot at us. And they hit. Look at the wing."

Revna angled them away from the nearest peak. "I'm a little busy." But the port wing shivered, as if agreeing with Linné's words.

Despite the shot, she couldn't help noticing that the flight seemed calmer than before. Some underlying piece of fear had broken off and burned with the Elda camp. Things were different now, somehow.

"I can't believe it. We fly too high, we freeze. We fly too low, we get shot." Linné's voice took on a more thoughtful tone. "We got shot at," she said again. And then Revna realized what was so different. They didn't buck and bob with every breath. Linné's anxiety no longer leaked into their lifeline. "We *got shot at*. I can't believe—" She stopped. But the Strekoza amplified her feeling, filling in the rest.

She'd missed it.

✳

Magdalena was the first to greet them as they landed back at the base. She ran toward the plane and hopped up on the wing to

204

squeeze Revna's shoulder, laughing with a joy that soothed Revna and the Strekoza both. Her grin split her face. "Full-on panic. The Elda are scrambling. Tamara wants you to hit the supply next. Any food stores or ammunition."

Linné cut the power. "We'll strand them."

Magdalena's smile dimmed as she remembered that Linné was there. "Yeah," she said. "Strand them. I'm loading explosives. Answer Olya's questions." She turned and nearly skipped off.

An army was scrambling because of them. Panicking because of eleven tiny planes on their very first mission.

We really can do anything, Revna thought. The secret bloomed in her. Let Hesovec rant at them now.

Olya popped up next to the cockpit, not nearly as happy as Magdalena. Her short hair stuck out of a knitted hat and grease smudged her forehead. She wore her irritated smile, a little one with a strained upturn to the mouth, and tapped her wrench against her palm. "What did you do to the engine?"

"It froze," Revna explained.

Olya flared her nostrils, as if Revna had frozen the engine on purpose. "That was stupid, wasn't it? The propeller's warped but maybe I can do something. Don't spark while I'm up there," she called to Linné.

"It felt off," Linné said. Revna twisted around to look at her. She was shockingly pale, and deep bags had already formed under her eyes. She massaged her bare forearm. A red welt had begun to rise at the edge of her rolled-up sleeve.

"Are you all right?" Revna said.

Linné turned on her signature glower. "I'm fine."

"It's just—you used a lot of extra spark, and—"

"I'm fine. I'm ready to go." Linné grabbed the throttle. "Point us in the right direction."

"What's this?" came Olya's outraged voice from the port wing.

"We got shot," Revna called back.

"Remember, if I get grounded, you get grounded," Linné said.

"I only—" Revna gave up. Linné would never understand her concern, and that wasn't Revna's problem. Her problem was the Elda, and she would utterly obliterate them. Because she could do anything.

Magdalena hooked more bombs underneath the Strekoza while Olya took a hammer to the propeller and got a patch kit for the wing. They didn't dawdle, but Revna and Linné were alone on the field by the time they'd finished.

"Come back safe," Magdalena finally said.

Linné fired up before Magdalena backed away.

✳

As they returned to the line, they began to hear the muted roar of hundreds of voices. Sweeping in from the east was a long dark mass—the Seventy-Seventh and Forty-Sixth had arrived. The Elda had set up sandbag barricades, and while their rifles cracked out over the taiga, targeting the approaching army, a searchlight flicked back and forth across the sky, chasing wings and tails.

"Food stores will be behind the line, if they're smart," Linné said.

"Which building?" Revna squinted at the contour of dark farm buildings, dodging as the searchlight swung their way.

"Hang on—I'll get out and ask."

"No need to be sarcastic," Revna said.

"What's that?" Linné's hand snaked over her shoulder to point. A pale blue cloud billowed up around the figures on the ground.

They realized at the same time. *"Gas!"*

The Strekozy scattered. Blue mist rose around them, reaching long tendrils into the cockpit. The acrid stench dizzied Revna. Her cheek tingled, as though it had been scraped raw and rubbed with sand. Something in her mind reached once, twice, then faded. Everything faded.

Linné's free hand clamped over Revna's mouth and nose. "Go," she choked out.

Go? She was supposed to go somewhere? Revna tried to push the ever-growing fog to the back of her mind. She twisted the Weave and they swung up, bombs bobbing under their wings. "Power," she managed through Linné's fingers. They sped toward clear sky.

Revna coughed as freezing air filled her lungs. Her brain fought for clarity. The Elda. The war. Food stores. She knew where she was; she knew where she was going. She righted the plane.

They'd been in the gas only a few seconds, and she hadn't gotten a proper lungful. The damage probably wouldn't be permanent. Whatever the damage was.

A blue wall rose in front of them, expanding slowly now that the initial blast had died away. They'd never get over it without freezing the engine, and they'd never get through it without—

"Gas masks?"

"Back at the base," Linné replied.

"Options?"

"We hold our breaths and try to make it through. Or we find a different target."

Revna swooped low over a few outlying buildings. The searchlight tailed them in vain. They dropped their incendiaries on a roof and caught up to the other Strekozy with a burst of speed. They were almost at the mountains when Linné broke the silence.

"Good flying," she said.

Revna resisted the urge to lift the earflaps of her helmet and ask for a repeat. She cleared her throat instead. "Thanks. And thanks for helping me with the—you know." She coughed.

Linné was quiet a moment. Then she said, "You're... welcome?"

Revna sighed. Progress was slow, but it was still progress.

✳

Magdalena ran up with the gas masks as soon as they landed. "We heard," she said. "Tamara's panicking."

"What does it do?" Revna took the masks and handed one to Linné.

"Daydream gas. You find it hard to concentrate and easy to get lost. You might think the clouds are the ground, or land in enemy territory." And everyone knew what happened to soldiers who landed in enemy territory. They were hauled away by the Skarov on suspicion of treason as soon as they came back. If they came back.

"Better this time," Olya said, popping out from behind the engine. Her smile had lost some of its angry luster. "Keep it up and our repairs might not be excessive." She tapped Magdalena's arm with her wrench. "Let's take a look at Katya."

"Come back safe," Magdalena said again.

"I don't mean to complain," Revna said as Linné fired up. "But how many runs are we going to make?"

✳

Eight. They made eight runs before Magdalena helped Revna out of the cockpit. Revna couldn't feel anything from the waist down. Her arms burned. She pulled off her gas mask, grimacing—her sweat had frozen the rubber ring to her face. Her residual limbs were slick inside their prosthetic sockets, and her knees felt like jelly. The cold was an unwelcome surprise after the protection the Strekoza had given her.

Linné didn't try to run ahead of them. She walked as if she'd carried the plane over the Karavels herself. Revna remembered Tamara's gray face as she'd flown training mission after training mission.

"Tamara made tea for us in the mess," Magdalena said, holding Revna's arm so tight Revna thought she'd unbalance and fall over.

Revna caught the sleeve of Linné's jacket. "Are you—" She stopped shy of saying *all right?* Linné would never admit to weakness and would hate her for even suggesting it. "Thirsty?"

"Revna," Magdalena whispered in her ear.

Linné eyed her, as though assessing whether she was joking or not, and whether it was worth it. "I could do with some tea," she said, and she said it with only a little reluctance.

The cold hit Revna's teeth as she smiled. Progress.

Three steaming cups of tea and fermented mare's milk had already been poured for them. But instead of the cheerful ruckus she'd expected, they were met with a sea of serious faces.

"What kind of party is this?" she said. Her false joviality fell flat.

Katya's hair had lost its curl and stuck damply to her head. Her nose was red. But her eyes were redder. "Pavi and Galina didn't come back."

Shock pierced Revna's heart. Of course this was war; of course there were no guarantees. But did their losses have to hit so soon?

Tamara approached and handed the teacups to each of them. It felt strange taking tea from the woman giving her orders, stranger to be taking it when two of her comrades most likely lay in the piling snow. "They didn't return from their second run."

Daydream gas. They could have flown too high, frozen their engine like Revna and Linné had, and been unable to blast free in time to regain control. Or they could have mistaken the ground for the sky. Or they could still be drifting, drifting farther into Elda-occupied territory, minds spinning in confusion.

The Night Raiders raised their cups together. Tamara took a deep breath. Her voice was hoarse, and as she spoke, tears slipped over her cheeks. Katya was crying, Elena was crying—even Olya had red-rimmed eyes and no smiles to give anyone. But Revna felt frozen. It didn't seem right that Pavi and Galina were gone. She hadn't seen them taken like her father or shot like traitors and ration thieves in Tammin Square. They simply weren't there anymore.

"I will wait for them tonight, and in the morning we will fly the Union colors at half-staff. They are gone because the Elda are here, and we won't let anyone forget that. Tonight we pushed the Elda hard. Hesovec's Day Raiders will help the Seventy-Seventh and Forty-Sixth finish the job. The Elda could be forced back toward Goreva for the first time during the war."

To this, the girls drank. Goreva had been in Elda hands for three years. Revna couldn't help wondering what it must look like now. Was there anything left of it worth rescuing?

"This is because of you. This is your victory. Commander Andrysiak of the Forty-Sixth and Commander Budny of the Seventy-Seventh extend their thanks for our capable assistance." This got a muted round of applause.

Tamara swallowed. "We shouldn't try to forget Pavi and Galina. But we have to carry on. We—"

The mess door slammed open. Two figures in mud-stained, oversized uniforms stumbled in. Pavi yanked the aviator helmet off her head and let her black braid tumble free. "Sorry we're late."

The room erupted. The girls surged forward, surrounding Pavi and Galina in an enormous hug. More than one shouted, "What *happened* to you?" Revna joined the outer ring, clasping someone else's shoulder, someone else's sleeve, pressing in, shocked to find she was crying at last.

When they broke apart, Pavi and Galina could do nothing for themselves. They were practically carried to their chairs, and two mugs were filled and put in front of them.

Magdalena pressed her fingers to the side of Pavi's nose. Pavi's nostrils were tinged with blue. "What happened? Tell us everything."

"It was the gas," Pavi said. "We were so close to the ground we could have landed when the Elda sparked it off. I think I forgot where I was for a good fifteen minutes. It must have been sheer luck that kept us flying. By the time we came to, we'd gone so far south we almost couldn't see the Karavels anymore. We set down and came back to our senses."

"It took you a long time to get back," Tamara said.

"We didn't want to fly through the gas," Pavi said. "We didn't know how far it had spread."

Galina nodded through the whole exchange. The circles under her eyes stood out like deep bruises.

Katya raised her glass. "Here's to us—all of us. We rule the night."

"We rule the night," they murmured. Everyone drank, even Tamara, though her smile seemed sadder than ever.

13

OUR REALM IS THE NIGHT

They should have gone to bed. They should have tried to get a few scant hours of sleep before they woke for training and the next night's mission. But when the cook came in to make breakfast, they got out their bowls. Olya turned the radio to state-approved jazz, where a woman's smoky voice crooned "Factory Girl's Blues." Revna moved to a chair by the wall and loosened the buckles on her prosthetics as the others set up their makeshift dance floor.

Katya heaved a sigh as she collapsed next to her. "Not dancing?" Revna said.

"In a minute. What do you think?" Katya opened her writing kit and pulled out the top sheet of paper. She'd drawn a girl in sharp profile—a girl with Revna's nose, Revna's eye and chin. A strand of dark hair had escaped from her aviator helmet and fluttered in the wind. The goggles on the helmet were cracked and smeared with smoke, but her eye gleamed with determination. The moon was partially obscured by the headline OUR REALM IS THE NIGHT. At the bottom, Katya had stenciled in THE UNION'S WOMEN FLY FOR YOU.

"I think I'll send it off to the Public Morale Committee," she said.

"With my face?"

"If that's all right. I like your nose," Katya said. "It's sharp, but small." She rubbed her own nose—perfectly normal-sized, Revna thought, but she smiled.

She imagined her profile pasted up outside her factory, where Mrs. Rodoya could see it every day, or on the lampposts on the street outside her house. She was surprised at how much she liked the idea. Not that she thought the Public Morale Committee would use it. "It's beautifully done."

The men started coming in for breakfast and clustered near the door, wary at the sight of Olya and Nadya dancing. Asya went up to the one at the front; he grinned nervously but allowed her to lead him to the empty floor.

Katya yawned. "Let me know if Linné's dark-haired pilot comes in." She leaned against the wall and closed her eyes.

The dance floor gradually filled. Some of the girls danced with each other and some snagged a boy to dance with. Tamara watched from the side, sipping her tea, more like an indulgent aunt than a commanding officer. Linné stood nearby. She studied the dance floor as if it were a problem.

"Excuse me, miss."

Revna looked up at a blue star pinned to a silver-covered chest. Her blood turned to ice. "Ah, yes?" *Oh, God—no, not God*, she corrected furiously, trying to push her thoughts onto the track of the innocent. Would they really arrest her now, after she'd had a successful night?

It was the blond Skarov, the one who always smiled. He was smiling now, too, and though his yellow eyes unnerved her, the smile itself seemed kind. Another thrill of fear ran through her. If he wasn't here to arrest her, why was he talking to her? Had something happened to Mama? Or Papa? Kolshek Prison wasn't known for its amenities. Many died there in service to the Union they'd never betrayed.

He extended a hand. "Might I request the honor of the next dance?"

"What?"

"A dance. I'm sure you're tired, but the problem is, if you turn me down, I'll have to parade on the floor with Dostorov. And he dances like a yak. He smells like one, too." He smiled, inviting her to laugh.

The other Skarov was nowhere to be seen. Maybe he'd danced his partner right off to an interrogation room already. Everyone else was on the dance floor or engaged in conversation. Tamara was examining a living metal glove with Magdalena. Linné was pulling off her jacket. The only person paying attention to them was Katya, and her eyes were wide with terror.

"I, um, didn't bring my dancing legs." *I left them under a cart.*

"I'll help you." He started to unbutton his coat. He wore a plain brown shirt underneath, like all the other recruits. Revna wasn't sure what she'd expected—a full military dress suit, maybe?—but that wasn't it.

You don't have any idea how to help me, she wanted to say. But no one said no to the Skarov.

She pulled up her trouser legs, showing off her prosthetics in all their glory. Maybe he would get uncomfortable and change his mind. She took her time rebuckling them, rubbing her calves and drawing the living metal snug, though it pinched her already sore skin. She winced when she stood. But Tannov was still there, looking as if dancing with her was the only thing he wanted to do with his morning. Maybe he'd dance her all the way into a cell, let his knife do the talking for the next eight hours.

He'd taken off his gloves. His hands were warm and dry. Revna resisted the urge to wipe her sweaty palms on her trouser legs.

A path cleared around them as they made their way to the floor. *Now* they were getting attention. She ignored it. *Breathe, walk.* Her prosthetics trembled. *Stay steady.*

A bright swing began with a blast of saxophone. Before the accident, she'd danced with more enthusiasm than skill. Now she didn't even have that.

Tannov rested his hand on her waist and bobbed back and forth. "Revna, isn't it?"

She coughed. "Yes," she said, trying to push some confidence into her voice. She was getting dizzy, watching him. He looked a little like a chicken. She bit back a hysterical laugh.

"And where are you from?"

Don't you already know? "Tammin."

216

"The factory town. I've spent so many hours in your palanquins I think I have 'From Tammin Reaching and Environs' stamped backward across my ass. Pardon the language," he added as she winced.

"It's okay," she said.

"I've never been to Tammin. Is it nice?"

She ought to say yes. But if the Skarov could sniff out lies, like everyone said, then surely he already knew how she felt. "I'm sure it's quite boring compared with where you're from."

"And you have family there?" he pressed.

Ice spread up her spine. Forget dancing; this was where Revna needed to watch her step. "I have a mother and a sister. Protectors of the Union," she added brashly, though he must know already. And he must know how they got their status back.

"No father."

Was there a question in his tone? Revna didn't want to offer up information freely. But her silence felt damning to her. Refusing to contradict him might make him think she was hiding something. Could she address it without rousing his suspicion?

"My father's a traitor," she said at last, in the harshest voice she could manage. She hoped Tannov would think it came from contempt, and not from heartbreak. "We don't speak of him." The voice in her head cried, louder and louder, *Now who's the traitor?*

"I see." His tone was neutral, but his arm went rigid, and his hand tightened around hers. He could probably break it with a squeeze of his fingers. "Important to uproot treason before it spreads to the whole family tree."

Her palms were slick again. She wanted to tear away from him.

217

She wanted to tell him to say whatever he was thinking and get it over with. But he still smiled, kind and carefree, and no one else seemed to think that anything was wrong. Revna risked a glance at Tamara. Tamara was still deep in conversation with Magdalena.

She should have known. No one would save her from this.

"The original arrest papers recorded my innocence. If you like, I can borrow Tamara's radio and send to Tammin for the documents." She tried to say it casually, but her voice cracked on *documents*.

"Do you think it's necessary?" he asked.

Another trick question. And the longer it took her to sort through her words for an answer, the more suspicious he would find her.

The song ended before she could come up with a suitable reply. Tannov bowed. When he released her, she stumbled back, suddenly cold. "It was a pleasure, Miss Roshena."

"Yes," she said. "I mean—"

He led her over to the door—by Linné, she noticed. Linné watched her strangely, she thought. What had happened? Had that been an interrogation or just a conversation?

"I need a cigarette," Tannov said.

"All right." Linné reached for her jacket, folded on a table.

Nerves spiked in Revna again. First the Skarov had singled her out, and now he was singling out her navigator. She doubted his conversation with Linné would be the same sort of family attack. He'd be asking about *her* instead. How well did Revna fly? What did she say in the cockpit?

Tannov went for his coat. This would be her only chance to talk to Linné before he did. "Did you speak with Tamara?"

"About what?" Linné pulled her jacket on, wrinkling her nose at its smell.

"You still want to switch partners, don't you?"

"Don't you?" Linné countered.

What should she say? *Not anymore* was a lie that anyone could see through. *Yes* might turn into an entry in the Skarov's interrogation notebook.

Revna didn't like Linné. Linné looked at her face and somehow saw only her feet. But they'd helped each other last night. And even with Tannov breathing down her neck, working together was better than being grounded alone. "I want to fly."

"Me too. And I'm not going to let Pavi strand me in Elda territory." Linné eyed Pavi and Galina skeptically. "And did you see Katya's last flight? I thought she was going to go straight into the side of the mountain." She paused for a moment to glare at Katya. Katya had found Linné's dark-haired soldier, and they were dancing together. "I might as well stick with you."

Yes, that was Linné. Entitled and miserable, like Magdalena said. But she wouldn't sell out Revna just because she didn't like her.

Progress.

✳

Linné and Tannov walked into the ever-lightening early morning. The clouds opened up to release slow-falling flakes that kissed her jacket and settled in her hair. She breathed in the cold, clean smell. The stink of the engineers' experiments had hung over Intelgard for far too long. "Where's Dostorov?" she said.

A little messenger skidded to a stop in front of them. It opened its bowl-like top, and Tannov plucked out the message inside. He scanned the note, then with a flick of his spark he ignited it, dropping it into the snow as the paper turned black. "He's here," he said. He fished his cigarette case out of his pocket, retrieved two cigarettes, and lit both before passing one to her. Then he pressed a hand to the messenger and sent it off with a flash of spark. "Coming?"

"Won't people talk?" Linné said.

"I highly doubt they'll talk about *me*." He offered her his arm.

She shoved it away. No need for him to start with all that. They walked. "I'm surprised you're leaving the party so soon."

"I collected the information that was relevant to me. Perhaps I'll be back when my work is complete." He paused. The heaviness of his silence surprised Linné. "Your flying partner seems rather lovely."

She'd seen them dancing and wondered at his game. "I suppose. Why do you care?"

Because he was a Skarov, that was why. Tannov chose not to answer. He exhaled a bluish puff of rascidine smoke with a sigh. "Revna Roshena," he mused as they passed the last building and set off toward the edge of the compound.

Linné snorted. "Truly, you are a great detective and secret agent. Did you really have to dance with her to find out her name?"

She heard rather than saw Tannov's smile. "I think you're jealous of her," he said. "For dancing with me."

A flush of spark worked down her arm. She put her hands behind her back so he wouldn't see the way it lit the end of her fingers. "Yes, and the gods will rise from their God Spaces and save us all."

The smile slid out of his voice. "Don't say things like that," he said. Sour smoke puffed around his face. "Even if you're joking."

"What are you going to do, report me?" Linné winced inwardly. She hadn't meant to say it out loud. In case the answer was *yes.*

Tannov sounded irritated. "I'm not the only Extraordinary Wartime Information Officer on this base."

"Yeah, but Dostorov has a better sense of humor than you."

She'd thought it would bring his smile back, but Tannov only shook his head. "You walk by agents every night, and you don't even know it. Not all of us wear flashy coats." He touched her shoulder briefly, squeezing with his gloved fingers until she felt the pressure. "Be careful, Linné."

Before she could say more, Tannov spotted something at the edge of the base, raised his arm in a salute, and strode toward the compound gate. Linné followed.

Between the inner fence and the outer fortifications squatted a long prisoner transport. Its living metal legs shivered in the early-morning air. Dostorov waited next to it, puffing a cigarette and stroking its side contemplatively, watching the sun rise. Next to him, an enormous dappled white cat lounged on the open driver's seat. Its tail flicked over the side. It watched Linné with large amber eyes as she followed Tannov through the gate. The cat twisted its head toward Dostorov; he looked, in turn, to Linné.

"She knows what it is," Tannov said. "Don't be such a stick."

She'd heard the rumors, but she'd never seen a Skarov in its shifted form before. It looked—well, like a cat. It yawned, showing off canines as long as her little finger.

Dostorov shrugged. "It's your head," he said. Then, to Linné, "You'd better not be selling army secrets."

That would be the day. She opened her mouth to tell Dostorov that she didn't think he was so funny, after all. But Tannov's warning, *Don't say things like that*, still hung in her mind. They were Skarov now. Skarov got respect and fear and obedience. She shouldn't be out here in the first place, and not because of some "army secrets" bullshit.

Tannov frowned at the trembling palanquin. "Can it go on in that condition?"

"Sure," Dostorov said. "We got spotted by one of their Skyhorses, took a little fire. It's frightened, but it'll calm down the farther north you get."

"We can have the mechanics look it over anyway," Tannov said.

"We're behind schedule," Dostorov objected. "Now that the—"

This time, Tannov was the one to shoot a warning look. *Something's changed*, Linné realized. And Tannov didn't want her to know what it was.

Tannov steered Linné away from the palanquin. "Will you be flying every mission with Miss Roshena?"

Why such an interest in her pilot? "For now."

"Linné, you have to stay clear of her," Tannov said.

I'm a person, not a liability. "She's a good pilot, and she's a good soldier. She can fly as well as everyone else, and better than Katya and Pavi." Shame heated the back of Linné's neck. She forced herself to meet Tannov's eye. "I'm lucky to fly with her."

Tannov didn't seem to be paying attention. He looked at Dostorov, then at the shifted Skarov. "Roshena's father has a life sentence on Kolshek."

Kolshek, the icy prison island. Where the inmates slaved in poorly dug mine shafts, excavating the living metal that the Union needed so badly to win the war. "Impossible. She'd have been demoted to secondary citizen." And secondary citizens couldn't serve in the army. "Or," she added, hoping desperately that it could somehow be true, "maybe he's on Kolshek, and she did something to get reinstated." Secondary citizens were reinstated only for acts of the highest bravery or sacrifice. If Revna had managed that, then she deserved her fresh start.

"She has her Protector status because she's here," Tannov said softly. "Tamara Zima personally requested her reinstatement." His eyes glittered with contempt.

Linné swallowed her nerves. "I trust my commander's judgment." She was pretty sure that was only half a lie.

"You should trust mine more. Roshena's father is a traitor to the Union. What did he teach her before he got arrested? If she defects, I don't want her taking you with her."

"Someone has to be her navigator," Linné said.

"Not you." His eyes searched her face, but what he looked for, she did not know.

"Why not?" she asked, afraid of the answer.

"Weave magic has been decriminalized only for the duration of the war," Tannov said. "Zima says the tangles you make won't be permanent, but what if they are? She's not half as safe as she tells you she is. Someone like Revna could be arrested in seconds. Don't affiliate yourself strongly with her."

"*I* decide who I fly with," she snapped before she could think better of it.

The big white cat lashed its tail. Dostorov removed his cigarette, raising a brow at Tannov. And Tannov's jaw worked, the way it used to when Koslen told him something he didn't want to hear.

They were arguing. And they were doing it in a place where she couldn't hear them.

So the telepathy rumor was true.

She couldn't follow the debate, but she knew two things. First, it was more than likely about her. Second, it was one more thing that separated her friends from the boys they'd been. From the people she'd cared about for years.

But they were still Dostorov and Tannov, and she couldn't bring herself to give them up.

"Eight successful runs," she said. "Congratulate me."

For a moment she thought the argument was still going, and they'd ignored her. Then Tannov said, "Congratulations" and turned away. He didn't sound as if he meant it. He grabbed Dostorov's arm, knocking the cigarette from his hand as he began to walk away.

"Hey," Dostorov began, but something shuttered behind his

eyes. He followed Tannov, pausing only to call over his shoulder. "Congratulations, Alexei."

Linné didn't bother to correct him.

✳

Linné watched Tannov and Dostorov go into Zima's office. She didn't need to be a mind reader to guess what they were doing in there. Maybe Tannov thought he was helping. She hunched her shoulders against the snow. She should never have gone for a smoke with him. He'd only pulled her away from the Night Raiders, and they were the ones she was stuck with, for better or worse.

She drew closer to the office. Though the walls were cheap and thin, she could hear nothing but a low murmur inside. Could Tannov really order Zima to make the switch? Could Linné beg her not to? Linné would look like a buffoon; then again, she was one.

This is such a bad idea, she thought. She had no plan. She couldn't knock, but pressing her ear to the door would be worse. Hiding until Tannov and Dostorov left would work only if they didn't spot her. But if she walked away, she wasn't sure she'd be brave enough to come back.

The door swung open and the boys stepped out. Tannov halted in the doorway when he saw her. Then he shook his head and passed her without a word.

Dostorov had already gotten a cigarette out. Linné had never been intimidated by him before, but as she looked up—and up— at his broad shoulders and thick arms, she couldn't help noticing that he wasn't the scrawny boy who'd signed her up for service. "You'd better watch yourself," he said. "Your father can only keep you out of some kinds of trouble."

Before she could think of an answer, he was gone.

She was in her commander's office before she realized her feet were moving. Tamara Zima sat at her desk, a blank sheet in front of her and a pen in her hand.

"What did they talk to you about?" Linné asked.

The creases around Zima's face deepened as she took in Linné. "Nothing to do with you," she said in a voice colder than the air outside.

"Would you tell me if it was?"

Zima's mouth drew tight. Her nostrils flared. "Out of bounds, Linné."

"Is it about Revna?"

The flat of Zima's hand slammed the desk, spraying ink over her paper. "I don't want to hear it. Not tonight. I don't want to hear you demanding what you have no right to know. I don't want to hear you begging for a different pilot or complaining about your regiment. The only words I want to hear from you are good night. Is that clear?"

Linné started to take in what she hadn't seen in her flustered entrance: Zima's red-rimmed eyes. The smudged handkerchief on the edge of the desk. Something bad had happened. Something very bad, something that Zima couldn't change.

"Good night, sir," she said, and fled as fast as she could.

Far across the field, she could see the palanquin and two figures beside it. As she squinted against the dawn, one of the figures began

226

to move, faster and faster. Far too fast for a man. Then he was a blur on four legs, disappearing past the trees outside the base.

She should have kept her mouth shut around Tannov. Now she was going to wake up and Revna would be arrested and it would be Linné's fault and she'd be stuck on the ground. And she would forever be the snitch who gossiped freely with the Skarov.

But when Linné woke that afternoon, Revna slept soundly in her bed. It was Pavi and Galina who were gone.

14

VICTORY COSTS

The elation of a successful first mission was marred when the regiment discovered that they'd lost Pavi and Galina yet again. The Night Raiders didn't chat much, and whenever they did, the words were halting and whispered, as though they expected someone in a silver coat to jump out and arrest them for seditious behavior.

"Of course it's them," Nadya muttered as she, Revna, and Katya folded laundry in the barracks. No one said *Skarov*, in case one of them was in earshot or had some kind of little messenger hiding around a corner. Revna wouldn't put that out of the realm of possibility.

"The nearest prisoner facility is in Eponar." Katya got out her sewing kit and started on Nadya's frayed cuff. "It would take them three hours to get there, three hours back. And that's if they didn't stop for anything."

"They could be on a special mission," Revna said.

"Their plane's still on the field," Nadya said. "Besides, they went missing in enemy territory. Those are the rules. You fall behind the lines, you might be a defector—ow!" Katya had stabbed her with a needle.

Katya didn't apologize. "That's what they get for risking their lives?" she asked. "What's the point?"

Revna watched her for a moment. What kind of Union girl was Katya, really?

And what kind of Union girl was Revna?

The good kind. Until her family was completely safe, she was the Good Union Girl. "The Union doesn't make mistakes."

Katya's blue eyes filled with hurt. "No," she said. "Of course not."

Tamara refused to speak of it when she briefed them for their new mission at nine bells. "Pavi and Galina need their rest," she said. "They've been taken to better hospital facilities at Eponar."

Eponar. How convenient.

"I need you to turn your attention to a special task, soldiers." Something in her tone made them all sit up a little straighter. Last night they'd been on the brink of a breakthrough in Goreva. Why abandon it?

Tamara read off a typed sheet. "The Elda have launched an attack on the western front, and all available air forces have been requested as backup for the defensive. We need to help our men reach safety. Your primary objective will be to make sure the Elda cannot use any facilities that might be surrendered out of necessity. Your secondary objective is to immobilize any large Elda equipment that you may encounter. You'll be directed via semaphore signals and flares. Do not attempt to engage with the Elda aircraft, particularly their Dragons, *particularly* if you're in an isolated situation. Retreat if they try to engage."

The girls gaped at her. Katya slowly raised a hand. "I don't understand," she said. Her voice lilted up like a question. Was Tamara really saying what they thought?

Tamara set the sheet down. "I don't like it, either," she said. "But this operation is under the direction of Commander Kurcik and his orders are quite clear. He and his aviators will direct you. I'll be coordinating on the ground with both Kurcik and your engineers, so listen to them when you return to stock up. Remember what you told me. Remember what I need. When you see an order, it must be followed. Clear?"

"Yes," they chorused, though some voices lagged behind.

"Good." She checked her watch. "Best of luck, ladies. I expect to see all of you back by dawn. Navigators, come to me for your flight plans."

Revna watched them shuffle out as she adjusted her prosthetics, shaking her head when Magdalena offered to walk with her to the plane. Linné hurried off without waiting for her, flight plan clutched to her chest. Revna tried to breathe deep and remain calm. *Pavi and Galina—surrendered out of necessity—remember what you told me.* She couldn't think about Pavi and Galina right now—about where they were, about what was happening to them, about whether she might be next. Pavi and Galina's situation only proved how tenuous her own was. Guilt still burned in her from the way she'd spoken of her father so callously to the Skarov. She'd betrayed his memory to protect Mama and Lyfa.

She had to keep pushing forward, keep doing what the Union said had to be done.

She finished with her legs and crunched through the snow to her Strekoza. And when she reached it, she nearly turned around and went right back to Tamara's office. Linné and Magdalena faced each other under the starboard wing. A bomb lay in the snow.

"Do your own job before you tell me how to do mine," Magdalena spat.

"At least we've proved I can do mine. What if that bomb had fallen off midflight, or hit the plane when we banked?"

"Well, if it hit *you*, we might have achieved some kind of victory!"

Everything stilled. "That's out of bounds," Linné said softly.

"Great. Tell Tamara all about it. The Skarov can find me in the laboratory." Magdalena stooped and grabbed the bomb, then hefted it easily up to the release trigger. It hooked in with a snap. She stalked over to Revna. "I hate her," she said. "I hate her, and I'll never not hate her, and tonight I hate her more than ever."

"What—"

"Come back safe," Magdalena called over her shoulder as she stomped away.

Revna pulled on the Weave and levered herself into the cockpit. "So?" she said, tapping the inside of her gloves.

Linné's voice dripped with false uninterest as she fumbled half a cigarette out of her case. "So what?"

Maybe Revna should let it go. She had enough to think about on the flight, and when she got back she'd hear Magdalena's side of the story anyway. "What happened?"

"Her mood could curdle milk while it's still inside the mare. Everyone's on edge tonight, but she's abominable."

Revna pulled her goggles down. "I'll talk to her."

"I can fight my own battles." She took one drag, then sighed and stubbed the cigarette back out.

"We're a team. We should be working together."

"I said I'll deal with it." Linné climbed into her seat and sat with more force than necessary, kicking the back of Revna's chair as she did.

Would she deal with it by reporting to Tamara, or by complaining to Tannov? "Power up," Revna mumbled, and tried to ignore Linné in favor of the welcoming feel of the Strekoza as it awoke.

They readied for takeoff. The silence between them was so thick Revna thought she could turn around and take a bite of it. She tried to break it instead. "What do you think really happened to Pavi and Galina?"

"Why do you think I know?" Linné's voice chilled Revna to the bottom of her spine.

Because your only friends are spies? "Because you're smart?"

"I don't know anything that you wouldn't if you'd joined the army to be part of it, and not to follow Zima around like a duckling. It's law—if you disappear in enemy territory, you have to explain where you've been and what you were doing."

"They were making repairs," Revna said.

"Then they have nothing to worry about in Eponar."

The Skarov would give them something to worry about, and something to pay for. And if Linné didn't know that, then she was willfully stupid or she was in their pocket. Either way, Revna didn't feel much like talking further.

They were silent until Tamara directed them off the field. As they lurched into the air, Revna said, "All right. Where are we going?"

"Teltasha Forest," Linné said.

Dread unspooled in Revna's belly. "That's a fair way away." *All the way back home.*

"I can get us there and back. Can you?"

"Everyone thinks so except you," Revna muttered.

"I've already told you I know you can fly." Revna felt the defensive undertone and the beat of Linné's heart pulsing erratically through the engine.

They stuck close to the Mariszkoy mountain range as they flew out, until the mountains became hills and the Intelgard plains became the Teltasha birch forest. Its leaves gleamed silver and white underneath them, hiding the ground beneath a sparkling canvas. A strong wind gave them clear skies and a bright half-moon, and Revna had to compensate to keep them from drifting off course. The open air was liberating after their stuffy mountain runs last night, but the light freedom Revna felt battled against Linné's amplified surliness. Her spark was calmer than their former flights, though, so Revna tried not to let Linné bother her. For now the world's problems couldn't reach up to touch her as she floated on the air.

The black winding ribbon of the Tolga River cut starkly through the land, engorged from the heavy snow. Revna could make out the way the Weave warped to fit around it, forming little tangles where the water burbled over rocks. Above them the stars collected into a massive river of their own that divided the night sky. The borealis glimmered green on the horizon. Revna looked up, searching for the constellations that Lyfa so loved. Maybe when the war was over, she could borrow a plane and fly with Lyfa, take her closer to the stars.

The trees thinned, revealing a blanket of crisp snow as the woodland gave way to the steppe. Snow lynxes, foxes, and hares left dotted tracks, the only interruption in the smooth white. Occasionally Revna spotted larger tracks, from the paws of some enormous cat, that glinted magical around the edges.

The first signs of war came thirty minutes on, with patches of dark mud where soldiers had trampled the earth. The sharp smell of sulfur pricked at Revna's nose. Soon after, they began to see bits of detritus, twisted metal strips and spars, dropped packs, pieces of shrapnel reflecting bursts of light.

Then came the bodies.

No one had bothered to make them pretty or presentable. They lay as twisted as the trash that surrounded them, in dark-stained snowbanks. Some were facedown, limbs askew. Others had turned their heads to the side, or to the sky, their arms outstretched as if they'd used their last moments to reach for something unobtainable. In the moonlight Revna could see slices of skull, slices of arm. Slices of middle. She wasn't sure where the bodies ended and the machines began. She didn't know whether to weep for them or rejoice at their deaths.

The trail widened as they followed it. Metal pieces took on shape and meaning, becoming the lower halves of rail guns or the insectoid legs of palanquins or war beetles or strange, slim Elda craft that Revna had never seen before. Some of them still twitched, energized by terror in their final moments. The bodies grew more numerous, and the mud was churned as though the earth itself had reached out to take part in the battle. The air began to buzz with the sound of Skyhorses on the horizon, little bees spreading fire. The smell of smoke grew thicker and the ground became hazy.

Something moved below. Long, feline bodies stalked through the snow, converging in packs and racing for the front. They left glimmering paw-prints behind them. Revna was about to point them out when she saw dark shapes loping over the ground, bearing in from the west. These creatures were a canine counterpart to the feline ones below. The dogs raised their heads and howled, and then they were a tangled snarl of bodies, spitting and growling.

"What are they?" she said.

"Skarov," Linné said. "Ours and theirs." Something in her tone made Revna shiver. "Look."

Red outlined the horizon. Smoke created a thin film over the stars as it dissipated. Tammin wasn't far.

The world around grew brighter, bright as the morning, and as they drew closer, the scope of the fire expanded until it seemed to stretch for kilometers. Revna imagined the red-gold scar marching across the front, pushing the Elda forward. The Strekoza dipped in sympathy. This was nowhere near any of the God Spaces the Elda claimed to want.

She choked on a lungful of smoke. The wind blew northward; if she angled up, they might escape the worst of it. But then how were they supposed to see the signals sent by Kurcik and his men?

A shadow loomed before them. A roar shook their plane in the air. A steel jaw as large as the Strekoza emerged from the smoke, and a seam split open. For a moment Revna was certain that the mouth would be lined with teeth like knives, ready to close on their little canvas-and-wood plane. But the inside was smooth and empty, save for a pipe at the back of its cold throat.

Red billowed in the pipe. *Fire.* She grabbed the nearest strand of the Weave and hauled on it with all she had. The Strekoza flipped up. Her shoulders slammed against the cage, and the engine cut as Linné screamed. Revna felt a burst of heat as fire spurted underneath them in a stream. The Weave flashed around them, eating the Dragon's surplus spark. She pulled them through a backward loop. "Power," she cried, aiming them up toward the sky.

"*Fuck*," Linné shouted.

Heat seared the side of Revna's face. She wrenched them around to port. The Strekoza evened out. Below, a long, dark shape eased through the shifting smoke.

Their first Dragon.

She took them farther up, trying to breathe deep and avoid the smoke and calm the pounding of her heart all at once. *Do not attempt to engage*, Tamara had said. Would the Dragon pursue them? A hysterical giggle broke out of her. The Strekoza shook as if it were on the verge of falling apart. Linné cursed.

"Do you have to swear like that?" Revna said.

Linné made a disgusted noise. "Do you have to fly like that?"

They'd survived, hadn't they? "I—"

"Get back on course so we can drop the payload."

As they drew nearer, sounds of battle penetrated the red fog. Shapes worked beneath the smoke. The thick walls of Tammin Reaching reared up on the starboard side, and men crawled along them like ants.

Oh, Tammin. It bloomed red and gold and black, the dull gray of its buildings replaced with streaks of soot, with spires of orange flame. The even pulse, the clanging and thumping and pounding that gave Tammin its heart and its purpose, had ceased. All her life, she'd felt the steady beat of Tammin like a clock. Now time stood still as the city died.

"There." Linné tugged Revna's collar and pointed. A young man, maybe younger than them, stood on the reaching's walls. He held a pair of filthy semaphore flags. Revna read panic in every line of his body. He gestured with the flags, then ducked as they flew over.

"Where to?" Revna said.

She heard the puzzled frown in Linné's voice. "I...Double back. He must have said it wrong."

Couldn't Linné admit that her semaphore skills were rusty? "It's hard to see, with all the smoke," she said, trying to sound understanding instead of irritated.

The confusion turned to cold disdain. "I saw him fine. He signaled wrong."

Revna took them back around. The world beneath was a painting in black and red. Hues shifted as the battle moved and fire erupted in pockets all around. The Elda must have dropped incendiaries before launching the attack. She imagined the shelters, bursting with terrified factory workers. But they were safe. She didn't have to think about—

"Revna," Linné said. Revna tensed and pulled them back on course.

Mama and Lyfa would be fine. This was what the shelters were for. The regiment would protect Tammin, and as soon as the mission was over, she'd write them a letter. She was here to save them, not think about them. She flew the plane back over the semaphore boy.

"Do another pass," Linné said. She sounded dumbfounded. The air in the Strekoza hummed with her confusion.

"Even I could see that he did the same thing twice," Revna said.

"Well, he's wrong."

"Maybe he's not."

"He's telling us to bomb the reaching." Linné's voice echoed, hard and unforgiving, in the speaking tube.

"*What?*" Revna strained against the Strekoza's metal fingers. The plane turned cold. "Impossible."

"For once we agree."

She thought of the factory, of the propaganda posters peeling black and blistered outside. She thought of the twisted living metal full of panic and pain. She thought of her little house, engulfed in flame. "You read the signs wrong."

The Strekoza sped forward with a burst of angry spark from Linné. "I know my semaphore signals."

"Then he's confused. Disoriented. What have the others done?"

The rest of the regiment had scattered in the smoke. There was no way to know.

Linné hesitated a moment. But when she spoke, her voice was steady, and her spark was, too. "We find the best Elda target, drop the incendiaries, go back."

"Drop them now, then."

"We can't just drop them. It's a waste."

Linné wasn't supposed to make her feel like a coward. The fact that she was right only made Revna angrier. She suggested whatever caught her eye until Linné agreed to a skirmish between Union soldiers and Elda palanquins. They punched a hole in a palanquin below and were rewarded with a cheer from the Union men.

They turned east and Linné put on a burst of power. Revna leaned forward as if that would speed up the plane. They had to get back to Intelgard. She had to tell Tamara about this mistake.

The light and the noise and the color receded. The air turned sweet and the silence pressed in. They flew over the Teltasha Forest, back over the glassy Tolga River so thick with snowmelt that Revna could hear its sated roar.

Revna concentrated on Linné's breathing, trying to remind herself she wasn't alone in the world. Trying to think of anything but Tammin, and the people she knew there, and the people she loved there, and the people who might be dead there.

They landed at Intelgard to find Tamara pacing the field. She took each step as if something on the ground had personally wronged her. She stalked over as Linné cut the power. The Strekoza ceased its humming, and the cage loosened enough that Revna could lean out of the cockpit.

Magdalena hurried over with an incendiary. Her face was paler than the snow on the ground. She passed Revna without a word and ducked under the starboard wing.

"Magdalena." Revna had to tell her about Tammin. But Magdalena didn't look up.

Tamara radiated rage. "Commander Kurcik is on the radio. He says he gave you girls clear orders, which hardly any of you followed through on."

Clear orders? Revna thought of the boy, frantically waving his semaphore flags from a crumbling wall.

Tamara glared past her into the navigator's seat. "Can you read semaphore signals?"

There was a moment of silence. Then Linné said, "Yes, sir," in clipped, cold tones.

"Are you sure?" Tamara said.

"You tested me. Sir."

"Yet according to Kurcik, you avoided the specified target and wasted your incendiaries."

"You can't mean the reaching—" Revna began.

Tamara's fist came down on the side of the cockpit with a slam that froze Revna's blood. "You promised to follow orders when you joined. You promised again when you began your training, and yet again when you finished it. Now apparently all of you

240

think you have a better grasp on the war than our high commanders? You made the entire regiment look foolish and unreliable. And now Hesovec is right. How are we supposed to win a war with soldiers like you?"

Mama. Lyfa. Reasons chased one another across Revna's mind, but words turned to ash in her mouth. Linné, for once in her life, seemed similarly speechless.

Revna couldn't tear her eyes away from the dash, but she felt Magdalena come up beside her and put a hand on the cockpit. She reached out and squeezed it with everything she had. "You can't ask us..." *You can't ask us to burn our home to the ground.*

"If the Elda take Tammin, they'll have access to major weapons factories and the surrounding farmland."

"But it's our home," Magdalena interjected.

"It's a target," Tamara snarled. "They cannot have it. No cost is too great."

"But we're supposed to protect the Union," Revna added.

"You're supposed to follow orders!" Tamara screamed. Every inch of her trembled—or maybe those were the tears dancing in Revna's eyes.

"Please, Commander," Linné said. She didn't sound angry. She didn't sound cold or matter-of-fact. She didn't sound like Linné at all. She sounded devastated.

Tamara gripped the cockpit so hard Revna felt the pressure through the living metal. "I'm not asking you, Zolonov. I'm telling you. If you're not willing to do the job, then you can go back to your palace in the capital and give your spot to another girl."

They were silent.

"Well?" she said, spreading her arms.

"We can follow orders, ma'am," Revna whispered.

Tamara took a deep breath. Then another. Then she rounded on Magdalena. "Get back to work. If I have to speak with any of you again, you'll all be punished for insubordination. Now stop wasting the night." She stomped toward the edge of the field, where a knot of engineers shrank away from her.

Magdalena's face glistened in the light of her lantern. "D-direct order f-from Kurcik," she stammered around her tears. "Destroy Tammin Reaching. Raze every building. Burn every crop."

The words were like a hammer to Revna's heart. "No," she said.

"Everything," whispered Magdalena. "Come back safe."

✳

So they burned everything. They started with the factories that remained, tearing the buildings apart brick by brick, shattering glass and blowing holes in the equipment. They watched as a munitions factory exploded, leveling the buildings a block in every direction. They dropped Union bombs onto Union buildings, at the direction of Union soldiers and under the watch of no Union god.

In the fire and shadow and smoke, she lost track of what she destroyed. She saw the shell of her palanquin factory, the husk of the commissar's office and the city hall. She saw a gaping crater where a shelter had collapsed, and turned her head away as they flew by. If she didn't see the bodies, she didn't have to know.

The offices were gone, the rich mansions long burned. The

homes nearest the reaching's wall had collapsed in the first bombardment. Only the workers' quarter remained.

The houses were stacked side by side like toys beneath them. Her hands shook. The Strekoza pulsed with nausea. Elena flew past her and a hole opened in a roof below, bursting with red and orange. Tiles spilled from it like tears. The city screamed like a beast in pain.

"Revna," Linné said. She barely heard. Her mind was static. "You have to line up the shot."

The buildings began to crumple, one by one. Smoke thickened, rising to swallow them. But Revna could spot one little house still standing. The birch tree in front spread its naked arms like a prayer.

"We have to. Tamara will throw you out."

Her heart beat thick and fast. *You're cursed, you're cursed.*

Linné's hand hovered by her shoulder. "Revna," she said again.

The Weave wrapped silky threads around them, tangling as they turned. Linné cut power and Revna brought them down in a perfect dive. Linné released the bombs and powered up. They flew away.

Revna didn't look back.

✳

They flew until the city was gone. Then Magdalena attached bombs of liquid fire, and they bombarded the farmland that had fed Revna all her life. The whole world crackled and roared around them. The stink of charred grass and roots, the too-sweet scent of the apple orchards burning, mingled with the smell of melting steel. And beneath it Revna caught a sharp odor, meaty and coppery and musky, acrid and thick, burning meat and seared liver and so much worse.

She didn't want to think about the smells. She didn't want to think about any of it.

They flew until the sky in the east was lighter than in the west. When Magdalena ran up empty-handed, Revna knew it was finally over.

She sagged in her chair as Linné cut the power. She didn't want to move, not even to stretch her legs. She could sleep in the cockpit for all she cared. Only she didn't want to sleep. She didn't want the dreams she'd have.

Behind her, Linné sniffed. Revna turned her head as far as she could. Linné rummaged in her pockets, then blew her nose loudly. Linné, crying.

Linné caught her staring. "It was a bad thing we did tonight."

It was, perhaps, the kindest thing she'd ever heard Linné say. The only reply she could think to make was "Tammin was my home."

But Tammin had also been useful and surrendered by necessity. The Union's orders on that were clear.

Linné unfastened her harness and used Revna's chair to push herself up. "I'm sorry." And she sounded as though she meant it. "I didn't join for this."

When Revna pulled herself from the cockpit, Linné was there with Magdalena to grab an arm, and they limped away together.

"I can't believe…" Magdalena didn't seem to know how to finish.

"We had to," Revna said. The words twisted her heart like a knife.

Linné opened her mouth, then closed it. Opened it again. "You flew well tonight," she said.

"Yes," Revna mumbled. She had flown well. The Union required it of her, after all. And what the Union demanded, she gave.

15

FAITH AND LOYALTY

Linné pulled off her gloves and rubbed her frozen nose as she headed toward the men's bar. She didn't care what stupid rules they had. She didn't feel like pretending tonight. Part of her had burned away under that relentless barrage of fire. And she couldn't feel most of her face.

It was near dawn and the bar was largely empty. A couple of aviators sat in the corner with warm cups. They raised their brows when she came in but turned away when she glared.

The soldier behind the bar was less sympathetic. "You've been in here before," he said, pulling out a glass and pouring himself a finger of dark sugar beet rum. "You know the rules."

"I'll pay you extra," she said.

"That's not the point."

"What'll they do, send you to the iron mines? Make you bomb your own side?" Her throat closed up as she spat out the words. *Not here.* No more crying, and not here of all places. She bit her tongue until the burn in her eyes subsided. "Give me something."

Maybe he gave her something out of respect or understanding. Maybe he gave her something out of pity. She watched him pour a measure of amber rum into a cup, then top it off with tea. When she handed him a ten-crown note, he passed it back. "Just tea, all right?" he said, and winked.

He was definitely feeling pity. "Take it," Linné said. "Make a tab."

The kindness in his eyes dimmed and his mouth twitched down. "Your father know you drink this much?"

What would her father have said about destroying their own? He must know. If he hadn't approved the strategy himself, he'd have heard about it by radio. She wondered if it weighed on him, or if it was a normal night. After all, he made decisions about the war every day.

She collapsed at a table by the corner. Her nose stung as feeling began to return to it. The radio played softly, a crooning love tune for the early hours of the morning. She wanted to kick it across the room.

A figure sat down across from her. "Go away," she said.

"Hard night," said Tannov. She hadn't seen him come in, but he'd gotten a drink, sugar beet rum without the tea. "I listened to the radio dispatches."

"Was that before or after you interrogated Pavi and Galina?"

Tannov raised his hands in defense. "Pavi and Galina are recovering in a fine hospital. I'm sure they'll be rejoining you in no time."

"Right."

"Don't punish me for Union law, Linné. Those girls were gone for five hours. Would you have let them go if you were in my position?"

Linné would never have been in his position. "What do you want?"

"You look like you've had it rough." His wide eyes seemed so innocent, so honest. Maybe this was how he got people to spill their secrets. How he kept getting her to take walks with him. "You look like you need a drink, which you've managed, and you look like you need a friend, which you haven't."

"Asshole," Linné said.

"What, are all the girls waiting outside to talk to you? Because they weren't when I came in a minute ago," he said, and now there was an edge to his tone.

Linné sipped her tea. By the time she lowered her glass, he was back to the no-cares expression he always wore.

"Sit with me awhile," he said. "It's not going to kill you."

She didn't know how to reply to that, so she didn't. She drained her glass and pushed it toward him. "I made a tab."

"Bad habit to get into, trust me." He carried her glass up to the bar all the same, and his own as well. The barman leaned around him to look at her, but if he had any serious objections, he didn't bring them up with the infamous Information Unit.

When Tannov returned, she took the cup he offered and held

it between her hands, leaning in so that the steam hit her face. The throbbing in her nose lessened. Was she imagining things, or did Tannov's typical smile seem forced around the edges?

"Would you have done it?" she said. "Bombed Tammin?"

The smile flattened. "Of course," he said. "An order is an order." That was the Skarov answer. The old Tannov wouldn't have been so quick to judge. But she saw uncertainty in the way he stared into his glass, sloshing the rum around inside. His amber eyes were wide and serious, and utterly impossible to read.

"Maybe it was a trick," she pressed. "Maybe we failed again."

Tannov shook his head, and the sad smile was back. He stretched out a hand to take one of hers. Linné pulled away. He didn't seem to notice. "The Elda already have a strong advantage with the Skyhorses and Dragons. If they captured our working factories, they could establish a supply line far too close to the front. The war would be over for us. It was the right thing to do."

It didn't feel like the right thing to do. But saying so might be treason, so Linné kept her opinion to herself.

"Nobody blames you for hesitating," Tannov said.

Did he mean it? Were his outstretched hand and earnest gaze all fake? "Commander Kurcik does," Linné said.

"Maybe," he conceded.

"And Zima."

"She would have hesitated, too. That's why she was so hard on you for it."

"And maybe Revna." She said this to herself, almost quietly enough to be masked by the croon of the radio. Almost.

Tannov brought his glass to his lips. "Is she still your pilot?"

"Who else would be?" She downed her cup. The tea was getting cold anyway. The alcohol buzzed in her, making her waspish. "What's it to you?"

"I told you once." He rose to get another round.

Revna *should* blame her. It was Linné who had refused to read the semaphore signal and gotten them in trouble. She'd never imagined an order like that. She thought of the scorched fields and torched houses her ground unit had seen as they marched from battle to battle. She'd assumed the Elda had destroyed her Union land. But what if the razing had been planned by the generals? By her father?

The Union always had reasons, she reminded herself. Kurcik hadn't gotten command of the Ryddan steppe by being a fool. FAITH AND LOYALTY UNTO DEATH, as the posters said. It wasn't her place to question.

Tannov slid back into the seat across from her with two glasses of amber rum. "Let's toast," he said abruptly. His mouth twisted in a bitter imitation of a smile.

"To what?"

"To a future Hero of the Union. You do what you have to do."

She resisted the urge to make a rude gesture. They clinked glasses and drank. The rum burned like lit lamp oil all the way down. Linné massaged her throat and concentrated on Tannov, waiting for the dizziness to stop.

"I do what I have to do," she said, but she wasn't so sure.

"You know I believe in you, don't you?" The bitter smile remained. His eyes shone with something like a fever. "Once, we said we'd be Heroes of the Union together. You can still do it."

250

Linné pressed a thumbprint onto her empty glass. "Of course I can." She barely stopped herself from saying, *Can you?* "Why wouldn't I?"

"Careful." He tapped the table. "Being the general's daughter only gets you so far."

"I seem to recall a cocky Information Officer telling me that all I needed to do was convince the colonel to let us fly." And look how well that had turned out.

"And you need to remain in good standing," he added.

"I am in good standing."

"As long as your pilot doesn't get in the way."

Tannov swam in and out of focus. Did she need one more rum, or one less? "What's that supposed to mean?"

"She disobeyed orders. She talked back to your commander."

"How do you know what my pilot says?"

"I know everything, Linné." Tannov leaned in. "It's not a good start to a military career. Do you want to go down with her?"

Faith and loyalty, Linné thought. "She lived there. What would you have done?"

"I would kill my own mother before I let the Elda capture her. Why wouldn't Roshena do the same?" He leaned forward. "Think about it. Her father's a political prisoner. She joined your unit because she was offered an incentive that would erase her family's criminal past. She could denounce her father a thousand times and I wouldn't believe her. It's us she hates. The Union. Maybe she wants revenge, or maybe she wants the Elda to succeed. Either way, she's not on our side."

"She did bomb her own reaching," Linné pointed out.

251

"On threat of disciplinary action."

Linné searched Tannov's face for any sign of sympathy. He really was different now. "If you're so sure, why not arrest her?" He was a blank mask, hard and foreign. "You can't," she realized. "Pavi and Galina broke rules, but Revna hasn't done anything." And Commander Zima protected her. "It's all conjecture."

"Revna hasn't done anything *yet*," Tannov said. "It's only a matter of time. Don't get caught in the crossfire. Don't put your life and career on the line for someone who doesn't even want to fly with you."

Faith and loyalty. She could put faith in her pilot or be loyal to her Union. She couldn't do both.

✳

Revna ought to have been sleeping. Not that many of the girls were. They lay in silence, breathing evenly, pretending together. Shapes swirled in the darkness, of fire, of headless men, of gutted buildings. Her mind supplied the screams, the crackling, the pounding of blood in her ears. She imagined her mother and Lyfa, limbs charring in the spark fire brought by the Dragons and the Strekozy. First her father had been taken away because of her. Now the rest of her family was gone at her hand. And all for the good of the Union.

It's not true, she told herself. *They're not dead.* But if they were—

Maybe she'd get a letter commending their ultimate service. Maybe she'd get nothing.

She began to tremble. She hated the Union and everything it

had done to her. The false hope. The promise of something better if she only fell in line. Her father might as well be dead, and nobody cared. Mama and Lyfa might be buried in the rubble of Tammin Reaching, and nobody cared. Nobody cared if she offered her life or her family or her everything.

There had to be something she could do. She rolled to the edge of the bed and fumbled for her prosthetics, pulling on the socks and pins, then the legs themselves. They might be all that was left of her family now. But she couldn't think like that. Grabbing her writing kit, she made her way out the door as quietly as she could.

It had snowed again after they'd landed and the ground was a fresh white blanket, crusted over with frost. Someone had sprinkled salt on the boards. She'd have to be extra careful cleaning her prosthetics later. They hated salt. She stepped carefully, toes crunching on the snow and chipping at the ice underneath.

The mess was empty, except for a bored cook cleaning a pot. Revna collapsed into the nearest chair. She didn't realize anyone had followed her until Linné took the seat next to her. "Couldn't sleep?"

Of course. Of *course* it had to be her. And she smelled sickly sweet, as if she'd been drinking. Revna mustered her best disdainful glower. "Obviously."

For a moment the mask slipped and Linné flashed a brief, bitter smile. Her eyes and voice were clear, for all that she smelled like cheap liquor. "You're thinking about your family."

"You don't know what I think." About the base, about the army, and yes, about her family. *Or about you.*

"Do you want some tea?" Linné got up without waiting for an answer.

It would be easier in the long run to try to make friends. But as she watched Linné face off against the cook, arms folded, something in Revna seethed and boiled. Linné always demanded her way. She never said thank you, and she never tried to learn from others. Maybe Linné could learn something from being treated the way she treated everyone else.

And Revna didn't have to talk to Linné. She was busy. She took out her writing kit and set a clean, cream-colored sheet on the table. Her fingers fumbled as she scraped her pocketknife against her pencil.

How did you address a letter to someone who might be dead?

The unwritten letter was a perfect abomination. Any thought she put down would mar its surface. But leaving it blank meant that she'd never send it. And maybe she'd never know if Mama and Lyfa had survived.

She scratched out words in a daze. Linné set a teacup down next to her with a clink. "Sorry," she muttered, though Revna wasn't sure what she was sorry for. Revna picked up the cup and took a gulp. Cold tea washed down her throat.

"Cook said he'd make fresh tea with breakfast, and not before," Linné explained, taking a sip from her own cup. She made a face. Revna pushed her teacup away and looked back at her page.

Dear Mama,
I hope you are well, and Lyfa, too. I am

She balled up the paper and flicked it away. How could she even think of writing soulless garbage like that to her family? They deserved better, and she knew she could do better. She pulled out a fresh sheet and tried again.

Dear Mother,
I heard about what happened to Tammin. I hope you could stay in the Protectors bunker. I miss you but things are going well and

She stopped again. She'd gone from garbage to outright lies. She imagined her mother clutching the letter with charred fingers, tears cleaning a path down her sooty cheeks, clinging to the hope that her little girl would save the day.

Linné took out a rascidine cigarette. "It's difficult." She spoke the words so coolly. As if she wanted to make casual conversation while she smoked. Her eyes rested on Revna's pencil.

Revna's hand convulsed around the paper, bunching it up into another ball. "Are you reading my letter?" Her throat closed off around *letter*, nearly choking her in her own rage.

Their eyes locked. And Revna saw, for the first time, a sort of sorrow, of sympathy. That Linné didn't understand her but could acknowledge the tragedy.

"Was . . . *is* your entire family there?"

"Everyone who's left," said Revna. She didn't feel like elaborating, and Linné didn't ask.

Linné took the crumpled papers and smoothed them out. "I

used to see this a lot in my old regiment," she said. "If you run out of paper, you'll have to formally request more, and it could take weeks. Practice writing on these. Then you can get a fresh sheet when you're ready."

Revna took them back, pressing on a wrinkled edge. Her head filled with memories of Lyfa pulling the covers over her head each morning as Mama drew the blackout curtains. Mama making rolls in the shape of cat faces. Papa, tall and broad, slim screwdrivers in his hands as he adjusted her prosthetics. Now each of those memories came with the twisting smell of fire and ash, smoke and melting metal.

Her pencil scratched over the paper without permission from her brain. She heard Linné's desperate voice saying, *He's telling us to bomb the reaching.* The squeal of the trigger as it released Magdalena's creation. She felt the weight of the Union pressing down until she couldn't breathe, squashing her until she lost the ability to do anything but obey. There was nothing, *nothing* she could write that would possibly encompass all she needed to say.

She didn't know how long she sat there. Linné sat, too, drinking her tea, looking bedraggled. Other girls came in and ate and left again. Revna ignored them. She ignored the bowl of porridge when it was set beside her, too.

"Eat," said Linné.

"No."

"Eat, or I'll have Zima take you off the evening roster."

"You wouldn't." Revna looked up. "You couldn't stand to miss a flight yourself." But now that her concentration was broken, the smell of the porridge made her remember her stomach. Dinner had been worlds ago. Her brain felt heavy, as if each stroke of her pencil had dropped a pebble into her skull. She pulled the bowl toward her.

"Good, isn't it?" Linné said.

"Needs salt," Revna grumbled.

Linné's mouth turned up at the corner.

"Why are you being so nice to me?" Revna said around a mouthful.

"What do you mean?"

"You got me tea. You got me breakfast. You've been sitting with me this whole time. Why?"

Linné opened her mouth to reply. Then she stopped. She seemed to rehearse the words in her head before she spoke. "If my home had burned last night, I know what I'd be doing today."

"What?" Revna said.

"I'd be screaming," she said. "Inside and out." Her eyes flicked away, down to the table, as if she were ashamed to be so frank. Then the space between her eyebrows creased.

Revna followed her gaze. Her two sheets of paper were filled to the brim with writing. Big letters, small ones, fluid ones, cramped ones. Creeping down the margins, written over one another, seething on the page. A crawling mass of thought.

One sentence, written over and over and over and over.

Please don't be dead.

"Please," Revna said. "I'm—" She couldn't say *fine*. She wasn't fine—even she knew that. Everyone knew that. "I can fly."

"I know," said Linné, but she was looking at her oddly.

"I need to do it." She'd rather see anything burn than Tammin, night after night. She needed revenge. Revenge against the stupid boy with his semaphore signals, against Tamara for screaming at them. Against Commander Kurcik, whoever he was, for making the order in the first place. Against the Union—no. *Never* against the Union, never again. But against the Elda for choosing Tammin as their next march. Against the Elda for turning the pale blue winter into a winter of soot and ash. "I can do it."

"I believe you," Linné said.

✳

Of course she didn't believe her.

Linné pushed out of the mess, nearly barreling into Katya and Elena as they opened the door.

"Watch it!" Katya snapped. Elena sighed peevishly.

She didn't want to watch it. She wanted to clear her head. She wanted to believe in her pilot. And she wanted another cigarette. Scratch that—she *needed* another cigarette. And she needed to talk to someone. But who? Revna was in no condition to talk to anyone. And she already knew what Tannov would say. The truth hung somewhere between them, and Linné did not know how to grasp it. Before Tammin, Linné would have trusted her Union, given it the faith and loyalty it demanded. Revna's grief was real, but why had she faltered in the bombing of Tammin?

You faltered, too. Maybe you're the traitor.

She clenched spark in a fist as she shoved a cigarette into her mouth. She *was* faithful. She *was* loyal. She'd proved it before and she'd do so again.

Clouds piled up against the Karavels and the wind hummed

over the plains. It slapped her face and wrapped around her neck like winter's scarf. The chill of it was enough to knock the breath out of her.

She heard a faint sniffling over the wind. Boot prints led around the side of the mess. *No*, she thought. *No, no, no.* She rounded the corner and almost tripped over the huddling figure. "Oh—" She barely stopped herself from saying *shit*. "Sorry."

Magdalena looked smaller and more miserable than Linné had ever seen her. She'd drawn her shoulders in and pulled her knees up to her chin. Her hair lay tangled against her arms, and her freckled cheeks were blotchy from crying.

"I'm fine." She sniffed. A fat teardrop slid down her jaw.

She came from Tammin, too. Linné slid down next to her, trying not to think of the mud stain she'd have to wash out of her uniform later. "You don't have to be fine." She drew on her cigarette, holding the sour smoke in her mouth as she thought about her next words. "It was the worst thing I've ever done." She could be loyal to the Union and admit that. The war had given her purpose, hope, friends, determination. It had filled every crack in her. But now the war itself was cracked.

Magdalena leaned in. For a paralyzing moment Linné thought she wanted a hug. But then she inhaled deeply. Linné sighed in relief and dug her cigarette case out of her back pocket. "Ran out?"

"Last night. I couldn't—" Magdalena's fingers shook. The cigarette tumbled to the ground.

Linné picked it up and wiped off the snow. She lit it with a touch of spark and handed it over. "You couldn't stop yourself." She'd been there. After the Thirty-First had been routed outside

Adovic, she thought she couldn't breathe without a cigarette. "You had a lot of family in Tammin?" Shit. Have. *Have.*

"Friends."

Linné winced. Friends would be even worse. She didn't want her father to die, and not only because he ran a large chunk of the Union. But she didn't share jokes with him. She'd never sworn at her father, or borrowed a cigarette from him, or gotten drunk with him. Her friends had been the family she needed for three long years.

And now the closest things she had were a suspect pilot and two Skarov agents.

"I don't know what you're going through," she admitted. "But Revna does. She could use your help."

Magdalena shook her head. Tears hung from her eyelashes, slid down her face when she blinked. "Not like this. I need a minute." She sucked on her cigarette. "I need to collect myself. She needs her friends to be strong."

Revna's neat letters scrawled across Linné's mind, over and over. Maybe Revna did need someone to be strong for her, to tell her that she was doing well. Or maybe she needed someone to tell her that she wasn't doing well and that she didn't have to be.

A man's voice echoed inside the mess, deep and angry. It was followed by a thunk. Someone screamed.

Magdalena was up in a shot. She grabbed Linné's hand and pulled her to her feet. They tore around to the door together and burst inside.

Revna, Katya, and several other girls stood in the middle of the mess. Revna's face was the color of fresh snow, her lips two bruises, and her eyes dark, hateful stars. She held her palms out, almost like a peace offering. The rest of the mess stared at her.

An aviator lay crumpled against the wall. His friends surrounded him. Linné recognized the good-looking ass who'd set off the shooting contest checking the aviator's pulse.

Linné crossed the mess to Revna in a few strides. "What did you do?"

Revna took one, two steps backward and fell into her chair. Magdalena knelt beside her and grabbed a hand. Revna didn't seem to notice.

"What happened?" Tannov's words fluttered in her mind, unwelcome. *Treason. Revenge.*

Revna wouldn't look at her. "I did everything," she whispered.

"Revna," said Magdalena, shooting Linné a warning look, "it's all right. Tell me."

"He called us deserters," Katya said. She wiped at a wet patch under her eye, but her voice was strong and clear. "He called us traitors."

"I did everything they asked me to," Revna said. Her voice was stronger, but it still trembled. "What have *you* ever done?"

"You crazy bitch," Good-Looking Ass said. Time on the base hadn't improved his temper. "You could have killed him."

Revna leaned around Magdalena. "So what? The Union doesn't care about you—"

"Stop it," Linné yelled. Revna's eyes shifted to her, and behind the grief she saw resentment. Revna thought she was siding with the boys.

261

Magdalena wrapped Revna in a protective hug. Revna's pale face screwed up, dangerously close to spouting real treason.

Fear punched an icy fist into Linné's stomach. *Revna hasn't done anything* yet. Maybe this was the excuse Tannov was waiting for. Starting fights, hospitalizing fellow soldiers, and bad-mouthing the Union? None of that would look good in her file.

Faith and loyalty. The air seemed to press in against her. Being loyal to the Union meant betraying Revna. But if she tried to protect Revna, what else would the girl do in her anger?

Linné didn't know who deserved her faith, but she wouldn't let Revna destroy herself.

The male soldiers checked on the downed man. "He's still unconscious," Good-Looking Ass said as he stood.

"So do something useful and take him to the hospital," Linné said. She was too weary to try another pissing contest. They all needed a rest.

Good-Looking Ass jerked his head at Revna. "What about her?"

"You're not her supervisor. I am," Linné said.

Katya's hand closed over her wrist. *Not now.* She tried to shake it away, but the girl's grip only tightened. "You can't," Katya whispered.

Linné maintained eye contact with the soldier. "Go help your man."

"Linné," Katya murmured as he turned away. "You can't report it."

The downed soldier groaned as he was lifted and carried out. Linné's shoulders slumped. "It's my job."

"Screw your job. Screw the rules. Something bad could happen to her."

Something bad had already happened. And lying wouldn't make it better. "Zima and Hesovec are going to find out," Linné said. "Everyone saw." And covering it up wouldn't make Revna seem more innocent. Their best hope was for Zima to pass judgment before the Skarov even heard of it. She tried to ignore the little voice that said, *And I'll be loyal, like I always am.* That wasn't the point. It wasn't. "I have to. I'm sorry."

Katya's mouth turned down in disgust. "Yeah," she said. "Right."

Linné saw Tannov in the distance as she hurried out of the mess. She felt his eyes on her back all the way to Commander Zima's office.

✳

The radio dispatches had poured in all night. Accusations, demands, anger. No one had bothered to distinguish between the Night Raiders and Day Raiders. It was all the 146th. The lack of distinction hadn't exactly pleased the Day Raiders, who'd felt their image slipping thanks to their counterparts. One had stopped to take a verbal shot at them as they huddled together in the mess. "I've never seen anyone train so much to shoot so little."

"Leave it," one of his companions had muttered.

It was too late. His ire had roused Katya. She stopped combing her fingers through her hair long enough to give him a death glare that would have made Linné proud. "We don't need to be lectured by a bunch of flyboys who slept through the night."

"Hey, we did our jobs. If you want to play at being deserters and traitors, you could have tried not to get us involved." He clenched his fists, as if he was ready for a fight.

The word *traitors* hung thick in the air. The soldier's friends sidled away, enough to create a gap.

"We're not traitors," Katya said.

"You're certainly not soldiers. You're pathetic," he sneered. "Fly home."

It was the word *home* that did it. Home was nowhere now; home was nothing. And he was nothing, too. Revna flicked her wrist, violently enough to send a thread of the Weave whipping forward. The edge caught him in the middle of his smug face, sending him straight back into the wall.

She hadn't meant to hit him so hard. But she didn't really care, either.

∗

Everyone who had been in the mess for the fight was called up before Hesovec. Revna heard half his rant and cared about none of it. As spit flew from his mouth, she imagined him in battle, fixed to the wrong end of a bayonet. Blood spraying instead of saliva. His life was worth as much—as little—as the soldier she'd thrown against the wall. Hadn't that been Tamara's point? No one was too important for the war. Not Revna, not the civilians of Tammin. She felt hollow. Nothing around her mattered.

After his rant, Hesovec sent the rest of the 146th to the field to wash down the planes. But Tamara called Revna, Linné, and

Magdalena to her office instead. The three of them squeezed through the door together and stood, hands clasped behind them.

Tamara poured them each a cup of tea. The thin golden liquid steamed in their tiny ceramic cups. Twelve hours ago she'd been raging at them, pounding on the Strekoza's cockpit. Now she acted as if it had never happened.

"You'll be happy to hear that Ludovic has suffered no lasting damage from your altercation," she said.

"Ludovic?" Revna echoed.

"The private you rendered unconscious. From what I understand, you quite lost your temper," Tamara said.

She guessed she had. But Ludovic had deserved it. He didn't take precedence over the war. And he didn't get to treat her as though she were a joke. Not after last night.

"I know Tammin was difficult for everyone. But I met the two of you in Tammin, didn't I?" Tamara said.

"Yes, ma'am," said Magdalena. She squeezed Revna's arm. A sliver of anguish pierced that hollow feeling around her.

"I understand your reluctance last night. And your temper this morning."

Revna wanted to explain. It was dark, it was Tammin, Linné made the call, *it was Tammin*—but one thing she'd learned from her navigator was that you put your head down and took your punishment.

"I will have to discipline you for your demonstration in the mess. But first I must be clear: Our pilots need to keep their calm. If you lose your head during a battle, it could mean both your deaths and the loss of our plane, and you know what a blow that would be to the regiment."

The hollowed-out shell around her broke. "I can fly," she said. "I only—he made me—"

"Are you clearheaded enough?" Tamara picked up her pen and pulled the evening roster toward her. Ready to eliminate them.

"I can do it." Revna hated the desperate edge to her voice. But she *could* do it. She *had* to do it.

"Can she?" Tamara looked to her engineer.

"Of course," Magdalena said without hesitating. Revna wanted to grab her hands and kiss them.

Then Tamara turned to Linné. Linné tapped the side of her cup as if she really were thinking about it. She'd say yes. She wouldn't accept sitting around the base while everyone else ran off to fight.

"No."

Revna's heart dropped like a stone. "What?"

Linné turned her cup around in her hands. A flush crept up her neck. "She can't. She needs time."

"I can fight." Revna leaned forward, grabbing the desk for support. "Please, let me stay on duty."

"Look at her," Linné said.

"*Shut up*," Revna choked out.

Tamara cut in. "That's enough. All of us feel the blow of Tammin, Revna. It's no shame that you feel it more than others. Your team is grounded until further notice. I recommend that you try to get some sleep, then report to me for your discipline. I'll reassess your situation in a week." She lowered her pen and struck a thick black line through their names.

Tamara's words left her ears ringing. A week? A scream swelled in her chest. She squashed it down. Screaming would only prove her unfit after all.

Apparently, a week was more than Linné had bargained for, too. "For all of us? Please, Commander, I'm more than capable."

"It seems you're more than capable of fighting. With anyone, including your comrades. I won't give you a new pilot and ground a different navigator. If you can find someone willing to switch, I'll approve it," Tamara snapped. "But don't burden me with your petty problems." She set her typewriter on top of the papers with a thud and began to type. "Good afternoon."

Linné was out of Tamara's office before she'd stopped talking. Magdalena shot off after her. By the time Revna got outside, Magdalena had grabbed Linné's wrist and jerked her around. "How could you?"

Red blazed in Linné's cheeks, but she met Revna's eye. "I saw how you were in the mess. Everyone else might be willing to ignore it, but I can't."

"And trying to abandon me?" Revna managed to say. She wasn't surprised, but the betrayal still stung.

"We never wanted to fly with each other anyway," Linné said. "You need time off. That doesn't mean I do." But her gaze dropped, and Revna heard the thinness of her voice. She was lying about something.

"I thought you cared about honor," Magdalena said. She pushed Linné so hard that the girl tripped over her own boots and landed hard on the boards. "Your pathetic begging is the most disgusting thing I've ever seen. Revna's lucky to be free of you."

"I'm trying to make sure she doesn't kill herself," Linné growled. She climbed to her feet, wincing, and shook out her ankle. "I'm trying to give her what she needs, not what she wants." Her boots crunched over the half-frosted plywood as she limped away.

Revna's anger boiled over. "How could you possibly know what I need?" she yelled at Linné's back. Right now she needed to hit something, to fly as hard and as fast as she could, to leave a trail of fire in her wake. She didn't need false friends who spent more time helping the Information Unit than helping her.

Magdalena wrapped an arm around her shoulders. "We'll fix this," she said.

"Yes," Revna said. They'd fix this. But she didn't know how.

✳

Revna had to submit to an examination by the base doctor, and then she was turned loose for three torturous nights. Her Strekoza sat lonely on the field, quivering next to Pavi's. Everywhere she turned she saw reminders of what happened to innocent people who ended up in the wrong place. Yet she was the most treasonous person she knew, and she still hung on to her position.

Tamara made her file papers but let her off after midnight, when Magdalena took her into the engineers' workshop to help pack bombs in crates of hay. Linné vanished somewhere, and Revna didn't care where.

When she couldn't take the noise of the laboratory, she went to the mess. She tried to write. She tried not to think about flying, about how free and powerful she felt in the cockpit. When she saw other soldiers, she tried to remember they were living instead of imagining them dead. Sometimes the cook brought her things, so she forgave him for gawking at her legs. She wished that his fixation made her angrier, but she was too used to that kind of attention.

Her reprieve came on the fourth day. Revna looked up from her blank letter as a group of engineers flocked into the mess, each arguing her own point as loudly as she could. She spotted Magdalena in the middle of them, looking grim.

"Freezing the guns will make them as useless as burning them, and maybe they'll freeze the soldiers, too," Nina said. "We should improve the cold design and make them battle-ready."

"Freeze a gun one day and it'll be working again the next," Olya argued. "Destroy it by fire and the Elda will have to wait weeks to get a replacement, if they can even get one at all."

"But Elda who are frozen to death can't use the replacements, either," Nina said.

Couldn't they shut up? She usually found their arguments funny, but today she wanted to shake each of them by the shoulders. Didn't they understand? The next person they froze or burned might not be Elda at all.

Magdalena broke away and headed for Revna's table, looking troubled. For a moment Revna thought she was coming to commiserate. But she pressed Revna's hand and said, "Tamara wants to speak with you."

Revna's first thought was a burst of hope. Maybe Tamara had news of her family. Her second was that they'd finally decided to send her north to Papa. Whichever it was, she might as well get it over with.

She let Magdalena walk her down to Tamara's office. They stopped at the door. "Do you want me to come in with you?"

"No." She had to be strong.

Tamara sat with one hand holding a telephone receiver and the other scribbling notes. She nodded as Revna entered and gestured to the chair. When she was finished, she set the receiver down and folded her hands. She regarded Revna without smiling, but there was a gentleness in her eyes. "We're halfway through the week."

So? Revna reined in her temper. "I'm feeling a lot better." She wasn't, but she hadn't had any more outbursts, and surely that meant something.

Tamara leaned across the desk and squeezed her hand. "I want to explain something. Goreva Reaching was my hometown." Revna winced in sympathy. "A lucky shot killed my navigator during the retreat. When we tallied our losses, there was only one thing on my mind: vengeance. I wanted to pick up my rifle and follow the boys to war, to see the look of suffering on the faces of the Elda, to burn their homes as they'd burned mine. I even wished I'd died there as a hero instead of living without everything I'd known. *I know* how it is." Except Tamara had tried to defend her home, and Revna had helped obliterate hers. "The anger can feel like your whole life. But it can't *be* your whole life. Do you understand?"

"I guess?" Why was Tamara telling her all this?

Tamara put her face in her hands. "I need to reinstate you early," she said through her fingers.

The fires bloomed hot in Revna's mind. Vengeance. "I'm ready."

"I can't have you breaking down on a mission, Revna. If you can't do it, there might be some other way..."

"To do what?" Revna said.

Tamara lowered her hands. Her red-rimmed eyes seemed to look everywhere but at Revna. For a moment she seemed so young. Like a university student. Her voice trembled. "The doctor has declared you physically fit to fly. If I don't approve you, the Information Unit has the right to investigate your mental ability."

Revna bit back the urge to laugh. It always came down to the Skarov. She could almost feel them, tightening the strings of an invisible noose around her. Maybe she should let them win. What more could the war take away from her?

But the Union demanded, and so she would give. If her family was truly gone, then this base and the people on it were all she had left. And perhaps she could give the Elda an extra dose of vengeance for herself. "I can fight. I won't break."

They locked eyes. Tamara nodded slowly. "If you say you're ready, I believe you. And we could use you tonight. As long as you can fly with Linné."

"Did she speak to you again?" Revna tried to keep the sneer out of her voice.

She evidently hadn't succeeded. Tamara pursed her lips. "Your navigator is valuable, and your plane is valuable. And you're valuable, whether you believe it right now or not. Do you swear that you can keep the three of you safe? On your honor, on your reaching?"

Tamara hadn't denied talking to Linné, and that was probably as close to an admission as Revna was going to get. "On all of it, I swear." She made fists of her hands, squeezing until the rage she felt went out of her words and into her palms. She *would* hold it together. If only to show Linné what a wrongheaded, self-centered harpy she was. If only to make the Skarov wait a little longer.

Tamara sighed. "Don't make me regret this, Miss Roshena."

16

FIRE AND GLORY

When Revna trudged into Tamara's office at nine bells, the muttering spread. She didn't look at anyone, not even when Katya leaned around Nadya to squeeze her shoulder.

"Tonight we have another special assignment," Tamara said. "I know that many of you want to strike back at the Elda, especially after what happened in Tammin. This might be our big chance. Fighting on the steppe has diminished and we've been requested to scout along the southern front. Ground scouts for the Forty-Sixth and Seventy-Seventh Night Armies have reported rumors of a new weapon being prepared near the front, possibly an aircraft even larger than a Dragon."

The room broke out in incredulous murmurs. "Impossible," Katya whispered.

"They're calling it a Serpent. It will be under cover, but not too far from the front. Spies have indicated that it lies somewhere between Korplin and Tavgard. We've located three possible targets, and we're sending three teams to each. One team will assist the Forty-Sixth and Seventy-Seventh on the southeastern front. If your team finds a potential target, your orders are to do everything in your power to destroy it." Tamara's mouth sagged. "No price is too high."

Revna knew what that meant. Not their planes, and not their lives.

"Once you've released your bombs, return to the base and report what you've found. Speed is essential here. Questions?" Tamara met each girl's eye in turn. Katya tucked a curl behind her ear and smiled bravely. Asya straightened her uniform. Elena looked slightly green, but Nadya puffed out her chest, ready enough for both of them. Revna willed all her strength, all her readiness into her posture. Tamara couldn't change her mind now. "Your assignments are here. Best of luck."

The girls surged forward. When the crowd had dispersed, Revna scanned the list for her name. She knew what she would find, but she couldn't help the desperate hope that hammered at her. Maybe Tamara had listened to them. Maybe one of the other pilots had taken pity.

ROSHENA - ZOLONOV - CHUIKOVA had been written under the last header, KORPLIN REACHING AND NEARBY ENVIRONS.

Magdalena gave her a half hug. "We're back on the roster."

"Yes." She should have felt triumphant. But all she could think was that she'd spend ten excruciating hours with someone she hated, and who hated her. It might have been easier to take if

Tamara had put them back in combat. But instead of revenge, she got reconnaissance.

"Are you all right?" Magdalena asked.

Revna pressed a sarcastic reply between her teeth and held it there. "Fine," she said. "I'm fine." And she would be.

She walked to the field with Magdalena. It would be her first time in the cockpit since Tammin. *You're cursed.* She pushed back against the thought. What did she have to be cursed about now? Her whole family was probably dead.

Katya and Elena stood at the side of the field, deep in discussion. Revna and Magdalena veered toward them. As they came up, Katya reached out to adjust Revna's collar. "I'm point. We thought you should be second."

"I've always been last in the lineup," Revna said. She had a sneaking suspicion why Katya wanted to change it now.

Katya and Elena looked at each other, then pretended they hadn't. "We..." Katya worked her mouth, obviously searching for a lie.

Elena resorted to the truth. "We wanted to make sure you're all right," she said. "Keep you on course, protect you from a sneak attack. Any nasty surprises that might come up."

They meant well. She knew they did. But her voice was flat and cold as she replied. "I know how to deal with nasty surprises. I don't need to be second in the lineup. I need to do my job."

Katya's hand went from her collar to her shoulder. "Revna, we know how you—"

Revna knocked her hand away. "No, you don't."

Katya and Elena glanced at each other. Katya bit her lip. "I guess we'll stick to the usual." She showed them a smile that was clearly forced. "Good luck, everyone."

"You don't usually get mad at people," Magdalena said as they walked away. "Other than Linné."

"Maybe I'm tired of being patronized." Of being "looked after." Of being told she was fragile, whether her friends said it out loud or not.

"I don't think they were trying to patronize you," Magdalena said.

"Don't you start," Revna muttered.

"I'm not," said Magdalena, looping an arm around her again. "I'm cheering for you."

Linné watched Revna wearily as they approached, a frown on her angry face, as if Revna was the burden she had to bear and not the other way around.

For a moment Revna thought she'd throw up if she had to get in the cockpit with her. But refusing to fly would either prove Revna a traitor or make her unfit for duty. Revna lifted herself off the ground before she got within speaking distance of Linné. She soared over her navigator's head and landed in the cockpit with a thump so jarring she'd be feeling it in her feet for the rest of the night.

Linné stared at her a moment, mouth ajar. Then she hopped up into the navigator's chair. "You really shouldn't use the Weave for stunts like that. You'll use up all your energy."

"Thanks for your concern." Revna parroted the angry sarcasm that Linné always seemed to have handy and was rewarded with an awkward silence. The air in the Strekoza tightened around her anger.

She secured her helmet and goggles as Magdalena prepared the plane. Linné said nothing, and that was more than fine by Revna. She'd rather spend the night in silence.

"Katya and Elena are cleared to go before you. Outer bay is equipped with incendiaries, inner bay with smoke and gas." Magdalena stood on her toes to squeeze Revna's hand, like always. "Come back safe."

Revna squeezed, too. "We will." Then she stuck her hands into the pilot's gloves. "Fire up."

They took off at the edge of dusk, with eight planes before them. The Strekoza multiplied her anger and fed off Linné's discomfort. More than once it drifted, and she felt Linné's sharp unease every time she made a hard or slightly clumsy course correction. She could almost hear Linné assessing her in her head.

The wind whistled low through the propeller, driving a gentle snow through the air. Despite that, it wasn't a bad night for reconnaissance. Clouds obscured the moon, but the snow was light, and it stopped before they reached the mountains. The Karavel range rose stark and bare, and the line of planes angled toward it.

"Look, I'm not sorry I grounded you," Linné said at last.

"Of course you're not," Revna replied. She meant to sound resigned, but an old bitterness crept in. A surge of resentment flooded the cockpit.

Linné's spark faltered, and Revna felt her anger pushing back. "Stop it," Linné said. "We have to be at our sharpest if we want to win. We can't be distracted or demoralized. It's what the Elda want."

She knew that, and she wanted to scream that she knew that loud enough for Linné's eardrums to bleed. She knew the war was more important. She knew the war called for sacrifice. But for her, there was another truth. She couldn't forget it and she couldn't justify it, no matter how hard she tried. The Strekoza flashed hot. "Everyone I know might be dead." *Because of me.*

"Which is why I didn't want you flying," Linné said. "If you can't concentrate, you might endanger the entire unit."

"*You* don't get to tell me how to do my job." Something inside her shook loose, pushed by rage and the fatigue that always, *always* something was wrong, or not good enough, or not for her. "Stop parading about like you're such a big thing. You're not better than me because you have real legs and you act like a boy."

"I—I don't think I'm better than you," Linné sputtered.

"Oh, please." Revna rolled her eyes. "Strutting around, handing out orders when Tamara's not looking—"

"She *told* me to help," Linné interrupted.

"Not to mention begging for a new team every five minutes. I'm human. I'm not a problem to be avoided."

There was a short, unpleasant silence. Then Linné said, "I wanted us to be taken seriously."

"Maybe you should have considered *taking* us seriously." Revna pulled them sharply away from a peak. Linné had no reply to that. "And don't you *ever* tell me what I can and cannot do."

"Prepare to adjust southeast," Linné said, and that was the end of the conversation.

They emerged from the Karavels onto the taiga. The Strekozy began to peel away, toward Adovic Reaching and the surrounding land. Soon only Katya's and Elena's planes flew in front of them. The snowy ground was dotted with larch, spruce, and the occasional elm. "Are you sure we're where we ought to be?"

"Yes," said Linné, in a voice colder than the frost on the cockpit's windscreen. "Bear southeast and stick close to the mountains."

"I can't see the Ava River."

"That's because it's frozen and snowed over." The Strekoza turned hot again. "Would you like to navigate?"

Revna bit back her reply. The Strekoza's nerves pulsed against her. She had to keep the plane from working into a frenzy, even if it was for no other reason than to prove she *could*.

They almost missed the base, a tiny cluster of buildings that lay dark and silent like any other hamlet on a night of war. Revna imagined families behind the blackout curtains, extinguishing the last candle before bed. Maybe they were making a mistake. Maybe this wasn't the outpost at all.

Or maybe it wasn't a mistake, and the Union wanted to destroy the area anyway. And if they did, Revna would obey without hesitating.

She hated knowing that about herself.

"Look," Linné said. "Corner of the large farmhouse."

Thin tracks led around the side of the farmhouse and to the field behind. The snow there had been trampled by enormous paws. As they drew closer, Revna began to pick out massive shapes, covered by tarps and canvas. War machines. Relief washed over her. The Strekoza felt almost comfortable for the first time on the flight.

"It seems abandoned," she said.

"Then their Serpent's not here. But I'm sure you remember what to do."

Revna pressed her teeth together so hard her jaw clicked. Up ahead, Katya winged around, making a full loop until she was beside Revna and Linné. Could no one trust her on this mission? She waved her wings. Katya turned her nose down in the Strekoza equivalent of a shrug, then sped up to take the lead as they neared the center of the village.

Revna plucked the Weave like a violin, taking them down for a reconnaissance pass. "Cut power," she said, and the noise dropped away. Linné's breath huffed in her ear. Her pulse thrummed.

They drifted closer. No searchlights—a good omen. Revna's heart spasmed as she spotted the antiaircraft, but it seemed abandoned. They flew over, silent and dark, following Katya and Elena.

A long shape curved over the ground, a shadow on black at the edge of the base. It had to be half again as long as a Dragon, a sinuous fuselage with a stylized, serpentine head. Her heart stuttered and the Strekoza wobbled in astonishment. That was it. The Serpent.

"That's our target," Revna said as they flew over. Ahead, Katya reengaged her engine and came about. "But why is it sitting there?"

"Maybe they weren't expecting us," Linné said as she wound her spark back into the engine. It kicked to life with a whine.

"They have two decoy locations and you don't think they expected us?"

"Maybe they got cocky. Maybe they thought one of the other decoys was drawing all the fire."

"You've always got the answer, haven't you?" Revna murmured.

She half hoped Linné would miss it in the whistle of the wind. But Linné sighed. "Don't start this again. We're in the middle of an assignment."

"Well, you don't have to one-up me every time I say something."

"*You* don't have to doubt me every time I—what's that?"

Revna opened her mouth to retort. Then she heard it, too, a faint thrumming. Like bees.

The air in front of them bloomed with fire. For a terrible moment she saw Katya's little plane illuminated at the center of the blaze, like the firebird she'd so meticulously stitched around one sleeve.

Linné let out a yell, feral and angry and afraid all at once. The air filled with burning debris, the smell of charred paper and burnt flesh. The wings of the firebird fell away, leaving dark shapes in a disintegrating fuselage. A blast of heat washed over the cockpit. And with that, it was over. The night turned black, and a few pieces of twisted metal and burning canvas fell to the ground. Lines streaked through Revna's vision.

The Strekoza spun upward like a top. Revna wrenched them out of their spiral.

"What was that?" Linné shouted. "What's happening?"

"I don't know," Revna said. "I don't know." Her entire body trembled. She did know what had happened. Katya was dead. Beautiful, brave Katya, who thought rules were for other people and wanted to look out for Revna. Katya, gone.

"They're activating antiaircraft. Avoid the antiaircraft!" Linné's spark surged.

"*I know what to do*," Revna yelled, blinking through tears and

281

the bright afterimages of the fire. Of Katya's last moments. The tears spilled hot, pooling in the rim of her goggles and smudging her cheeks.

"Look out!" Linné screamed.

Revna had enough time to think, *I've never heard her voice go that high before.* Then the air in front of them exploded.

She grabbed the Weave and pulled the Strekoza up, letting fear steer them. Beneath them, the wings broke off the burning shell of Elena's plane. Her fuselage tumbled toward the ground.

Linné shouted again. "Watch out!"

Revna couldn't watch out for anything. The next burst of flame missed them by less than a meter. Linné screamed some wordless curse as heat seared their faces. Her power flooded into the plane, kicking the engine into high gear. Even so, every movement of the Strekoza seemed painfully slow, hopelessly inadequate.

The Strekoza flew into a low cloud bank. The cover gave Revna a moment of relief. She grabbed for the Weave and pulled.

She could do this. She could stabilize them. She could bring them home, as she'd promised Tamara. *Find the antiaircraft,* she thought. She had to focus on one thing or she'd lose out to her fear and kill them both. *Find the antiaircraft.*

A soft sound from above them. The flare of someone's spark on the Weave.

A fuselage flashed overhead, metal jaws opening to release a gout of flame.

Revna pulled on the Weave with all her might. "Skyhorse!" she screamed. The Strekoza made a tight roll to starboard. The sky lit up where they'd been.

"*Fuck*," Linné said. She sounded almost appreciative.

"Watch your mouth," Revna said. She pulled them sharply around.

"Now? You want to get into this *now*?"

"You're breaking my concentration!" She fumbled with the Weave. Something dripped from her chin. Was it blood? She drew her hand out of the glove, felt the wet heat. The Skyhorses were better planes with more experienced pilots; they were—

Linné grabbed her shoulder with an iron grip. "The payload, Revna. We have to drop the payload."

The whisper of the engine took on stability again. Even the Strekoza was trying to help. *Breathe*, Revna told herself. She sucked in air and put her hand back into the glove, giving her plane a thankful squeeze as the glimmer of the Weave sharpened again. Linné was right. They had to get rid of the payload.

The outpost was still dark under cover of night. But now they were close enough to see tiny shapes running through the compound, toys that Revna could blot out with one thumb. An anti-aircraft gun clunked. If the soldier manning it spotted them, their chances of survival would plummet. But if they retreated, they might lead the Skyhorses back to the base.

"Can you see the Skyhorses?" Her voice sounded miraculously calm to her own ears.

Linné leaned around the back of her chair. "I...yes. One coming in at two o'clock. And the other—" She peered at the side mirrors. "The other's at our six and gaining."

"Okay." Revna took another deep breath. The Strekoza steadied a little under her. She couldn't afford to panic now. She had to be precise. Her fingers worked at the threads of the Weave, feeling them out. "Okay. Cut power."

Something flashed on their two. The Weave, as their enemy pilot made a course adjustment. The night fighter sped toward them, a dark shape against a dark sky.

"Revna," said Linné urgently.

Revna took a light hold of two threads. She nearly had it. Nearly—

"Revna, we're going to die."

She pulled. The Strekoza dove toward the ground. The Elda aircraft roared over, far too fast. Flames blazed against the night above. Linné screamed again, a splitting sound that left Revna's ears ringing.

Revna hauled them level with the ground, leaving them with a few precious moments over the Serpent. "Now," she shouted.

Linné kept screaming. The triggers on either side clicked, and the bombs fell away.

They rushed back toward the sky, back toward life and cold and freedom. Revna checked the smudged wing mirror. Smoke poured out of the corner of a barn.

They'd missed.

The antiaircraft popped as it began to fire again. "We have to go," Linné said. "Back to Intelgard. We'll get the rest of the regiment."

They couldn't take on the night fighters alone. Even before she said, "Increase power," she felt Linné's spark intensify. Maybe they'd turn into a real team in time to die. She took them away from the base.

"Someone's on our tail," Linné said.

"Cut it again." Revna felt the flow of energy drop away. The Skyhorse behind them *clunk*ed as its engine stalled. It roared back to life a moment later, and as the enemy aircraft streaked by, Linné reached out her arm and let loose a blast of spark.

The Skyhorse tore away, igniting as it flew, and streamed toward the ground like a meteor.

"One down, one to go," Linné said.

Revna thought of Katya, a shadow in the middle of a blaze, burning alive. The air whined as the last Skyhorse sped toward them.

The world before them flared bright. But it wasn't the bright of fire. It was a dazzling, blinding white, a white that turned the shapes of the world inside out. "Searchlight," cried Linné.

"Thanks for the warning," Revna shouted back. She let Linné's power flow through the throttle, throwing them toward the dark sky at top speed, spinning to port and to starboard. But Strekozy had never been fast, and the searchlight followed them, dazzling them, dancing with them no matter how she fought to get back to the night.

"Can you take it out?" If they could destroy the searchlight, it might make them invisible enough to get away.

"I can take out anything," Linné replied. "Just give me a clear shot."

Revna brought them around in a sharp ninety-degree turn. The night striped from dark to light to dark. She pulled them into a dive. The ground rushed toward them, black and bright and black and bright.

They came in over the searchlight, slowing a fraction as they approached. Revna squinted into the hulking shape of the light, hoping against hope that the Skyhorse wouldn't dare follow them.

Linné's spark flashed in a fireball, punching through the casing of the searchlight. The world plunged into merciful darkness. Revna prayed that her instincts would take her up, not down.

She waited for the hit. And waited. But it didn't come. Maybe they'd survive after all. Behind her, Linné sighed and relief filled the plane. "Let's go—"

The world bucked, lifting Revna up and slamming her back against her seat. Her right prosthetic plunged into open space.

The bottom of the cockpit was gone.

The Strekoza shook as she'd never felt it shake before, fighting to keep its living parts together. Its cage began to release from around Revna's chest. She was cold suddenly. So cold.

Linné screamed. Again. "Hit! We've been hit!"

"I *know*," Revna yelled back. *Don't think of stupid Linné. Don't think of Katya. Don't think of Elena. Think of the problems, girl.*

Problem: The plane spun and the Weave flickered in her sight as the Strekoza lost consciousness.

Problem: Her living plane was dying under them.

Problem: They had no parachutes.

"*Revna*," Linné screamed.

Solution. She pulled one hand from its glove. She'd been here before, in a haze of smoke and fire, faced with something falling and a hard death. She hadn't died then. She didn't need to die now. She shoved the Strekoza's cage away from her body and brought her legs up to crouch on the seat. She seized Linné's free hand. "Hold on."

Linné twisted, trying to push herself up without letting go. Her mouth formed around a curse, but the wind whipped it away. Revna leaned into her and punched the buckle on Linné's harness. "When I say, jump. Don't let go."

Linné wrestled free of the harness, then grabbed Revna again, squeezing her fingers until the bones ground together. "Revna, we'll die."

"No, we won't."

"We don't have chutes!"

"We don't need them." *Hopefully*. Staying in the Strekoza was certain death. Her idea carried only a 90 percent chance.

The Strekoza gasped fury and pain and sorrow. Then Revna felt nothing at all, except the tilt of their bodies in the air. The earth rushed up in a swirl of darkness and fire. "Now!" Revna shouted.

They jumped.

She snatched at the Weave and her fingers wrapped around a handful of threads, pulling them into the air. With a sucking sound, the throttle tube disengaged from Linné's arm. The Strekoza fell away, and they were hanging.

Linné hugged Revna around the chest, squeezing so hard Revna felt her ribs creak. "Holy *shit*." Her breath tickled Revna's chin.

The threads slipped. Revna caught a few more with her free hand and they swung. "We need to find somewhere to land." Her arm already burned.

"How?" said Linné.

"Find me a spot." The threads slipped from her hand, and her shoulder jerked as she let go of Linné to grab with the other. Linné squeezed tighter. Revna reached for a little tangle to secure them.

The world beneath them was dotted with fire. The Elda Skarov howled. Wherever Revna and Linné landed, the canines needed to be upwind. Maybe if the dogs couldn't smell them, the Elda would think they were dead.

"There." Linné pointed to a dark patch on the ground, devoid of fire and people and war machines. Only 150 meters away, and as good a spot as they could hope for.

Revna pulled toward the open spot. Her shoulder was going to pop out of its socket and her legs dragged on her calves. They slipped off course. She'd practiced using the Weave on others, but only for scant moments at a time. Now her fingers were slick with blood and sweat and fear, and she kept thinking about the roar of the planes, the singeing heat of the fire.

"I can't believe we're flying," Linné said. She gazed down, wide-eyed.

"We fly every night," Revna pointed out. Her arms trembled.

"This is different. You know what I mean." Linné tightened her grip and Revna cringed. "Are we going to break our legs?"

"Only if you don't let me concentrate." Or if they landed wrong. Or too fast. Revna released a few strands. They fell another meter. Linné stifled a curse. Revna thought of Katya and Elena, lying somewhere on the field with Asya and Nadya. Maybe falling was all their fates.

The sound of the Skyhorse's engine died away. It obviously

288

thought the fight was over. But noise surrounded them—the crackle of fire, the shouting of men, the yips of the Elda shape-shifters.

"Revn—ow!" Linné seized against her as they fell another few meters. "We're falling too fast."

They'd drifted over the corner of a roof. Revna's finger hooked around a Weave strand. "It's not as easy as it looks—" Then the last thread slipped from her grasp.

Linné clipped the edge of the roof with her foot. She yelped a curse and grabbed for the corner. Revna's shoulder popped as Linné's hand fastened around her wrist and pulled her up tight. Her back slammed into the side of the building, driving the air from her lungs. She heard a brittle *snap* and gasped. It felt as though someone had driven a knife up through the soles of her feet.

Her hand tore free from Linné's. She hit the sloping top of a war beetle and tumbled through the air. Then she was rolling, over and over, through a sucking warmth, until finally she came to a stop.

Pain radiated from her chest. The universe closed around her, dark and hot. Fire in her legs, fire in her ribs. She couldn't see; she couldn't breathe. She didn't know whether she was living or dead.

Fire flickered in a patch of sky above. The war beetle loomed over her, one leg raised. Revna threw her arms up to cover her face. But it didn't move. It was unmanned, and when she touched its flank, she felt its panic, latent and thick, ready to activate at the touch of a driver.

The universe began to expand again. The wetness around her was mud; the darkness was the shadow of the war beetle and the ash that smeared her goggles. Smoke covered the ground. She clapped her hand over her mouth and nose. The world flickered between red-orange flame and shadow. Her legs blazed.

Voices called to one another in Eldar. Revna peered out from under the war beetle.

"Linné?" she whispered. A dread rose in her that had nothing to do with the beetle above. Her navigator was gone.

17

OUR REALM IS THE AIR

Revna pressed herself against the underside of the war beetle. Her eyes stung. Around her the Elda soldiers rushed to put out the fire they'd started in the old barn.

She heard a cry, faint and desperate. Linné. *Be quiet,* she prayed silently. *I'll come to you.* Linné might have broken something. She might be trapped under a beetle or fallen debris. She might be stuck on the roof. Revna leaned into the smoke. Was the cry getting closer?

A shape moved toward her. She shrank under the beetle's carapace. If it was one of the Elda Skarov, it would nose her out from under the war beetle and tear her to nothing.

The boots came to a stop not a meter from her face. Revna caught a sense of fear, anger, an undercurrent of hard determination. It felt like their cockpit. Just in case, Revna reached for her issued pistol. Then Linné shouted her name loud enough for half the base to hear, and Revna started so hard she cracked her head on the beetle's undercarriage.

She grabbed Linné by the ankle and pulled. Linné went down with a yell and rolled under the beetle. Sharp nails dug into the skin around Revna's throat. For a moment Revna locked eyes with a feral beast. Linné held her gun like a club, her mouth twisted in a snarl.

"Don't—" Revna choked.

Linné's eyes widened. She snatched her hand away, taking small chunks of Revna's skin with her. "What did you do that for?" Her voice shook. "I almost killed you."

Revna touched her stinging neck. "Why were you running around shouting for me? Now they'll know we're here."

"Oh, excuse me for trying to save your ass from this situation, which, I will remind you, *you* put yourself in." Mud spattered the right side of Linné's face, and ash streaked the rest. She wiped at it uselessly.

Giddiness bubbled up. Maybe it was the smoke. "You care."

"Quiet," said Linné. She crouched near the hind legs of the beetle and peered out.

"Not until you—"

"*Shh.*" Revna heard three choking coughs from up ahead. "How do we get out of here?" Linné whispered.

Revna thought of the Strekoza, falling away from them. They weren't going to walk out of the base—fire surrounded them, and where there wasn't fire there would be Elda. She clenched her fists. "I need to think." But really, she needed to keep herself from thinking. About the lancing pain in her legs. About Katya and Asya, about how Elena and Nadya might still be alive if she'd agreed to fly in second position. *You're cursed.*

An Elda Skarov barked somewhere in the smoke. "We don't have time to think," Linné said. "What are the options? Escape?"

"How do we get home?"

Linné scowled. "Good point. What about this thing?" She tapped the hind leg of the beetle, lip curling. She didn't seem too enthused about her own suggestion.

"I don't think it wants to go anywhere," Revna said.

"Who cares? We can make it go."

"And then what? Get blasted by Skyhorses on the way to the mountains?"

Linné peered out as footsteps thundered by. "What's your brilliant suggestion, then?"

Revna put her muddy palm to the undercarriage. Linné would have to drive, and the war beetle would probably throw them both off in its panic before she managed to get in and take control. It would definitely draw unwanted attention. And even if they got it off the base, the Elda could fly after them in their Serpent.

The Skarov barked again. Linné grabbed her hand. "If you don't have a better idea—"

The Serpent. "I do, actually." Revna tried to pull her feet under her. But her prosthetic bent against her calf, and she fell on Linné with a strangled cry.

"Shh," Linné hissed in her ear, juggling to hold on to her gun as she helped Revna right herself.

Revna pulled her hands free and rolled up her left trouser leg.

The leather buckle at the top of her calf was torn, and the sock protecting her residual limb had ripped. She tried to ignore the red skin underneath, prying the inner part of the prosthetic away from the sweat-soaked cloth. The pin had snapped. The leg was broken. She lifted it to her chest, stomach heaving.

"How bad?" Linné said. "Can you walk?"

Revna cradled the leg. "I don't know."

"Then I'll have to carry you. Put it back on."

Revna drew away from her, stung. "Let me try."

"We don't have time," said Linné.

Revna thought of Mrs. Rodoya. *Speed over pride.* She'd thought she was through with others dictating her mobility. "I can walk."

"Fine, but—" They heard the crunch of more boots on debris. Linné waved her hand. Her impatience pricked at Revna, as clear as if they were flying together. *Get on with it.*

Revna reattached her leg with shaking hands. She thought about her father, his features hazy in her mind, fitting her oversized legs to her frame. Holding her hands as she learned to walk on her new feet. Cradling her when the tears spilled forth. He'd gone to prison for making her these legs. And now she'd broken one.

She tied the buckle as tight as she could with a scrap of wool from her coat lining. The living metal squeezed, igniting a faint hope. "We can make it to the airfield without you having to carry me."

Linné looked at her long and hard. "I trust you," she said finally, rolling the words around in her mouth, sounding uncertain. Then she slid out from under the war beetle.

Revna took her hand again and used her good leg to push herself up. She leaned on the war beetle to test the broken prosthetic.

Her leg tried to work with her, living metal straining, but the shift of her weight sent it twisting to the side.

"Revna," Linné warned her.

"I need to readjust—"

A shape cut through the smoke. Linné pulled her backward, stumbling behind the war beetle, wedging them between the metal and the wooden wall of the farmhouse. Linné pressed the barrel of her gun over Revna's mouth, a brief warning to be silent.

The shape resolved into a man. Revna's breath caught. Next to her, Linné moved her gun by degrees, sliding her finger over the trigger as she aimed.

A rough voice shouted from the other side of the barn. The man shouted back and ran past them.

Revna sagged in relief. Then she shoved Linné. "Don't drag me around."

"Can you move that thing or not?" Linné said.

"It's not a thing," Revna said hotly. She wrapped her left arm around Linné's shoulders and clung tight. Linné holstered her gun, and they staggered in what Revna hoped was the right direction. The broken pin in her left leg slid around in its socket and her residual limb burned and scraped, but the living metal held together. She could walk. Smoke stung their eyes and noses and bit their throats. Revna tucked her face into Linné's shoulder. At least the smoke obscured them from the Elda.

Fire dotted the ground, filling the air with the stench of hot metal and burning wood. Revna strangled a cry as her broken prosthetic scraped the raw skin of her calf. They limped along the farmhouse, leaning against it. Elda shouts dimmed and swelled as the fire roared. Linné checked the corner. "You're going to have to handle any trouble."

Revna unclipped her holster, pulling her pistol free.

A wave of heat seared their shoulders. There was no time to wonder if she could do this. Together they stumbled around a palanquin and came face-to-face with the wreckage of the searchlight.

A war beetle next to the searchlight had flipped onto its back, and its legs still twitched in its final throes. The warehouse to their right spouted flame, and a few men engaged in a futile attempt to freeze out the fire with cold spark.

They took refuge behind the smoldering jumble of metal and wire, and Revna leaned against a low sandbag wall. The smoke had thinned to a veil, and through it Revna could see the edge of the field. The Serpent was there, not two hundred meters away.

"They probably think we're dead, and they're too busy with the fire to look for our bodies," Linné said. "But we haven't got long." She put her hands on Revna's shoulders. "Are you sure you can fly it?"

Revna wiped sweat from the back of her neck. "I can fly anything. Just give me a clear shot."

"Ha." Linné favored her with a grim smile that faded as quickly as it came.

Men moved around the Serpent, checking the wings, the engine. "They're getting ready to fly," Revna said.

"Well, fuck."

Revna couldn't find it in herself to reprimand Linné.

The Serpent stretched out, scale upon scale of living steel

hammered into plates the size of her torso. Its tail ended in a sharp point that looked nearly as dangerous as its slender maw. Each wing spanned as long as three men lying end to end, and spines gleamed on its back like starlight.

Linné crawled to peer around the corner of the antiaircraft. "Shit," she said, and Revna couldn't resist a quick look of her own. A man was walking around the plane. His eyes narrowed and he reached for his gun, starting forward.

Revna fumbled with her pistol, but Linné was quicker, whipping hers out and firing two shots. He crumpled. Revna couldn't tear her eyes from the heap of limbs, the sudden lack where there had once been life. She'd have killed that man without even thinking. She hadn't only because Linné had been faster.

Linné put her gun away again and looped Revna's arm around her shoulders. "Someone will have heard that. Come on."

Revna clung to Linné as they limped past the dead man. *Revenge. I want revenge.* And revenge was a line of Elda soldiers, facedown in the mud. But she thought of her family, engulfed by fire, and she could not be glad.

The Weave flashed and tangled in the aftermath of their battle with the Skyhorses, and the steel of the Serpent glittered in the firelight. They hobbled onto the field together, breaths hitching. "Eya," a man shouted from the other side of the Serpent. Revna stumbled, trying to keep up as Linné broke into a jog. Her prosthetic slammed against her skin. She couldn't keep her balance, and her gun tumbled out of her hand. No time to pick it up—she pushed forward, gritting her teeth.

More shouts sounded behind them. But they were almost

there, the Serpent filled her vision, they were in the shadow of the wing—

Revna gripped the wing with one hand and pulled on the Weave with the other. She soared up to the hatch at the top, fumbling it open and falling in. Her legs smashed against the floor. The cockpit was huge and hollow, a cockpit for giants, with two seats at the dash and one behind.

Linné scrambled into the navigator's seat beside her. The empty third seat must've been for a gunner. "Let's go, let's go."

There was no cage to hook into Revna, just a slender tendril with two points like teeth, hanging next to her chair. Revna pulled her goggles down and reached for the flying gloves. She saw only empty space in front of her. God, God, *God*, how was she supposed to fly without them?

There was a hinge in the dashboard. She pried open the top and pulled out two thin mesh gloves, connected to the dash by a wire. This was it? She pulled them over her fingers. On the back of each hand was a small wing, stretching from thumb to pinky. The wings of the Serpent. A third glove had a tiny model head of the Serpent attached. She tossed it to Linné. "Find the feed." They had to get off the ground before they got shot.

Linné shoved her hand into the throttle in front of her. "Found it. Get us in the air." Without waiting for Revna's order, she fired up.

The Serpent hummed as the living metal woke. The tendril of the pilot's feed slithered under Revna's sleeve and punctured her arm, sliding deep into the vein. A searing cold spread through her, and the Weave brightened as she hooked in to the living metal.

The Serpent could tell she wasn't its usual master.

It was not pleased.

The metal itched against her skin, and the air inside the cockpit flashed warm. A sick feeling twisted in her belly, the feeling of wrongness, that she'd done something terrible and would pay the price in her own blood.

She pushed against the Serpent's resistance, opening up to the Weave. But it moved too sluggishly. "A little more," she said.

"I'm trying," Linné bit back. Revna could feel Linné's spark thundering into the Serpent. But whatever she gave, it wasn't enough. Linné hit the dashboard with her gloved fist.

The Serpent's sinuous head darted forward, and the cockpit lurched with it. Revna gripped the dashboard. "Don't do that," she said. Not yet, anyway.

A man sprinted from the edge of the field, a look of incandescent rage on his face. He brandished his pistol. A shot bounced off the nose of the plane and cracked the windscreen.

"Do something," Linné said through gritted teeth. "You said you could fly anything."

She should be able to fly the Serpent. She had everything she needed.

Except enough power.

The third seat. She craned her head to make sure. Yes, it had a feed, too, just behind her chair. This ship needed both a navigator and a gunner to give it spark.

They were, in Linné's words, screwed.

"What are you looking—" Linné caught sight of the extra power duct, too. "Is that what I think it is?"

Revna nodded. Panic was starting to claw its way up her throat.

A soldier ran toward the Serpent's nose. Linné swung her gloved hand, and the Serpent's head hit him with a wet thunk. He fell to the ground. Someone else grabbed a wing. More men appeared from the smoke with murder in their faces.

"You'd better deliver, firebird," Linné muttered. She peeled the glove off and tossed it onto the dash. Then she leaned back, shoving her shoulder into the gap between their chairs.

"What are you doing?" Revna cried.

Linné closed her eyes and took a deep breath. Light gathered in her palms and spread in a shiver over her, illuminating her skin. It spread up her neck, to the roots of her hair. For a moment she looked like a god. Then she shoved her hand into the spare throttle, and the fire shot down into the engine.

The Serpent woke like a dream ending. Revna felt its landing gear dig into the ground. They bucked as its long body rippled. It launched into the air, and men fell away like ticks. Fire moved beneath Linné's skin. She roared, bracing her back against the chair as her spark wound down the throttle.

The Weave pulsed around them, so bright it was nearly blinding, and Revna's skin tingled with stolen power. They soared over the heads of the Elda and into the night sky, leaving the bewildered soldiers to curse and shout below.

✳

Linné was dying. No military career, no saving the day, no Hero of the Union medal. But she didn't care. She'd doubted Revna, and she'd betrayed Revna. Now she would get her pilot over the mountains and back into Union territory if it was the last thing she accomplished on Earth.

Her spark tore out of her. It churned through the engine and flashed out along the Weave, making the lines ripple and thicken, lingering for long seconds in her vision. She fixed a singular image in her mind: Revna, sitting in the mess, writing a letter to her family. Safe. She pushed, and the Serpent sped overland.

"God," said Revna, leaning out to look at the world as they soared. The Serpent heaved, lashing them back and forth. Revna hissed as she forced her control. Her anger and wonder bled together, but Linné could barely feel it over the bold hate of the Serpent.

"You should watch your mouth," Linné said. The words slurred on her tongue.

Revna barked a laugh. "You're one to talk."

Linné looked at her arms. Long ropes of spark undulated beneath her skin. Power flushed her veins as it drew out of her, filling her with an addictive heat. She was burning. Give her an Elda and she'd turn him to ash with a touch. She really *was* a firebird now. She'd be drunk on her own spark if she didn't know it was killing her.

Sweat trickled down the back of her neck and the side of her face. Black started to dot her vision. "Keep going." It was so hard to talk. "We have to get back to Tamara." If they returned with the Serpent, they wouldn't be in trouble. The Union would obsess over the technology, its renewed chance in the war. And everyone would leave Revna alone.

Revna concentrated on fighting the Serpent as it twisted against them. She hated Linné. She thought Linné hated her. And even though Linné didn't care about the fight, about surviving, about getting some stupid medal, there was one thing she needed before she died.

"Revna?" Her voice was a whisper when she wanted to shout. She couldn't pull back. The Serpent seethed, leeching spark. The world was turning gray. The taiga stretched below, crumpling in the dim outline of the Karavels ahead. They came ever closer, but not close enough. "I'm sorry." Something wet slid down to her chin.

"Why are you sorry?" Revna said. Her voice grew louder and softer, as if she were on the other end of a malfunctioning radio. She was supposed to say, *It's okay*. She was supposed to forgive Linné. "You can pull back a bit. We're safe." The Serpent's head whipped back and forth, and Revna's hands went rigid as she kept its wings steady. *Concentrate*. Fog closed in on Linné's mind. "I'm sorry for trying to switch. I'm sorry for thinking you couldn't..." She fought for the words, but they fled her. Why couldn't Revna say it was okay? "I can't—"

Die next to someone who hates me.

"Linné?"

Everything was far away—the anger, the sorrow. The pain of her spark, draining from her. And the Karavels still loomed before them. Linné tried to tell Revna to push for the mountains. But she whispered, "Don't hate me," instead. *I don't want to die like this.*

I don't want to die.

Revna leaned over, and the Serpent rolled with her. They

tilted in the air until the clouds were a gray ocean beneath them. "Please," Linné mumbled. "I'm sorry."

Revna's hand was hot against her forehead. "Linné, *stop*. You're killing yourself." She tugged at Linné's forearm. But it was no use. The engine was greedy, and the Serpent wanted her to suffer.

"Saving you." Linné's head sagged against the back of her seat. It was getting too difficult to keep her eyes open.

"Not like this," Revna said. Her hands closed around the gun at Linné's waist and jerked it free. Revna pushed the barrel of the gun against the base of the gunner's throttle.

An alarm flashed in Linné's brain. She couldn't do that, they had to get over the mountains—

The sound of the shot broke through her gray world. Everything turned white.

✳

Revna wrenched them back on course as the wing of the Serpent lit up like the sun. Her left glove burned and she grabbed for the Weave. She hadn't considered that her forced disconnect might set the aircraft on fire.

Then she saw planes darting around them like silverfish, flashing against the Weave as they fired. This time, the Serpent wasn't trying to kill them—Skyhorses were.

Next to her Linné collapsed in her chair, heaving. Spark flushed back up her arm from the ruined gunner's throttle. Revna could only hope it was enough to keep her alive. "Linné? Are you with me?"

Linné's head bobbed. "You—" she murmured.

The night lit up as the Skyhorses fired again. The Serpent

flopped in the air. Weave threads whipped around them. Revna gripped the edge of her seat as her legs slammed from side to side. She *felt* the decision, the clean disconnect of the burning wing from the rest of the plane, tumbling through the air to crash into the underbrush of the taiga. They began to spin.

Linné tried to push herself up in her seat, then collapsed back. Her face shone with sweat. "What did you *do*?"

Revna ignored her navigator and pulled with all she had. No good. The Serpent tilted toward the ground. Above them, Skyhorses circled and danced. She steered toward the slight indent in the snow that Linné had identified as the Ava River on their flight out.

"You shot me," Linné accused, incredulous.

"I shot the plane," Revna corrected her.

"Why?"

Was she serious? "You were about to die!"

"Now *you're* going to die!"

"No, we're going to land." Again.

Linné looked from the Skyhorses to the ground. "In the river? Are you joking?"

Landing gear. *Ignore your ungrateful navigator and get the landing gear down.* The hatred of the Serpent cut through every command she tried to give. It was palpable in a way she'd never experienced from any other living metal. She gripped the Weave until the living steel gloves cut into her palms. The metal links seared her skin. The Serpent *would* obey her. And as they tumbled down, she pulled and pulled, and ignored Linné's screams, and she prayed to any god, legal or illegal, that might be listening.

They hit the river with an impact that punched a hole in the ice and sent water cascading in waves. The windscreen cracked from the bottom up, bursting in and showering them with glass. The living metal screamed as they struck rocks, roots, and the riverbank, grinding against the earth until they came to their slow, final halt at a bend in the river.

Linné sagged against the dash. Her skin had a tint like ash, and when she pulled her hand from the gunner's throttle, blood ran from beneath her sleeve.

Revna slid down in her chair, heart thundering. She couldn't get enough air, no matter how she gulped it in. Her entire body shook.

It took her a moment to realize she was laughing.

She'd saved Linné. She'd saved them both. Twice. "We're not dead."

Linné looked at Revna. "You're bleeding everywhere."

"I'm fine." Revna giggled. She was better than fine. It was a glorious night, and she'd lost her plane, and they were trapped in the taiga, and everyone thought they were dead.

Linné leaned forward and traced a slick line down Revna's face. Dots of blood speckled her own cheeks, tiny cuts from the shattered glass of the windscreen. "It can't be serious." Revna laughed. Because tonight was a glorious night.

"Let me take a look." Linné scooted to the edge of her seat. The Serpent rocked, ice clinking against its fuselage. Linné inspected Revna's neck, wiping at a stinging cut under her ear. Then she probed her shoulders and chest, unzipping her jacket to check her shirt underneath. She felt her knees and her residual limbs, running her finger around the line where the prosthetics began. "You seem to be all right," she admitted.

"Because tonight's a glorious night," Revna said.

It *was* a glorious night.

And they were trapped in the taiga.

And everyone thought they were dead.

18

THE MOTHERLAND IS CALLING

Glass lay scattered over the cockpit. The Serpent pinged as the dead metal cooled against the ice. They were alive.

Linné continued to check Revna. It was easier than thinking about how her own body felt like a bag of sand, or that the world was still a study in gray. It was easier than looking her pilot in the eye. Revna had been thinking about *her*. Not about getting home safe. Not about saving herself. And Linné had wanted her grounded.

Glass had ripped through Revna's jacket, but her cuts looked superficial. It seemed luck was with them. Revna still giggled, but Linné felt more like crying. If she'd been a better navigator—if she'd been stronger with her spark, more trusting of her pilot—would they even be here?

Wind blew in through the shattered windscreen. It would

be warmer on solid ground, and they'd need to conserve heat as much as they could. Linné could be ashamed of herself later. "All right?" she asked Revna.

"Of course," Revna said, as if she were stupid for even asking.

"Of course," Linné muttered. She needed a cigarette. But when she patted her pockets, they were suspiciously flat. Her coat pockets were empty, too. It was apparently too much of a miracle to expect her cigarettes to survive a crash, a heist, and another crash.

All she could do instead was move, distract herself. The sky was clear above them—the Skyhorses must think them dead. She leaned forward to pry open the dash and liberated the compass and flare gun inside. The seat behind Revna looked empty, but next to that—a metal hatch, leading to the body of the plane. And it looked undamaged.

"Stay here," she said. Revna snorted as if she'd told a joke. Maybe she had; where else was Revna supposed to go?

Come back safe, she thought. Revna was supposed to go home. They might have to make it to the other side of the river and over a mountain, but they would get home.

Linné crawled into the back. Her head still pounded and she wasn't sure she could stand. The hatch door stuck, but when she levered it with her shoulder, it popped open and she fell through.

The space beyond was blacker than the night. Linné reached for her spark. Her palms flickered and her head spun, but her power hid from her. *Or it's gone.* Maybe she'd used too much; maybe it would never return.

She gritted her teeth. *I need you now.* And even though it made her ears ring, she shoved until the faintest glow illuminated her palms. Her veins burned. Using the side of the hatch to steady herself, she pushed to her feet and took a tottering step.

She moved down the long compartment. The living metal shifted under her feet, thrumming and angry and sliding on the ice. Over her head, two bars hung from the ceiling, with a dozen straps dangling from each. Twenty-four in all. Empty harnesses lined the walls on either side of her.

Her foot connected with something squishy. Linné grabbed for her gun. Her holster was empty—Revna had taken it. With a sigh she crouched down, touching the floor to steady herself.

She'd kicked a survival kit, a pack for the cold winter. When she lifted her hand, she saw more jumbled against the end of the fuselage. Enough for each harness, and for the men in the cockpit. Parachutes hung from the wall.

This meant something terrible for the war. But right now, it might save their lives. Linné hoisted the pack, pulling it on even though her muscles screamed. As she reached for a second pack, something cracked near the front end of the plane. The fuselage rocked.

At first she thought it was the ice. Then she heard Revna scream.

She spun, and her feet were moving before she realized what was happening. She tumbled through the hatch shoulder-first and collapsed in the gunner's chair. Revna had thrown her arms over her face. The front of the cockpit was covered in earth, and the far side of the bank drifted away from them in a widening patch of steaming water.

"Skyhorses," Revna said. Linné looked up through the shattered windscreen. The Weave shimmered as it ate up spark. Long bodies spun above them. One dipped down, and red fire filled her vision.

Shit! The spark hit the ice in front of them with a crack, grazing the cockpit and making it jolt. A wave of heat came from the other end of the Serpent as a second blast of spark hit near the tail. Linné imagined a whole fleet of Skyhorses, flashing as they circled closer and closer. "Come on." She pushed on the hatch above them, dislodging more glass and dirt.

"I can't walk." Revna's breathing grew quicker.

Her leg. Shit again. "The wing. We'll crawl." Linné's arms shook. Revna edged through the hatch and slid down onto the wing. Linné followed her, scraping her legs on the overlapping scales of the fuselage. The stolen pack threatened to tip Linné sideways. The Skyhorse engines roared, far too close, and the Weave illuminated the sky as the Elda navigators pushed more power through the throttles.

Beneath them, the ice groaned.

"Go, go," she begged. Revna scrambled, she was nearing the edge of the wing, they'd make it—

The buzzing intensified as a Skyhorse dove. "Get off the plane," Linné shouted.

"The bank's too far," Revna said, looking back. "It's all ice."

Well, it wasn't water. Linné jumped.

She waited for the break, for the numbing shock of the water beneath. Instead she hit the surface hard and her feet slid out from under her. Her shoulder throbbed as it struck the frozen crust of the river.

A flash lit the sky. Spark blazed down. It punched through the cockpit and split the ice with a sound like a gunshot. The whole plane slammed forward and Revna shrieked. She tumbled from the wing.

Linné launched herself up and ran, sliding as she grabbed Revna by the arm again. Revna got her good leg under her and together they scrambled to the bank, cutting through the soft snow to solid earth beneath. They turned in time to see thin lines skitter across the surface of the ice.

The Serpent sat in a rapidly widening circle of dark water. Fire flickered at the front end, a golden beacon in the night, as the fuselage tilted into the river.

"I can see colors again," Linné realized.

Revna burst into tears.

✳

Cursed. Family killer. The words chased themselves through Revna's head as she readjusted her prosthetics. First she'd destroyed her home. Then she'd gotten four girls killed because she hadn't been willing to trade places in formation. Now she'd stranded her navigator in the middle of the taiga. Everyone around Revna seemed to die, and she survived whether she deserved to or not.

The taiga was slipping into the cold gray of dawn, and the noise of Skyhorse engines had diminished to a faint buzz. The pilots must have been convinced that Revna and Linné were dead.

Next to her, Linné ignored her snuffling tears in favor of taking apart the survival pack. She pulled out a blanket, a tarp, a hatchet, a pistol, and a pitiful ration of oats, jerky, and dried fruit. Linné holstered the pistol and hooked the hatchet to her belt, then rummaged at the bottom of the pack. "No cigarettes," she muttered. She turned to Revna. "Did you lose my gun?"

Revna sniffed. "Sorry." She wiped at her face, smearing mud and reopening half a dozen tiny cuts on her cheeks. She retied the strip of wool around her broken leg. The living metal pressed in, supporting her. It wouldn't work for long, but it was better than nothing. Cold was already beginning to seep through the holes in her jacket. Her hands were dotted with cuts, too, from the mesh gloves of the Serpent. It hurt to move them, but she forced herself to roll her trousers down, to pick up the rations Linné had found in the pack.

Linné frowned at Revna's leg as if it were a problem. Revna resisted the urge to snap at her. "I'll make you some crutches," Linné said.

What's the point? she thought as Linné went off to find suitable branches. If Linné left her and went ahead, she could take news of the Serpent back to Intelgard. She could save the others. She could change the war. She didn't need Revna for that.

No one needed Revna now.

When Linné returned, Revna tested the crutches in the soft snow. Linné stood at the bank, looking at the remains of the Serpent on the other side. The fire in the cockpit had died out, and ice was beginning to re-form around the fuselage. She lifted her hands and the spark trickled out of her, weak. The shadows under her eyes turned the color of a fresh bruise. Revna took an experimental step. "What are you doing?"

"I'm—" Linné shook out her hands. "Nothing. I'm ready to go.

If we can get back to Intelgard soon enough, Hesovec and Zima can send a salvage team."

Soon enough. "Do you think that would save us?"

"Save us from what?" Linné said.

"Interrogation. Torture." Revna tried to say the words matter-of-factly, but her throat constricted. If they made it home, she'd spend the rest of her short life in front of a Skarov brutalizer, begging to die.

"We won't get tortured," Linné said.

She probably believed it, too. Revna couldn't imagine that the general's daughter would be tossed into prison forever. Linné had influence, for all she pretended she was any other child of the Union. But Revna's enlistment had come with a caveat.

Linné slid the pack on and they started to walk. They'd taken only a few steps when Revna's crutch slipped on a patch of ice, jerking her sideways. Her bad prosthetic bit into the ground, and she stifled a curse.

Linné ducked under her arm and levered her up. Revna pushed her away. She'd walked on her own for years, and it stung for Linné to help without asking.

"I guess I shouldn't get too far ahead," Linné said, eyeing her critically.

Revna's temper flared. "You can do what you like," she snapped. "Don't let me ruin your chance to heroically make your way out of the wilderness."

She knew it was the wrong thing to say as soon as the words left her mouth. But she clamped her lips on an apology. Linné didn't deserve one. Linné's eyes narrowed. "Shut up," she said, and they set out.

✳

The taiga shone cold and bright in the early morning. Branches glistened with frost, scattering the rich orange-red of sunrise over the ground. The snow-covered forest was a blank tapestry, and with every step, Revna and Linné stitched their story into it.

They followed an old hunting trail throughout the day, walking in silence on gently tilting terrain. When the shadows turned the world purple and the snowy landscape blurred, Revna couldn't help feeling that they hadn't gone far at all.

They mounded snow to make a shelter, and as it settled, Linné gathered wood for a fire. Revna found a tiny cooking pot stuffed at the bottom of the pack, then gathered their rations—enough for one man over a couple of days. Maybe the Elda had expected to live off the land.

In the fading light, Revna eased her trouser legs up. Her hands burned, even when she pressed them against the snow or her cold prosthetics. Her right leg came off with a pop. She peeled away the sweaty sock and sighed in relief as her raw skin was released. Her phantom legs ached. She'd have to wash her calves with snow and hope that she didn't have too many blisters or a skin fungus by the time they got back to Intelgard. *Or maybe the Skarov would love it. Maybe they'd let my legs fester.*

There was a sewing kit in the pack; she could try to repair the torn buckle with it. But she couldn't fix the pin, which had bent and snapped at the bottom. The socket holding the pin in place had broken, too, and she could hear fragments rattling in the leg when she shook it. The pin wouldn't stay put in the damaged socket, and though the living metal might help her stay upright, walking would make things worse.

Linné dropped a bundle of sticks on the ground. "We eat, we dry out. Then we sleep. Hand me the pack."

Revna watched her build a pyramid with moss and twigs, then dig around for a box of matches. They were silent until the fire caught, and they boiled some oats and meat with snowmelt to make a thick porridge. Revna fumbled with the spoon, trying not to let Linné see the cuts on her hands. The porridge scalded her tongue. "Not bad."

"Needs salt," Linné replied. They finished in silence.

Revna couldn't figure her flying partner out. They'd been through battle together. Linné had put her own life on the line for Revna. But they couldn't have half an hour of conversation here on the ground. Perhaps Revna would never be able to speak to Linné. Perhaps no one could. *Except the Skarov.*

Linné scrubbed the bottom of the pot out with snow, then held it over the fire to dry. When she judged it finished, she stuck it in the pack and scooted over to Revna. "Let me see your face. I want to check for glass."

Revna wiped her filthy face with snow, inhaling sharply at the sting, and tilted her chin down.

Linné's fingers were a gentle pressure as they pressed at a cut on her forehead. "How's your leg?"

Revna toyed with the frayed cuff of her trousers. "Broken."

Linné made an impatient sound, moving to her ear. "Very helpful. Turn your head."

Revna turned. "How much do you know about prosthetics, anyway?"

"Good point," Linné said.

She checked Revna's neck, behind her ear, and the top of her shoulder, then started on the other side of her face in silence. The pause was awkward and Linné had actually been trying, so Revna finally admitted, "I don't know how broken." If they got back to the base, she'd see what Magdalena could do with it. The thought made her heart wrench.

She probably wouldn't need to try. Revna knew what awaited her in Union territory. And she knew from personal experience that the Skarov wanted confessions, not truth.

"Maybe you should go by yourself," she said.

For a moment she thought Linné hadn't heard. She frowned at a spot on the right side of Revna's face, pressing until Revna made a strangled sound. Then Linné said, "Go where?"

"Over the mountain. Back to Intelgard. You'll—travel faster alone." Revna almost faltered. *Don't be a coward.* She didn't have to be the curse that killed her navigator. "You can take the news back to the regiment."

Linné stopped, fingers tightening around Revna's chin. "Not without you."

"Why?" Revna asked it curiously, but as she continued, her voice grew hard. "What the Union asks, we give. Don't you believe that? Why shouldn't you leave me behind?"

316

Linné pulled her hand away. "Because I *don't*. I don't leave people behind."

Revna's voice rose. "You left me behind a million times at the base!"

"I never left you to die!"

Revna picked up her leg. She didn't want to look at Linné. "I guess that depends on what you told your Skarov friend."

There was a short silence. The fire crackled, tantalizing and warm, reminding her of nights in Tammin in front of their wood-stove. "What are you saying?" Linné said.

Revna rallied her courage. "Did you tell him I was a liability? Did you tell him I couldn't handle the war?"

"Of course not. I…" Linné trailed off. Revna felt a coldness that had nothing to do with the taiga.

"Whatever you said to him, he'll use it. Do you really think it's better to let me be interrogated and tortured than leave me out here? This way you can tell everyone I died a loyal servant to the Union."

"I didn't talk to him," Linné said.

"Don't lie—"

"I *didn't*. He talked to me."

"About what?" *About me.* Revna did look at her now, seeing if Linné could bring herself to answer.

She couldn't. Linné swallowed, then said, "It's your turn to check me."

She sat, more still than Revna had ever seen her, as if she were afraid to move as long as Revna's hands were on her skin. Revna probed at her face with the tips of her fingers, pushing as lightly as she could. As she worked, Linné said, "Anyway, he's never tortured anyone. We'll go home, we'll be interviewed, we'll follow standard procedure."

"Like Pavi and Galina?" Revna said. "They were standard procedure, too, and they never came back from Eponar." She checked a dot of blood at the side of Linné's nose.

Linné hesitated. Then she said, "We'll explain what happened. We haven't done anything wrong, so we have nothing to fear."

A bitter anger rose in Revna's throat. "*You* have nothing to fear, *Zolonova*." Linné's glare was murderous. Revna could feel her anger as palpably as if they were connected by their Strekoza. She didn't care. How often had she heard that line from the Union or one of its mouthpieces? "How are you so sure that I won't drag you down? That I won't be a liability for you, too?" *I am a curse, after all.*

She expected Linné to shout, to put some of that murder into her voice. But to Revna's surprise, after a long moment, she sighed. The rage left her. "You're not a liability. I—" She fidgeted. "I shouldn't have said that."

Her eyes darted up, hopeful. As if she'd said enough. "Apology not accepted," Revna replied. Linné would have to try harder.

They lapsed into silence as Revna finished checking Linné for glass. Then Linné shifted and collapsed the fire with a spare stick so that they could relight it. "Whether you accept my apology or not, we still have to share a blanket. So maybe we can get some sleep and continue insulting each other in the morning?"

"Can't wait."

Linné made a snow bed in the shelter while Revna washed her legs. Her phantom feet still itched and burned, and they would only get worse the longer Revna and Linné were stuck out here. They spread the tarp out and pulled the blanket over themselves, then lay down side by side, without speaking. Revna thought of Mama, cupping the back of her head, snuggling Lyfa between them. Mama had been proud of her, then. Would she be so now?

They'd studied survival at Intelgard, but after half an hour, Revna started to wonder if they'd made their shelter wrong. Her teeth felt as if they were freezing to her lips. She tried to warm her hands with the spark, but they seared and pulsed and she gave up. It was probably for the best; she didn't want to set fire to their blanket and accidentally incinerate Linné. Who would take their story back to the Union?

The ache in her muscles spread to her bones. She tucked her nose under the edge of the blanket and pulled her goggles down over her eyes, tearing the scabs there. Whenever she breathed in, it felt as if the cold had formed a fist that punched the inside of her chest. Linné's body was rigid next to hers, so still that Revna was half-convinced she'd already frozen.

"It's too cold to sleep," Revna said at last.

She expected Linné to ignore her. But she said, "Yes."

"If we're going to die out here, you might as well tell me why you got me grounded."

Linné huffed a warm breath in her ear. "We're not going to die out here."

"Well, I want to know anyway. Whatever you've got to say, I've probably heard it." The laundry list of reasons she wasn't fit for this or that—for factory work, for school, for piloting, for love.

Linné shifted, rustling the blanket. "Why was your father sentenced to life on Kolshek?"

Of course. Of course Tannov had told her. Revna wasn't surprised that Linné knew, not really, but she was surprised at the way it hurt. Her father. Her poor father. "He used to smith living metal at a factory. After my accident he saved the scrap to make my new legs."

"It is treason to steal from the factories. We're at war," Linné reasoned.

"We weren't then." The words came out sharp, unforgiving. Her father had sacrificed everything for her. Linné couldn't possibly understand. "And the metal wasn't going to be used for anything. But the Skarov still came for him when the war started."

"They let you keep the legs?"

"The formal accusation was dissidence. Papa's foreman convinced them that they didn't need to take my legs." *My daughter is your age*, the foreman had told her, the day she'd learned that Papa was gone.

The blanket tugged on her as Linné scratched something. "Was your father a dissident?"

"Of course not." They'd wanted him because he could work living metal. The northern coast was rich with it, which made Kolshek an ideal prison. Ice dotted its waters year-round, and no one could hope to survive the swim to shore. And living metal could be temperamental. The Weave worked through it over thousands of years, and then men forcibly removed it from its natural

320

space. Entire mines had collapsed in the past because they were staffed with men who didn't understand how to keep it calm.

He could be dead already. She'd taught herself not to think like that in Tammin, but on the taiga, only a few steps away from death herself, the concept held some comfort. He might be waiting on the other side of life. She imagined Mama and Papa and Lyfa taking her somewhere that wasn't so abysmally cold, where her phantom limbs didn't hurt all the time. "When you get home, will you tell them I died in the crash? I want my family to keep Protector status," she said. If they were still alive.

"I'm not telling you again," Linné said.

"Please."

Linné pretended to be asleep.

19

WE WELCOME THE ADVANCE OF COMMANDER WINTER

She couldn't breathe. The cold beat in on every side, and her residual limbs ached and itched. The space under her arms felt puffy. Panic jolted through her. She couldn't move; she couldn't breathe—she tore her eyes open. A silhouette loomed over her.

"Don't shout." Linné pulled her hand away from Revna's mouth. She picked up Revna's prosthetics and held them out. "We have to get moving," she whispered.

Revna pushed herself up, gasping a little as hot knives of pain stabbed through her palms and feet. Her stiff muscles faltered. "What's happening?"

Linné spoke in a low voice as Revna pulled on her socks.

"Planes have landed in the taiga. I heard them when I went out for a piss. I think it's a salvage team."

And only the Elda knew they'd crashed in the first place. "Do you think they'll come looking for us?" Revna took the prosthetics and began to fit the inner sheets over her calves. Her prosthetics shivered. The right pin clicked into place; the left rattled. Her hands screamed.

"They won't find bodies in the cockpit. It hasn't snowed since we crashed, so there's no cover for our tracks. It'll be easy to find us." Linné rummaged in the pack until she found a bit of jerky, then tossed it on Revna's lap. "Can you eat quickly?"

Revna looked down at the jerky, then back to Linné's silhouette, black against the glow of the snow. "I'll never outrun an Elda search party on a broken leg."

For a moment she thought that Linné would disagree. But she said, "I'll think of something."

Right. Revna nodded and took a bite. Linné folded the blanket and tarp, then shoved them back into the pack. Revna should tell Linné to go without her, to let the curse of her end in the taiga. Instead she ate her jerky and they collapsed the shelter together. When Revna broke the top layer, the cold air hit her so hard she thought her heart would stop. Sunlight had barely penetrated the canopy.

Revna shoved more snow on the remains of the fire. The cold soothed her palms. They'd crusted over with scabs in the night, and when she pressed one with her thumbnail, a thick white fluid oozed up. If her hands were infected, what did that mean for using the Weave? Revna found a strand and tugged on it. The thread seemed to cut through her, leaving a burning agony behind. A pathetic clump of snow dislodged from a tree branch and fell with a soft puff to the trail beneath.

"I don't think that's going to help," said Linné.

Revna's very bones felt bruised, and cold wormed through her torn jacket. Her heart pounded. Problem: She was trapped in the taiga and powerless. At any moment some Elda tracker would come up that path, and only if she was lucky would she die right away. "What's your great suggestion, then?" she said as she pulled on her gloves.

Linné sat in the ruins of their shelter with a huff. She took a piece of jerky and chewed, staring at the trees. Revna strained to hear the sound of feet on the forest floor. She could almost feel Linné's tightly wound mind spinning, searching for a solution.

"We'll probably have two men on our trail, maybe four. Hopefully not more. But they'll come in pairs. Pilot and navigator, right?" Linné said. Revna nodded. "If we want to overcome them—" She took a deep breath. "Hatchet or pistol?"

Revna frowned. "What?"

"We need the advantage of surprise. While they're examining the trail, we use their distraction, and—" Linné pulled the hatchet from her belt and swished it through the air. "Hatchet or pistol?"

Revna's stomach curdled at the thought of swinging the little hatchet into someone's flesh. Maybe she could use the Weave, the way she had on the private in the mess. Her hands twinged. She reached for the pistol. "Better if I don't have to dodge," she said.

Linné nodded. "Focus on one. I'll take care of the other."

Revna swallowed. "What if there are more than two?"

Linné tapped the leather cover of the hatchet against her thumb. Her gloves were torn across the knuckles, exposing dry and cracked skin beneath. When she looked at Revna, her eyes were cold and serious. "If we can't kill them, shoot me. Then yourself. No prisoners."

"I—" The pistol seemed suddenly heavy in her hand. She knew what happened to prisoners of the Elda: interrogation and torture. All the same, she still hadn't shot anyone yet.

Linné eyed the gun, doubtful. "Can you do it?"

The war doesn't care about you. Or her.

"Do you want the hatchet?"

"No." Revna's hand tightened around the pistol's grip.

"Not so loud," Linné hissed.

"I can do it. No prisoners."

They set Revna up next to the shelter's remains. She'd have a little cover, even though she'd have to lie on her belly. Linné hid the pack behind a bush, then took up her post behind a spruce on the edge of a path. They settled in to wait.

And wait. Revna's throat grew raw, and the front of her thighs started to numb. Her head rang with a mix of fatigue and adrenaline; her prosthetics shivered; her phantom limbs pulsed. Crows and waxwings called out from the trees, and branches swayed overhead as martens and squirrels scuttled through the canopy. Somewhere out of sight, a moose bellowed. The forest resonated with the rustling of small things, but her ears strained to hear something larger come stomping up the path.

Maybe the Elda wouldn't come at all. Maybe the Serpent had

broken free of the ice and drifted downstream, or maybe some animal had disturbed their tracks and the Elda didn't even know they'd survived. Maybe they were going to sit here, steadily freezing until they couldn't move anymore at all.

Or maybe the Elda would come and overpower them anyway.

Linné held a finger to her lips, then slid the cover off the hatchet. Around them, the forest stilled. Linné edged to the side of the tree, away from the path. Revna wriggled down in the snow, trying not to squeal as a few clumps got under her collar. She clenched her hands around the gun, focusing on the way they cracked and seared until they stopped shaking. She only had to shoot one man.

Unless she had to shoot herself and Linné.

Revenge. She wanted revenge, didn't she?

Soon she heard them, too. They moved with confidence, and why wouldn't they? The trail was hours old, and one of their quarry was clearly injured. Every so often, they spoke; their voices lilted like birdsong through the trees.

Linné's hands shifted around the shaft of the hatchet. She leaned back, a coiled spring.

The soldiers came into view.

Revna stifled her sigh of relief. There were only two of them. And they were young. Revna could have gone to school with them in some other life. They wore their uniforms poorly, so baggy and wrinkled that even the Night Raiders would feel ashamed. The thin blue fabric was obviously no kind of winter uniform, and as they stopped, the Elda on the left ran his hands up and down his arms. He said something that made his companion laugh. They were comfortable together, friends. They could have been taking a walk through the woods.

Revna put her thumb on the hammer. *One man.* She could hear her own heart. And when the Elda stopped, she was half-convinced they heard it, too.

The boys examined the trail. The one closest to Linné pointed at the remains of the shelter. "Da haren de gesojvet," he said. Then his eyes locked on Revna. They widened.

Linné sprang out and swung. The hatchet connected with his stomach with a soft thud. He doubled over, gurgling. Revna pulled the hammer back. The second Elda shouted, she raised the pistol and shot—

She missed. The forest erupted as birds squalled and took flight. The Elda tore at his own holster, turning toward her. Her fingers fumbled to find a Weave thread. Linné roared, swinging again. Revna ducked her head, but she couldn't block out the sick *thump, slurp* of the hatchet burying and dislodging, nor his wet scream.

Two bodies hit the ground. It was finished. Footsteps crunched over the snow, then Linné crouched beside her. "We have to go." Her voice was surprisingly gentle. "If anyone's at the crash site, they heard the shot." She took the gun from Revna and shoved it into her holster.

Revna sat up. Fire chased ice over her body. Her mouth flooded and she leaned over to spit in the snow. She concentrated on the ground, on her breath, on trying not to vomit. When she could finally speak again, she risked looking at Linné. "I'm sorry."

"At least you fired. We can work on your aim back at the base."

327

There was a harsh sort of humor to Linné's voice as she passed Revna the crutches. The edge of one sleeve was soaked and dark, and blood dotted her coat and flecked her skin. Her face was pale, making her freckles stand out. They wound across the bridge of her nose like stars. She stood and offered her hand.

Revna took it and cried out. Her hand slid from Linné's, tearing the scabs away, and she came back down on the snow. Linné crouched. "What's wrong?"

Revna tugged off her gloves and turned her palms up in the still-pink morning light.

"Holy shit." Linné touched a blackened scab, wrinkling her nose when it cracked. "What happened?"

"Parting gift from the Serpent." Revna tried to ignore Linné's stricken look. "Will you help me up?"

Linné gripped Revna by the upper arm. "We *have* to get you home."

Revna stumbled to her feet. Her whole body was a combination of aches, clamoring for attention. "What's the difference? If we stay here, we get sent away and tortured. If we go home, we get sent away and tortured."

Linné's mouth drew down. The blows they'd traded yesterday were fresh bruises. She still had faith—that the Union would believe them, that they'd be called heroes instead of traitors. "We can treat the infection at Intelgard. And if the Elda have started the salvage, it's even more important that we take the news back before the evidence disappears completely."

They started walking. Revna waited for Linné to refute her, to spout off the virtues of the Union or promise that they cared about the truth. But Linné didn't say anything, and she could feel the disquiet in her as clearly as if they were bonded in flight.

✳

They walked in silence. The sounds of the morning had ceased at the shot, but slowly they returned, as riotous as before. Their racket wasn't enough to drown out the other noises that Revna remembered. The *thump, slurp* of a man buckling around a sharp blade. The slushy gasps of the soldier Linné had killed first. The thud, like a cleaver on a prime cut. They caught in her brain, playing over and over.

"Don't think about it," Linné advised her after a while.

Revna's laugh sounded like a rusty pipe. "That's easy to say." If she didn't think about the dead men, she thought about her hands, or the fact that her phantom feet hurt more with every step. What if the Serpent had ruined her connection to the Weave? What if she returned to the Union without the one skill the Union valued in her? She stabbed with her crutch at a piece of icy ground.

"Fix your mind on something else. Talk to me."

You talk, Revna thought, but she said, "About what?"

"Anything. Tell me about your prosthetics. What happened to your legs?"

Revna tightened her grip on the crutches. "What makes you think I want to talk about that?"

Linné made a strangled, guilty sound in the back of her throat. It was almost enough to make Revna laugh again.

"It was an accident. I don't remember much about it." She remembered the shadow of the cart, the enormous horse and its ropy mane eclipsing the sun. She remembered waking in Tammin's hospital, next to the weeping form of her father. She remembered wanting to throw up the first time she saw where her legs ended too early. She remembered reaching for her toes in the middle of the night, crying at the needling sensation of her phantom limbs. She remembered the pain of her first prosthetics digging at her skin. And she remembered the other pain, the new and raging pain, when she realized no one would treat her the same ever again.

But she didn't feel like sharing all that with Linné. So she said, "I got crushed by a cart."

"Sounds pretty shit—I mean, terrible." Linné moved ahead to clear some fallen branches out of the way.

"I started experimenting more with the Weave after that," she said. "I might not be here if it wasn't for the accident."

"And who'd want to miss out on this?" Linné muttered.

The cold and the fear and the memories cracked Revna's temper. "You don't have to be here. You could run back to Intelgard and tell them all about the Serpent and be the big hero. Don't act like you're stuck."

"Soldiers don't abandon their brothers." Linné kicked a branch, sending it skittering into a tree. Sunlight limned her profile, down to the snow that clumped in her eyelashes.

"Well, don't act like it's not your choice. For a general's daughter you didn't learn much about manners. Or did you get your conversational skills amputated?"

330

Linné went still. Revna watched emotions flip across her face, as if she was trying to choose one. Anger, guilt, hurt. When she spoke, she had a measured, almost conversational tone. "My father told me to be respectful, but everyone in the Union was always bowing and scraping to him, so he never set much of an example. And it frustrated my tutors to be rude, so it was extra fun."

"Your mother didn't have anything to say about it?" Revna asked.

Linné's shoulders hunched and a flush brushed over her cheeks. "My mother didn't stick around after I was born. She went back to the Doi Ungurin."

"Oh." Now Revna felt as though she'd asked an unwanted question. She'd never heard anything about General Zolonov's wife, and she floundered for something to say as she started forward again. "You never visited her?"

Linné fell in line with her. "Bayabar Enluta is a designated enemy of the Union," she said.

Revna snorted. "*That's* your mother?" The Doi Ungurin had consented to be an affiliate member of the Union after decades of on-and-off warfare. Eltai Bayabar had negotiated peace, and his daughter Enluta had refused to abide by it. "I never heard that story."

"It was part of the peace settlement, but she left before it became official and he didn't want anyone to know. Failed marriage contracts aren't really a part of my father's image." Linné paused, surveying the landscape. "He found some farmer willing to be his wife and everyone assumed she was my mother. I didn't find out until she died." Were her cheeks red from cold or something else?

Bayabar Enluta was the very image of insurgent in the Union's eyes. Revna wondered how Linné must have felt, realizing her birth mother was the antithesis of everything she believed in. How she must have heard her father tell lies about their family. "I thought lies were the enemy of the Union. Aren't you angry he didn't tell you the truth?"

"Faith and loyalty are also important, and my mother had neither." Linné blew out a cold breath, and they started up again. For a little while they walked in silence, and Revna thought the conversation was over. Then Linné said, "Maybe he worried I'd turn out like her."

Revna forced a laugh at that. "You're the most straightlaced person I know." *It's what makes you so little fun.*

Linné shrugged. "I left him, like she did. I ran off to fight, like she did. Nobody thinks I look like him. He wanted me to be a lady, the perfect Union girl."

Revna had never expected that Linné might feel uncomfortable being a Union girl, too. "I'm sure he's proud of you."

"I don't care whether he's proud or not," Linné replied, far too quickly for Revna to believe her.

They came to a tree that had begun decomposing over the path. "You have to laugh," Revna said as Linné hopped across.

"I disagree." Linné offered a hand to steady her as she climbed over.

"*I* have to laugh. Your mother's hiding a rebel army in the steppe, and my father's the one serving a life sentence on Kolshek." Not to mention that if they made it over the mountains, Linné would be let off because of her father, and Revna all but convicted because of hers.

✳

The Karavels glowed in the sunset like the fire of the gods. Across the sky, clouds gathered on the horizon, striped gold and red and purple and orange. They made for a spectacular dusk, and they portended a killer storm. "Will we be on the mountain when it hits?" Revna asked.

"We'll get over before that." Linné stopped, glaring from the mountains to the path in front of them. "It's going to be fine." Revna didn't know who she was trying to convince. Linné wore that expression that meant she'd never be the first to give in. But it didn't matter what sort of demands she made on the world and the weather. Those were the two things she couldn't intimidate into submission.

Even when both of Revna's prosthetics had been securely attached, wilderness trails had challenged her. Now the pressure on her residual limbs made her want to give up before she even started on the path that cut back and forth across the mountain slope. Every movement she made was a balancing act, parts touching but not working together. Her hands felt as though tiny barbs pricked at her skin. And what was she even fighting to get home for? Her breath huffed in and out, a reminder. *You're cursed, you're cursed.*

She went first, stepping with care, relying on the living metal to give what she needed. She concentrated on her feet and tried to ignore the small surge of hope every time she came to another turn. Mud gave way to frozen ground, which gave way, in turn, to ice. When her crutch slipped, Linné had to lunge forward to keep her from toppling.

"These don't have much grip," Revna said.

Linné took a breath. "You can hold on to me."

She looped her arm under Revna, squeezing around her ribs. Her touch was hesitant at first, but her grip tightened as they took a step. They moved their legs together, slowly. Linné stank of sweat and mud and unwashed hair, of stale smoke. Revna doubted she smelled any better. Pain assaulted her every time she moved. Her palms burst with it as she made a fist around Linné's coat. Her phantom feet made her want to cry. Her working prosthetic rubbed against her residual limb, scraping at the already raw skin. She could feel a long blister forming near her knee. Another had already punctured. Her bad leg gripped at the ice, but her residual limb kept sliding off its center of balance. The prosthetic had become a shackle.

Sweat collected at the edge of her cap and dripped around her collar, freezing when the wind brushed her. The air thickened as the storm neared. But they made it a meter, then another. And then they'd reached the crest of a false summit, with the main part of the mountain beyond.

They stopped, facing the summit. "It's a long way," Revna said. The mountain was a deep blue shadow, a cutout overlaying the darkening sky.

"Less than it looks. We'll reach the top tonight."

"And then what?"

Linné patted the pack. "We'll set off a flare."

"And all the Elda will see us?"

"Or maybe Intelgard will see us," Linné replied. She wore her favorite expression, the one that meant she'd made up her mind and wouldn't change it. As Revna opened her mouth to speak, Linné shook her head. "Don't waste your breath. I don't—"

"Leave people behind," Revna finished. "Even if I'm asking you to do it?"

Linné's hand tightened on her jacket. "That's treason. They'd strip your family's rights as soon as I reported it."

Revna was too cold to be angry. She hurt too much. "You can't be loyal to both me and the Union, Linné. You have to choose one."

She'd expected Linné's silence. It was the shot that took her by surprise.

Her left knee wrenched and her body was jerked forward. A scream scraped her throat raw as she hit the snow, and the mountain erupted in flight as birds fled the sound. She rolled, bringing her arms up to protect her head.

Linné twisted and yelled, reaching for her gun.

The Elda boy stumbled up the trail but stayed on his feet. He held one hand over the hatchet wound in his stomach, fingers clutched around something dark and glistening. Hate radiated from his blue eyes. His pistol shook in his hand.

Linné fired. Two bursts of red bloomed on his chest. His gun fell. Linné didn't lower hers until he'd sunk, first to his knees, then to his face.

Then she dropped down beside Revna, shoving her pistol back into its holster. "You got shot." Her voice trembled.

Revna sat up. Her prosthetic foot spasmed and she blinked through tears. "I'm okay," she said, fumbling for her crutch. Linné grabbed her arm, trying to lift her without touching her hands. The moment Revna put pressure on her left prosthetic, it buckled again. Her heart crashed, and she took great gulps of air. Terror and pain wound tight around her.

"Let me," Linné said. She pushed up the tattered end of Revna's trouser.

Revna's knee was scraped and bloody, but intact. Her upper calf was a mass of bruises from walking wrong on the prosthetic. And below that—

Her left prosthetic had been ripped apart right below the end of her residual limb. The metal sheet on her calf had crumpled. The bullet had torn all the way through, leaving a twisted hole. She couldn't walk on it now. She'd never be able to walk on it again.

"Fuck," she said, deliberately.

Linné took off her pack. "I can carry you. We can still get to the summit—"

"Leave it," Revna said. A new sort of numbness began to fill her. She ran her fingers over the frayed edge of the bullet hole. She was so tired. Tired of walking, and walking, and never getting anywhere. Tired of dragging down the people around her. Tired of the thin line between treason and loyalty, tired of the demands of her Union, tired of wondering whether her family was alive or dead. She was tired of remembering, tired of hurting, tired of her disability.

"I'm serious," Linné said.

"So am I," Revna snapped. "Stop trying. You don't have to save me. I'm not your brother in arms. I'm not your ticket to some medal."

In the fading light she couldn't see Linné's expression, but she felt the blow land. Linné flopped down beside her. "I don't want to stop trying."

Oh, Linné. She never gave up. She wouldn't admit defeat, even when it might save her life. And she didn't stop to think about what Revna might want. Revna had already lost one whole family. Now she was starting to lose another. This war wanted to take everything from her.

Her voice came out hoarse. "There's nothing you can do. I can't walk without this leg, but if you go now, you can get over the mountains before the Night Raiders finish tonight's run. You can tell them about the Serpent. You can tell them what happened." Linné could change the war, and wasn't that all that mattered? What was the worth of one cursed girl by comparison? The regiment would forgive Linné. The propaganda would love her.

And the Union would finally leave Revna alone.

Linné shook her head, balling her fists on her thighs. "I won't leave you. We can do it together. I'm not trying to win some medal—"

"No," Revna cut in. "You're trying not to feel guilty." Her voice rose. "You're so busy thinking about yourself, like it's your fault if I die. You want me to live, but you don't care what happens after. Going to prison, facing the Skarov—I have to deal with the consequences, not you. So if you're going to leave me, leave me now."

"*Don't tell me what I have to do.*"

Revna twisted to face her. "But you should tell me? I joined to protect my family, and I—" *Mama. Lyfa.* Everything she knew, burning. What could have survived that, and what was the point in hoping? "I killed them. You want to take me home so I can dig two empty graves and stand trial for treason."

Linné reached out, but she didn't seem to know where to put her hand. Her eyes were hard and angry and desperate. "We can find out what happened to your family. Don't give up because you don't know."

"I *do know* what happened!" she screamed. Linné recoiled. Revna pulled her knees into her chest. The broken prosthetic dug into the back of her thigh, but she didn't care. This was all she had left of her father. Her poor father, taken from her piece by piece, scrap by scrap. Memory by memory. "I happened," she whispered. "I'm a curse. On everyone. My father's in prison. My home is gone. Katya and Elena and Nadya and Asya would still be here if it weren't for me." Linné would be safe at the base.

"It's not your fault," Linné said.

"It's still my doing."

Linné shifted. Her finger scraped in the snow, drawing a Union firebird. Revna wanted to shove her off the side of the mountain. She was sick of Linné shouting, snapping, spouting Union rhetoric, and swearing like a Union soldier.

But when Linné finally spoke, her voice was soft. "You're not a curse on me."

Revna fought to breathe. Her skin was too tight and her eyes itched and she couldn't say anything. She shook her head.

Linné's voice picked up strength and certainty. "You're not. How many times did you save my life? You irritate me in almost every way. You're a wet blanket, you're long-suffering, falsely modest about your powers, and the one time you decide to grow a spine is when we're stuck halfway up a fucking mountain. But you're not cursed, and dying won't fix anything."

Revna felt Linné's eyes come back to her. She couldn't look up. The world started to blur. Linné's hand landed on her arm. "It doesn't matter if we're friends or not. You joined the Night Raiders to protect people, and you've always managed to protect me. I can't walk away."

"What do I have to go home to?" What the Union asked, she would give. One way or another, they'd have her death. "I won't be a prisoner of the Union. You can't make my choices for me. Not here." She made herself look at Linné, and Linné met her gaze. Her eyes had lost their anger. Instead they were filled with a hopeless pleading that Revna almost couldn't stand. But she didn't break away, and as she watched, the pleading in Linné's eyes became less, and the hopelessness became more.

Linné broke eye contact at last. "You're right." She looked down at her trembling hands. "But this doesn't have to be the end for you." Revna shook her head again but Linné pushed on. "I know things look different for you on the other side of the mountain. If you come back, you will stand trial. But you'll stand trial with me, and when we're through, we'll find out what happened to your family. I won't abandon you then, and I won't abandon you now. I have faith in you."

Linné's hope was so earnest, so unlike her. Something within Revna reached for it. Maybe they could stand trial together; maybe they could search for her family.

But she was afraid of what they'd find. "You said no prisoners."

"Revna," Linné whispered. The last hope behind her eyes flickered and Revna felt the understanding click into place. She knew Revna was right. But she wouldn't leave, not unless Revna froze to death.

Or died some other way. "Give me the gun."

For a long moment Linné was motionless. Then Revna heard the snap of her holster, and Linné's hand rested lightly on her knee, fingers curled around the gun.

The Elda pistol swam in and out of focus. Guns were such strange things, death in small packages. And the first thing she'd manage to hit would be herself. An irrevocable ending, a fate she couldn't try to change. The weight of it pushed against her arms. But she reached anyway.

She wanted to die with a comforting thought in her head. Of her mother and father and Lyfa, all whole and happy again. Like they never would be, because no one ever returned from Kolshek, and Tammin Reaching was no more.

The air smelled like metal and snow. She lifted the gun with her cracked hands.

Shaking. Her hands were shaking. She turned the gun over

and over. Her thoughts fluttered from place to place. Magdalena, arguing cheerfully with the other engineers. Her scabbed fingers scraped against the trigger. Cabbages and the firing range and abhorrent food in the mess. The barrel, long and thin and wicked. The silver of the Weave under her wings.

And Tamara, believing in her. Tcerlin believing in her. All the girls believed in her. And she believed in them, too.

Even in Linné.

Revna wasn't a curse. The Union was her curse. She could let it unmake her, or she could march back to Intelgard demanding a soldier's welcome and a list of Tammin's survivors. The war was eternal, but the war was also her. Her and everyone else who might do something outside the perfect Union plan. She could give up, or she could hold her head high. She could make the Elda someone else's problem, or she could bring the curse of the Union down upon them like no one had before.

And if the war didn't want her, the war could go screw itself.

She set the pistol back down on Linné's leg. Linné's hand clamped over it as she breathed out. Relief flowed over Revna, mixed with fear that she might change her mind. Even without the Strekoza, she was in her navigator's head.

Revna sniffled. Her cheeks were stiff with quick-freezing tears. She began to shudder. Linné leaned over with an awkward cough and dabbed under Revna's eyes with her dirty sleeve.

"You're brave, you know," Linné said. "I mean it. You're more than your legs."

Revna hiccuped. "I *know*." And she did know. Everyone

made such a big deal out of it and *of course she fucking knew* she was more than her legs. She was furious with everyone for thinking she wasn't, furious with Linné for saying it as if it were some revelation.

And furious with herself, for forgetting it for even a moment.

20

YOUR BROTHERS WON'T ABANDON YOU

Linné took the flare gun out of the pack and strapped it to her belt. Then she kicked the pack off the side of the false summit. She knelt with her back to Revna. Revna almost asked, *Are you sure?* But that was the thing about Linné. She was always sure. Revna wrapped her arms around Linné's collar and Linné looped hers under Revna's knees.

Linné grunted as she struggled to her feet. "You're heavy."

Revna's arms tightened. "Didn't your father ever tell you not to mock a girl's weight?"

Linné didn't laugh. She set out resolutely, planting her feet firmly with every step. Revna kept her duties to clinging.

As they went up the mountain, the path grew steeper, and soon Linné was pushing through snow up to her calves. The noise of the birds diminished as the trees thinned, and the only sound in the air was Linné's labored breaths, huffing in and out to the beat of Revna's heart. The cold had settled in her bones, so deep she thought it might never thaw. Her eyes felt puffy and she wanted nothing more than to close them, to let herself drift off on Linné's shoulder. She ached. Her arms and phantom limbs ached from holding on; her head ached from fatigue. Her heart ached for the things that had happened and the things yet to come.

The night deepened, but Linné didn't stop. Weak moonlight filtered down through the clouds, giving the world a ghostly cast. Linné pushed a sickly spark through her hands that gave only a little light to the path in front of them. Revna waited for the first flurries of snow. They had to get down the mountain before the storm broke.

"We're almost there," Linné panted. "Almost there." She muttered it as she walked, until it became a whispered chant, and then steady breath as they went up and up. The breath became Revna's clock. They made it another meter, and another. *Almost there, almost there.* Her legs and hands stopped burning. She didn't think that was a good sign. But she locked the thought away. First they had to get to the top of the mountain, then she could worry about hypothermia. *Almost there.*

Then she heard the faint sound, bouncing from peak to peak. Buzzing.

She twisted her head as far as she could. "Skyhorses."

Linné leaned on a tree and turned to look over the false summit and the hills behind. The Skyhorses drifted below the clouds, flitting and flashing. They made tight circles, passing over and under one another like dancers. Spark flashed from their jaws. "What are they doing?" Revna said.

Revna and Linné watched the Skyhorses dip, turn, dive. A flare of yellow-orange caught in the trees near the Ava River and stayed there, like a beacon. The Skyhorses' circle became a little wider, flame spouting.

"Shit," Linné said. "Shit, *shit*—"

The Skyhorses were burning the Ava River. The Serpent, their evidence. And they were moving methodically across the taiga toward the mountain.

"Don't you dare let go," Linné said. She pushed up the path. The buzzing behind them grew louder. Revna clutched Linné with all she had.

The forest spat and crackled as trees succumbed to the flames. Birds and foxes screamed. Heat began to nudge at the back of Revna's frozen neck, and the thick scent of charred pine filled her nose. The gray sky illuminated, bright as daylight. "Almost there," hissed Linné. They tottered around a slanting formation of rocks.

The mountain fell away in a seemingly impossible face. The plains spread out below them, pale as the surface of the moon. Revna dug her chin into Linné's shoulder as she looked down. "God," she whispered. Linné winced against her. "What now?"

"Down the mountain," Linné said.

"I don't see a path."

"We don't have a—" But Linné never finished. The thrum of a Skyhorse made Revna's bones shake.

Linné slipped and fell in the snow. Revna's shoulder hit the ground and her grip on Linné loosened. They tore away from each other. This really was how she'd die. With the long neck of a Sky-horse above her and with flames behind her.

The clouds parted, death streaming in.

Only, it wasn't death. It was a little fat plane of canvas and wood and metal. Spark popped like gunfire on the fuselage—the 146th Night Raiders. The Strekoza spun away, rolling wing over wing as the Skyhorse tried to retaliate. Smoke poured from the Skyhorse's tail, and the Weave stuttered in and out of sight as its navigator fought for control.

The Skyhorse's engine choked. It roared with rage. The scent of smoke and storm filled Revna's nose. The Strekoza was coming back around for another pass, and this time it came with company.

The Skyhorse took its chance as the Strekoza flipped under its nose. A long flame sent a scorching wave of heat blasting over the top of the mountain.

Linné scrambled over. She looped one of Revna's arms around her shoulders. "Let's go!" She dragged them both to their feet.

But it was too late. Revna's curse wanted one last try.

A second Skyhorse passed over them, so close it blotted out the world. Its engine hummed like a swarm. It winged around the injured plane, herding its friend away. A Strekoza flew below its underbelly, undaunted, blasting spark against the Skyhorse's wing.

"Down," Linné yelled in Revna's ear. *Down the mountain.*

"How?" Revna shouted back.

The Skyhorse screamed, and fire lit the sky. The ground trembled.

"However we can!"

The snow beneath them began to slide. Revna lunged for the safety of the rock formation. It was already gone.

Linné was gone, too.

Then she was gone. Tumbling down the slope of the mountain, caught up in the avalanche.

She had to swim, to swim with the snow. But she hadn't swum since she'd lost her legs. The snow dragged on her prosthetics like a tide, and she went under. Her nose and mouth filled with it as she tumbled. The snow slid under her jacket, up her trousers. Her left prosthetic snapped. The roar of the battle became the rush of a cold white sea.

She struggled to free her arms, reached and hoped she was aiming for the surface.

Her chest exploded with pain as her ribs cracked. The snow broke over her head and she sucked in a grateful, agonizing breath. She'd hit an evergreen tree. She clutched it like her salvation.

A final wave of snow washed over her. And then, all was still.

Revna dug up frantically until she broke through a thin crust of snow. For a moment she couldn't tell whether she was looking at the sky or at the earth. Everything was gray, and everything hurt. No sign of the fighters. Where was Linné?

Hypothermia. Suffocation. Head injury. All the ways in which Linné could be dead or close to it. Revna had to find her.

Pain hammered against her when she tried to push herself up. She could add *ribs* to the growing list of her physical injuries. Revna gritted her teeth. Time to think of the problems. She wasn't unconscious and she wasn't vomiting. It couldn't be that bad. She could move, or she could die.

"*Linné,*" she wheezed. She tried to draw in breath to shout. The corners of her vision turned black.

347

Far away, she heard the roar of a plane. But the mountain was silent. It was pointless.

No, not pointless. It couldn't be pointless. Linné had refused to leave her behind. Now it was Revna's turn. She *wasn't* a curse. She'd used the Weave on people before, and Linné wasn't just anyone. They had been connected by metal and magic, by faith and loyalty.

She closed her eyes. Her torso throbbed every time she inhaled. She focused on the silence around her, trying to find peace in it rather than fear. The erratic pulsing of her heart settled into a rhythm.

She touched the Weave with cracking fingers. She didn't have time to think about the agony she felt every time she plucked a string. If it was the last Weave magic she ever did, it would be enough. *Linné*. Night Raider. Fighter. Comrade. Maybe friend. She sifted through the Weave, picking apart the strands that made up the world, searching for her one lost thread.

She thought of their plane. Linné's white-knuckled grip and spark streaming across the sky.

She thought of Linné clutching her in the air, falling from the wreckage, staring down at the world on fire. *We're flying.*

She felt—not heat, but some kind of warmth all the same. Something she recognized. She knew the way Linné moved, the way she breathed.

The Weave cut at her and she tore off her gloves, forcing her hands to obey, biting her lip until teeth went through skin. Her whole body convulsed as she shivered. But shivering was good. Shivering meant her body was fighting for her. Her fingers curled around the Weave's invisible threads and she pulled on them, one by one, tugging Linné's body from the snow.

Nothing changed in the white expanse. Revna tried to swallow her panic. It wouldn't help Linné if she lost all sense. It wouldn't help *her*. "Come on," she whispered. She *knew* Linné's body was on the other end of the line, but it resisted her. Like Linné always did.

If only she hadn't been so stubborn. If only she'd gone ahead when Revna told her to.

Well, Linné wasn't going to ruin Revna's final moments by making her feel guilty. "Screw you sideways," she breathed, and the flush that came with it gave her strength to heave again.

She felt the snow shift before she saw it. For an instant she was numbingly cold, too cold to think, surrounded by white.

She cajoled the Weave around her into a cradle, pushing the threads this way and that as they tried to escape. Then she bundled them all in one hand and yanked. The muscles in her arms screamed. Her palms oozed. She set her teeth, braced her back against the tree, and tried again.

Snow puffed up as Linné's limp body emerged from the mountainside. She lay only a couple hundred meters away. Revna could get to her. She had to. But the snow was a vicious opponent to her infected hands and prosthetic legs. And she didn't know what had happened to her chest, but she knew crawling would be agony.

She wasn't going to lose this one. She could win against her allies; she could win against her enemies. And now that it had dumped an avalanche on her, she'd compete with nature, too.

One more thing, she promised her arms. She felt them tremble as she took hold of a strand. Her body came a bare inch off the ground. But an inch was enough.

Her broken prosthetic scraped over the snow. Revna caught it on the edge of a stone and lost her grip. Invisible knives drove into her hands and phantom feet. She kept trying. She pulled, pulled without thinking, pulled until her body came free again. Eternity passed. Black spots popped in and out of her vision. But she was still shivering. Shivering was good. And finally her body was next to Linné's.

Linné's face was terribly cold. Snow had gotten into her jacket and gloves, and probably into her boots as well. A nasty bruise was forming in the space around one eye socket, and her cheek was scraped raw.

Revna put her ear against Linné's mouth. A faint breath tickled her cheek. Linné was still alive. For now.

She sat in the snow next to Linné. The whole world was blank, like the entrance to some underworld, some dream. Of her broken prosthetic, only the tattered calf was left. The shivering was beginning to subside, but her exhaustion made it difficult for her to care. Maybe she should lie down and sleep. She'd known she wouldn't make it over the mountains, after all.

She couldn't sleep yet. There was something she had to do. Linné needed her. Linné wasn't going to ruin her death by dying, too. Revna's fingers fumbled with Linné's belt, where the flare gun was strapped to her hip. She managed to tear the flap open on her third try.

The cold metal of the grip burned her palms. She pointed the barrel toward the gray sky. Maybe they'd see it in Intelgard.

Maybe not. She had to wrap two fingers around the trigger to fire.

A bright ball of red burst from the gun. The flare sailed up, turning the heavens the color of the Union flag. If they died, they'd die in the homeland.

She pulled Linné close, propping Linné's freezing forehead against her neck. "I'm glad it was you," Revna mumbled, even though speaking was the worst, even though she knew Linné couldn't hear.

Something wet pooled and froze on her face. Tears? Blood? Revna touched it gingerly before tucking her hands into Linné's pockets. What did it matter?

She tried to think of her family, of the good times from before her father had been taken. She tried to think of the girls, dancing to the radio in the mess.

Linné's head shifted, just barely.

"Look." Revna's voice came out as a bare whisper. Snow fell on her upturned face like ash. "The storm broke."

✳

Footsteps crunched over the snow. A man. "Who is it?" a strange voice called.

"It's her." The man bent down over Revna and began to excavate Linné from her grasp.

"Alive?" asked the first man.

"Get the blankets."

Revna couldn't even scream when they lifted her into a palanquin next to Linné. Someone began to remove her jacket. She pushed at him with her frozen hands. She needed it.

"Stop it," he snapped. Tannov, the friendly Skarov. The one who'd danced with her, then told Linné about her father. He stripped her methodically, taking her jacket, pulling off her prosthetics and her trousers, and then piled blankets on top of her and Linné both. Then he disappeared. A few moments later an enormous cat hopped up onto the palanquin bed, radiating heat. It settled over Linné's chest.

The man up front barked an order, and the palanquin began to pick its way down the mountainside, talons chipping into the ice. Every time it jostled, Revna wanted to scream.

She wondered how much she'd lose this time. She tried to feel the ends of her legs. But she couldn't fight through the blankets. She gave up and brushed one finger against Linné's arm. She was still there. She'd be all right.

The cat lowered its head onto Linné's belly. Revna could have sworn it was purring.

21

LIES ARE THE ENEMY OF THE UNION

Linné recognized the stale smell of disinfectant before she opened her eyes. For a moment all she cared about was the warmth, the softness of a real mattress under her and real sheets around her. And if she didn't open her eyes, she didn't have to think about what was wrong with her.

But she'd never been good at avoiding her problems.

She moved her feet—still had those. And they didn't hurt too badly, for all she felt as if she'd been run over by a war beetle.

They'd been going up the mountain. Revna was with her. But then—

Revna. Where was she? And if she was here, where was *here*?

Linné pulled on the thin curtains around her bed and got the answers to both her questions. Revna lay in a bed next to her, pale as a wraith but still breathing. The flag of the Union hung on the cheap board walls behind her. They were in home territory.

The door opened and the nurse came in. She smiled when she saw that Linné was awake. Linné wasn't sure how she felt about that. People didn't smile at her.

"Welcome home," the nurse said. "The girls went mad when they saw you."

They'd made it to Intelgard. Only—the others had been happy to see her?

Linné coughed. The nurse brought her a glass of water and tilted her head up to help her drink.

"You've been through quite a lot. How are you feeling?"

"I have to report to Commander Zima," Linné said.

The nurse bobbed her head, as though she heard this all the time. "I've been keeping her updated on your status. I'm sure she'll be happy to know you're awake."

"It's about the mission," Linné said. Her head pounded. "Please."

"Perhaps you'd like some dinner?" the nurse suggested.

"I'd *like* to talk to the commander." Her stomach rumbled. *Traitor.*

The nurse checked on Revna's bandaged hands, clicking her tongue at what she saw. She drew the curtain around Revna's bed, then turned. "I'll get you food. *And* your commander," she added before Linné could complain.

Food. Real food. Better than boiled oats with no salt and bits of venison that tasted like tree bark. Linné imagined caribou steak and crispy fried cabbage with bacon and tea with sugar beet rum.

The nurse came back with beef soup. It wasn't the stuff of

Linné's dreams but was still better than the oats. The nurse helped her sit up, and Linné spooned down mushy onions and barley with an eagerness she'd never felt for army cooking before. For an instant, this was a perfect life—soft bed, warm food. Safe friends.

Tamara came in as she scraped her bowl clean. "Welcome home." She was smiling, but the deep rings under her eyes spoke of long nights, and the upturn to her mouth seemed forced.

Linné put the empty bowl aside. "We found it."

Tamara leaned forward. "Tell me."

She described the Serpent, and Tamara fetched a map so Linné could point to where they'd crashed. For a few minutes, Tamara's forced cheer was replaced with an intense concentration as she traced the path of the Ava River, calculating current and ice flow. "We'll have to tell the colonel and the Information Unit immediately. If we act fast..." Her frown was back.

Even if they sent a salvage team right away, Linné wasn't sure what they'd find. She remembered the heat of fire, the kiss of snow. How long had she been asleep? And if the salvage team found nothing, what would that mean for an interrogation?

"If you're finished with your very important debriefings, it's time for Miss Zolonova to rest," the nurse said. She nodded to the door.

Tamara opened her mouth to object. She seemed to change her mind under the steely eye of the nurse. "We'll write a full report in a couple of days." She leaned forward to pat Linné's arm. Linné tried not to wince as she hit a bruise. "Well done, Zolonov."

"How's Revna?" Linné asked as soon as Tamara had gone.

The nurse looked over at the curtain. She forced her lips into a smile much less genuine than when she'd seen Linné. "She'll be fine. She needs a little more rest."

No one had ever called Linné skilled with people, but that might've been the worst lie she'd ever heard. Linné settled back against her pillow. She tried to tell herself that it was the food that nauseated her, not the drawn curtain next to her.

✳

She slept again; she ate again; she managed to sit up on her own again. Revna slept through everything, even the pilot with the broken leg, who was brought in howling the next morning. Listening to his short scream as they set the bone made Linné's skin crawl.

"When can I leave?" she said when the nurse came in to check on them.

"Don't even think about it," the nurse said. "You need your rest. We'll see how you're doing in a few days."

A few days? Where did she think they were, a general's estate? If Linné couldn't be in the air, she could be doing something. Packing crates or loading bombs. But the nurse would hear nothing of it. She bustled out to tend to the broken-legged pilot. Through the thin walls, Linné heard her say, "Sorry, dear. You can't go in. They need their rest."

A moment later Magdalena slid into the room. They stared at each other—Linné from the bed, Magdalena from the door. Magdalena's uniform was rumpled, as if she'd gone to bed in it. Her eyes had the wild look of someone who hadn't slept.

"I'm glad to be back," Linné said pointedly.

Magdalena turned red. "Sorry. I didn't realize—" Her uniform was stained with oil, and her eyes were hopeful as they flicked to Revna's bed. The hope dimmed at the sight of the pale girl, sleeping. For a moment Linné thought Magdalena might try to act as if all their animosity had never happened, but she took a deep breath and said, "I guess I should go."

"It's okay," Linné said. Revna would want Magdalena to stay.

She expected Magdalena to make some excuse and abandon her anyway. Instead, Magdalena approached and sat awkwardly in the chair between her bed and Revna's. "How are you feeling?"

Why do you care? Linné wanted to ask. But they were all here for Revna's sake, and that she could understand. "Like I fell off a mountain. Which I figure is kind of what happened."

"You figure?"

Linné had never been able to do small talk, and Magdalena didn't want to hear it. So she didn't try. She began to tell the story as if she were reporting to Tamara again, but soon she found herself getting derailed as Magdalena interrupted her with questions.

At first it irritated her to jump back and forth. She had to keep reminding herself of Revna. Revna had saved her, so Revna should wake up to find that her navigator had managed to be civil with her unit. After a while she realized that Magdalena listened because she wanted to, not because she had to, and things became a little easier after that.

When Linné got to their ascent of the mountain, silence caught up with her. She hesitated.

"What happened then?" Magdalena prompted her.

Linné's mind faced a blank wall. "I'm not sure," she said. She remembered fire and the rumble of the mountain. She remembered

Revna handing back the gun; she remembered wanting to cry with relief and fear.

"So you don't remember how you got here?"

She looked over at Revna. "I remember being cold."

"I wish I'd been there," Magdalena said softly.

Linné didn't reply. She doubted anyone would truly want to hike through the taiga for two days in the early winter.

Magdalena's cheeks colored as she looked at Linné, and she set her jaw defiantly. "I mean it," she said. "I'd still fly with her. I'd always fly with her."

"You'd have to fight me for the privilege." Her chapped lips cracked as a smile tried to pull at one corner of her mouth. Revna would be proud. They'd finally found common ground.

Magdalena's eyes glistened. *Please don't cry*, Linné thought. The rest of it she could deal with, but not that. Magdalena didn't cry, though. "I—I'm glad you're back," she said to the floor.

Linné didn't care what she thought. She never had. But this was a different kind of not caring. Before, she'd wanted to prove everyone wrong. She wasn't angry anymore. She didn't mind. And if Magdalena wanted to offer peace, the least she could do was take it.

The nurse's muffled voice came through the thin wall. "She hasn't fully recovered. The commander's visit was a special allowance, so official business or no—"

The door opened. The nurse froze at the sight of Magdalena, who was trying her best to pretend she'd wandered in by accident. The nurse's eyes narrowed. "I see," she said. "Well, I suppose there's nothing I can do." She took a clipboard and pencil from a gloved hand and signed with an angry flourish.

Tannov leaned around the door frame. His silver coat was buttoned all the way up to his throat, showing off his blue star. Magdalena went stiff and gripped the edge of Linné's bed. Linné couldn't help glancing at Revna. *Stay asleep*, she begged silently.

"You look cheerful." Something about his carefree tone felt flat. Maybe Magdalena didn't see it, but Linné knew him. "I don't think you've made friends with the nurse," he said.

"With any luck I won't see her for the rest of the war," Linné managed.

His easy smile widened. "Fortune is with you. She's signed your discharge papers so that you can take a walk with me."

"Where to?"

He shrugged. "Wherever the day may take us."

She tried to wipe her sweaty palms on the sheet without drawing his attention to them. "I'd rather stay where it's warm."

"I can arrange somewhere warm," he said, raising one eyebrow.

She'd have flushed at the suggestion before. She'd have told him to go screw himself. But it wasn't funny. Revna's leg was ruined and she slept and slept, and Linné couldn't convince herself that she'd wake up again. "My comrades have died. If you'd like to pay your respects, you may join us. Be an ass somewhere else."

She saw Magdalena's eyes widen in alarm. *Too far*, they seemed to say. But Linné didn't care. Tannov *was* being an ass, and if he was here for the reasons she thought, he should be honest. As a friend.

Tannov stopped smiling. The room was so still that Linné could hear her own heartbeat. "Come with me, Miss Zolonova."

"You can't—" Magdalena said.

"It's fine." Linné pushed the blankets off. Vertigo spun through her. "I need a minute." Tannov ducked out as she swung her legs to the floor.

She had to lean against the wall to get dressed. Magdalena handed her items of clothing, one by one. By the time she got to her boots, she was too out of breath to even lace them, and Magdalena bent down to help. "Leave it," she said. She took one last look at Revna's bed. *We'll stand through the charges together.* She pressed a hand to her temple and pushed away from the wall, hoping she wouldn't collapse.

Tannov held the door open for her as she walked out. He still didn't smile.

The cold air outside hit Linné with a blast that left her gasping. Snow drifted down in thick clumps. No flying tonight.

The snow had been dug out around the boards, leaving them to walk through little tunnels that came up to Linné's thigh. The killer storm had grounded everyone, by the looks of things. Linné wondered if the snow had stopped the forest fire, and what that meant for a salvage team.

Tannov led the way, striding over the iced boards, slowing only when he realized she lagged behind. The air cleared her head, but she moved ponderously, heavy on her feet. As the fog lifted from her brain, she became aware of the way the silence stretched.

She supposed she should make the peace offering. "I guess I shouldn't have called you an ass."

"You probably shouldn't have." He didn't sound angry. Just neutral.

Linné knew she wouldn't make things better by fighting with him. But she'd never really been able to hold her tongue. "Their deaths aren't a joke. And neither is Revna's life. She did incredible things to keep us alive. And she's my friend."

"That's all quite interesting to hear," he said. Collecting information on her.

Linné stopped. After a few more steps, Tannov turned to face her. "If you want to ask me something, ask it," she said.

He considered her for a moment. Then he dug his cigarette case out of his pocket. "Have one," he said, holding it out.

She stopped herself from shoving his arm away. "I'm being serious."

"So am I," he replied. "Last chance. Their black market value is high."

A snowflake settled on her nose. "Are you out here with me as a friend or as a Skarov?"

His smile twisted bitterly. "You know it doesn't work that way." He flipped open the case and took out a cigarette for himself. She could almost smell the sour tang as he slipped it between his pale lips. He lit the cigarette with a flash of his fingers and exhaled a puff of blue smoke. "Let's go." They headed away from the infirmary, toward the officers' block. Linné forced her shoulders back, her chest forward, out of habit. A light flickered in Hesovec's office. Next to it, Tamara's was dark.

She followed Tannov all the way to a little door on the corner of the block. The building looked like any other on the outside.

But the inner room was cold, dark, and barren. A table stood in the middle, flanked by two chairs. "We can do this in the hospital," she said. "We can do it in the mess. I've got nothing to hide."

He held the door open, leaning forward in a little bow. As if they were going to the theater, not the interrogation room. "Please make yourself comfortable." She hadn't heard him sound so stilted since they'd assisted in a field surgery outside the Goreva farmland. They'd tried to stuff a man's intestines back inside him. They'd both cried afterward. Then they'd pretended it never happened.

"Tannov," she said. If she went into that room, something would break. It might be their friendship, or it might be her.

"Please go inside," he said. "Don't make me write that I had to force you. Please, Linné. Please."

She'd never heard him say *please* so many times in one go. She hadn't expected him to sound so much…like himself. But every word twisted the invisible knife deeper into her gut. Revna had warned her. And she'd known all along—Skarov didn't have friends. As Tannov said, it didn't work that way. But it still hurt. She pushed past him and went inside.

The wooden chair was cold and hard. She couldn't get comfortable, no matter how she shifted.

"I'll get you something warm to drink," Tannov said. "I won't be a moment."

The room darkened as he closed the door.

＊

He came back hours later.

Linné's ass had gone numb long before. She'd given up on

summoning her spark after the first half hour, and she spent the rest of the waiting period trying to convince herself that it didn't matter if her spark never returned. When she heard footsteps on the gravel outside, she tried to shake off her shivering, and folded her hands in front of her. She knew the tactics the Skarov imposed. She'd heard of them from her father when he talked to his ministers and thought she was too young to really listen. The empty room, the hard chair, the cold oven. The waiting and waiting. She was almost offended that Tannov thought she'd break so easily.

"Sorry about the wait," he said as the door scraped open. He carried a steaming cup of tea in one hand and a bag in the other. She set her face to a look of composure. He put the cup down next to her hands, then opened the bag. He took out a lantern and sparked it to life before he closed the door. He fixed the lantern to a swinging hook over their heads. Then he reached into the bag again, retrieving a soft black cloth case. Something metal clinked inside. He sat, folding his hands. Mirroring her.

Linné nodded to the case. "What is that?"

"It's only standard procedure," Tannov replied. "Don't worry about it."

Have you ever tortured someone? she'd asked him, not so long ago.

Give me a break, he'd said. He hadn't said no.

She was tempted to throw the tea all over his smooth silver coat. And she was tempted to wrap her hands around the cup and let the warmth burn all her shivering away. But she didn't touch it. She stared at the black case, and Tannov stared at her.

The minutes stretched out. For the Skarov, it was all about the wait. And at first Linné was willing to play the game. But she'd always been the impatient one. The honest one. She tore her eyes away from the case. "You got grayer since the last time I saw you." Silver streaked through Tannov's honey-colored hair, a thin line at each temple.

"Long week," he replied. "Why don't we get started? On behalf of the Union, it is my pleasure to officially welcome you back to the land of the living."

"Never left it," she replied.

"You were gone for two nights and two days. We were convinced that you and Miss Roshena had perished in the raid."

She shrugged and spread her arms. Tannov leaned away. She smothered an angry laugh. Did he really think she'd attack? Instead she reached for the tea. She couldn't help herself anymore. "Who would you rather believe?" she said, and took a sip.

He shifted, and Linné tensed—but he only drew a small notebook from his pocket. "I'd like to hear the story in your own words. Why don't you tell me what happened? Go slowly, if you need to. I want to hear everything. Any detail you can remember, tell me."

"I'll tell it more thoroughly if I'm warm and full," she pointed out.

He paused with his pen a centimeter above the page. "Are you saying you'd like another four and a half hours of isolation?" His eyes flicked to the case at the edge of the table. Things could definitely get worse from here.

Linné's hands tightened around her cup. "Honestly, I didn't think you'd be so uncivil right from the start." Here was where she found out exactly how far their friendship would take her. *Better to know now.* If only she could convince her pounding heart.

Tannov pushed his chair back and went over to the door. He opened it a fraction and leaned out.

A minute later he stepped back and pulled the door open wide. A man came in with an armful of split logs. He loaded them into the iron stove before scurrying away. Tannov lit the fire with a blast of spark.

"So," he said, sitting again. "The room is getting warm and a meal is on its way. Every excuse you make is something I have to write down. Something that makes you appear less willing."

She hated the way he looked at her. So earnest, so distressed. As if he truly wanted to help.

"Start from the beginning," he said. "What happened to your plane?"

She related the story as well as she could remember, beginning with Katya and Elena. She tried to describe the layout of the camp, the movements of the Skyhorses. Tannov never interrupted her, never shook his head, never did anything but write. His pen scratched and scratched at the cheap brown paper in his notebook, and the only sounds he made were the marks of his pen and an occasional rustling as he turned a page.

She spoke for a quarter of an hour before her voice began to crack. The tea was long gone. Tannov unclasped his hip flask and handed it to her. She took a swig without checking what was inside. Brandy. The cheap stuff. She coughed and sputtered. Tannov was part of the Information Unit. Couldn't he get his hands on some nice black market booze?

When the food finally arrived, she kept going around mouthfuls of cabbage, beef, and onion cooked to oblivion. She paused to lick the bowl clean. Tannov watched her with a mix of pity and horror. "You try two days of Elda rations," she said as she set the bowl down.

She finished her story, then she sat back and waited as Tannov flipped through the pages of his notebook.

"It's quite a tale," he said at last, knitting his brow.

"Put it in the papers. People will love it."

"Perhaps." He scanned a page, lips moving as he read. Then he lowered the notebook. "Are you sure there's nothing else?"

"Like what?" This was what the Skarov relied on. The thought that maybe, maybe she'd done something wrong. The overanalysis of little lies to cover up imaginary infractions that would turn into bigger lies that would be cracked open like chestnuts, with the help of a black case.

"No Strekoza pilot has ever survived a crash. Our attempts to unlock the secrets of Elda aircraft have been universally thwarted. And the way you claim Miss Roshena manipulated the Weave… it's an advanced tactic that's practically unthinkable for a girl of her age and background."

Cold crawled up her spine. *Don't show fear.* "Why stop there?" she said. "Tell me what you think about our time in the taiga."

Tannov tapped a page in his notebook. "You said that one of Miss Roshena's prosthetics broke in the crash."

"I did say that."

"Yet the two of you climbed a mountain."

"It was a small mountain," she said. "And we sort of rolled down the other side." As far as she could recall.

For long minutes they were silent. Linné prepared bombast

after bombast, snide replies to every question he didn't ask. The room grew too warm as the wood burned merrily.

She knew the game. She knew its rules. But she'd never liked it. "If you're going to accuse me of treason, do it," she finally said.

The mask slipped. Tannov's eyes glistened. Then he swallowed and his composure snapped back into place. He leaned in over the table, letting her see the gold detail around his blue star. His hands seemed bigger than she remembered. Suited to breaking limbs. "Did you commit treason?"

She forced herself not to lean away. "If I had, wouldn't I have come up with a more plausible story?"

"That's not a no."

Linné gripped the edge of the table. "No."

"Did Miss Roshena commit treason?"

"*No.*"

Tannov shut his notebook with a snap. "Why was the Serpent unguarded?"

Even breaths. "They were getting it ready for flight. They didn't know we were alive."

He raised his eyebrows. "No one saw you?"

"The world was on fire. Our plane had crashed. No one was looking for us."

He let out a dry husk of a laugh. "How convenient. And two girls under twenty did what no Union engineer has done so far."

Linné felt sweat gathering under her arms and collar. If she took off her coat, she'd only look as if she was getting flustered. "It had already been prepped for flight."

"For three people."

She nodded.

"And you powered it all by yourself, *and* conveniently crashed it."

"Get me a map. I showed Tamara—I'll show you. Didn't you send a salvage team?" *Please, didn't they find anything?* She began to tremble. She wanted to hit him. Back in the day, before she became a woman in his eyes and he became…whatever he was, she would have hit him. It probably would have resolved the argument nicely. She let go of the table and put her hands in her lap, but she couldn't keep the hurt from her voice when she said, "We did everything to get home. And now—" And now Revna's predictions were about to come true.

His pen snapped. Tannov tossed the pieces onto the table and propped his face in his hands, pressing his palms against his eyes. This time, the silence wasn't a waiting game. It was a game of control and who could regain theirs first.

Tannov could, of course. He straightened and pulled out his cigarette case. He took one and pushed the open case toward her. A cigarette would be so good. She could taste it. But it was still Tannov on the other side of the cigarette. And she wasn't sure what that meant anymore. "No, thanks."

Tannov lit his. "I want to help," he said.

"Then believe me."

"I do," he said, and he sounded so pleading that she almost fell for it.

Sour rascidine tickled her nose. She flared her nostrils, trying to breathe it in without showing how desperate she was. "Then why am I here?"

"Because no one else will believe you," he said. "You disappeared in enemy territory, and you disappeared with a traitor's daughter. Between her father and her illegal magic, it's a lot easier to believe that you concocted this story. But if you told me a truth..."

"I'm telling you *the* truth," she said. "Don't you want to go back to Mistelgard dragging the corpse of a Serpent behind you?"

"We've sent the salvage team," he said. "We'll take care of the Serpent, or what's left of it."

She made a disgusted sound in the back of her throat. "But we won't get credit for it."

"Trust me—you don't want credit for it."

Her hands closed around the cup. Her first instinct was to throw it at Tannov's face, but she had enough control to know what that would get her. She squeezed the cup instead, so hard she thought it would shatter. "Lies are the enemy of the Union."

"Your truths will get you thrown in prison." He tossed the notebook on the table, making her jerk back. "Don't you see? How could Revna possibly have known what would get the Serpent in the air? How is it that she survived a crash that no one else could? How do you know she didn't plan to lead the Elda here?"

"I know her." Linné held to the thought of Revna, asleep in her sickbed, relying on Linné. *We'll get through the charges together.* "We spent days fighting for our lives. You should remember what that's like. Or do they pull that out of you with a little black tool kit?"

He paled but pressed on. "When I go to Mistelgard, all they'll hear is that two girls disappeared in enemy territory and came out again with an impossible story. When you add the fact that it's Roshena—"

369

"Leave her alone." Linné slammed her hand on the table. The teacup fell to the floor, splitting neatly down the middle. Tannov's eyes bored into her. Swallowing, Linné bent down and retrieved the pieces, pressing them together. If she pushed hard enough, the crack was almost invisible. Almost.

Tannov closed his eyes. The space between his brows furrowed. "Help me, Linné."

She thought of Revna pulling them through the air. Really flying. "She saved me. She fought for me. And for her I'll fight anyone. Whoever I have to." *Even you.*

"I don't want to fight you." He reached halfway across the table before he stopped himself. His expression was earnest, begging. He sounded like the friend he had been, once.

It's a lie. The Skarov were trained to lie. Tannov was using their shared past. That was all.

He reached again and caught her hand. She pulled away. "Please, Linné," he said, voice cracking. "You know this is standard procedure. You know we do this every time someone goes missing in enemy territory. And you know that if I'd followed protocol, I'd have taken you straight to Eponar and left you with some skull breaker who didn't know you, who'd have opened that case and gotten to work. I want more than anything to go back to Mistelgard and tell everyone what a hero you are. But I can't go back with this."

She looked down at her hands. "It's the truth," she whispered.

They sat like that for a while.

"Well," he finally said in a raw voice. "You won't lie for me, and you won't lie for yourself. Maybe you'll lie for her." The firelight

370

turned his eyes to liquid gold. "You're a general's daughter. Your father will pull strings for you. But Revna has no one. And with her background, she'll never see the outside of a prison cell again."

Heat flooded her. For a moment she thought the spark would push through her skin, returning in a glorious blaze. "Are you threatening her?"

"I'm telling her future," Tannov said. He turned his palms up, a gesture of peace. "Unless you choose to save her. What's a small lie in exchange for the life of your friend?"

22

YOUR SOLDIERS, YOUR COMRADES, YOUR FRIENDS

And so the general's daughter sat down with the Information Unit, and together they lied to their country. Tannov flipped back to the beginning of his little book and went through the written account, line by line. "No one's going to believe that Revna single-handedly got the Serpent flying. We've been working on Elda mechanisms for years."

"Single-handedly? I guess I was there for my glittering wit." Linné rubbed the place where the Serpent had sucked out her spark.

"No one's going to believe you could put in that much power, either," Tannov pointed out. "The other girls on your mission died, didn't they? There's no one to say you didn't fly your issued Strekoza until it became too damaged to continue. The others shot the Serpent down."

And Linné got to watch her achievements be diminished and given away. Again. *It's for Revna*, she reminded herself. "And the lost days?" The night in the taiga and the walk to the mountain?

All the things she wished she hadn't said?

"Blown off course," he said. "You made an emergency landing in Union territory. You rested, recuperated, and later crashed on the slope of the mountain attempting to get back to Intelgard without being spotted by the enemy. I can verify that pieces of your plane were found in the snow."

"And your underlings happened upon the Serpent?"

"I see no reason you wouldn't have remembered where you shot it down."

"You have a convenient lie for everything," Linné said bitterly.

"Think of it as a different way of getting the truth back to Mistelgard." Tannov's mouth turned down as he crossed out half a page. "Not the truth of how it happened. The truth of your convictions. The truth of your loyalty."

Linné didn't need her loyalty publicly verified. "What about Revna's loyalty?"

Tannov looked up. His eyes were so different, and it wasn't just the color. They were cold, uncaring. Foreign to her. "Can Revna handle this story?"

Her heart tapped out a quick double rhythm. "She can handle anything."

Tannov smiled as though he couldn't quite believe that. "As long as she doesn't contradict the official report, she'll be safe for now. But I can't step in for her every time. One day, you'll have to choose who you believe."

Linné didn't answer. She already knew who she'd choose. Not long ago she'd believed in the perfect Union.

Now she believed in her pilot.

So she focused on the notebook and thought, *This is what happened. This is the truth.* She would memorize the story and repeat it to Revna until she'd memorized it, too. And by the time they were flying again, there would be no other truth to tell.

Tannov closed the notebook. "I'll take the report to Mistelgard myself. Dostorov has a prisoner transport to make, so he can drop me off on the way up north. You should be cleared to fly again in three days or so. A week at the most."

"A *week*?" After all this, she still had to wait on bureaucrats who wanted to see her fail?

"Standard procedure," he said firmly. "You can't fly, and you can't leave the base until your status has been cleared."

"Send it by radio," Linné pleaded.

Tannov laughed outright at that. "You know that's not possible. I'll do what I can. In the meantime, do remember that flying will get you a prison sentence."

"Screw you," she said indignantly.

He didn't smile. For a moment she thought she'd gone too far again. Sadness was etched in the lines of his face, the turn of his mouth. "I'll do what I can, Linné."

A knock sounded on the door. Tannov whipped it open. "What?"

Dostorov poked his head in. "What crawled up your ass?" He nodded to Linné. "Heard you were back."

"I think I like his greeting better than yours," she told Tannov.

Tannov shrugged, but she knew it bothered him. "Everything

ready to go?" he said. He turned back to the table, scooped the black case into the bag, and extinguished the lantern.

Dostorov nodded. "Need a drink first, though. It's a twenty-hour ride before I can get rid of you."

"So sweet." Tannov held out a hand to Linné. She stood without taking it. "Come get a drink with us."

"I beg your pardon?" She folded her arms.

"Call it an apology drink. Or whatever you want, Linné. You can spend five minutes enjoying yourself."

"Come on," Dostorov said. He smiled, one of the rare times. It made him look so much younger. "We want to welcome you home."

And they wanted to keep her home. She knew Tannov could have sent her to Eponar. He could have interrogated Revna first, and he could have ruined her. He hadn't, because of Linné.

"To be clear," she said, "I'm doing this for Dostorov, not for you."

Tannov shrugged, smiling, the carefree, easy smile of a soldier who loved victory no matter the cost.

The night had passed while they were inside, and dawn was right around the corner. Cold bit at her nose every time she inhaled. She tucked her hands into her armpits to keep them from freezing and followed close behind the flapping silver coats of her friends until Magdalena's voice drifted over to her.

Magdalena ran across the compound, sliding on the slushy ground in her too-large boots. She skidded to a halt in front of Linné and managed a half-hearted salute to the Skarov men before she burst out, "She's awake."

Linné turned toward the infirmary. She'd promised Revna she wouldn't abandon her. She had to make good on that promise.

Magdalena grabbed her arm. "We can't go in. I heard her talking but the nurse sent me away." Her smile nearly split her face and her voice came out in short huffs, as though she was trying not to laugh. "She needs rest. Tamara isn't even allowed to visit. But she's awake."

Linné could feel heat under her eyes. She thought the relief would spill over her cheeks and freeze to her face. "Thank you."

Magdalena dug her toe into the ground. Her cheeks flushed. "I didn't do anything."

"You stayed with her when I could not." Linné didn't look at Tannov.

"I could say the same to you." Magdalena's foot stilled. Silence grew between them. But it wasn't the usual stony silence. It was an embarrassed silence. Like things had been said that they both regretted.

Magdalena rubbed the back of her neck. "I should go."

"No." Linné was half-surprised to hear herself say it, and all surprised to hear that she meant it. "You should come have a drink."

Magdalena raised her eyebrows. "With... you?"

"With us. The gentlemen have agreed to buy."

Distrust flicked across Magdalena's face, though she did her best to hide it. She glanced at the Skarov, then back.

"I only agreed to—" Tannov caught Linné's well-practiced glare. "To do whatever you like. Of course we'd be honored to have your company, miss."

He offered an arm. Magdalena didn't look as if she believed him, but she allowed Tannov to lead her toward the bar.

That left Linné with Dostorov. They walked in the companionable silence at which Dostorov was so accomplished. But his steps were purposefully slow, and when Tannov and Magdalena were sufficiently ahead, he spoke.

"We'll still have to talk to Roshena."

"Why?" she asked, even though she knew why.

"He's postponing it till he gets back. To give her a bit of time to prepare."

Prepare her story? Prepare for the cold room and colder welcome? "Quite generous of you."

"You know he didn't want to do this."

Not you, too. "I know," she said, and she didn't try to hide the bitterness. "He didn't want to leave me in the dark and cold for hours, or to interrogate me, or call me a liar, or threaten my friend, or any of it. He made sure to tell me it was all standard procedure."

"He already showed you favoritism. He could lose his job if he showed you more," Dostorov replied. "And you don't really lose your job in our line of work, do you?"

Everyone knew what the Skarov did, the power they had, the price of their failure. But Tannov had become one anyway.

Tannov and Magdalena waited outside the bar. Dostorov waved for them to go in. Then he stopped. "He asked to come to Intelgard because of you."

Her blood turned to ice. "He—you didn't even know I was here." She thought of Tannov stalking over the ground, shouting, *Excuse me, miss.* Grabbing her hand in sheer delight. *Look who I found.*

Dostorov shook his head. "We know everything, Linné," he said, and took her inside.

The tiny bar had more men than chairs, and all of them were staring at Magdalena and Tannov. Tannov didn't seem concerned. Magdalena's face was the color of the Union flag, and she fixed her gaze on the floor, scratching her leg with the side of her boot.

The barman grimaced when he saw Linné. "You can't keep coming in here. I told you before."

Linné went up and leaned in his face. She didn't know what exactly made him step back, but she liked it. She gestured to the boys around the bar. "If they get a drink, I get a drink. And pour one for my engineer."

✳

The next pilot grinned as he seated himself across from Magdalena. He downed the rest of his beer in one gulp, then set his elbow on the table, hand out. Magdalena mimicked him, right down to the belch she let out as their hands clasped. Linné had worried about her at first, but she fit in better than Linné did.

The pilot looked over at the referees. "First one to touch the table is out?"

"Like the others," Linné said. "On three."

Tannov raised his glass from the bar. "One," he called. "Two."

Magdalena's opponent forced her hand back. Months of hauling bomb crates and heavy equipment had made her stronger than he'd bargained for. The muscles in her arm rippled, and her descent slowed.

"Three," Tannov called, saluting them both.

Magdalena was locked at the three-quarters position. Linné almost heard the bones of their hands grinding together.

"What sort of winning present do you give to the men who beat you?" said the pilot, waggling both eyebrows. Linné could hear the strain in his voice.

Magdalena was more than a match for him. "Don't know," she said, smiling. "Haven't met any men." The soldiers around them crowed. Slowly, her arm moved upward, forcing him back to the starting position. He bared his teeth.

Linné couldn't help her self-satisfied grin. It was Magdalena's victory, not hers; all the same, the looks on the faces of the first five men had been priceless when their hands had slammed on the table. And this one would be no exception.

The man flexed to no avail. Sweat glistened on his forehead. Magdalena squared her shoulders, preparing to end it all.

The soldier leaned back. Too late Linné saw his friend, right behind Magdalena. He reached enormous hands around and grabbed a breast in each, squeezing generously.

Magdalena's eyes became the size of dinner plates. Her opponent jerked his arm, trying to press his advantage. The crowd screamed. Even Tannov laughed incredulously, sliding off his stool to come help her.

But it wasn't enough, and it wasn't funny. Linné took in everything: the laughing crowd, Magdalena desperately uncomfortable, twisting away from the man's hands and trying to hold on to the one thing, the competition, that might keep their respect.

Rage had always been Linné's friend. And now she reveled in it. Heat poured through her arms, gathering at her fingers, sharpening to a point at the end of her hand. Her smile was of bitter victory. Her spark had returned to her.

She whipped the blade up the offending man's back, slicing through his jacket and singeing his skin. He arched with a yell, releasing Magdalena. Linné used his overbalanced weight to flip him over her knee. She kicked a chair at him for good measure.

Then she turned and kicked his friend in the face.

She couldn't keep track of what happened after that. She kicked a lot of people, and punched a few more, and threw the contents of an entire table in a blast of the spark. At some point Magdalena joined in the fray, shoving the soldiers with arms used to carrying bombs and lifting planes. Someone cracked Linné on the jaw, and someone else got a good jab at her stomach, but by the time Tannov pried her away from the crowd and jerked her arms behind her back, she figured they'd caused more damage than they'd gotten in return.

She kicked behind her, aiming for Tannov's knees, but she missed. "Calm down," he shouted in her ear.

"Get off me," she spat. She tried to spark heat through her arms, but as soon as it reached her hands, it was replaced with a cooling sensation, like flowing water. He was counteracting her.

She saw Dostorov wading into a fight between Magdalena and one of the men she'd trounced. Dostorov shoved Magdalena away. The man Linné had burned came at him, murder in his eyes. Dostorov faced him, and the man backed up. He knew enough to let the Skarov officers have their way.

Linné tried to twist out of Tannov's grip again, but it was futile. He held her tight and she couldn't surprise him with her spark.

He shouted at the crowd. "Contest is over. Fix this mess or get a write-up."

His news was not well received. As Tannov steered her toward the exit, someone said, "They started it."

Tannov didn't bother replying. He shoved Linné through the door and into the cold night, Magdalena and Dostorov close behind. His hands tightened on her wrists. "Are you calm?"

"I'm fine." It wasn't true, but she wasn't about to punch Tannov. Not now, anyway.

He let her go. His tawny eyes challenged her. "Are you sure all of you came back? From the mountains?"

Linné rolled her eyes. "Give me a break."

"It's the biggest loss your regiment has sustained so far. You must have made sacrifices to stay alive—"

"You know exactly what we did to stay alive. We spent the whole night discussing it." She pulled her spark back, letting the excess flash out on the Weave. She needed to keep her temper. Unless one of those assholes came out of the bar.

"It's got to hurt," he said gently.

Of course it hurt. But it was a different kind of hurt. She looked out to the Karavels. The sky was beginning to lighten in the east. "What hurts is that Magdalena would've been the biggest man in the bar tonight. Except she's not a man. So they laughed at her, and they grabbed at her, and when it upset her, it was *her* problem. That's us. It always will be."

Magdalena stood silently next to Dostorov as he smoked a rascidine cigarette. She was crying, silently and furiously, smearing her face with grease as she wiped her eyes on her sleeve.

Tannov sighed and got a cigarette of his own. He seemed

deflated. He didn't touch Linné, and she was grateful for that. "Welcome to the world, little lion."

She'd earned that nickname with her yell. Now it seemed that whenever she yelled, someone was there to tell her to calm down. "Don't call me that."

Tannov removed the cigarette from his mouth and examined its glowing tip. "Listen to me, Linné," he said. "Not as a boy, not as an officer. As a friend. Don't go back in that bar by yourself. Stop and think for five seconds before you go on some angry rampage, even if what you see isn't fair." He looked up at her, and his eyes crinkled into an almost-smile. "You can't hospitalize every soldier on base. Some of them have to go to the front."

Dostorov bent and stubbed out his cigarette on the snow, then put the remaining half back in its case. He sauntered over. "It's time."

Tannov nodded and flicked his cigarette to the ground. "Don't even think about flying. Zima knows you're banned."

Linné shrugged. Tannov offered his hand, but she shrugged at that, too.

He forced a smile and shoved the offending hand into his pocket. "I'll be seeing you, soldier."

"Bye," said Dostorov.

She stood next to Magdalena and watched the two men walk to the edge of the base, where another silver-coated Skarov guarded a hulking palanquin. They climbed in. The palanquin's six living metal legs creaked as it pushed off the ground. It lurched down the road and into the dawn.

Linné and Magdalena watched until it was gone.

Magdalena spoke first. "Sorry for ruining your night."

She deserved something better than a brush-off. "You were brilliant," Linné said, trying to bring some warmth into her words. "A credit to the regiment and the best brawl mate I ever had."

Magdalena turned pink.

"Come on." Linné nodded toward the infirmary. "Let's go see Revna."

✳

Revna propped herself up against the headboard and waited for the room to cease spinning. Her ribs pulsed with every breath. Her hands itched against their gauze, but they'd stopped burning.

Her prosthetic was propped against the wall, stiff and cold, covered in grime. Her broken leg lay on the floor next to it, little more than a couple of straps and half a metal sheet. Looking at it felt like poking a raw wound. She focused on the room instead—the Union flag, the empty bed next to her.

She picked up a muffled argument outside the closed door. "—can't go in," her nurse was saying. "I don't know how many times I'm supposed to tell you."

It must be Tannov. He was probably salivating at the chance to interrogate her.

Only it was Linné who slid around the door—and Magdalena trailed close behind. "We won't be long," Linné said over her shoulder.

"Any amount of time is too long," the nurse said, following them into the room. She interrupted herself with an irritated sigh when she saw Revna sitting up.

"I didn't think it would be you." Revna leaned forward, even though it made her right side scream. Seeing Linné and Magdalena together lifted some of her weariness. She didn't realize she was grinning until her cheeks started to hurt.

"Who else would it be?" Linné said. Her shoulders drooped. Magdalena's eyes were puffy and red, her hair disheveled. Bright scratches ran down the length of her arms.

Something was wrong.

"What happened?" Had the Skarov already come? She imagined Magdalena and Linné, in separate blank rooms, sporting fresh bruises and fighting to keep their spirits up.

"Everything's fine," Linné said. She forced a smile. It didn't fit her.

"You sound very cheerful," Revna said.

Linné shook out her hand. The knuckles were scraped. "Do I?"

Yes, something was definitely off. "What happened?" she repeated.

Magdalena let her thick hair fall into her face. Her eyes settled on the place where the sheets flattened below Revna's residual limbs. Revna tried not to shift away.

"Nothing. We're tired. Not everyone got to lie in bed all night like you did," Linné said. Her classic sharpness was back, but one side of her mouth twisted. It might be a genuine smile this time.

"The others are asking about you. Shall I tell them you're doing well?" Magdalena said finally.

"Very well," Revna said, and the lightness came back. "I'll be out of here in a couple of days."

"No, you won't," the nurse put in from behind them.

"Get better, all right?" Linné blushed at Revna's smile. "You're my ticket to shooting things. I don't know what I'll do until we fly again."

Revna did. "You'll scowl in the mess."

Magdalena giggled. Linné looked daggers at her.

"That's enough," the nurse said. "Revna needs to regain her strength."

"Can't they stay? I promise they'll be quiet." She didn't want to be alone, nursing her injuries, remembering the last few days. Worrying about what would happen next.

Magdalena pressed her lips together. Linné folded her arms.

The nurse flared her nostrils. "At least I can keep an eye on you," she said to Linné. Linné lifted her chin in defiance. "Did they let you off, or send you back here to rest?"

"That's none of your business." Linné took the chair next to Revna's bed.

"What's she talking about?" Revna asked as the nurse left.

Linné shared a look with Magdalena that Revna didn't understand. She didn't like it. Why was everyone acting so bizarre?

"I'll go now, too. I'm supposed to be inspecting glass for gas canisters. I'm, um, a little behind." Magdalena coughed, then leaned in and wrapped her arms around Revna's shoulders, pressing tentatively. Revna breathed deep. Her friend smelled of sweat and oil and smoke—and liquor? Magdalena's nose pressed into the top of her head. "I'll see you tomorrow," she said into Revna's hair. She looked at Linné one last time. Her eyes filled and she blinked furiously before turning away.

Revna watched her leave. "Did you two fight?" she said as the door swung shut. It would be typical Linné to antagonize Magdalena as soon as she got back.

"Not each other," Linné said.

"What's that supposed to mean?"

Linné opened her mouth, then closed it again. She clasped her hands, squeezing until the skin of her knuckles broke open and filled with red.

Her uncertainty was more jarring than her silence. "Did you tell Tamara about the Serpent?" Revna asked to distract her.

Rage gleamed in Linné's dark eyes. Something in her spoke to Revna of despair, of helplessness, and slowly the anger diminished until she could force her hands apart. "We didn't fly the Serpent."

"What are you talking about?"

Linné opened her mouth once more, and the story came out. She told Revna about her interrogation in broken sentences, falsely casual, as though it had been nothing more than a conversation between her and Tannov. Revna knew better. The Skarov never chatted.

She listened, and the hollowness in her grew the more she heard. Everything was different. Everything was a lie. "So all this was for nothing?"

"No." Linné hesitated, then lifted her hands. They fell, heavy and awkward, on Revna's shoulders. But the longer they stayed there, the more they seemed to fit. "I told you I wouldn't abandon you. This…" She met Revna's eye. "This is going to keep us flying."

It was going to keep Revna out of prison. But somehow, it felt like an empty trade. The Union stood for truth and obedience, faith and loyalty. Her family had been destroyed for the tenets of the Union. She'd lost her leg for the Union. Now the Union didn't want to hear the truth at all. Anger made her vision swim.

She put a bandaged hand over Linné's scraped one, pressing until she could feel the pain in hers. Linné's eyes shone with grief, raw and real, for all they had done and could not say.

"We still know," Linné said. "It's enough for us."

They both knew it had to be.

She didn't mean to start sobbing. And when panic flashed over Linné's face, her tears turned into a gasp of laughter, for a bare moment. She couldn't help herself. She leaned into Linné's shoulder, shaking.

Linné's arms closed around her, tentative. One hand rested on her head, then slid cautiously down to the nape of her neck. "I'm here," she said in a soft voice Revna had never heard before. It only made her cry harder.

Later she could do anything. Later she could be stronger. But now she sobbed, and Linné stroked her hair and held her until she fell asleep.

AUTHOR'S NOTE

There is a trite saying that truth is stranger than fiction, and another trite saying that the best lies are often laced with truth. This elaborate lie I have spun is inspired by the truth, and while much of that truth is strange, it is also tragic, uplifting, and incredible in its own way. The women who inspired this novel were not called firebirds, but Night Witches, and they flew night missions at the Soviet front during World War II. Flying outdated training planes, they dropped bombs on the German lines to keep their enemies from sleeping, and it was the Germans who gave them their iconic name. The Night Witches met resistance from their enemies, their own army, and their country—but they never stopped fighting, and they never stopped caring, even when it seemed the Union didn't care about them.

Reading about their friendships and their hardships made me want to write a book about women who only needed one another, women who worked hard to do what everyone said they couldn't, women who struggled and suffered for a country that would never repay them. The books that most inspired me were, first off, *A Dance with Death* by Anne Noggle, which is the closest we can get to hearing the words of the Night Witches themselves. I also found

Wings, Women, and War by Reina Pennington and *Soviet Women in Combat* by Anna Krylova to be essential reading to understand the full significance of the Night Witches and their sister units.

This novel is, of course, very loosely inspired by the story of the Night Witches and is not meant to be historically accurate.

ACKNOWLEDGMENTS

The very first people I'd like to acknowledge are my family. Mom, Dad, Liz, and, of course, Grandma, you've always encouraged me to keep writing, to share that writing with the world, and to work on my dream of becoming a published author. Honestly, how many moms say to their girls, *I still think you'll make your living off writing*?! I love you all, and I miss you all.

Second, to my husband, Elias, who was the one who actually put up with my writing habits, let me sit down at the computer at all sorts of inconvenient times, who watched me set ridiculous goals for myself and helped me achieve them, who talked me through difficult plot points, who read my strangely horrific short fiction, and who can always mortify me by performing my novel in a voice loud enough to wake the neighbors. I love you, too.

Thank you to Kurestin Armada, my amazing agent. You didn't just see my book—you saw where it was, and where it should be, and how to get there, and you were the first who did. I'm so grateful to work with you. Here's to many more historically inspired fantasies!

And thank you to Hallie Tibbetts and Lisa Yoskowitz, my editors at Little, Brown. Hallie, you never gave me a comment that didn't stick. You pushed me, you had faith in me, and you gave me the tools I needed to make a book I'm still proud of. Lisa, having you on my side was wonderful, from our first conversation to our cover discussions and beyond. It's been a pleasure from the first phone call. Thank you.

To the Little, Brown team who made this book a book: Jen Graham, Anna Dobbin, Virginia Lawther, Karina Granda, cover artist Billelis, and the publicity, marketing, and school and library teams. Thank you for cleaning up my messy writing, keeping everything on task, and giving me a beautiful interior and exterior.

A lot of research was conducted while writing this book, and a good chunk of it involved marginalized individuals, particularly amputees. A special thank-you to the people who allowed me interviews and discussed the social and practical realities of disability, and a special thanks to Kati Gardner for your sensitivity reads. Any remaining errors, in fact or in judgment, are mine, and for them I apologize. I will always be striving to do better.

Writing can be lonely, but it doesn't have to be! A big thank-you to the sci-fi and fantasy writers' group in Copenhagen, to the Storied Imaginarium, and to the Brainery, who all played a big part in helping me to understand my strengths and weaknesses. And often fed me cake.

And to the Novel Nineteens and the Class of 2k19, who have been a place of cheer and happiness, who have been supportive through my fears, depressions, and elations: I got a different but no less important kind of writing support from you, and I look forward to seeing where our writing takes us all.

I'd probably better acknowledge Sabaton, Swedish power metal band and fantastic live performers. And Crystal, for giving me your extra ticket to go see them. Maybe I would never have heard their song *Night Witches* otherwise. Maybe I'd never have gotten curious. Maybe I'd never have written this book.

And finally, one last thank-you to the women themselves, the *Nachthexen*, the Night Witches, who risked it all in total war. I'd never heard a story like yours. I hope I've stayed true to the spirit of it.

Turn the page for a sneak preview of

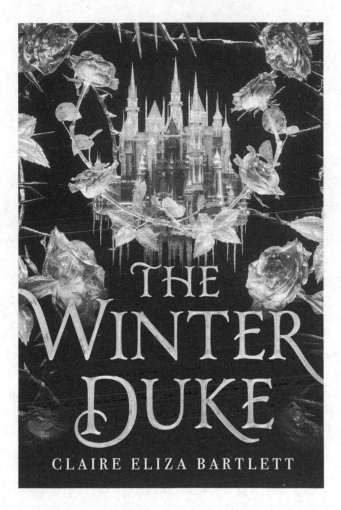

THE WINTER DUKE

CLAIRE ELIZA BARTLETT

CHAPTER ONE

The night could be worse, considering. The likelihood of a public death was low.

All the same, I kept my opulent coat buttoned up, despite how my neck itched in it. The more layers I had between me and my sister Velosha, the better. Last week she'd nicked our brother Kevro's arm with a poisoned stiletto at Wintertide mass, and I wasn't about to let her try her tricks on me. "Ekata," she whispered. I pretended not to hear.

My favorite tutor said that other people's siblings were noisy, argumentative telltales. *My* siblings tried to murder one another.

But not this night. Tonight we had a strict no-murder policy. Tonight we had a brideshow, and the world was watching us. And nothing said *get out of here* like an unstable, bloodthirsty family. I should know. I'd been begging my father for the chance to leave from the moment I was old enough to take a place at a university. He'd promised that when the brideshow was finally over, I'd be free to do it. Provided I lived so long.

The brideshow candidates stood on the long, narrow balcony that ran around the Great Hall—fifteen people who thought that marrying into our family was a good idea. Some of them giggled with one another. Some observed the floor, pointing out their delegates to the candidates next to them. More than one looked tired of waiting. A pretty girl with a dark ponytail and an emerald-and-gold riding suit covered a yawn with her hand, earning a laugh from the girl next to her. Her arms were bare, tan from the kiss of a foreign sun. A bold choice for a palace made of ice. But something about her *seemed* bold. When she caught me watching her, she raised an eyebrow. I rolled my eyes at the absurdity of it all. Her mouth twitched into a lazy smile.

My stomach lurched. I flushed, looking away before I could cause a scene. I had no desire to create an international incident, and she was here for my brother, not me.

Mother had sent written invitations to twenty empires, duchies, and kingdoms. Fifteen of the invitations had been answered with delegations, who now stood on the floor of the Great Hall and waited for the festivities to finally begin. Most eligible royals would be interested in a deal with Kylma Above and access to trade with the prosperous duchy Below. Kylma Below was the only source of distillable magic in the world, which meant that our cold, tiny country on a frozen lake commanded policy alongside kingdoms a hundred times our size.

Even so, it surprised me that fifteen people could be interested in Lyosha. That, more than anything, was a clear indication they'd never met him.

The restlessness was infectious. We'd been waiting for my father, mother, and brother for half an hour, and up on the royal dais, we didn't talk. I glanced at my maid, Aino; she lifted her chin, and I did the same. Aino had never steered me wrong at a social function.

A door on the side of the Great Hall opened, but it was only Prime Minister Eirhan. He'd been prime minister longer than I'd been alive, and his oily demeanor left me with a sour taste every time I had to speak with him. That was happily rare; I preferred the study of bones and trees and the denizens Below to the study of politics.

Eirhan spoke to a guard next to the door. The guard, dressed in ceremonial silver and blue, struck his iron-tipped halberd on the ground. The guards lining the hall took up the movement, creating the iron tempo that announced my father.

The hall went dark, and whispering began. A dark hall heralded magic, for magic did not work well with fire. The candles burned low in their sconces, reflected like diamonds by the ice walls.

Light descended from above, instead, in round pearls that fell like feathers. They glittered as they drifted, shimmering blue one moment, orange the next, clumping together like the thick pollen that blew in from the mountains during what passed for summer in Kylma Above. There was a great intake of breath from the hall, and I tilted my face up to catch some of the pearls as they fell. My father was the only man in the world Above who could refine magic and control how it manifested, and it never failed to mesmerize. It was his declaration of wealth, his declaration of power, and it reminded the rest of us what magic could do, if we only had the imagination for it.

The pearls turned into flower petals, filling the air with a sweet scent. *Rosaeus brumalis*, I thought, breathing in the faint smell of winter roses, the only kind that grew here.

Before they kissed our faces, they burst apart again, showering us with needled points. I covered my face with my sleeves. A few of the delegates shouted. A crack shook the palace walls, and dark wings snapped above us. An enormous eagle winged around the top of the domed ceiling, golden eyes flashing in the dark. Its cry made my ears throb, and its wingbeat nearly blew me into Velosha.

The eagle pulled its wings in and hurtled to the ground. Delegates stumbled out of its way, and even I, who'd seen my father's displays at least twice a year, flinched. With a screech, the eagle raked its talons across the floor, leaving deep gouges that would stay long after the bird had disappeared. The power of magic: It was temporary, but the effects were permanent. And only my father had the secret to it.

I hated him for that more than I hated him for other things.

The eagle launched back into the air, knocking over the nearest delegates, and sped toward the ceiling. I was certain it would slow down or disappear—but instead, it crashed through the dome. Ice shattered and plummeted toward us. We ducked again, but the ice slowed and spun, turning into snowflakes that dusted our shoulders like sugar. Wind howled through the cracked dome, but winter roses grew over the cracks, smoothing the wall; ice climbed toward the starred sky. The hole became smaller and smaller until the last of the roses knit together, leaving us with our ice dome and sealing us off from the elements once more.

Light flared. The room became golden and warm. The show was over, and the grand duke stood before us. Everyone knelt.

That was Father's grand trick for our guests. Show them the power of magic—its constructive, destructive, and transformative glory. Because magic was our most exported resource, Father wanted the wealthy delegates to imagine what they could do with it. They could impress kings. They could bring down city walls. With the correctly refined pearl, they could change the world.

My father's very presence demanded silence. I'd feared him for almost as long as I could remember. Where he walked, the air seemed thin and sparse, as if his broad shoulders and fur coat pushed it out of a room. As if it tangled in his snow-and-stone beard or got bitten off by his sharp teeth when he smiled. As if his brown eyes could pin it down.

Mother stood next to him in a dress of white doeskin. She and I shared the same pale hair and skin, the same gray eyes, the same pointed chin and nose. I hadn't managed to inherit her elegance, but I made up for it by being less abhorrent. And on Father's other side stood Lyosha—eldest brother, heir-elect, and groom for the brideshow—who had Father's height and dark hair and pale skin, but still looked like a weasel in a coat. Unlike the rest of us, he wore the brown-and-white wool that was spun from the shaggy goats we kept at the base of the mountains, eschewing the bright colors and fine-spun cottons that could be purchased from abroad. Lyosha liked to consider himself a man of the people—provided the people wanted nothing from him.

My father motioned for the hall to rise. I straightened reflexively. As Father began his welcome speech, I kept my hands clasped in front of me; I knew if Lyosha caught any of us fidgeting, he'd have harsh words and harsher actions for later. As subtly as I could, I let my eyes and mind wander over the motifs on the walls. They told the story of the duchies—the duchy Above, and the duchy Below. Our duchy, which sat on a frozen lake, and the land that thrived beneath the ice.

More than anything, I wanted to see what truly lay Below. But I would never get the chance. Only Father was allowed to enter that realm.

I focused next on a hunting scene with a former grand duke and a cornered bear. I recalled bones, starting with the bear's nose. *Nasal, premaxilla, maxilla. When ground, stabilizer for liquids that tend to curdle. Incisors, canines. Amulets for strength with no demonstrable benefit.*

I was nearing the ilium when the patter of applause interrupted me. The speech was over. I joined in, lifting my chin so that I could look properly impressed. Father offered Mother his arm, and she took it with barely a sneer. They stepped down from the dais together. The brideshow had formally begun.

Prime Minister Eirhan came forward and bowed perfunctorily before murmuring something in Father's ear. Father nodded coldly to the Kylmian ministers, who clustered off to the side. It was no secret that Father and Lyosha fought over the ministers; they fought over everything. Lyosha couldn't mount a successful coup without the majority of the ministers on his side, but Mother's support lent him strength; a coup had been rumored for years. My maid, Aino, had been predicting it once a night for weeks. After all, it was the traditional way for Kylmian children to inherit the dukedom. Poor Aino had taken to double-locking my door each night, and she spent hours fretting right inside it. As though *I'd* be the first one slaughtered in a coup.

It doesn't matter anyway. The coup wouldn't take place in the next five days, and after that, I'd be down south at the university, where the world was civilized and people didn't kill their relatives as a matter of course.

As the brideshow candidates filed down from the balcony,

the first of the guests began to greet my father. King Sigis of Drysiak approached, and I slunk behind Velosha. Sigis was an observer, not a delegate, but in my opinion, he was more of a royal pain than anything else. He'd oiled his golden beard to catch the lamplight, and aside from a scarlet-and-diamond pin that signified his own colors, he wore our family blue. He'd fostered with us for five years, learning to swagger like Father and manufacture "accidents" leading to broken legs and broken skulls among more than one sibling. Father favored Sigis over any natural-born child of his own, and he had taught him the worst of his tricks. Maybe it was the cruelty they had in common. The Gods knew arrogance was something we all shared.

Sigis embraced Father, and Father clapped him hard on the back. "Welcome, as always."

"As always, I am honored to be welcome," Sigis said. I didn't snort at that. I didn't want to attract attention. But Sigis's politeness was always an act. He always made me think of a bear—except he lacked the bear's manners. "I was surprised by the size of the magic display."

"It's only the preliminary night," Father said. "I've saved a more impressive show for when the rest of the delegates arrive."

Sigis's eyes glinted strangely. "I look forward to it."

As he moved away, Father leaned over to speak in Mother's ear. "I could have gotten him to stand up in the brideshow."

"Sigis doesn't like boys," she replied out of the side of her mouth.

Lucky boys, I thought.

Father rolled his shoulders. "I could have done it."

"Maybe you should have given him a daughter when you had the chance." Mother sneered. Father shot her a murderous look in response. How those two stayed in the same room long enough to make thirteen children, I'll never guess.

My dress itched in a number of awkward places, and the noise that bounced off the ice walls threatened to give me a headache. But I had to stay until each of the brideshow guests had been greeted and we'd been dismissed from our formal duties. I curtsied to the first candidate, a blushing, stuttering boy. He muttered a name too soft for me to hear, though I ought to have known it from the crest on his shoulder, a wheel flanked by rearing horses. Father and Mother treated him courteously; Lyosha dismissed him with a curled lip. I didn't know much about the candidates, but I did know this: My parents and my brother each had a favorite, and it wasn't the same person.

"Show respect," said Father as the boy retreated. His voice was soft—dangerous.

Lyosha's lip curled. "Why? Omsara is a paupers' kingdom. We don't need them."

"The point of the brideshow is to strengthen friendships, not create rifts," Father said. "I asked you to think about that when you started considering your choices."

The next candidate came up, a girl who was graceful and tall, brown-skinned and wide-eyed, and dressed in a white-and-green shift dress. It looked loose and free compared with the tight bodices we wore under our coats. She dipped a curtsy to each of us, smiling. I stifled a sigh as I curtsied back and pressed her hand. This was going to take *hours*. I could be spending the time packing, or studying, or making my university portfolio. Maybe I could persuade Aino to claim I was ill. Anything would be better than pretending I cared about a brother who thought I'd be more convenient dead and about the poor person who was about to marry him.

I spotted Farhod, my alchemy tutor. Like me, he tried to eschew major functions; unlike me, he usually had more success. I rolled my eyes for his benefit. He shook his head reproachfully. His dark, wide eyes were uniquely suited to disapproval.

"I like her," Lyosha said as the snowdrop girl retreated. "She can be considered."

"Not so obviously, my love," Mother warned him. "Everyone needs to start off on equal footing."

"They're not equal," Lyosha replied. "And I don't see the point in wasting my time."

"Then perhaps I should select a different heir," Father replied. "Being grand duke is a balance, not a life of doing whatever suits you, and when."

Lyosha stiffened, as though he'd been hit by a blast of cold wind. Rage gathered around him like lightning waiting to ground on something. "The future of the duchy is mine. My choice. I don't have to run it as inefficiently as you have."

The next candidate faltered. Father motioned them forward with a gracious sweep of his hand, but I couldn't blame them for moving with reluctance. They introduced themselves in a hurry and retreated as soon as they could.

"Come, now." Mother touched Lyosha's shoulder, on Father's side for the first time in years. "There are many considerations to be met. We can't afford to offend anyone before we know what they're offering for the marriage."

Lyosha sulked. "You just don't like her because she's not *your* choice."

"We talked about this," Father said.

Lyosha spoke in a voice not quite low enough, not quite practiced enough to reach only our ears. "*You* talked about this. You didn't bother to ask."

"This is a political endeavor—" Father began.

Lyosha's voice rose. "I have my politics. I make my choices." A small circle of space began to grow around us. "And if I can't make my own choice, I'll make no choice."

"You are jeopardizing years of statecraft," Father growled.

"The duchy doesn't need outdated relics deciding statecraft," Lyosha choked out. "And neither do I." His words slid through the air like a red sword. The brideshow candidates stared. The tan, dark-haired girl in the emerald-and-gold riding suit no longer smiled. Lyosha's anger crackled, so palpable I could almost see it. "This isn't your brideshow."

"This isn't your duchy," Father replied. He sounded almost contemplative. "And the more you try to take it, the more I think it never should be."

The whole hall was silent for a breath, waiting for Lyosha's lightning to finally ground.

"The brideshow's off," Lyosha called, his voice bouncing off the hard ice walls.

Noise rippled across the hall. Father grabbed for Lyosha's arm, but Lyosha had spun on his heel and was already striding through the candidates, who scattered and regrouped like a herd of animals.

Father clapped his hands. In response, the guards around the hall slammed their halberds against the ground with a *crack*. In the silence that followed, he said in an impossibly calm voice, "The brideshow will resume tomorrow. Please enjoy yourselves."

By the time he was finished, most of the foreign delegates had begun to shout.

"Excellent," Velosha murmured beside me, and I shuddered. If Lyosha lost the title of heir-elect, she'd look to win it through a process of elimination—specifically, by eliminating her sibling rivals. Half the court ministers disappeared; the rest decided to settle the matter by arguing at the top of their lungs.

A hand gripped my elbow and yanked me sideways. Aino. She was supposed to stand at the edge of the hall as a lesser lady, but she'd squeezed her way over to me. "Come on," she said, pulling me toward a side door. She elbowed past the minister of the people, and I tripped over the minister of trade's robe. He stumbled past me, steadying himself by putting a hand on top of my head for balance. Had it been a normal night, I would have confronted him for his rudeness.

Aino dragged me past anxious servants to the corridor, barely letting me get my feet under me. The flickering lamps set into the walls caught the red in her auburn hair, and her knuckles were white around my arm. We hurried past officials and servants who rushed the other way, alarmed, no doubt, by the noise. "Slow down," I protested, tripping over the heavy hem of my coat. Aino didn't answer. "Aino!" She wrenched me around a corner, nearly dislocating my shoulder. The iron grips on the bottoms of my shoes dug into the ice.

She didn't slow down until we reached the royal wing and passed beyond the guards there. We scurried down corridors carved with the scenes of my family—grand dukes battling with enemies, treating with the duchy Below, choosing brides from their own brideshows. Winter roses twined above us, their ice petals stretching into a two-thirds bloom.

Aino dug out a key and unlocked my door with trembling fingers. Then she shoved me inside.

The fire was out. The ice walls of my rooms glowed blue-white in moonlight that streamed through thin windowpanes. Aino dumped firewood into the metal basin that served as the fireplace, then started the fire with dry moss and a flint.

The fire basin sat on a thick stone shelf to protect the ice floor beneath, and white and blue tiles lined its chimney. A bearskin rug lay in front of the fire, and I sat in the oak chair there, shifting a blanket to one side. I slid my feet out of my wooden shoes and dug my socks into the rug. A tightness began to uncoil in me. No siblings to murder me, no Father or Mother to examine me, balancing my usefulness and irrelevance against my potential as a threat. I pulled diamond-studded pins from hair that had Mother's paleness but not its curl.

My rooms always meant safety to me, but not to Aino. She locked the door, slid the bolt, and heaved a chair from next to the door until it blocked the handle. Then she went to lock the door to the servants' corridor.

"What are you doing?" I asked.

"Making sure no one separates your head from your neck in whatever happens tonight." Aino's braid had come undone, and she pinned it back up with thin-lipped determination. "This is a coup, and Lyosha and your father are in the middle of it. You don't have to be. How packed are you?"

"Fairly packed." My trunk sat in a corner of the room, stuffed with all the things I thought I'd need at the university—clothes, books, sketches of the biology of Above, a few plates with detail on flora from Below sent up as a sample and gift to Farhod. I was still working on copying his dissection report, a recent—and generous—gift from the duchy Below to expand our academic knowledge.

"Good. We'll set out tonight, and we won't come back until one of them is grand duke and one of them is dead."

No one could boss me around like Aino could. She was

more of a mother to me than Mother. She was shorter and slimmer than our family, with wide blue eyes that always looked alarmed and a nose made for poking into my business. She knew the intrigues of Lyosha and my parents before I did, and she made sure I was always well dressed for events of the court, well versed in what to say, and well protected from the worst of my family's wrath. She tasted my coffee every morning and ran her fingers along the seams of my new clothes to check for razors my siblings might have slipped in. Worrying for my safety lined her mouth and forehead and streaked her hair with gray before its time. In recent weeks, she'd looked more and more worn out as she updated me on which minister backed which family member and how many siblings were trying to get involved in the imminent coup.

I didn't pay much attention. I cared less for Lyosha's political ambitions than I did for a vial of wolf urine. At least I could learn something interesting from wolf urine. And as long as my chief interests were the flora and fauna of Above and Below, I doubted any ministers or ambitious family members cared about me. All the same: "I can't leave yet." Even if I had no interest in the duchy, I had a duty. Our family *was* Kylma Above, and we had responsibilities to uphold. Father had stipulated that I could go south when the bride-show was over, not before. If I violated his order, he might find some way to prevent me from going at all.

I went over to my desk, skipping across the floor in my wool socks. "What are you doing?" Aino asked.

"I might as well get some work done." I pulled my technical drawings from the middle drawer of the desk. I was annotating Farhod's technical drawings, and I had to finish them before I went south. They'd be part of my university portfolio and application. Farhod had warned me that gaining admittance was hard, even for the daughter of a grand duke—but detailed dissection notes of a creature never seen before was sure to catch the attention of scholars and professors.

"You ought to rest." Aino checked the door, then paced back to the fire, dispersing the logs with a poker. "We shouldn't have lit this. What if someone realizes you're here?"

I rolled my eyes as I lit the little candle under my frozen inkwell. Aino was back to her favorite hobby: fretting. "No one can see me, and no one's going to care. Fetch my robe, won't you?"

She stomped off, muttering about ungrateful brats and coups and heads. I was restless, too, and opened the window next to my desk, leaning out to let the cold air sting my cheeks.

The palace was quieter than usual. Maybe we really were on the cusp of a coup. Or maybe the brideshow was canceled, and nobody wanted to celebrate. From here, I could just see the bridal tower, and I wondered if the candidates had retreated to it. The girl in the riding suit didn't seem like the type to retreat from anything.

A lone figure hurried across a decorative wall, and four stories beneath me lay the thick ice sheet that separated Above and Below. I wanted to crack that ice so badly that it split my heart to think about it. Beneath that ice swam undulating bodies with serpentine legs, vague shapes I could nearly recognize when I walked on the lake's frozen surface. The duchy Below was our closest ally and our dearest friend. It was the only political matter I had any interest in. It was the greatest thing Father had denied me—and denied me, and denied me.

Aino draped my robe around my shoulders. "Shut the window," she said, reaching past me to do it herself.

I pulled my head inside. "No one's going to shoot me from the palace walls."

"Honestly, Ekata. If there is one night my worrying might save your life, it's tonight." She cinched the robe around my waist. "You've never been the sweet, obedient type. Humor me."

"I'll keep the doors and windows locked." I forced myself not to roll my eyes again. "But don't call for a sled. And let me work for a few hours before bed. There's nothing unsafe about sitting at my desk."

"You can work for half an hour, then I'm dousing the fire. And if anyone knocks, say nothing. You're not here."

I shook my head and tucked my chin to hide a smile. "All right."

I didn't hide it well enough. "Don't treat this like a joke, my lady," Aino snapped. She only used *my lady* when she was really cross. "I'm concerned about your life, and all you can think of is livers and cross sections." She curled her lip at the sheet on my desk, on which Minister Farhod had painstakingly drawn a number of internal organs in a hand so fine they still seemed to glisten.

I licked the nib of my pen. "Aino, relax," I said. "The kitchen boy's more politically involved than I am. Whatever occurs tonight, it's hardly going to concern us."

As it happened, I was wrong.

CLAIRE ELIZA BARTLETT

grew up in Colorado. She studied history and archaeology and spent time in Switzerland and Wales before settling in Denmark for good. She is the author of *We Rule the Night* and *The Winter Duke*. When not at her computer telling mostly fictional stories, she works as a tour guide in Copenhagen, telling stories that are (mostly) true. Claire invites you to visit her online at authorclaire.com.

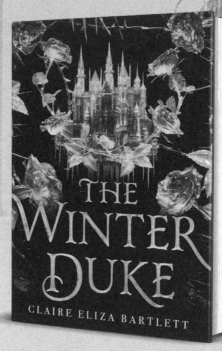